A BURNING DESIRE

"I want you more than I've ever wanted anything or anyone in my life," Chase whispered, his voice hoarse and throaty, "but I—"

"There's no but about it." She interrupted before he could say another word. "Because I want you more than you could possibly imagine."

Ever so gently, he pulled her to her feet. His eyes never strayed from the delicate angles of her face. Dare held herself tall and proud as he began to undress her. He moved slowly, almost worshipfully, as though he, too, wanted that special moment to be savored.

His fingers moved in tiny, teasing circles as he undid the buttons of her blouse. *Hurry, please hurry,* she wanted to cry out, but the words simply would not come.

"You're even more exquisite than I imagined," Chase murmured as he caressed her satiny skin.

His touch was maddening. Contained within his hands was the power to make each bit of flesh he touched sizzle. His lips taunted and tantalized, filling her with such incredible sensations that she felt faint. She moaned as ecstasy and passion flowed through her like sweet, liquid fire.

Rapture's Raging Storm

BY
JOLENE
PREWIT-PARKER

ZEBRA BOOKS
KENSINGTON PUBLISHING CORP.

ZEBRA BOOKS

are published by

Kensington Publishing Corp.
475 Park Avenue South
New York, N.Y. 10016

First printing: January 1985

Printed in the United States of America

To my parents,
Sue and Edward Prewit

Chapter One

Dare MacDade sat slumped over the big, roll-top desk that had been salvaged from a sinking freighter thirty years before. Thick tresses the color of Cuban coffee spilled onto the ledger in front of her. As each clap of thunder bombarded the skies, she felt her world was about to come crashing down. She was at wit's end! Her spirits were taking as much of a beating as the twin gables on the roof. Knowing there was little she could do to remedy matters only compounded the situation.

Hoping against hope that for once she had made an error in addition, she tallied the columns a third time, then a fourth, but the total remained unchanged. The accounts payable far outweighed those receivable.

After sending her pen flying across the room, she collapsed against the velvet backing and massaged the dull throbbing in her temples. Perhaps the financial status of the Sea Palms Resort would improve once the Yanks began their winter migration to the Florida keys.

Her head sank deeper into her hands. Indulging in wishful thinking would only make matters worse. An end to her money problems was not in sight, and there was no point in deceiving herself. It was not likely that wealthy Northerners would flock to the southern tip of the United States as they had done in seasons past, and she couldn't much blame them. Key West resembled a war port, not a tropical haven for vacationers seeking refuge from the cold. Uniformed soldiers patrolled the streets day and night, and the word coming out of Fort Taylor was that it would only be a matter of time before these fighting men saw action. Moored outside the harbor was the USS *Maine*. Common sense told her it was no coincidence that the battleship with a reputation for being the staunchest armored cruiser in the entire fleet had been selected for a routine tour at that particular time. It didn't take a military strategist to figure out why the pride of the Navy had been ordered to the port of Key West, where the ship would be only ninety miles away from the turmoil erupting in Cuba should the nation's commander in chief elect to intervene in the controversy between the island and its motherland.

Dare picked up the *New York Journal*. The latest edition had just arrived by mail boat from Tampa. The longer she thumbed through it the more infuriated she became. Publisher Hearst was hellbent on goading the country into war. She couldn't remember an issue that had not carried stories of

Spanish atrocities. Just last fall an entire edition had been devoted to Remington sketches of customs officers disrobing and searching an American woman on vacation in Havana. That such practice was routine and that female officers conducted the search had been shrewdly omitted. The coverage had become even more slanted since. Apparently, sensationalism sold more newspapers than objective reporting! Hearst and Pulitzer used yellow journalism to boost their circulations, and they successfully duped their readers with this tactic.

Dare leafed to the editorial section. The letters were even worse than last week's, and the number had nearly tripled.

She skimmed them quickly, becoming more enraged by the minute. Hearst had the people so riled up they were chafing at the bit. Public sentiment was demanding that America rally on behalf of the Cuban insurgents who were struggling and dying for their independence. Angered by the bloodshed, some Americans accused President McKinley of being a coward. They warned him that unless he sent troops to Cuba he could forget his aspirations to a second term in office. "Hurl the dirty Bourbon flag from the hemisphere" seemed to be the latest patriotic slogan. "A war with Spain would boost our economy," wrote one industrialist. A history professor suggested that conflict with such a world power would inspire Americans with love for their country and would, thereby, unify states which had never been truly unified since the Civil War.

Dare tossed the newspaper aside in disgust. Damn Hearst, Pulitzer, and the whole lot of them! They had carried the whole notion of freedom of the press way too far. Because of them, war was inevitable, she decided grimly; and the likelihood that her island paradise would be drawn smack-dab into the middle of the conflict troubled her.

She returned to her accounting, more depressed than when she'd paused to rest a few minutes earlier. It was obvious from the numbers before her that she wasn't the only one who sensed an impending war. Last year the Sea Palms had been packed with guests who'd made reservations well in advance to celebrate Thanksgiving, Christmas, and the New Year under the shade of a palm frond. This year, however, rumors of a bloody confrontation so close to the shores of the U.S. were keeping tourists at home and out of harm's way should Spain decide to violate the neutral waters zone.

The chimes in the courthouse tower tolled midnight a short time later, and Dare slammed the ledger shut. Even if she were to spend another five hours with her eyes glued to the long columns, the outlook would be no brighter. She could multiply and divide until she was blue in the face, but the truth was . . . there simply was no money! Expenses had already been shaved to the minimum; there were just no more corners to be cut. She'd never thought the day would come when she'd be praying for Yankee boarders, but she saw no other way to clear up her money problems.

She frowned. Northerners weren't her only alternative, but even they seemed more appealing than the proposal made by Señor Eduardo Ferrer. How had he phrased his offer? Ah, yes. "A friendly business arrangement that would prove mutually beneficial to both of them." Humph! She had told him in no uncertain terms just what he could do with his proposition.

The sky is darkest just before daybreak. That was what Mac always said when she was feeling low. Things would take a turn for the best. They had to. That was all there was to it. If they didn't, well . . . she'd just have to worry about that when the time came!

She poured herself a brandy, then scuffed across to the window and flung open the shutter. The festivities had already commenced. Boisterous cheers and applause erupted throughout the mud-soaked streets. Fireworks, a blazing kaleidoscope of colors, exploded in the rain, and across the way in the harbor, the *Maine* discharged another volley to welcome in 1898.

Snifter in hand, Dare curled up in the window seat. She watched the display below with a detached interest. It was hard to be merry. She could think of very little worth celebrating. With Mac gone, nothing was the same. Christmas had just been another day, and there was no reason to think that New Year's Day would be any different. He had been more than a father, he had been a mother and best friend as well. After twenty years of closeness it was difficult to realize the person who was so important to your life was only a memory. She remembered crying herself to sleep night after night when her mother had died of the fever. She had been a child. Mac had comforted her then. Now she was a woman. She couldn't afford to be weak.

Her gaze swept across the room to a portrait of a grizzled-looking seaman. She extended her goblet in its direction. "Happy New Year, Mac," she whispered.

Tears welled up in her eyes. She swallowed hard. "Damn you," she cursed with soft tenderness. "Why'd you have to get yourself drowned? I told you there was a storm brewing, but you were too pigheaded to listen." She took a slow sip of her brandy. "I love you," she said a moment later as she blew him a kiss. "I'll take good care of this old place. You just wait and see. The Sea Palms is going to be the most popular wintering spot in the entire South."

After a few quick blinks and a hard swallow, she turned her attention to the action outside. The joy seekers with their funny hats and silly, tooting horns did not interest her. What lay in the darkness beyond the reef was far more exciting. Somewhere out in the pitch black blanketing the Gulf Stream there was a steamer furrowing the swells. And on it—at least she hoped they were on board—were those moneyed tourists she so desperately needed to insure that her father's legacy remained in her possession! She didn't need many. Maybe just a dozen or so. That would be enough to tide her over until all the nonsense of war died down.

One hour dragged into the next, and still there was no sign of the Mallory liner. Undoubtedly the weather had delayed the ship, she reasoned. The moment the storm lifted, the skies would be lit by reflections from the steamer's lights.

Dare stood, gazing out the window awhile longer,

but her lids were growing heavier and heavier with each passing minute. A blast of thunder that sounded like artillery fire jolted her from her sleepy state. A last look revealed no trace of a ship clearing the reef. Most likely, the captain had chosen to wait out the storm rather than risk entering the harbor under the present conditions, she told herself. After all, navigating the reef-filled waters at the entrance to the harbor was difficult enough in broad daylight.

Dare dragged herself out of the room. Just as well the ship was going to be late, she thought as she began to climb up the stairs. A good night's sleep was just what she needed after laboring over the books. She couldn't very well greet guests in her present mood anyway. The Sea Palms could do without a grumpy hostess. It already had more than its share of problems.

A loud banging at the front door halted her midway up the stairs. "Who's there?" she yelled, racing back down.

"'Tis me, lass. Open up."

Dare smiled. She recognized the familiar brogue immediately. Poor Uriah! He sounded as though he had really tied one on tonight.

She unbolted the latch. A gust of wind threw the door open, and in staggered her father's lifelong pal. "What are you doing out in this?" she scolded good-naturedly. "You'll have pneumonia for sure."

"The Mallory liner . . . she's hit the reef off Loggerhead Point . . . She's sinkin' fast."

"Oh, dear God, no!" she gasped. "Somebody's got to get out to her."

"I know," he said, finally catching his breath. "I

13

could only round up six sober men. They're already down at the boat house." He hesitated. "We need the *Blue Runner*, lass. My old tub'll never make it in these seas."

Dare nodded. She understood the reason for his hesitation. The *Blue Runner* hadn't left the dock since Mac's death. "You didn't need to ask my permission. Of course you can use it." She jerked her slicker down from the peg beside the door. "Let's go."

"What?" Uriah caught her by the arm and whirled her around. "Be ye crazy, lass? That sea's no place fer a woman."

"You can lecture me on the finer points of womanhood tomorrow." She pulled away and darted outside. "Well, what are you waiting for?" she called out over her shoulder. "Come on. There's work to do."

"I've a good mind to get one of me boys to throw you o'er his shoulder and tote you back home where you belong," threatened Uriah when he finally caught up with her.

"I'm not a bag of potatoes!" She scrambled onto the deck with the rest of the crew. "Besides, you know as well as I that it would take more than one of these lugs to get me ashore."

Uriah pointed to the cockpit. "Sit. And not another word out of ye!"

"But—"

"No buts about it, lass." He hushed her protests with a wave of his hand. "This ain't a fishing trip. Ye might be the owner of this vessel, but don't ye forget who's captainin' it. I haven't had a mutiny in forty years, and I don't aim to start now."

Dare took her place in the cockpit. "Aye, aye, sir!"

The crew snapped to attention the moment Uriah manned the helm and bellowed out orders to get underway. Within minutes, the lines were cast, the sails unfurled, and the anchor weighed.

Her timbers creaking, the *Blue Runner* lunged away from the dock in one gigantic motion and was pitched into a swirl of white caps that lashed unrelentingly at her sides.

Dare held onto her seat scarcely daring to breathe. Each time the bow plunged into the water seemed certain to be the last! Waves rose up to meet them, dumping gallons of water onto the deck. Hurricane-force gusts battered the sails and sent them flapping out of control. Every few moments the sky sent forth a barrage of thunder while crackling whips of lightning charged around them. Violent swells tossed the sloop from one roll to the next as if she were a toy boat. They were totally at the mercy of a furious sea, and Dare had a feeling the worst of the tempest had yet to be unleashed.

Her father had often warned her that the sea loved to seduce sailors into a watery hell. She could almost hear Mac's voice rising above the tumult to deliver those same words. Each wave that catapulted across her brought with it visions of Mac washing up on shore, his face purple and bloated, his flesh clammy and shriveled.

She wondered if she were doomed to a similar fate. For one brief instant, she regretted having insisted on accompanying Uriah, but she quickly shook such notions from her mind. There were people drowning

15

on the reef! She had an obligation to rescue them.

Dare glanced over her shoulder a short while later. The other vessels which had put to sea were gaining on them. Soon, they would be close to the *Blue Runner*'s stern. It had been nearly a year since the last freighter had foundered on the reefs. The seamen were hungry for a lucrative haul. Please, please let us be the first to reach the steamer, she prayed over and over. The law of the sea gave the first ship to reach a vessel in distress possession of its load, but she was confident that with Uriah in charge, survivors would be given top priority over the storehouse of wealth in the hold. He was just like Mac! Neither of them would salvage a vessel until every possible attempt to locate and rescue all those on board had been made.

Uriah skirted one protruding patch of coral after another, meanwhile cursing the drunken lighthouse keeper whose carelessness had damned still another ship.

Dare closed her eyes. She couldn't bear to watch. The slightest change in wind direction could easily ram the *Blue Runner* into razor-sharp reefs that would sliver the hull into hundreds of pieces.

"Dear God in heaven! Would ye look at that!" exclaimed Uriah.

Dare opened her eyes just as they cleared the reef and rounded the point. She couldn't believe the sight that lay ahead. The Mallory steamer had broken amidships. Her bow section had been carried into the shallows of the bay side while the stern half remained perched, on its side, atop the reef.

"She must've rammed it head-on at full steam," remarked Uriah quietly, almost reverently, before calling out to the men to drop anchor.

Dare felt her way to the starboard side. Agony clawed at her heart with sharp talons when she peered over the rail into the billows churning beneath her. Cargo and supplies from the ship's stores littered the sea, and riding the waves facedown alongside bales of cotton and casks of liquor were lifeless forms. It wouldn't take long for the sharks to catch the whiff of death, converge upon them, and tear them to shreds in a feeding frenzy.

Uriah pulled her away from the railing. "Are ye a'right, lass?"

She nodded. Her senses were dulled. There was no way any of those on board could have been spared Neptune's wrath. No way! "Those poor devils . . . They didn't have a chance, did they?"

"N'ary a prayer!" He took a silver flask out of his coat pocket and raised it to his lips. "We need to get on about our business now," he mumbled as he wiped his mouth with the back of his hand.

Dare nodded. She understood. They had been too late. The ship had broken apart too quickly. There was no one left to save. The objective now would be to salvage everything still afloat.

Uriah shouted for the launches to be lowered. "You stay here," he told Dare sternly.

She offered no objection. Her job, she knew, was an important one. She would have to keep an eye on the lines the entire time the *Blue Runner* lay at anchor. If a line slipped, her responsibility would be to maneuver the sloop clear of the reef.

Dare watched as Uriah went over the side to join the rest of the crew. He gave her a quick salute as the boat headed in the direction of the wreck.

She took her position at the helm. From her vantage point there, she could observe the flurry of activity around her. The *Blue Runner*, undisputedly, had been the first vessel to reach the wreck, and as such, Uriah had taken complete charge of the salvaging operation. No one seemed to mind his bellowing, for each man knew that regardless of who was in command, an equal amount of the haul would be distributed to each and every one of them.

Feeling as though every nerve in her body had been numbed, Dare watched as furniture and machinery were secured and towed to vessels that could accommodate their weights. If there were any survivors, Uriah would find them, but not once had he signaled that a body showed any sign of life.

There was no turning back. Dare knew she had to stay right where she was until the casks had been hoisted on board. Minutes dragged into hours, and she realized that she had lost all track of time. She did not know just how long she had been manning the helm, but she did know this would probably be the longest night of her life.

Sometime later she caught sight of an object bobbing up and down off the port stern. Her first glance assured her it was nothing more than a channel marker, the very same one she had sailed past at least a hundred times on her way to Conch Key. Still, every time she glanced away she felt drawn back to that marker.

She leaned over the side for a closer look. Good Lord! Was that a man clinging to the buoy?

Dare yelled for Uriah—for anyone—but the roar of

the storm combined with the commotion around her drowned out her pleas.

"Hold on!" she yelled as she scrambled back across the deck.

Dare grabbed a life ring from the cabin door and knotted a rope around it. If he would only grab hold, she could tow him the rest of the way to the boat.

Three attempts to get the line out to him failed. The rope just wasn't long enough to cover the distance to the float. She yelled for Uriah until she was hoarse, but the wind carried her cries farther out to sea. The man couldn't hold on much longer, not with the waves crashing against him. She might not be able to summon help in time. There was only one thing to do, and unless she acted quickly, he would perish like the others.

Deciding to take matters into her own hands, Dare pulled one of the big, bulky life preservers over her slicker. She secured the straps tightly around her waist, and grasping the rope with the life ring attached to it, she tied that securely around her waist.

She ducked under the railing. Without hesitating she plunged feet first into the inky abyss.

Dare surfaced, gasping for air. The ferocity of the waves rolling over her stunned her, and the temperature of the water chilled her bones. Collecting her wits, she told herself that someone depended on her for his very life. She knew there were sharks nearby just waiting to attack. Mac had always told her that they never attacked unless provoked. God, she hoped he had been right.

She battled the distance separating the sloop from the buoy with strokes as powerful as the current would allow; yet it seemed that for every yard she covered she was pushed back two. Sudden surges washed over her every few seconds, leaving her choking on the brine.

It seemed an eternity before she finally closed the gap between the sloop and the man. With all the strength she could command, she made a final lunge for the beacon. Her arm stretched out as far as it could. The tips of her fingers could not quite touch his shoulder.

She took a deep breath and tried again. Another billow, this one even more ferocious than the last, broke over her. She saw it coming, closed her eyes, and waited. When she reopened them, she was alone. The man had been swept away! She had reached him seconds too late!

Her fingers dug deeper into the marker. She clung to it knowing full well that now her own life was at stake. How foolish she had been to think otherwise! Frantic, she scanned the water for the body that had been washed out of her reach. It was no use! The sky and the sea were both the same color—tourmaline. There was no trace of him. Soon, she feared, there would be no trace of her, either.

Minutes later, just as she had given up hope of finding him, she spotted him behind her. He was a few yards beyond her reach. So close, yet so far away, she thought, feeling more and more at the sea's mercy. She knew he could not tread water much longer. Each time a wave swallowed him, she had a sickening feeling it would be the last. She had to reach him, even if it meant they would both share the same doom.

Determinedly, Dare pushed herself off the buoy. Her limbs seemed weighted. She couldn't move fast enough.

She watched the man's head go under again and waited for it to reappear, but it did not. She stroked faster, this time reaching him. Taking a handful of hair, she jerked his face out of the water. One hand held up his head while the other struggled to stuff the ring over his shoulders.

Keeping a secure grip on the rope, she paddled back against the current fighting with every stroke to keep herself afloat. The load she was towing was as heavy as dead weight. Never before had she realized she was capable of such strength.

When she collapsed against the beacon she realized all her energy had been expended. She feared her chances of making it to the *Blue Runner* were nil. Suddenly a surge of strength replenished what had drained out of her. She had come too far to give up now, she told herself. She'd make it! She had to! She was Mac MacDade's daughter, wasn't she?

"Hold on. Just a little while longer," she yelled to the form drifting up behind her. "We're almost there." She knew her words of encouragement were intended more for herself than for the half-drowned man. She didn't expect an answer. He looked as though he had already resigned himself to the fate of his companions. Only an occasional gasp for air told her she had not rescued a corpse.

Dare held onto the buoy for dear life. She was not sure what to do next. She could not bring herself to leave the float. Never had she been confronted with a more difficult choice. If she attempted to reach the

Blue Runner and failed, the two of them would be carried out to sea. If she stayed where she was, it might be hours before someone spotted them.

Time seemed to slip away as quickly as the water that lapped through her fingers. Still, she could not decide what must be done. If only she could close her eyes and sleep! Surely, she would wake up and find this had been a bad dream.

As time passed the rain, which had pelted her face seconds earlier, turned into a fine drizzle. The wind stilled, and the fury of the sea abated as if at the command of a more omnipotent force. The hush enveloping her was eerie; the pall of death seemed to hang over the stilled waters.

Dare opened her eyes and blinked quickly. Was it over? Had her life on earth ended so effortlessly, so painlessly, she wondered.

Dazed, she stared out over the water. Was that a launch rowing toward them? She couldn't be sure. Fatigue could create all sorts of illusions.

"Hold on lassie! I'm a'comin'."

Relief flooded her. There was no mistaking that voice!

A pair of arms snatched her up out of the sea and swung her into the boat. She watched wordlessly as the man was reeled in behind her and laid out on the deck.

"Is he alive?" She braced herself for the answer she dreaded. Something told her her efforts had all been in vain. Already, his face had taken on the waxen glaze of death.

Uriah felt for a pulse. "Aye, lass. He's alive." His usually gruff voice cracked. "But he won't see dawn."

22

Dare dropped to her knees. "He can't die! I won't let him!" She gathered his lifeless shoulders close to her breast and rocked him gently as though she were cradling a baby. "You can't give up. Not after what we've been through. You made it over the worst of it." A steady stream of tears trailed down her cheeks. "Fight, damn it. Fight!"

Chapter Two

Fight, damn it! Fight!

The same words kept echoing over and over inside Dare's head from the instant the skiff pulled away from the *Blue Runner* and headed toward shore. How she hoped Uriah's prediction would prove wrong! The man had to live! He must! If he didn't, a little bit of her would die with him.

Even as she gazed down at the head her arms were cradling, she feared the man could not hold on much longer. His cheeks were hollow and had turned the same gray color her father's had been when he'd been washed up by the surf. Her fingers trembling, she smoothed pale shocks of hair away from his face. She cringed. Already his flesh had the clammy feel of death.

Dare studied him closely. He didn't look more than eight or ten years older than she. He was still young, so young. He had braved the worst of it.

Surely, he would live, she kept telling herself. It seemed only fair for him to make it!

"Faster, please," she entreated the two sailors Uriah had assigned to row her and her charge to shore. "He needs help fast. We must hurry."

She checked his pulse. It was weak, but at least there was one.

Perhaps with proper care, she told herself, he stood a chance. She knew she could not allow herself to think otherwise. He hadn't given up. Not yet. He was a fighter. The way his chest rose and sank with each labored intake of air told her that he wanted to live just as badly as she wanted it. He was determined. That in itself should buy him that little extra time.

Dare sat back and waited. She could see the pier just ahead. They were almost home!

Dawn was about to break across the horizon. The sea and the sky were both iridescent pearls. One could hardly be distinguished from the other.

She shook her head in disbelief. It was hard to think of last night as being anything but a bad dream, a nightmare. But she knew that it was not, nor could it ever be viewed in that manner. Today, the waters were mirror calm, and the wind was nothing more than a gentle breeze helping the skiff along, but the victims of last night's savagery had sunk to watery graves. The horrors she had witnessed would remain in her memory as long as she lived.

At last, the boat glided up to the dock.

Dare felt as though a tremendous weight had been lifted from her shoulders. Smiling, she gazed upward. The sky glowed like a fiery opal. Uriah was wrong! It was daylight, and the man was still

26

holding on.

While she secured the lines, Uriah's two mates lifted the limp form out of the skiff.

"Easy. Be careful! Don't jar him," she cautioned as they carried him into the Sea Palms. "Bring him in here," she instructed, directing the way into one of the guest suites downstairs. She hurried on ahead and turned down the covers. "Jamie, you get him out of those wet clothes and dry him off. Jason, go fetch Doc Edmundson. Tell him it's an emergency!"

With that, she took off up the stairs. She opened the door to the room that had belonged to her father and waited a moment before going inside.

The scent of his pipe still lingered within. Its subtle fragrance evoked a feeling of desolation she knew time could never heal. The room had remained untouched since Mac's death. It looked as though it were waiting for him to return. The pouch of cherry tobacco on the bureau had not been disturbed. *Moby Dick* was still open to the last page he had read, and his robe still lay draped across the wickerwork rocker in which he had whiled away so many hours.

Dare took a deep breath to collect herself. Now was not the time to dwell on her loss.

She pulled a nightshirt from the black lacquer cabinet Mac had acquired on his last trading expedition to the Orient and then sped back down the stairs.

"Put this on him before he catches pneumonia," she told Jamie.

Jason, out of breath, barged into the room a moment later. "Doc Edmundson . . . he's off the island . . . fishing up at Manatee Key . . . won't be back until Sunday."

"Damn!" she cursed under her breath. "That man cuts open more fish than he does people!"

Dare rolled up her sleeves. She had no alternative but to tend his injuries as best she could.

"You need us for anything else?" asked Jamie.

"We've done as you told us," Jason added timidly.

Dare shook her head. She knew they were anxious to return to the excitement of salvaging. "I can manage from here. Thanks for your help."

She stood looking down at the sleeping man for the longest time. She wasn't quite sure what she was supposed to do. The only nursing she had done was bandaging the cuts and icing the bruises Mac and Uriah had often acquired when Saturday night poker games turned into brawls. She had never even been alone with a man who was in bed, and knowing he was half dead did nothing to make the situation any the less awkward.

She swallowed hard, determined to do what had to be done. His welfare was her responsibility. Now was not the time for modesty, she reminded herself, easing down onto the bed.

Hands trembling, she lowered the quilts one by one.

"You poor, poor man," she whispered, catching her breath at each snap she unfastened.

She was afraid to touch him. It was painful just to look at him. He looked as if he had rammed the reef. Large, swollen bruises darkened his chest with blues and purples. Blood and pus oozed from the deep, ragged gashes that slashed his chest.

Her fingers barely skimming the skin, Dare

sponged his chest with hot alcohol. Closer examination revealed the lacerations were not nearly as severe as she had first thought. They could be tended to quite easily. Ammonia and alcohol would draw out the fire of the coral, and salves and bandages would minimize the infection.

She examined his head for any bumps or bruises. Nonetheless, what concerned her most was what she couldn't see. If he had sustained internal injuries, there was nothing she could do. She didn't need Doc to tell her the reason for his unconsciousness should be her primary concern. If he had suffered a concussion, he could easily remain in this state for days, perhaps months, and even then there was no guarantee he would ever emerge from his sleep.

A low, muffled groan escaped his lips when she laid his head down on the pillow. She leaned closer. What was it he was trying to say?

She stroked his cheek with a gentleness that came naturally. "There, everything's all right. There's no reason for you to be afraid," she whispered to him. "You're safe. I promise. I'll take care of you."

She wasn't really sure if it was her imagination or if the tension in his face eased at the sound of her voice. Even if he was in no condition to comprehend her words, he could surely sense her presence. Perhaps having someone with whom to share his pain would ease his suffering.

She pulled a rocker up to the bed and settled down into it. She'd stay there until he drifted into slumber. After what he had been through, she wasn't about to abandon him now, she mused as she took his hand in hers and gave it a tender squeeze.

As the minutes ticked by, she found that her gaze was focusing on him with far more boldness than she would have permitted herself had he been awake. She studied him as though she were trying to memorize every detail. Hair the color of sea oats fell away from his face in waves and framed his head like a lion's mane. The creases of pain that etched his brow did nothing to mar his handsomeness. Instead, they seemed to enhance the hard set strength of his features. His chest looked as solid as the coral that had scarred it, and his wide, powerful shoulders made him look commanding even as he slept. His likeness to the Robinson Crusoe she had imagined upon first reading Defoe's novel was astounding. She wondered what the color of his eyes might be. Blue, she would imagine, a Nordic blue to match his Viking characteristics.

Flurries of feeling excited and confused her with each observation she made. Even in his present condition, the stranger radiated an aura of manliness which piqued heretofore alien sensations in Dare.

She could not wrench her eyes from him. There was something very special about this man! Just what it was she couldn't quite put her finger on. Under the circumstances forming such an attachment to someone she had rescued seemed natural. Why shouldn't she feel protective toward him? she asked herself. But she sensed that more was involved. His identity and everything about him might be a mystery, and yet there was no denying that strange, inexplicable bond linking them together. Their paths had crossed for a reason. Fate had brought them together. She might not understand why, but nothing could convince her otherwise.

If only she knew something about him . . . his name, if nothing else. Was he a William, a Richard, perhaps? Where had he come from, and what had brought him South? She wondered if he would have stayed at the Sea Palms, and if they would have met had he decided to room elsewhere. Question after question posed itself. She wished she knew the answers!

His clothes! she exclaimed to herself. Of course! Why had she not thought of that sooner? They would surely give her a clue to his identity.

Careful not to awaken him, she tiptoed across to the window where Jamie had hung his garments to dry. The shirt was nothing more than shreds of linen. His trousers were still wet, but at least they were intact.

Should she? She hesitated. She must. How else would she know? she asked herself as her hand dove into a pocket.

A gold clip that secured a wad of bills had somehow managed to remain inside. Never had she seen so much money. With what was there, she could easily pay off the note at the bank and still have enough left to tide her over until next season, she mused as she thumbed through the cash.

Dare stold a glance at the bed. Good lord! Suppose he awakened and saw her with his money? He'd think she was robbing him.

Quickly, she stuffed the roll as far down in his pocket as it would go. Her fingers brushed something that was circular and metal.

Curious, she fished out the object. It was a gold

pocket watch. The initials CH were engraved on the cover.

She turned it over and held it up to the light to read the inscription on the back.

"To Chase. Yours forever, Nessa."

She reread it softly, her fingers fidgeting nervously with the clasp.

The face of a fair-haired young woman deep in meditation sprang up at her. The casing opposite the miniature held a timepiece with Roman numerals. The hands had stopped at a few minutes past one.

Upset with herself, Dare snapped the cover shut and dropped the watch back into the pocket where she had found it. She felt like an intruder on his private life. Curiosity was a poor excuse for rummaging through his pockets, she chided herself.

She laid the clothes out on the window ledge, her fingers lingering across the folds of his trousers. Was Nessa his wife or his sweetheart, she wondered, and had the thought of her driven him to battle death so fiercely? She wondered why a twinge of envy had overcome her when she'd seen the pale beauty in the locket.

She returned to his side. He seemed to be resting much easier. Perhaps at that very moment, he was holding his Nessa close in his dreams.

Dare lowered herself into her rocker ever so slowly. Why should that thought fill her with such sadness and leave her feeling so empty? she asked herself as she rocked rhythmically.

She heard herself mumbling his name under her breath a moment later.

"Chase."

Its sound against her lips made her feel warm and tingly.

She leaned over to him.

"Chase," she repeated, this time a little louder.

Her hand was on his cheek before she even realized it had left her lap. The surge of emotion sweeping over her left her mind cloudy. His name had the power to draw her to him. She felt as though she were slipping under some kind of a spell. She had no control.

She stood up. Her legs were shaky. She couldn't understand what was happening.

She took several steps away from the bed. A magnetic force beckoned her to return. It took more resolve than she had expected to fight it.

A long soak in the cedar tub at the back of the house was just what she needed to sort out her thoughts. As soon as the man . . . as Chase . . . was well, he'd go about his life and she would do the same. He'd accomplish whatever he had come to Key West to do, then be about his business. To think otherwise was pure nonsense!

She donned a skirt and middy blouse and concentrated on her household chores, fighting the urge to return to the room. Late in the afternoon, she could no longer resist and she ventured back inside.

She settled into the rocker after pulling it away from the bed. In the same motion she opened and closed the book of poetry she was holding. Byron, Shelley, and Keats simply were not as fascinating as the man before her . . . as Chase.

Uriah peeked in on her at supper time.

"How's the patient, lass?"

Her fingers to her lips, she eased out of the room. "You were wrong," she told him as they stepped outside onto the porch. "He made it past dawn. But I'd sure rest a lot easier if Doc were here to have a look at him," she added, sighing.

Uriah gave her arm a fatherly squeeze. "Ye've done the best ye can do, lass. The rest is up to him."

Dare sank down into the glider. "I only hope my best is good enough."

"It will be. Ye're a MacDade, aren't ye?" He dropped down beside her. "Ahhh, feels good to give these old legs of mine a rest," he said, stretching them out in front of him. "I feel like I've been at sea for a year. No, two years." He shook his head sadly. "Salvagin's not as easy as it used to be. Reckon I'm just gettin' old."

Dare tucked her arm around his. "Old? Don't be ridiculous! You'll never get old. Why, when you're a hundred, you'll still be barking orders."

"Maybe, but it'll be from the old seaman's home up in Tampa," he said wearily. "That steamer was so crammed full o' machinery and equipment it took us all day to salvage her. Lucky for us the storm stopped when it did or we'd have lost most o' the cargo." He crossed his arms over his chest and expelled a heavy sigh. "I've never seen so rich a haul. She must've been headed to one of those plantations in South America."

"Were there any more survivors?" asked Dare, suspecting she already knew the answer.

"Nary a one. Just the young fellow ye found." He paused. His head hung low. He looked much older than his sixty years. "Counted thirteen bodies still

34

afloat. God knows how many others there were."

"All those deaths because of Ezra Bower's carelessness," she reflected aloud.

"Aye, lass. 'Tis a pity. Hazard of the profession, I reckon. Never knew a lighthouse keeper yet who could stay away from the bottle. A sailor neither, come to think of it," he added, pulling at the gray shag curling onto his collar. "Say, do ye think I could trouble Calpurnia for a cup of chowder? If I don't eat soon, I'm going to waste away to nothin'."

"So I see," laughed Dare, pinching a fold of flesh thickening his middle.

"Hey, watch it, lass," laughed Uriah as he pushed her hand away. "Calpurnia! Calpurnia!" he bellowed. "Get out here."

"Shhh. Keep your voice down," she said sternly. "There's a sick man in there."

"Sorry, I forgot." He peered around the corner into the house. "Where is that old battle-axe, anyway?"

"I had to let her go," she announced quietly.

"Ye what? What on earth got into ye?" he asked, surprised. "Granted, she's a bit cantankerous at times, but she's been with the family for years. Why, even when the Yanks took over the town, she stood on this very porch cursin' Cap'n Randolph. Said she didn't want to be freed, and the only way she was going to leave the Sea Palms was in a wooden box."

Dare waited until he was finished with the story she had heard a hundred times before. "You're not telling me anything I don't already know, Uriah, but if you'll give me a chance, I'll explain."

"I should hope so," he exclaimed indignantly.

Dare rolled her eyes and chuckled to herself.

35

Sometimes Uriah was just as headstrong as Mac.

"Calpurnia's tending to Clayton Jarvis's wife while he's up in Tallahassee. She's bedridden, you know."

Uriah gave an impatient nod. "Aye, get on with it."

She took a deep breath. "That's all there is. Calpurnia thinks it's only temporary, two, three weeks at the most, but the truth is, I just can't afford to keep her. She'd be all too happy to work for free, but I'll have none of that. When Mr. Jarvis returns, I'm going to see if he can use her full time."

Uriah's weathered face unwrinkled. "I didn't know you were strapped for money, lass. Ye never said anything about it to me."

Dare crossed her arms and leaned back in the swing. "I kept thinking things were bound to get better, what with the season starting and all. I guess I was wrong."

He took her hand in his two calloused ones. "Tell me about it, lass. Let me hear yer worries. Ivy MacDade was like a brother to me. Ye were always the daughter I would have given anything to have had." His voice cracked. "Besides, now that Mac's gone, we've got no one but each other."

Dare smiled. She could have kissed him. He was right. They didn't have anyone but each other.

"The truth is, Uriah," she began as she moved the swing back and forth slowly, "Mac was so sure this was going to be the year to surpass all others for tourists that he overextended himself. A lot of expenses were accumulated over the past six months, and when he died . . . well, it became my responsibility to pay them off."

Uriah scratched his whiskers thoughtfully. "Aye, I was wonderin' where the money came from for another bathhouse, those family cottages, the lounges and the umbrellas for the beach, a new—"

She held up her hand. "Please, don't remind me."

"Surely, in light of what happened, Morrow and the rest of the fellows would hold off demandin' payment for a while longer," suggested Uriah.

Dare made a face. "What do you mean? Would hold off? Mac wasn't even cold in the ground before they converged on the Sea Palms like a group of vultures and demanded payment."

"What?" demanded Uriah in disbelief.

She nodded. "To make a long story short, I had to take out a loan of a thousand dollars from the bank so I could pay them what Mac owed."

"Why those bastards! Those good for nothin' bastards!" Uriah rammed his fist into the palm of his other hand. "I'll teach them a thing or two."

Dare patted his arm. "What's done is done, Uriah. We can't change that any more than we can bring Mac back to life."

"You should have come to me, lass," he said, his tone mellowing. "I don't have much money, that's for sure, but between us, we'd have found a way out of that fix."

Dare tried to put on a cheerful face. "I know exactly what you would have done, Uriah Robertson, and that's the very reason I kept it to myself. A captain without his ship is as helpless as a fish out of water," she added, tucking her arm around his.

"Aye, and without this place, ye'd be no better off."

His sun-burnished face eroded into a smile. "Come Saturday though and all yer worries'll be over. Ye just leave everything to me."

She forced a half-hearted grin. "That's only four days away. I didn't know you had a knack for miracles."

"Who said anything about miracles? We are goin' to have us one hell of an auction." His face lit up. "I can see it now. Folks from as far north as Savannah will come down here all ready to bid. Ye just mark my word."

"What auction? Oh, you mean for the goods you just salvaged?" she asked with uncertainty.

"That's right." Smoke-gray eyes came alive with mysterious sparkles. "As owner of the first vessel to reach the wreck, ye're entitled to the biggest percentage of whatever we make from the sale of her goods."

"Don't talk nonsense, Uriah. I didn't captain the *Blue Runner*, and if I remember correctly, I wasn't even invited to participate," she teased.

"That's neither here nor there, lass. With yer thirty percent added to my thirty for captainin' er, we'll have enough to pay off the bank note," he announced, looking pleased with himself. "Well, what do ye think?"

"I think that you're a very sweet man to offer me your share, but—"

"But what?"

"But I just can't let you give me your money," she declared firmly. "I'm sorry, but the Sea Palm's money worries are my problems, and I refuse to let you, or anyone else for that matter, pay off my debt."

"Mac's debt," he corrected quickly. "And don't ye give me any of this business about your responsibility. I have a responsibility, too, ye know," he said, shaking his finger in her face. "Mac was the best friend I had. That gives me a claim to some of his daughter's burdens, don't ye agree?"

Dare's expression remained unchanged. "I appreciate what you're offering to do. Really, I do, but I just cannot let you give me your money. I'm sorry."

"Give it to ye? Is that what's bothering ye?" He threw back his head laughing. "So that's it! It's that cursed MacDade pride, ain't it, lass? Give it to ye, indeed. Why, I intend to make me an investment in this here seaside resort."

"An investment?" she asked, confused. "What on earth are you talking about?"

"It won't be long before that little skirmish across the way peters out, and when it does those rich Yanks'll be beatin' yer door down." He crossed his hands knowingly over his stomach. "And I figure ye'll be needin' yerself a partner, then. Someone to take out the fishing charters, keep the boats repaired, things like that, ye know."

Dare started to object, but decided instead to take his proposition under consideration. With Mac gone, she would need someone to captain the charters. She could handle the *Blue Runner* as well as any man, but there was no one else in the keys who could find schools of marlin like Uriah. Besides, she reminded herself, dealing with Uriah would be much more pleasant than fighting off Señor Ferrer's advances. Still, she wanted Uriah to know what he was getting into.

"And what if that little skirmish, as you call it, blazes up into an all-out war."

Uriah didn't blink. "Then we'll just have to wait until it's over before we start baiting the lines." He tugged at his chin. "Besides, lass, ye know as well as I that my days of wrestling the sea are over. I'd like to sleep in a bed for a while rather than a hammock strung over the deck."

Dare nodded. She understood exactly what he meant. His remark about the old seamen's home came to mind. "The Sea Palms has always been your home. You know that." She started to tell him just how disappointed she was that he would think he had to bail her out of debt just so he'd have a roof over his head, but changed her mind, and smiled instead. The Robertson pride was ten times worse than the MacDade.

"I'd be honored to be in business with you. Partner," she added, throwing both arms around him.

"All right, all right! Enough's enough!" His apple-plump cheeks blushed like a schoolboy's. "Now will ye feed me? All this business transacting makes me hungry!"

She gave him a salute. "Aye, aye, sir." Dare smiled to herself. It would be nice having Uriah around the house. Mac couldn't have planned it better himself!

On her way out to the kitchen, Dare paused outside the guest room and peered in at Chase. He seemed to be resting comfortably. His breathing was less strained, and no moans came from his mouth. Barring any complications, he should come to tomorrow, she told herself with a sigh of relief.

"Will you be back later?" Dare asked Uriah when he pushed back from the table after a supper of conch fritters and chowder.

"'Fraid not, lass. As much as I'd like a soft mattress under these weary limbs tonight of all nights, I can't afford that luxury. Not right yet, anyway."

She followed him out onto the porch.

"As much as I be dreadin' it, I intend to sleep at the warehouse until all that cargo's been auctioned off. When that much money's involved, it doesn't pay to be too trusting." He tipped his cap. "Remember what I said now. Saturday's the day, so no more worryin', ye hear. That's an order," he barked as he went sauntering across the lawn.

Dare leaned over the balustrade at the front of the house, her eyes following Uriah's short, stocky frame until it rounded the corner and disappeared from sight behind the turtle kraals.

Dusk fell across the spread of Spanish laurel canopying the house a short while later. The sky caught fire and exploded into purples and reds. Dare curled up in the glider, one leg tucked under her while the other moved the swing in rhythm to the offshore breeze fanning her face.

No longer being in danger of losing the Sea Palms should make her happy, but she wasn't. Granted, the Mallory liner would have hit the reef and sunk regardless, she mused, but it just didn't seem fair to prosper from the misfortunes of others even if she had not caused their bad luck. On the other hand, she reminded herself, Mr. Morrow at the bank would profit from her misfortunes if the note wasn't paid off in full in the spring.

41

Ye gotta be practical, lass! That's what Mac had always said. Like it or not, she'd do well to take his advice, she told herself. Come Saturday, the Sea Palms would be able to pay off all its debts, and then she could get down to the business of making it the most fashionable seaside resort on the entire east coast.

How she loved that old house, she sighed to herself. She had forgotten just how much it meant to her. It was more than just a roof over her head, it was a symbol of her mother and father, of their love for her and for each other. As a little girl, she had pleaded with Mac to tell her the story of the house time and time again. She must have heard it a thousand times at least, and each time Mac's eyes sparkled like dewdrops when he spoke of his beloved Victoria and how he had taken his bride's family home apart and floated the cyprus and madeira sections across from Abaco just so his beloved wouldn't get homesick for the Bahamas.

Dare studied the house thoughtfully, as though she were viewing it for the first time. She loved everything about it, the low ceilings, the delicate balustrades on the porches, the large, shuttered windows, but most of all the twin gables on the roof. It was a real Bahama house. Most of the homes in Key West were much too ornate for her liking. The red-bricked edifices with all their towers and verandas looked sad and lonely by comparison. The simple dignity of the Sea Palms seemed to beckon to friends and strangers alike with open arms.

Dare smiled to herself. Even now, she could feel Mac's presence. As long as the Sea Palms remained in her possession, she'd never really be without him.

As she strode back into the house she experienced an inner peace that she had not known for quite a while. Maybe problems did have a way of working themselves out!

Faint, broken moans drew her attention to the guest room. Chase was still unconscious, but he was tossing from one side of the bed to the other, his arms flailing and his legs kicking. He looked as though he were still thrashing against the current in an attempt to save himself from being sucked under. Dare wondered if his garbled words were cries to his Nessa. Had she been on board with him, or was she waiting his return home?

Her hands pressed his shoulders gently. "Shhh, lie still. Everything's all right now. You're out of danger. Nothing will harm you, I promise."

She could feel the tension drain from his chest.

"Good, good," she cooed. Her head dropped closer to his. "Try and get some sleep now. Tomorrow, everything will be just fine." Her lips brushed his brow. He was so hot! So feverish! He must have been out of his mind with delirium.

Dare jerked up quickly. Good Lord! She had kissed him. What on earth had possessed her to do that?

Her gaze fell onto his face. Eyes bluer than sapphires met hers.

Her face fired. She felt like a fool. Words of explanation wadded like cotton in her mouth. "I'm . . . sorry . . . I . . ."

His lids blinked shut.

Relieved, Dare left the room without glancing back.

Chapter Three

Dare awakened with his name on her lips. *Chase* . . . Even as he slept, he had had an unsettling effect on her. *Chase* . . . During the night, he had frequently appeared in her dreams as if to remind her of his presence in the room below. Not that she needed any reminding, she mused as she threw back the covers. A man like that could not be forgotten easily.

For once she didn't dress in a mad rush. Instead, she found herself devoting a good deal of attention to her toilet. She couldn't remember the last morning she had stood in front of the chiffonier's mirror. Now, she was dallying there.

Dare chuckled softly to herself. It was pointless to deny the reason behind such extra care. She just couldn't seem to get him . . . *Chase* . . . out of her mind, and she suspected she wasn't really trying very hard to do so.

Humming cheerfully, she examined her wardrobe. The skirts and middies all looked too matronly. What she needed was something bright and gay! Chase was going to regain consciousness today. She just knew it! And when he did, she must look her absolute best.

A few minutes later, she slipped into her favorite frock, a lavender lawn dress with a wide sash the same shade of damson as her eyes. Its glovelike fit accentuated each fine detail of her hourglass silhouette. Balloon sleeves tapered tightly from her elbows to her wrists, and the tiny green stripes that ran down to the hem made her look as if she were on her way to an afternoon garden party.

It was fun being a woman, she decided as she sashayed in front of the mirror. Mac had always told her the time would come when she'd feel that way, but she certainly hadn't expected to be almost twenty when the moment finally arrived.

Dare viewed her reflection from every possible angle. The image staring back from the smoke-tinted glass awed her. Almost overnight, she had blossomed into a woman, a real woman! She had always thought of herself as plain. How funny that assessment seemed now! Her image did not match her mental picture of herself. Striking, not plain, was the word that best described her at that moment. Not necessarily beautiful, but striking!

She studied her face critically. It was neither frail nor dainty. Each feature was definite and contained a composed sort of strength which enhanced her femininity rather than lessening it. She even fancied herself as looking a bit exotic when her lashes, dark as her hair, fell across her sun-kissed cheeks, and shuttered the wide, expressive eyes that revealed her every mood.

Her gaze swept down to breasts that rode high and proud, then to her naturally cinched waist and her hips, rounded and ripe, perfect for childbearing, or so Calpurnia had told her. One thing was certain, she decided, a half-grin, half-frown on her mouth. The days when she could pile her hair under a cap, don a pair of trousers, and go out turtling with some of the boys she had grown up with were long gone!

Yet, something was still not quite right. She scanned the total effect again. Of course. Her hair! She had outgrown the braid down the back. She swirled the silken plait into loops and pinned them loosely to the back of her head. There. Perfect, she mused as she curled a few wisps down around her face. Just the way Nessa had styled hers!

One more pirouette, and then Dare waltzed down the stairs, her petticoats swishing around her ankles.

She waited outside several minutes before venturing across the threshold of his room. Her insides were all aquiver. She hadn't felt this giddy the first time Richard Davis came calling.

Finally, she summoned enough courage to turn the doorknob. Would Chase notice her? she wondered as she stepped through the doorway, and if he did, how would she compare with the woman who had given him the pocket watch?

She stood over him a moment later not knowing quite what to do. His sleep was sound. Thank God for that! But she couldn't help feeling just a bit disappointed. She was so certain he would be conscious by now.

Warm sensations shot down her spine as the seconds passed. As she watched him sleep odd changes came over her. Her breasts grew taut; her legs were like jelly. Feelings of guilt and excitement assailed her at the same time. It was as though her body were coming to life for the first time.

Gathering her wits about her, she tried to repress the urges gnawing at her. Her association with the stranger could never be more than a friendly one, she reminded herself. The fact that he wore no wedding band on his left hand mattered little. There could be a dozen explanations for that. Even without one, he belonged to the woman who had vowed her love to him forever. Yours forever, Nessa. Had he pledged his undying devotion in return? Dare asked herself, inching forward.

She sensed that his eyes would open a few seconds before they did, but she hadn't the strength to step back. She watched, her mouth half open, as his weary lids lifted slowly. He didn't seem the least surprised to see her hovering above him. It was almost as though he had expected her to be there when he awakened.

Their eyes held. Hers refused to let go. His wouldn't permit even a wink. Dare felt as though she were being hypnotized by the fathomless blue of his gaze. Her resolve was rapidly slipping away, and she felt as though she were falling under some sort of spell. Even if she'd had the will to look away, she knew that would not lessen his magnetism, but at that moment, she didn't want to do anything to break their trance. There was something magical, mystical, about this exchange. Her innermost thoughts were certain to be betrayed each moment her eyes lingered, but she found this to be of little concern.

He stretched out his legs, and his face contorted in pain.

"Why do I get the feeling I must look even worse than I feel?" he asked, sucking in his breath and releasing it slowly.

Immediately she was at ease. "You do, but don't let that alarm you. I'm sure the way you feel is only temporary. You've been through a lot these past twenty-four hours." She pulled the rocker up to the bed. "Have you any recollection at all of what happened to you?"

His pale brows pulled tightly together. "I'm not sure exactly what happened, to be honest with you."

Dare longed to reach out and erase the lines of agony. Instead, she made sure her hands remained locked firmly in her lap.

"One minute I was in a poker game with a few of the Mallory executives, and the next, I was fighting to keep my head above water."

He winced with each word. Obviously remembering pained him greatly. If only there was something she might do to comfort him!

"It was well past midnight," he continued, frowning. "We had just decided that would be our last hand. All at once, a horrendous noise came from below. It sounded like the keel had rammed right into a rock wall." Shadows deeper than the cuts dug into his face. "The next thing I knew, water came pouring in from all directions. Panic set in quickly. Everywhere men were being sucked under. Their prayers and desperate pleas were louder than the storm." He caught his breath with much effort. "I swam as hard as I could. Waves kept pounding over me and dragging me back to the ship. I swam until my arms and legs refused to move at all. Luckily, the tide carried me to the channel marker. Holding on proved as hard an ordeal as swimming. There was a schooner anchored nearby," he said, looking directly at her for the first time since beginning his story. "At any other time I could have swum to it with no effort at all, but by then, I was too exhausted to do more than keep my head out of the water. I waited, praying that one of the launches that had set out from the schooner or from one of the other craft that had gathered around would see me. I yelled until sound would no longer come, but I could not be heard above the commotion." His brows knotted. He looked at her as though he could not believe his memory was serving him correctly. "Finally, someone did come. I remember thinking that I was hallucinating because of my fatigue. I thought she was a mirage."

Dare sat up straight. He remembered more than she had expected. "Yes, go on," she urged softly.

"Tales of mermaids rescuing drowning sailors at sea always fascinated me," he said, reaching for her hand. He laced his fingers weakly through hers. "Somehow merely saying thank you can't possibly express what I feel. I owe you my life."

"You owe me nothing," she said, her words barely audible. She knew she should withdraw her hand, but she just couldn't bring herself to unweave her fingers from his. "Were . . . were you traveling alone?"

He nodded. "The others?"

She shook her head. "I'm sorry. By the time the shore patrol spotted the vessel, she was already well under."

His sigh was troubled. "I was afraid of that." He released her hand. "I wonder why I was chosen to survive."

"Sometimes it's better not to question things we cannot change." She searched for words to ease his grief. It was obvious he was hurting inside, and there was nothing she could do to remedy it. "It's best to accept things just as they are, and to be grateful that, for whatever reason, you can go on living." She thought of Mac and smiled. Giving advice was one thing, taking it an entirely different matter.

"Wise, brave, and beautiful. Quite a combination of attributes," he remarked, rolling over onto his side to face her.

Dare felt her temperature rise. No man had ever told her she was beautiful.

"I seem to have embarrassed you. I apologize."

Her face caught the flush of the sun at midday. How unsophisticated he must think her! "You didn't embarrass me at all," she assured him, leveling her gaze with his.

"Good. There's no reason for you to feel the least bit leery of me, you know." His blue eyes prodded deeper and deeper.

She felt herself slipping under his spell once again. "Considering my present condition, if I were

51

anything but a perfect gentleman, you'd have no trouble putting me in my place. Friends?"

His smile was contagious.

"Friends."

"Excellent."

Was that how you and Nessa began? she wanted to ask. As friends?

His eyes refused to release hers.

Dare could not muster the strength to break the spell. Finally, she could endure the unnerving silence no longer. "Are you . . . are you still in a great deal of pain?"

"The pain is there, but I welcome it," he said gravely. "At least I am alive to suffer. Thanks to you," he added, his gaze once again settling on her. "You know, last night I dreamed of a woman, of a very beautiful woman, nursing my injuries and sponging cool water across my face. Her touch was so gentle, so kind."

Dare's face paled. Oh, please, let that be all he remembered!

"And do you know what else I dreamed?"

Her heart ground to a halt. The room had become an unbearable inferno. Dare felt herself wilting under his scorching stare. She was afraid to move a muscle.

He did not wait for an answer. "That very same beautiful woman soothed my hurts with a kiss."

"I'm not at all surprised your sleep was filled with dreams." She tried her best to keep her expression unchanged. "Your fever was extremely high."

A mischievous gleam played in his eye. "My fever? Yes of course. That would certainly explain my dreams." He rolled over and folded his arms across his chest. "Here we are, chatting away like old friends, and I don't even know your name."

Her pulse raced. "My name is Dare . . . Dare MacDade," she replied, feeling her resolve weaken.

"Dare," he repeated slowly. "Your name suits you well. Few men would have braved those seas to rescue someone who was already half dead. Few, indeed," he echoed thoughtfully.

"I only did what had to be done. You mustn't make such a fuss over it. Really," she said, embarrassed.

He looked puzzled. "What do you mean by what had to be done?"

"The sea had to be deprived of at least one soul," she answered, her voice distant.

"You speak as though you've experienced the sea's wrath before," he said in a softened tone.

She nodded. "I have. I lost my father to the sea last fall."

"I'm sorry."

She could sense his words were genuine and not spoken to be polite. "Perhaps, if had I gone out with him that day, the result might have been different." Her words trailed off to a whisper. "He asked me to, but I was too busy. Too busy," she echoed softly. "I don't remember him ever telling me he was too busy to do anything with me." Tears glistened in her eyes. "Anyway, he went alone. I think a water spout must have capsized his boat and he was just too far out to swim back to shore."

Dare collected herself quickly. She wondered why she had bared her soul to this man? To a complete stranger. Why on earth would she tell him of her

53

guilt at not accompanying Mac on his fishing trip? Why? She had never even told Uriah that she felt partly to blame for Mac's death.

The man struggled to sit up. "Had you gone, you could have done nothing to change the outcome." His quiet voice was filled with understanding. "Besides, think how unbearable the end would have been for your father had you been suffering beside him."

"I've never really thought of it that way," she responded.

"This must be a very trying period for you and your family," he said.

"There is no one else. My mother died when I was a little girl."

He reached for her hand. "Then it must be very difficult for you."

She smiled. The kindness she saw reflected in his eyes was strangely comforting. Accepting his hand seemed quite natural. "I suppose that, given time, adjusting will become easier."

"A lot can happen." He gave her hand a pat, then released it. "Given time."

His words resounded in her ears. Given time . . . What had he meant by that? she wondered.

"How about some breakfast?" Dare asked suddenly, realizing she had been involved in her thoughts.

"I thought you'd never ask," he replied cheerfully. "I am starving."

"Wonderful. That's a sure sign you're well on your way to recovery."

He looked concerned. "I certainly hope it doesn't

come too quickly."

"Oh?"

"I find that I'm enjoying the attention, not to mention the company," he grinned. "You will join me, won't you? For breakfast, that is. After what I've been through, it would probably prove very traumatic if I had to dine alone."

Do not misinterpret his kindness, Dare cautioned herself. He's grateful, that's all. You must not forget there's someone else.

She frowned to herself. How could she possibly forget about blond, beautiful Nessa? He would not!

"I thought I had been abandoned," he remarked cheerfully when she returned to the room with a tray in each hand.

"That hungry, were you?" she laughed as she positioned one of the trays across his lap.

"That, too," he returned matter-of-factly.

Dare backed into the rocker. His smile had the power to start and stop the beating of her heart, she decided as she balanced the tray on her knees.

"What? You're not going to feed me?" he asked once she was comfortable.

"I think you can manage that on your own," she laughed.

"I suppose the least I can do is give it a try." He began buttering his biscuit. "Incidentally, in case you're curious, my name is Matt Colby."

Dare choked on her tea.

"Is something wrong?"

She shook her head. "The tea. It's much hotter

55

than I thought."

Her answer seemed to satisfy him, and he resumed eating.

Perhaps he had won the watch in a poker game, she reasoned, slowly sipping her tea. That would explain it. She frowned to herself. Of course, it would be difficult not to think of him as Chase. Oh, dear. Calling him by that name in her thoughts had become a habit. Guarding against such slip-ups in the future would be difficult.

Her mood suddenly lifted. Wait! If his name were not Chase, then he could not possibly have been the man to whom Nessa had vowed her love.

Mixed feelings flooded her thoughts. Why that deduction should secretly please her was perplexing indeed! No man had ever caused such a commotion within her. She liked being courted as well as the next girl, but she didn't have much use for all the nonsense that usually went along with it. For as long as she could remember, she had always fancied herself destined for greatness. Such was always the fate of first-born MacDades, or so Mac had said. Why should the fact that she was Mac's only offspring, and a daughter at that, alter that notion? Besides, she had never pictured herself as a wife and mother. Being a successful resort owner was far more appealing. So why was she now having second thoughts, she asked herself as she spread sea-grape jelly onto her biscuit.

She popped a bite into her mouth and stole another glance at Matt. He fascinated her. She couldn't deny that. No man had ever piqued her interest so. Not even Richard Davis, and he had come calling twice weekly and at least once on the weekends, she remembered fondly.

As Dare chewed her biscuit she silently considered the young men who had vied for her hand both before and after Mac's death. Perhaps accepting one of the proposals would have offered her the financial security she so desperately needed. Still, she had resigned herself to a life alone, she reminded herself, swallowing hard. That was what she wanted. The decision had been made of her own choosing, not of necessity. She would do well to remember that more frequently, she told herself, her eyes lifting from her plate only to intercept his.

"So what brings you South, Mr. Colby?" It took a moment for her to recover from his stare. His blatant perusal of her had caught her off guard.

"Mr. Colby? Must we be so formal?" He gestured to his nightshirt. "After all . . ."

Her face flamed. She fought to keep her composure. "If you think that I was responsible for your change of clothing, you are wrong," she said as lightly as she could manage. "That was accomplished by one of the sailors who helped bring you here."

Matt grinned sheepishly. "I assumed as much. If I offended you, I certainly didn't mean to. I was only teasing. Can't we be on a first-name basis? I'm hardly thirty, so I'm not quite your elder yet . . . Dare."

She nodded. "Of course." The way he said her name made warmth surge through her.

He reached for another biscuit. "To answer your question, I'm a correspondent with the *New York World*."

Her mouth suddenly went dry. "Oh. I see."

He seemed surprised. "Do I detect a note of disapproval?"

"Disapproval? Of course not. I suppose you've come here to cover the controversy in Cuba," she remarked flatly.

"As a matter of fact, I have." He looked puzzled. "Does that bother you?"

Dare hesitated.

"It does." A forkful of grits stopped in midair. "I can see it written on your face."

"What bothers me," she calmly began, "are the private vendettas waged by several of the major publishers. It seems to me that of late when there are no newsworthy events, they create them."

"You're referring of course to the civil strife in Cuba?"

His smile was disarming. "Yes, I am."

"Which major publishers are you speaking of?" he asked.

"Mr. Hearst." His smile brought one to her own lips. "And your Mr. Pulitzer."

"So what you're saying in fact is that the news we report is biased?"

She held her ground. "Yes, it is. Objective journalism has become more the exception than the rule." She waited for a response. When none came, she continued. "It seems to me that the decision to intervene in Cuba must rest with our nation's leaders and certainly not the press."

The grin had yet to leave his face. "Good thing I was in no condition to show you my press card night before last. You would have let me drown for sure," he remarked, reaching for another biscuit.

"Sorry. I seem to get a bit carried away with the politics in Cuba."

"Tell me, where do your sympathies lie? With Cuba or with Spain?" he asked between bites.

Dare met his gaze head on. "Neither one, to be quite honest with you. My loyalties lie with my island. If our nation goes to war with Spain, it will be Florida, in particular Key West, that will be most affected by the war. Washington and New York will both be far removed from the action."

Matt said nothing.

Dare sensed she had offended him. She wasn't quite certain whether she should apologize or not, but she did not, feeling that she had a right to voice her opinion.

"Being a newspaperman must be very exciting," she said finally, hoping to shift the conversation to more neutral grounds.

"It is," he agreed. "Then again, it's a high pressure business as well. You're always rushing to meet one deadline or another, and you hardly have time to breathe between one newsmaking event and the next." He winked. "Plus, one must be very creative. If everything on the home front is dull, we have to fabricate all sorts of rebellions abroad."

Dare laughed. Thank goodness she hadn't insulted him.

Matt lifted his cup to his mouth. "But the places I visit and the people I meet," he remarked, gazing at her over the china rim, "make all the demands less strenuous."

She felt as though a flight of butterflies had just been set free in her stomach. "The people I meet," he

59

had said, looking right at her.

"Are you acquainted with Mr. Richard Davis?" she asked quickly, trying to calm the flitting inside her.

Matt thought for a moment.

"He and his associate, Elliot Harris, spent some time here on their way to Cuba," continued Dare. "Their mission was to infiltrate guerrilla camps and interview rebel leaders for the *Journal*."

"Yes, yes of course," he said, nodding. "But only professionally. Dick and I collaborated on several Washington assignments last year. Back in May," he added as he turned his attention to his breakfast.

Dare shook her head. "No, it couldn't have been May."

"Oh?" He looked surprised.

"He was here that entire month," she informed him as she moved her tray to the bureau.

"You're certain?"

"Positive."

Matt gave a curt nod. "In that case I stand corrected. Is something troubling you?" he asked a few moments later when she'd made no other comments.

Dare looked puzzled. "Isn't it highly unusual for two journalists from rival papers to confer on assignments?"

"Not really," he answered. "Hearst's and Pulitzer's feuding is strictly between the two of them. We journalists are an entirely different breed."

"Oh, I see," she said quietly. That certainly wasn't what Richard, who hated to be called Dick, had told her. "It's a bit stuffy in here. I think we could do with some fresh air."

She was conscious of his eyes following her as she crossed to the window and opened the shutters.

Matt inhaled a deep breath. "Fresh air! Good for the body and the soul."

Dare relieved him of his tray. "Would you care for anything else? More tea?"

"No, thank you. Everything was delicious." A devilish gleam danced in his eyes a few minutes later. "By the way, when do my bandages get changed?"

His smile was certainly disarming. "Later this afternoon, I shall explain the entire process in detail. It shouldn't take you long to get the knack of it," she couldn't resist adding.

"You're not leaving now, are you?"

She was certain she had detected a note of disappointment in his voice. "I'm afraid I must," she said, stacking the trays. "You need your rest, and I have some chores to do."

"Don't you want to take my temperature or to put cold compresses on my head?" he asked, refusing to release her from his scrutiny.

"To be honest with you, I know very few of the basics of doctoring." She could feel her temperature rising steadily.

"But what if I have a relapse?"

"I would suggest that you wait until Doc Edmundson returns from his fishing trip before your condition takes a turn for the worse." Her eyes remained on the dishes. It was becoming increasingly more difficult to avoid his stare. "He can deal with such matters far better than I."

"I'll try to prolong the suffering as long as I can."

Dare couldn't help but chuckle. "How brave

61

you are!"

He shrugged his shoulders. "Just courageous."

"Do try to rest, won't you?"

He nodded. "When will you be back to check on me?"

"Never, if you don't do as you're told."

Matt settled himself beneath the covers. "All right, Miss MacDade, you win. You are a miss, aren't you?" he asked as an afterthought.

She opened the door. "Yes, I am."

"One more thing."

"Yes, what is it?" she asked, sighing.

"The clothes I was wearing . . . where are they?" he inquired, sitting up in bed.

Dare pointed to the window. "I don't think you're quite up to a stroll around town."

"I couldn't agree more. As a matter of fact, I would venture to say that if Doctor Edmundson were here he would prescribe one week's bed rest and instruct the nurse to treat the patient with as much kindness as possible."

"We'll seek his professional opinion when he returns," she said lightly.

"Sorry to be such a nuisance, but could I trouble you to hand them to me?" he asked, pointing to his clothes.

Dare set the trays outside the door, then did as he requested. She pulled her rocker away from the bed, watching with curious interest as he drew the watch from his pocket.

"Good thing I wasn't the one to stop ticking," he said, closing the cover and slipping the watch back into his pocket.

She kept her voice firm and steady. "I hope your pocket watch wasn't a family heirloom," she said matter-of-factly.

He shook his head. "It was a Christmas present from a friend of mine."

"Oh, I see." Her heart plunged. "I really must go now. I'll check in on you later."

"Don't forget I'm here," he called out cheerfully.

"I won't."

Dare closed the door behind her. Her thoughts raced wildly. How can I forget about you, Chase, or Matt, or whoever you are?

Chapter Four

Breakfast tray in hand, Dare stalled outside the guest room. Her emotions were divided. On the one hand, she wanted to rush into the room and give him a good morning peck on the cheek, while on the other, she wanted to keep her distance from him and maintain a strictly professional relationship. She so desperately wanted to see Chase or Matt—whatever he called himself—but she knew she'd fare far better if she just left well enough alone. As much as it perplexed her, the fact remained. He had purposely deceived her. Regardless of the reason, he had lied to her, and there could be no excuse for that. So much of what he had told her simply did not pan out. More than once, he had been snared in his own web of deceit. Had he been introduced to Richard Davis, he would have been informed right from the start that Richard hated being called Dick. His name was Richard, and that was that. Period. Not Dick, Dicky,

Rick, or Ricky. Richard! Furthermore, the *Journal* and the *World* were such bulldog competitors that no one from either paper would collaborate on an assignment with someone from the enemy camp. According to Richard, Hearst would fire anyone known to have mumbled a polite hello to one of Pulitzer's reporters, and the same held true for the publisher of the *Journal*.

As Dare inched closer to the door, she knew there was no denying what really hurt the most. It mattered little whether his name was Chase or Matt, the watch still belonged to him. He had casually mentioned that it had been a Christmas present, and who else could have possibly given it to him but the beautiful young woman whose picture graced the inside— Nessa. It had been the watch, not his money, that he had reached for first. No doubt the woman who had pledged herself to him forever had been foremost in his thoughts. One look at his lovely Nessa and his suffering would be tolerable.

Oh, why could she not stand back and be nothing more than an objective observer? wailed Dare as her hand reached for the doorknob then pulled back in the same motion. Why should a man she hardly knew be able to elicit such unsettling sensations from her? She had always been poised, self-assured, and confident in any situation. How could she be so easily disarmed now? She had been unable to think of anything but him all day yesterday although she had gone out of her way to avoid him. He would have to be blind not to notice, and she would have to be blind to his lies not to avoid him. At breakfast only twenty-four hours ago, she had taken him a tray, then hurriedly excused herself on the pretense of having errands in town. Thank goodness Uriah had appeared at noon. The two men had become fast friends over green turtle soup. Uriah had found a spellbound audience for his seafaring tales. Had her own absence been noticed, Uriah would have mentioned it, but nothing had been said. When Uriah had gone back to the warehouse for the evening watch, she had once more been left alone with her patient. His supper had been delivered in a rush. Accounting chores awaited her, she had told him when he'd asked her to dine with him. For the rest of the evening, she had moped around in the room above his, regretting over and over her decision to keep her distance. At one point during the evening, her hand had been only a fraction of an inch from the thick oak door of his room, but her good sense had kept her from knocking. What would she have said? I know you lied to me, so fess up and everything will be just fine? No, of course, she couldn't. If he'd done it once, he could easily do it again, she reminded herself. Damn him! He had her thoughts running around in circles, but why did he have to put her heart into a tizzy as well!

Her heart fluttered. Good sense had discouraged her from knocking, but it hadn't kept her from peeking through the keyhole. He had looked so lonely sitting up in bed and staring out into space, his arms neatly crossed over his chest and a forlorn— no, a wistful—expression on his face. Concluding that his reverie had most likely involved the girl he'd left behind, she had tiptoed back up the stairs only to lie awake most of the night, anticipating the slightest noise from below. Once the springs creaked and her heart pummeled her ribs. Thoughts she had never entertained before whirlwinded inside her head. She probably slept about two hours that night.

It would take tremendous willpower to keep her relationship with him in perspective. Of that she was certain! Still, it was better to realize that now than later. In a few days, he'd settle the business that had brought him to Key West; then he would be on his way. Right now such a thought was unbearable. If she didn't guard against her feelings, that same thought would be agonizing forty-eight or seventy-two hours from now.

Dare took one last deep breath to steady her nerves before positioning her fingers around the brass knob. It was all well and good to tell herself he'd be gone soon, but acceptance of his impending departure didn't make the inevitable any easier to face. Nor had it made her grooming any less meticulous. An hour earlier, knowing precisely why she had done so, she had flipped through her everyday attire of skirts and middies and had chosen one of the dressier, more flattering outfits in her cedar wardrobe. She had selected a gown with a straight, fitted skirt and a full bodice that bloused above a tight belt, thereby making her slim waistline look even smaller. As small as Nessa's waist? she asked herself. However, it had been the color, not the style, which had prompted her choice. The satin was the same vibrant shade of blue as his eyes. When she took the same care dressing as she had the past two mornings, she knew why she did so, just as she knew why she had been wearing her hair unswept as of late. She wanted him to find her attractive! She wanted him to . . .

Stop it! Dare shouted silently to herself. Enough of such nonsense. Why should she care what kind of impression she made on him. Humph! Why, indeed!

She cleared her throat and, standing erect, delivered a trio of firm, decisive taps on the door.

The moment the words "Come in" were spoken, she felt a weakening in her knees. Her entire resolve turned to jelly the moment she heard his voice. Mustering all the courage she could manage, she pushed open the door and stepped inside.

Just seeing him sitting up in bed with the covers folded neatly around his waist sent her pulse racing. Nervously, she moistened her dry lips with the tip of her tongue. "Good morning," she managed to say as she strolled toward him, attempting to act nonchalant.

A pair of dimples suddenly jumped at the corners of his mouth. "And a good morning to you as well," he returned softly. "I was beginning to think you had forgotten all about me."

His deep, sensuous tone sent a response rippling through her. His words had cut through her hard defense. Her misgivings vanished. There was no use deceiving herself any longer. What she was feeling for him was an emotion she had never before experienced. He was the only one who could quiet the storm blustering inside her.

She broke into a wide, friendly smile in spite of herself. "I do apologize for leaving you on your own for so much of yesterday," she said, positioning the tray across his lap. "But I'm afraid my absence could not be helped. My duties can't be neglected."

He held up his hand. "Please, you owe me no apology. If anyone is to blame it is I for demanding so much of your time, but it seems I . . ." He hesitated.

"Yes, go on," she encouraged.

She could have sworn she saw a tinge of rose play on his cheek.

"It seems that I felt quite lost without you." He unfolded his napkin and positioned it across his chest. "Your friend, Uriah, is some storyteller. He kept me in stitches most of the afternoon, but . . ." His fork stopped midway to his mouth.

She felt herself consumed by a look that was bold and assertive.

"The truth is, I looked forward all day to seeing you, and when you breezed in and out so quickly, I was rather disappointed."

His own words seemed to make him uncomfortable. The forkful of johnnycake found its way to his mouth. He chewed it hurriedly, then jabbed another chunk.

Dare pulled the rocker to a respectable distance from the bed and lowered herself slowly into it, holding on to the arms. Her eyes were drawn to him, while her palm pressed a tiny wrinkle from her dress. She could feel droplets of moisture beading on her forehead. When she had been dressing a short while earlier, she had rehearsed many clever remarks she intended to use to lighten their conversation. But now, no matter how hard she tried, not one of those witty comments found its way past the lump in her throat.

"How are you feeling?" she asked finally. It had not been part of her plan to ask him about his health.

He seemed to sense the hesitancy in her voice. He looked up at her, his gaze thoughtful and kind. "Thanks to you, my recovery has been most speedy. As a matter of fact, such a quick return to good health may not prove to be in my best interest," he added, a pair of deep, worry lines forming between his eyes.

Once more her composure was waning. Those sapphirine blue eyes had a way of penetrating right into her soul. "Not in your best interest?" she echoed questioningly. "I don't understand."

A mysterious smile curved his mouth. "No, I don't suppose you would. But no matter." He resumed his breakfast with sudden vigor.

She felt as though she had been left dangling, but from what she wasn't quite sure.

"Tell me, did Uriah drop off any packages for me?" he asked, hungrily attacking his breakfast once again.

Dare couldn't decide whether she were relieved or disappointed that the topic of conversation had been altered. Her arms resting on those of the rocker, she lounged against the wicker backing. "Just what kind of a conspiracy are you two involved in?" she asked, becoming more relaxed. "I caught him sneaking in here with an armful of boxes when he was supposed to be out checking crab pots. When I asked what he thought he was doing, he said you had asked him to pick up a few things at Josh Curry's. But, he wouldn't tell me what," she said, eying her patient suspiciously. She folded her arms around her waist. "You know, I have a feeling I know just what was in those packages, and if I'm right it's no one's fault but your own if you drop dead on the street."

71

His chuckle was unrestrained. "I think you've made your point loud and clear. Perhaps I should wait another day or two before getting on with my assignment," he announced, shrugging his shoulders. "After all, I'm lucky even to be in the position to decide when I will or when I won't get back to work."

There was a relaxed silence between them. For the first time since he had come to, she was starting to feel totally at ease with him. If only he hadn't lied to her, she mused, then maybe she . . . maybe they . . .

She quickly erased such thoughts. The same sea that brought him to her would soon carry him away. Constantly reminding herself of this fact would surely alleviate the anguish when he left.

A few minutes later, she heard her name tagged onto the end of a sentence. She looked up, her face flushed with embarrassment. "I'm sorry. What were you saying?" What excuse could she possibly make for having heard his words without having comprehended their meaning. "I, I was just thinking what an exciting life a journalist must lead," she added hastily.

"Oh?" His very tone questioned the truth of her remark. "You had such a sad expression on your face just then."

"Did I?" Her laughter was forced. "Goodness! I can't think of any reason at all why I should be the least bit sad."

"No. I suppose not." His gaze lingered on her face, its intentness holding her eyes captive with each sweep.

A moment later, he gestured to his bandages. His grin was laced with sarcasm. "I suppose I'm living proof of that."

"Of what?"

"Of reporters leading such exciting lives," he told her.

Her cheeks flamed. Now, she really did feel like an idiot.

He continued, however, as though not a single awkward moment had passed between them. "You know something. I'd bet that a story with a personal slant—say, how I survived a shipwreck—might just have human interest."

"If you do decide to write one along those lines, I hope you'll put in a good word for the Sea Palms." Her smile was weak. "As you've noticed I'm sure, business is a bit slow these days."

He gave a knowing nod. "No doubt the trouble in Cuba is to blame for that."

"Either that or last year's horde of vacationers decided to build snowmen rather than sand castles," she said, a hint of bitterness in her tone.

He reached across the space separating them, nearly upsetting his tray. "Worry no more," he said, closing his fingers around hers. "The week after that story hits the newsstands, you'll have such a flood of tourists, you'll curse the day you dragged me out of the ocean."

"Oh, I doubt that," she said quickly. Then her cheeks patched scarlet. Her gaze fell to the arm of the rocker, to her hand swallowed by his.

A moment later, she chanced to lift her lashes and her look collided head-on with his. Try as she might, there was no way she could wrest her eyes from his gaze. Nor was she sure she wanted to.

It was he who broke the spell their eyes had woven. "I was telling you about the nature of my assignment a little while ago. Shall I continue?" he asked, his voice almost hushed.

Dare nodded. She did not trust herself to speak. It was difficult enough to concentrate on what he was saying. Doing so with his hand atop hers would prove even more challenging. This was not the first time a gentleman had held her hand, but never before had such sensations been evoked by masculine flesh. Panic, unlike any she had known before, surfaced in her throat. Flames which she had never suspected existed inside her suddenly came alive. Had such feelings as these caused her friend Caroline Lowe to run off to Savannah with her cousin's fiancé only two days before the wedding?

Blinking rapidly, she tried to concentrate on what was being explained. If he sensed the maelstrom building inside her, he gave no indication. Thank heavens for that!

"The way I see it, those who've escaped Spanish domination and settled here in Key West can give me a better insight into the situation in Cuba," he continued as he finished his breakfast. "From here, I hope to go to Cuba myself and appraise the situation firsthand."

"When you do," she began, her voice as serious as her expression, "please keep in mind that the way the story is presented to the American public greatly influences their decision to ally themselves with Cuba or to remain neutral. If people continue to demand the former, then President McKinley will, in all likelihood, declare war and—"

He completed her sentence for her. "And Spain could easily retaliate by invading the southern part of Florida, namely Key West." He gave her hand a reassuring squeeze before letting it go. "I'll proceed with that in mind. You can count on me."

"I'd certainly appreciate that." Her gaze dropped to her lap. Her hand quivered from his touch. His promise echoed inside her head. You can count on me, he had told her. You can count on me. Could she? she wondered.

At that instant, the turmoil in Cuba was far from her mind. Had Chase . . . Matt . . . been referring solely to the crisis in Cuba, or had there been a hidden message in his words.

You'll do well not to dwell on such fantasies, she told herself and prepared to depart. "Now, if you'll excuse me, I—"

"You're not going so soon, are you?"

His fervency caught her off guard. "Since you've finished your breakfast, I thought I'd . . ."

He quickly took his knife and fork back in hand. "I'm not finished. I'm a very slow eater," he told her as he cut the remaining piece of johnnycake into a half-dozen tiny morsels. "Besides, I was hoping you'd be able to give me a little background information on the political scene here. You do seem to be rather well versed on such issues."

Dare couldn't help but smile. "Had you tagged 'for a woman' onto the end of your statement, you'd have the rest of the coffee poured over you."

"Well, have you a few extra minutes to spare?"

She nodded. After all, she told herself, what harm could there possibly be in staying another five or ten minutes. She wouldn't be able to concentrate on the ledger anyway.

Folding her hands in her lap, she waited for his first question.

"Not there. Here," he said, patting the edge of the bed. "I'm not going to bite. Word of honor."

"What is it that you'd like to know?" she asked as she stiffly positioned herself on the spot his hand had patted.

"For starters, you can tell me how you and the rest of the Key Westerners feel about the sudden influx of refugees."

Feminine intuition told her that he was using his assignment as an excuse to detain her. Furthermore, the ploy did not annoy her at all.

"There's nothing sudden about the flight of the Cuban patriots," she said, allowing herself to relax somewhat. "In fact, it began nearly thirty years ago. From the early seventies to the mid-eighties, some fifteen thousand of them sought political asylum in Key West. Of course, not all of them remained. Many traveled upstate to Saint Augustine and then on to Tampa." She tried her best to avoid direct contact with his eyes, for every time their two hues of blue collided, their gazes locked. "As far as community reaction is concerned," she continued, her fingers entwined in her lap, "Key Westerners as a whole accept the Latin community. Many of the Cubans have made great civic contributions in the areas of business and commerce. Their influence is even more apparent in apparel, cooking, and architecture."

"It is said that the birth of the Cuban revolution was not in Havana as one might have expected, but here in Key West," he remarked, positioning himself so she would have no other alternative but to meet his stare head-on.

"I am sure there is much truth in that statement."

His eyes mesmerized her. The deeper she delved into them, the more at ease she became. The longer she permitted such a frank confrontation, the deeper she could feel herself slipping under their spell.

Keeping her mind on the matters at hand was becoming increasingly difficult. Momentarily gaining control of her wits, she cautioned herself that she must not allow him to have such a tremendous impact on her.

"Many of those who came here," she continued as she smoothed a fold in her skirt, "dream of one day returning to their native land. Their dream can only come true, however, if the Spanish are driven from their soil."

He seemed to be listening more to the sound of her voice than to what she was saying. "What thoughts have you concerning Spanish domination of the island?"

"I do not feel as though I'm qualified to voice an opinion one way or the other," she said after a long pause. "Horrible atrocities are committed every day. That's true. But both sides, not one, are at fault. I have both Cuban and Spanish friends in Havana, and basically, both groups are alike. Peace is the main objective. Unfortunately, it is one that cannot easily be attained."

"Why the pessimism?"

She frowned. "The revolution is in the hands of several hotheads who have become crazed by the whole notion of Cuba Libre. They are opposed by Spanish generals who want to make the entire world an armed military camp. An emotional American public aggravates the situation. I don't think peace can be achieved without great cost."

Dare waited for a response. When none was forthcoming, she permitted her eyes to travel the path they wanted to take. "You must be thinking that I sound like a crusader myself," she remarked, her gaze fastened on his.

"Quite the contrary."

She wanted to ask him why he was staring at her in such an intense manner, but couldn't bring herself to question him.

"It's rare indeed to find a woman, especially so young and beautiful a woman, who can intelligently discuss matters unrelated to fashions or recipes. Rare, indeed." He studied her freely and without reservation, raking her with his gaze. A look of appreciation glimmered in the hypnotic blue pools of his eyes.

Dare felt herself sinking deeper into the mattress. Thank goodness she was sitting. Had she been standing, her knees would have buckled.

She needed a moment to compose herself. True, his forthright appraisal of her was unnerving, yet at the same time, it was not entirely unpleasant.

"If you wish to interview some of the refugees," she began, deciding it was safer to change the subject to something other than herself, "I will be happy to arrange an invitation for you to lunch at the San Carlos Club with some of the Cuban leaders."

His expression remained unchanged. "I'd appreciate that." His words were flat. Enthusiasm flickered only in his eyes.

Dare watched, not speaking, as the rise and fall of his chest quickened. He seemed to be as entranced with her as she was with him. Something drew her closer and closer to him. How much longer could their eyes remain locked? she wondered. She could make up her mind to guard against an emotional attachment to him, to keep their relationship strictly impersonal, but to carry out that decision she had to be completely committed to it. A half-hearted approach simply would not do. To take the first step in that direction she must return to her own chair and remain a respectable distance from him, yet she had neither the strength nor the inclination to do so.

An involuntary sigh escaped her lips. How difficult it was to be so close, hardly an arm's length away. How wonderful it would be to reach out to him . . . just for a minute.

She listened quietly, her head tilted in his direction, and pretended to be totally engrossed in all he was saying about his upcoming trip to Cuba, but the sounds coming from his mouth were mere words without meaning. Those deep, deep blue orbs demanded her total attention. Nothing else mattered. His mouth might be relaying one message, but his eyes were communicating another that had nothing to do with infiltrating rebel forces. She had detected that sort of message in men's eyes before, but never before had she seen a reflection of her own desire.

He studied her intently, his gaze sliding down her face, past her shoulders, and onto her breasts, those full, soft mounds which lifted even higher under his scrutiny. His every look was caressing. Her skin tingled from a touch that was transmitted solely by his eyes, which held her captive. She could not escape them, nor did she want to do so.

With a nervous flick of her hand, she pushed a wayward strand of hair from her ear. Her breath caught. There was no mistaking the nature of the glance that passed between them. She had witnessed the same, starry-eyed exchange often enough between Caroline and Phillip to know what that sort of look led to!

He leaned toward her slowly, his motion as intent as his eyes.

Unable to resist, Dare surrendered to the force beckoning her. A sigh of sweet complaisance left her lips. All the pent-up emotions that had been swirling madly inside her since she had first set eyes on him were quietly being released.

Violet eyes absorbed depthless blue pools. Eager lips parted a bit more. She knew she should leave the room that very instant, leave it and never look back, never give another thought to what she was leaving behind! But she could not. She just could not! An act of fate had brought them together, an act which could just as easily separate them forever.

A dilemma faced her. What would be the lesser of the two evils, she wondered over and over again as her heart pounded loudly against her breast. Falling in love only to be abandoned one day, or never knowing such precious moments?

Her face now only a fraction of an inch from his, she made her decision. The time had come to listen to her heart. Life is a gamble, it was saying. Without risks, life is dull. Without love, it is hardly worth living.

At first, his kiss was hardly more than a whisper, a feather-light touch of his lips on hers. Then strong fingers caressed her cheeks, their touch gentle and soothing to her flesh.

A contented sigh rose in her throat. Never had she dreamed a kiss, even one so light and airy as this, could be so moving, so stimulating. It alone had the potency to retard or accelerate the beating of her heart.

As his strong, sensuous mouth possessed hers, her womanly intuition was quick to make up for her lack of experience. Back arched and anxious arms wound tight around his neck, she gladly imprisoned herself in his embrace, determined to savor each moment.

His mouth pressed hungrily onto hers, its pressure flattening her lips and drawing out her own life's force. She drank in the sweetness of his kiss, reveling in its passion, determined to hold nothing back.

A manly arm tightened around her. Powerful fingers molded themselves to her curves, and then bit by bit, inched toward her breasts.

Dare turned slightly. Shivers of desire raced up through her. There was no mistaking his hand's destination, and, eager for it to find its goal, she gasped as his fingers roamed over her breasts with a delicious possessiveness. Swollen from the passion building inside them, her rock-hard peaks welcomed his caresses.

Tremors shook her. Those hard-to-believe sensations Caroline had described in such detail were suddenly very real!

What's happening to me? she wondered, feeling as though she were floating a good ten feet above the bed. What havoc was being played with her senses? First she was cold, then she was burning up. One moment, she could hardly breathe, and the next, her lungs were filled with more than enough air.

Expert hands sought the buttons of her blouse. She had no intention of voicing an objection. Instead, although impatient, she restrained herself from lending him assistance.

Suddenly, without warning, his fingers ceased their wonderful wanderings.

Her eyes opened instantly, and she waited, afraid to lift her head.

Buttons, only seconds before undone, were being closed up again.

What's wrong? she wanted to scream out at the top of her lungs, but the words stuck in her throat and reverberated loudly inside her head.

A few seconds of agonizing silence, then she felt him tilting her cheek to his, tenderly forcing her to meet his look. She tried to look away, to focus on anything but him, but she could not.

A chaste kiss on the tip of her nose was his only explanation. Swallowing hard, she braved a look at his wonderfully handsome face. One glance, and she knew why he had curtailed his passion. Certainly he desired her, but he was a gentleman, a gentleman in every sense of the word. So he had restrained himself.

She was relieved that he had done so, still, she could not help but feel the tiniest twinge of disappointment as she sat there watching him from the corner of her eye.

Neither pulled away. Instead, their bodies rocked in gentle harmony one with the other, and he whispered her name over and over, the words a sad reminder of what had almost been.

For the longest while, she said nothing. As far as she was concerned, everything worth saying had already been said. At that moment, she was certain that nothing could give her more pleasure than to spend an eternity locked in his embrace. Now she knew exactly what Caroline had meant when she had said that she couldn't bear to be separated from her lover even for a minute. Her best friend's sentiments echoed her own. For an instant, his very essence had flowed through her veins, and because of that brief encounter, she'd carry a bit of him with her for all time.

He hesitated before loosening his hold. "Angry?"

She shook her head. No words could convey the ecstasy she was feeling at that very minute. She longed to tell him that she had never imagined a single show of affection could have such a powerful impact. Instead, she remained silent. How unsophisticated she would surely seem in comparison to Nessa if she let the truth be known.

His hands gently pushed her a few inches away. "If you were angry, you know, I wouldn't blame you in the least," he said softly, his eyes dwelling on hers. "As a matter of fact, you'd be perfectly justified if you threw me out in the street this instant for taking such liberties with your kindness."

Her forefinger brushed his lips into silence. "Shh. Don't be ridiculous. Liberties indeed!" Her grin broadened. "The fact is I quite enjoyed it."

She waited with bated breath for some reaction, any reaction, from him. Had she made a mistake by confessing her innermost feelings to him? she wondered.

Finally he spoke. "I, too, enjoyed it." A frown shadowed his mouth. "That's the problem. I liked it much too much."

"Problem?" Her back stiffened. "I don't understand."

At that instant, her eye caught sight of the gold pocket watch that had been placed on the bedside table. For one brief, wonderful moment she had forgotten.

She pulled back from him. How ashamed she felt. Another few minutes and she would have been all too eager to oblige his every wish. A kiss would have been only the beginning.

"Of course. I understand," she heard herself say.

His fingers brushed the side of her face. "How could you understand? I don't fully understand myself. You see, there's something you must know. I am not—"

Dare rose quickly. Under no circumstances must she let him continue. She would have enough trouble as it was coping with the pain of wanting another woman's man. "Please, there's no reason for explanations or apologies." At that moment, she would have liked nothing better than to disappear. Never had she experienced such humiliation. How could she have been so naïve? "As a matter of fact," she concluded tersely, "the less said, the better. I suggest we simply forget the entire incident."

Fighting to hold back her tears, she picked up the tray and walked quickly out of the room. She closed the door behind her, then collapsed against it. If she lived to be a hundred, she would never forget those few precious moments. If she were never again kissed, she could exist solely on this memory the remainder of her days.

Chapter Five

Dare sat at her desk later in the afternoon and penned a long overdue letter to Caroline. There was so much to report to her friend, but the words were slow in coming. Her mind simply wasn't on the task at hand. Trying to block that kiss from her mind only served to implant the memory of it more firmly, and even when she was not thinking of him, his agonizingly handsome face would suddenly be conjured up. She continually recalled the intimacy of his lips and her mouth ached for the feel of his, her lips still burning in the aftermath of his fiery possession. Reliving that moment was wrong, so wrong, she kept trying to convince herself, but she did not really believe that. How could something so wonderful be wicked?

Oh, why do I have to be so sensible? she wailed over and over. If only I were more like sweet, impetuous Caroline.

Lucky Caroline! Her letters spoke of nothing but love and passion and a promise of happiness and togetherness for ever and always. Always! Such a little word for such a very, very long time!

Vowing once again to put the past behind her, Dare threw down her pen in disgust. Recounting the past few days was just too complicated. A three-hour, face-to-face conversation was what she needed to explain all the twists and turns of the recent days. Caroline would think she'd lost her senses, feeling so strongly for a man she hardly knew, a man who'd told her his name was Matt but who was probably concealing his true identity.

A knock at the front door distracted her from her thoughts. She waited for Calpurnia to answer it, but remembering after the third knock that her dear old mammy was no longer in her service, she hurried from her office.

She opened the door. "Yes?"

Her smile of greeting froze.

"Good afternoon, Señorita Dare." Her visitor had a heavy Spanish accent. "You're certainly looking well."

She made no effort to disguise her displeasure at seeing him. "Señor Ferrer," she acknowledged stiffly. "What can I do for you?"

A mouthful of bright, white teeth flashed at her. "I believe the question might be better phrased: What can I do for you?"

She felt the hair on the back of her neck bristle. "I'm afraid I don't understand at all what you mean."

"Then permit me to explain matters to you."

Without waiting for an invitation, he stepped inside.

Her fists clenched at her sides, Dare followed him into the sitting room. "I have little time for a chat," she told him coldly. "I've an appointment in a quarter of an hour."

His onyx walking cane positioned in front of him, Ferrer lowered himself onto the edge of the settee and folded his hands over the silver-studded handle. "No matter," he said, his strident tone taking on an air of uncharacteristic pleasantness. "What I wish to discuss with you will take but a moment of your time."

Sitting down on one of the wicker-backed lounges opposite him, Dare studied her visitor closely as he removed a cigar from inside his coat.

Eduardo Ferrer was without a doubt the most despicable man she had ever encountered. He was by far the wealthiest man in the Keys, perhaps even in all of Florida. Most of the islanders speculated that the enormous wealth he had amassed in the few short years he had lived in Key West was not derived from his cigar manufacturing company.

He was not a very old man, in his early forties at most, and he was not unattractive. His tall, lean stature and dark, Latin features were agreeable enough. Still, she could think of few people she had so disliked. Except for a band of turquoise around his wrist, he was dressed entirely in black. Dare was certain he purposely dressed in such a morbid fashion to present a picture of doom and gloom to all those with whom he had dealings. She could think of no redeeming quality he might possess. He prided himself on his ability to goad those whom he deemed inferior. Mac had often said that he had been spawned by the devil. Having been the object of his lecherous intentions on more than one occasion, she wasn't so sure that he wasn't Satan himself. Ferrer smacked his thin lips together loudly as he took a long pull on his cigar. "Since you are pressed for time, allow me to come straight to the point."

"By all means," she said, giving a curt nod.

"It has come to my attention that the Sea Palms has been experiencing some very serious financial problems since the death of your father."

"I hardly see how my personal finances are of any concern to you, Señor Ferrer," she responded, her temperature rising steadily.

"Eduardo, please," he insisted as he slicked his crow-black hair back from his forehead. "Surely you must know by now how I feel for you, Dare."

She fought to maintain her poise, refusing to give him the satisfaction of knowing he made her uncomfortable. "No doubt you're referring to those . . . those proposals you've made on numerous occasions."

His smile was cold and calculating. "You mistook my intentions. What I proposed was an amicable business association. Nothing more."

Dare felt herself shiver. His eyes had the ability to see right through her, and his thoughts were written all over his face. "I have no wish for a partner . . . business or otherwise."

"I see." He shrugged his shoulders indifferently. "What a pity! I was certain you would be pleased when you learned what I've done. So pleased, in fact, that you might even be persuaded to allow me to escort you to the party at the San Carlos Club tonight," he said, sucking harder on his cigar.

Her eyes blazed red. "Regardless of your news, I have no intention of accompanying you there."

"A woman with fire. I like that." His gimlet stare narrowed itself to her breasts. "Where there's a flame, there's spirit."

Dare sat up straight, her hands folded tightly in her lap. Under no circumstances would she be bullied. "My time is limited so if you would get to the point, please."

"By all means." He drew a piece of paper from the pocket of his waistcoat, took his time unfolding it, then handed it to her.

"What's this?" she asked.

"Read it." His thin lips turned up in a sneering grin. "I'm certain every detail has been explained."

Puzzled, she scanned its contents. Her eyes grew wider with each sentence she read.

Upon finishing, she folded the piece of paper and returned it to him. "This is completely unacceptable." Her jaw was set square and tight. "What you have proposed is entirely out of the question." Her stare locked onto his. How dare he! she thought angrily. He wasn't about to get away with something as sneaky and underhanded as that. Not if she had anything to say about it! "I would advise you to tell Mr. Morrow that under no circumstances, none at all, will I sign something so blatantly ridiculous. I refuse to be a party to it. Period. That's that," she announced in a voice that was decisive and strong. "Now, if I've made myself perfectly clear—"

"I am afraid that is entirely out of the question," he

countered, ignoring her refusal.

Ferrer leaned back in his seat. "Negotiations were conducted between myself and the bank's board of directors." His cat-that-ate-the-canary grin grew wider. "Everything has already been finalized. Your signature is merely a formality."

She threw back her shoulders. "Then I shall go down to the bank myself this very afternoon and set Mr. Morrow and the whole lot of them straight."

"Morrow has nothing to do with this. Not anymore. As a matter of fact, he was all too happy to oblige me." Ferrer touched his slick mustache. "You see, my dear, you are no longer indebted to the bank. I repaid your loan for you. Consequently it is I, not the bank, who must be reimbursed." He looked very pleased with himself. "It's all very simple."

"Simple?" she asked, struggling to maintain her control.

He nodded. "Unfortunately for you, the bank considers the Sea Palms a bad risk," he said gravely.

Dare grew numb with rage. "A bad risk?" she repeated, hardly believing him. "Our debts have always been paid."

His turquoise-wristed hand gave a helpless gesture. "I am only repeating what I was told."

Dare shook her head. "No. You're lying," she said, her tone flat. "The Sea Palms is one of the oldest businesses in town. We were well established even before Mr. Morrow and that fancy bank of his came to town."

Humor quirked his mouth. "You're forgetting about that hotbed across the way. Because of conditions in Cuba, you will have no tourists.

92

Without tourists, the Sea Palms has no hope of surviving . . . without a little assistance, that is. Assistance which I shall lend you."

"Obviously you believe the Sea Palms to be a good, sound investment despite problems in Cuba?" she asked, her voice tinged with sarcasm.

Ferrer's frown was deliberate. "In all honesty, I am in agreement with the bank." He expelled a long, heavy sigh before continuing. "However, I am prepared to take the necessary risk."

"For a tidy profit, no doubt," she remarked bitterly.

"Señorita Dare! You misjudge me." White teeth gleamed with amusement. "I want nothing more than to be of some assistance in your time of crisis."

I'd as soon trust a shark, she was itching to say, but restrained herself. "And what might your terms be . . . if I might be so bold as to inquire," she added tersely.

"Why, the same as the bank's of course," he replied smoothly. "You'll have until April fifteenth to repay the note in addition to the one percent interest you would have been required to pay the bank. Fair?"

She was none too anxious to reply. Ferrer had not earned a barracuda reputation because of fairness.

"If you are worrying about the possibility of being unable to repay the loan by that date, please, I beg of you, do not trouble yourself with such minute matters." One oily brow arched suggestively. "I am more than certain we shall be able to work out the incidentals to our mutual satisfactions."

She clamped her teeth tighter. At that moment, she would have liked nothing better than to spit in his face. The nerve of that bastard! How dare he even think such a thing! She'd just as soon torch the Sea Palms than have that disgusting slob bed her!

Her breathing slowly returned to a steady rhythm. Why should she be upset? she asked herself. After all, on Monday all her worries would be over. He would not have the last laugh.

"Your concern for my welfare is touching, Señor Ferrer," she said, managing a tight smile. "My debt will be repaid in full, I assure you."

"But of course," he said, his voice patronizing. "And if, by chance, you should find that a shortage of funds makes that too much of a hardship, you will find me a most generous man."

"I feel certain it will cause me no undue hardship, Señor." She stood up, her head held proudly, her eyes boring into his. "You shall have your money no later than Wednesday of this coming week."

His greedy smile froze. "Wednesday?"

With a forced smile of confidence, she nodded. How rare for someone other than Ferrer to have the upper hand, she thought triumphantly. "That's correct," she told him, trying to keep her gloating from being evident in her voice. "My partner and I intend to pay off all debts as soon as possible."

"Partner?" he rasped angrily. "I was told nothing about a partner. Who is this partner of yours?"

Dare glared back at him. "He wishes to remain anonymous. A silent partner, shall we say?" Her smile was syrupy sweet. "Now, if you will excuse me, Señor Ferrer, I do have an appointment to keep."

He rose, emitting a disgruntled "Humph" and followed her to the door with steps which were heavy and abrupt.

"Until Wednesday," she told him as she pushed open the screened door and motioned him outside.

He clicked his heels together and, with a perfunctory nod, left.

"Bastard," she mumbled under her breath as she watched him steam down the street, his onyx cane jabbing the coral paving.

"I take it he's not one of your favorite people," said a pleasant voice.

Dare whirled around.

Matt stepped out from beside the staircase, his mouth fixed in an almost boyish grin.

Seeing him standing there, shaved and fashionably attired in a pair of navy milled trousers and a pale gray shirt, took her breath away. He was even more handsome than she had thought he would be.

"What are you doing up?" she asked, unable to control the pounding in her chest.

"I took a good, hard look at myself in the mirror and decided that in order for my health to be improved, my appearance had to be restored." A broad grin still affixed to his mouth, he held up a mango and an orange. "Besides, I got hungry."

Dare rolled back her eyes. "Of course. You haven't eaten since breakfast. Time seems to have completely slipped away from me." Tingling sensations reminded her that she had spent most of the morning trying to exorcise him from her thoughts. She took a step away from the stairs. "I do apologize. It'll only take a moment to prepare your lunch."

He caught her by the arm as she started past. "Just a minute."

Blood rushed to her face. Her arm ached. Not from the pressure of his fingers, she decided immediately, but because her flesh yearned to be really held by him. She dropped her gaze. She dared not look at his eyes. To do so would reveal her innermost thoughts.

He seemed to sense her discomfort and he released her. "You've been very kind to tend to me these past few days, and I appreciate it immensely but . . ."

Her heart sank. Oh, no. Surely he wasn't going to tell her he was leaving. Not yet. Not so soon!

"I've imposed on you long enough."

No, no, no! she wanted to cry out. Don't leave. Not yet.

"It's been no imposition," she told him quickly. "None at all. Really."

He lounged back against the railing. "Good. I'm glad to know that!"

Mesmerizing blue eyes held hers. A strange flicker of realization sparked between them.

"I wouldn't take advantage of your kind hospitality for anything in the world, Dare."

The sound of her name on his lips sent her senses reeling. "I know that," she whispered, aware that she was being drawn closer to him.

"Good!" he exclaimed cheerfully. "Now that that's resolved, let's go sit in the glider and you can tell me all about that miserable creature who was just here."

Dare hesitated. Mac had always told her not to burden others with her problems. Besides, she certainly didn't want him to think she was incapable of taking charge of her life. "What about your lunch?"

He held up his fruit. "This should tide me over for a while."

"I . . . I really don't want to trouble you." She hesitated.

"I insist," he said firmly as he took her elbow. "He's obviously made you very unhappy, and anything that makes you sad upsets me. After all, we're friends. Remember?" he said, giving her arm a squeeze.

Nodding, Dare allowed him to lead her outside. Friends! Why could that sort of a relationship not be enough? she asked herself. Why did she want more? So much more!

"Are you certain you're up to being out and about?" she asked as he led her to the glider.

He turned her around and gently pushed her into the swing. "Absolutely, and not another word about that," he replied, playfully shaking his finger at her. "Getting out and about is just what I need to relieve the kinks. After all, I haven't been in bed for three days running in my life. I don't intend to start now," he announced as he sat down beside her. "Now, tell me all about your friend, Señor Ferrer."

"That . . . animal is most definitely no friend of mine!" Hands tucked together, she proceeded to tell him about Ferrer's conniving to gain control over her through her beloved Sea Palms. "There are no words foul enough to portray him," she concluded vehemently. "I can't wait for the auction to be over so I can pay him off in full." An embarrassed smile flushed her face. "I'm sorry. You must think I'm terrible to want to profit from others' misfortunes."

97

"You're talking about the Mallory ship going down?"

She nodded. "And all those lives being lost."

His large hand swallowed hers.

Her heart fluttered. For a moment, she thought it would stop beating. All those wonderful, wicked secrets Caroline had confided in her were finally making sense. If Phillip had held her hand the way Matt was holding hers now, no wonder the temptation of forbidden moments had been too hard to resist.

"I don't think you're terrible at all," he replied, his eyes seeking hers. "Quite the contrary. You had nothing to do with the ship going down. You and the rest of the salvagers did your best to save those on board. As far as the cargo goes, it would have just sunk to the bottom and been of no use to anyone." He squeezed her fingers one last time before releasing them. "And my fate would have been no better than that of the cargo had you not happened along when you did."

Dare smiled. The tiny glimmer in his deep blue eyes reflected the twinkle in her own. According to the ancient Greeks, the eyes are windows to the soul, and as far as Dare was concerned, hers was not the only soul that had been bared.

"What are you thinking?" he asked, his voice soft and velvety. His eyes probed more deeply. "At this very moment," he added.

Dare started to answer. She wanted to tell him but she was unable to put what was on her mind into words—what had been on her mind ever since the night when she had brushed his cheek with her lips as he lay unconscious. Perhaps, there were no words to express her feelings or to explain why her breath caught each time he spoke.

She could do no more than smile. Her eyes held his. She was confident that they revealed the message she wished to relay.

She watched the pulse throb at the side of his temple. Perhaps, he, too . . .

She shook her head, freeing her mind of such intimate thoughts. Nessa. Remember Nessa she told herself.

He leaned closer, his face only inches from hers. "Would you think ill of me if I were to tell you that I hope the same thoughts occupying my mind fill yours as well?" His breath was as sultry and caressing as an onshore breeze in mid-July.

Good sense cautioned her to tell him that she had no idea what he was talking about, but her heart pleaded with her to do otherwise, to throw caution to the winds and let come what may.

"I don't believe I could ever think badly of you."

The look on his face was enough to convince her that the inscription on the watch and the photograph of the woman who had composed those words no longer mattered. If he had, indeed, lied to her, then he must have had a good reason for doing so, she reasoned. At that moment, she didn't care if he were John Smith, alligator hunter. He wanted her, and God, she wanted him! Never before had she thought it possible to experience such a conglomeration of feelings, feelings that took control of her body and soul.

As though he read her thoughts, with the familiarity of an old lover, he folded her tenderly to his chest. She breathed deeply of his scent, so manly and intoxicating! Her eyes appraised him openly, honestly, with no fear or shame. She wanted to commit to memory each handsome feature, every angle and plane of his perfectly hewn visage so that she would be able to conjure up his face in the days to come when he was no longer with her.

His hot palms burned through her gown. Her breasts peaked at his touch, eager to be molded and shaped by his hands. On fire with an unquenchable thirst, she pressed herself closer, positioning one leg underneath her and dangling the other over the edge of the swing.

Their breathing quickened. Their temperatures rose in unison, and muffled moans of delight passed from his mouth to hers as he reclaimed her lips with a crushing kiss. Ever so gently, his tongue slipped between her teeth, tenderly parting them, and probing deep inside her mouth.

Burning with a fire which could not be easily extinguished, she devoured his lips voraciously. The message her kiss relayed was loud and clear, as she intended it to be, and she was confident there was no way he could misinterpret its meaning.

One hand held her tightly while the other crept down her leg rustling fold after fold of satin en route. At her knee, it stopped to bunch the material in his palm while his adventuresome fingers stole beneath her skirt, their tips blazing a trail of fire as they followed the curve of her inner leg.

Cleaving to him and hardly able to muffle her moans of delight, she sank deeper and deeper into the vortex of the wonderful pressure building in the center of her body. It was all she could do to keep from guiding his hand right to the very spot it sought. What she was feeling, what she was wanting, was definitely not what a proper, well-bred woman of twenty should be feeling and wanting. He had touched nerves never before aroused, stirred sensations never before awakened. Instead of pulling away to extinguish the flames which blazed higher and higher under his expert stoking, she found herself fantasizing an even deeper ecstasy, one that would calm the storm of passion rising in her.

Prompted by a sudden chuckle, she quickly opened her eyes.

"What's so funny?" she demanded, uncertain whether to be amused or annoyed.

Covering her leg with one quick swish of satin, he nodded in the direction of the street.

Confused, Dare turned around to see the object of his amusement. Two giggling youngsters were standing a dozen yards away, their hands covering their mouths and their eyes glued to the front porch of the Sea Palms.

"Oh, damn!" she laughed. "Those are the Bryan twins." She waved, then sat up straight, doing her best to look proper and respectable. "Their mama's the biggest gossip of all of Monroe County," she added in a lower tone.

He wove his fingers through hers. "Think I've tarnished your reputation?"

Dare nestled close to his chest once again. "I doubt it," she sighed. "I've been told more than once that a block of ice down at Morley's has more fire in it than I have."

His teeth nipped her ear. "Is that so?"

Smiling and content, Dare closed her eyes. Her head found its way to his shoulder. Spending the rest of the day in that position would be delightful. Come to think of it, she mused, it would be a pleasant way to spend the rest of her life!

Chapter Six

Waving and calling out cheerful greetings to some of Mac's old fishing pals as they hauled in their day's catch, Dare pedaled her bicycle along the waterfront toward the Sea Palms. Seeing all the conchs gathered around Lowe's dock swapping stories and telling tales about the big ones that got away brought back fond memories of the days when Mac was right there matching wits with the best of them. More than once, she remembered pedaling down to the wharf to fetch him home for supper.

She biked on down the street, her heart heavy. When Mac had died, a part of her had died too. The loss she had suffered was irreparable, but at least she was learning to live with it, she told herself. Mac wasn't coming back. Not ever. But he wouldn't want her to go around moping for the rest of her life.

A smile lit her face. The two of them had shared so much happiness. He had been father and mother to her while she had been a son as well as a daughter. He often told her he had gotten the best of both sexes and none of the worst of either one. Not many girls went out fishing off the bank with their fathers or sailed to Havana on trading trips, she mused. Life is for the living, he had told her many times after her mother's death, and she knew she'd do well to heed that advice now. Life is short and it can be snatched away so suddenly. Live each day and let tomorrow worry about itself.

That was exactly what she would do from now on, she resolved. Let tomorrow worry about itself! Chase . . . Matt—whatever his name was—might very well have a sweetheart waiting for him at home, but Nessa was several thousand miles away, while she was living in the same house with him in Key West. He might leave tomorrow, or next week, or the week after, but until then, he'd be here with her.

Her feminine intuition had told her that he wanted her as much as she did him. Perhaps she was in love with him. Maybe she had fallen in love with him the night she'd dragged him out of the sea. If what she was feeling was indeed love, how would she know? she wondered. After all, she had never had such strong feelings for a man before, nor had she so desperately wanted a man to take full possession of her body and soul. How difficult it would be later to lie in bed knowing that he was just downstairs!

She rounded the corner of Elizabeth Street, thoughts of Matt still occupying her mind. The temptation to confess her feelings was great, but if he rejected her, she wouldn't be able to endure living in the same house. If only women were not supposed to be so reserved and subtle, she reflected miserably. If only they could forgo the games and deal directly with the subject of love on a one-to-one basis, with each party involved regarded as an equal.

But such was not the way things were done in Key West in 1898, she reminded herself as she pedaled past the cannery. Perhaps society's view of women would broaden in the twentieth century, and those of the fairer sex would be free to speak their piece without fear of scorn or ridicule. Maybe they'd even be given the right to vote for their nation's leaders and to have a say in matters other than those relating to the home and family.

Dare chuckled to herself. Lordy, the twentieth century was only two years away. The changes she wanted to implement in a paternalistic society would probably not come for another century.

Still, she decided, maneuvering the bicycle around piles of sponges spread out to dry, she wasn't about to wait another day before she told Matt how she felt about him. If he were to reject her or think her any less a lady . . . well that was the chance she'd have to take! If not . . . She smiled softly at this thought. If not, then the advantages of being a woman might be far more numerous than she had imagined.

A few moments later Dare squinted ahead. Surely that wasn't Matt coming toward her, she mused, frowning. She swerved in behind the turtle kraals and peered out from around the corner of a gigantic turtle tank to get a better look. It can't be, she told herself. He had declined her invitation to visit Uriah at the warehouse because he had wanted to nap a few hours. The short while he had spent up and about had fatigued him, or so he'd said, she recalled. Her brows knotted together. There was no doubt about it, she decided. It was him!

What on earth could he possibly be up to? she asked herself as she ducked out of sight when he neared her hiding place.

She waited until he was well ahead of her before venturing from behind the tanks. How do you like that! she thought as she pedaled after him. He had lied to her once again. That little quirk of his was becoming a habit!

Pedaling slowly and being careful to remain a safe distance behind, she followed him down to the harbor. Each time he stopped or looked in any direction except straight ahead, she'd turn in behind the nearest mule-drawn streetcar or wagon until his lengthy stride resumed.

He halted at the pier a few minutes later, and she parked in front of Pendleton's News Stand. Pretending to be interested in the rack of magazines, she watched as he exchanged a few words with a young man who wore the starched whites of a sailor before proceeding out to the end of the dock.

Curiosity getting the best of her, she pushed her bike across the street. Matt spoke briefly to another crisply uniformed sailor who had just tied a dinghy to the dock, but she couldn't quite make out what was said. The second seaman nodded, then hopped back into the boat, Matt following him. Moments later, the two of them were rowing out in the direction of the *Maine* which lay at anchor just outside the channel.

It took only a second for this sight to sink in. She

experienced a sick feeling in the pit of her stomach. He's leaving, she wailed silently.

Don't jump to conclusions, she warned herself as the launch pulled away. After all, he was in Key West on assignment, she reminded herself. Supposedly!

More confused than ever, she pedaled the rest of the way home. Matt had lied to her again, but why? If he had wanted to go out to the ship to conduct interviews with the crew, it would have been easier to say so than to sneak out of the house the moment her back was turned. Matt Colby, or Chase somebody, sure was hard to figure out.

However, despite her doubts, she knew that nothing had changed. Her feelings for him were as strong as they had been a few hours earlier when she had been held securely in his arms. That was even more baffling than his actions!

Matt breezed into the house late that afternoon carrying a wicker basket and sporting a sheepish grin.

Dare came out from behind the *Key West News* long enough to give him a quick smile and a mumbled hello, but behind her façade her heart leapt. He hadn't left!

If he noticed her coolness, he gave no indication of it. He acted as though he had not been absent most of the afternoon, and finally, he set the hamper down in front of her.

"Aren't you even going to ask what I have in there?"

Dare could feel her resolve weaken. She couldn't be annoyed with him even if she tried. Deep down, she knew he'd tell her what he was up to in his own good time. Until then, she had no alternative but to wait patiently until he believed the moment was right. After all, she reminded herself, she had no claim on him. She had towed him out of the sea and nursed him back to health but that did not mean that he was obligated to feel for her what she felt for him.

A smile tugged at her lips. "Oh, all right. What's in there?" She started to take a peek, but he gave her hand a playful smack.

"No fair," he scolded. "Guess."

Her smile broadened. If her sense of smell was correct, the scrumptious aroma wafting through the woven cane was that of arroz con pollo. "Umm. Smells like my favorite," she said, taking a deep whiff. "Chicken and yellow rice?"

A pleased look on his face, he sat down on the divan beside her. "With fried bananas, black beans, and flan for dessert."

"Is that your subtle way of telling me that my culinary skill does not particularly impress you?" she asked with a chuckle.

"*Au contraire, madame,*" answered Matt as he scooted closer. "I thought a quiet, romantic picnic on the beach would be a splendid way to bring an absolutely wonderful day to a close."

A strong, manly arm wrapped around her, and she melted into it, reveling in his closeness.

"From what I understand," he continued, his words drifting through her hair, "the sunset over Key West is unique. I can think of no other person with whom I'd rather share it."

Nessa included? she wanted to ask but bit down on her lip instead. "I think that's a marvelous idea," she exclaimed cheerfully. No use worrying about Nessa, she told herself, leastwise not tonight.

"Good!" He gave her a quick peck on the nose then stood up. "Why don't you go get yourself a wrap, and I'll find a blanket; then we'll be all set and ready to go."

Dare left the room with an uncharacteristic little bounce to her step. He has only been here for three days, she mused happily as she bounded up the stairs two at a time, yet what a difference he has made in my life. How easy it was to smile and tease and be happy around him. Lately, the only time she became glum was when he was not with her, and she was certain such occurrences were not coincidences.

An hour later, her face was still aglow with smiles. Matt was stretched out in front of her, his head nestled in her lap. His eyes were closed, and his mouth was turned up in a happy smile much like her own. She could hardly take her eyes from him. She longed to run her fingers through the pale blond shocks of hair falling onto her lilac skirt. If only time would stand still for just a short while, she thought as her eyes feasted on his strong-featured visage. How easy it would be to lower her head and brush her lips over his. But she dare not move for fear of spoiling that wonderful moment.

The setting could not have been any more perfect if she had created it in her imagination. An hour ago, the sky had exploded into a kaleidoscope of oranges and violets. "A spectacular display just in your honor," she had told Matt. The giant palm fronds that canopied the cozy little cove where they had spread their blanket rustled ever so slightly with each subtle breeze. The scent of perfumed jasmine wafted across the sand, and never-tiring waves lapped against the low-tide surf. Surely, paradise has just been found, Dare reflected with a quiet sigh.

The moon had cast its reflection over the mirror-calm waters by the time Matt finally opened his eyes. He grinned up lazily at her. "Fine company I turned out to be. Why didn't you pinch me?" he asked, lifting his head.

She smoothed the wrinkles from her skirt. "You were sleeping so soundly, I just couldn't bring myself to disturb you." Besides, if you were awake, I couldn't have treated myself to such an in-depth study of your wonderfully handsome face, she thought.

He leaned back on his elbows, his head even with her shoulders. "I dreamed about you while I was napping," he said matter-of-factly.

"Oh?" she asked, barely able to utter a single syllable.

"I dreamed we were marooned on a deserted island. We had only each other for company." He rolled over onto his side, his right hand reaching up for her cheek.

Dare felt herself drifting toward him as though she had no control over her actions. The next thing she knew, she was reclining on her elbows beside him.

"Don't you want to know how the dream ended?" he asked, his face a fraction of an inch from hers.

She shook her head. "I believe I already know," she whispered.

His mouth smothered her words. Strong arms grasped her waist and pulled her over onto him with a power that was forceful and gentle at the same time. Her soft curves molded to his firm contours. Clasping her even tighter with one arm the adventuresome fingers of his other hand explored her soft breasts.

She could no longer muffle her moans of pleasure. With each cry of delight, she felt her yearning grow. Her lips instinctively found their way to his a second time, and when he recaptured them, she knew that all he had to do was ask and she would succumb to his every wish. For all she cared, she could remain locked in his embrace until doomsday. She was his! All that remained for possession to be complete was the single act of consummation, and she could tell by his heavy groans it would not be long in coming.

Ever so gently, he rolled her over and blanketed her with his strength.

She lay under him, welcoming his weight with open arms and praying that that moment would never end. Lingering in his embrace, savoring kiss after kiss, was sheer heaven. The night carried with it a promise of hours and hours of togetherness, and she would let no one, not even memories of Nessa, come between them now or ever!

Her back arched in response to his movements. She might be inexperienced, but she'd show him just what an apt pupil she could be, she decided as she wrapped her limbs tightly around him and pulled herself as close to him as possible.

"Oh, Ch—" She caught herself just in time. Calling him by that name in her thoughts had become a habit. She waited, desperately hoping he had not heard her.

To her relief, his lips did not miss a single beat as he showered kisses down her throat, into the pulsing hollow of her neck, and as far onto her shoulders as her blouse would allow.

Thank Heavens, she sighed, relaxing and again reveling in his caresses. Regardless of who he was, where he had come from, or where he was headed, nothing would ever separate them, she vowed, squeezing him as hard as she could. Nothing! No one!

Her sudden burst of passion made him raise his head. He looked surprised, confused. His face revealed his uncertainty. The turmoil inside him was impossible to mask. "I want you more than I've ever wanted anything or anyone in my life," he whispered, his words hoarse and throaty, "but I . . ."

Her heart skipped a beat. Please, oh, please don't let him mention her name. "There's no but about it," she said before he had a chance to get out another word. Her eyes bored into his. Damson and violet melted together in fiery purple hues. "Because I want you more than you could possibly imagine!"

There! She'd said it!

Her eyes refused to break contact with his. Her gaze patiently searched for some flicker of guilt behind his stare, but she could find none. Perhaps Nessa wasn't as important an aspect of his life as she had imagined.

He said nothing.

She froze. She had really made a mess of things! How forward he must think her. What if she had frightened him by her honesty? Even worse, what if he thought her some kind of shameless hussy.

Caroline had told her that sometimes a woman should be the aggressive one. Obviously, she had never come across a man like Matt.

"I'm sorry," she mumbled. She turned her face from his. "I didn't mean to sound like a—"

His kisses quickly silenced her. "Shhh. There's nothing to apologize for. The only reason I was so silent is that I could not believe my good fortune. Ever since I opened my eyes and saw you, you've no idea how much I've wanted you. Just having you sit beside me on the bed was pure hell. You came very close to being ravaged on more than one occasion," he teased, a wicked gleam dancing in his eyes. His expression sobered quickly. "The only reason I restrained myself was because I wanted to make certain your wishes coincided with mine."

"They do," she whispered huskily.

Fingers, never before so brazen, began unbuttoning his shirt, their tips lingering on each bit of inviting flesh revealed. Playful teeth nipped at his hair-roughened flesh. She smiled to herself. Her actions alone should dispel any doubts he might have.

Ever so gently, he pulled her to her feet. His eyes did not stray for an instant from the delicate angles of her face.

Dare held herself tall and proud. She wanted him, damn it! She did not want to play at being coy, nor did she feel afraid or ashamed. Any misgivings or uncertainties she might have had were erased by the tender, adoring gaze she was receiving at that instant.

Holding her at arm's length, he began undressing her, slowly, almost worshipfully as though he, too,

113

wanted this to be a moment to be savored.

Her knees felt as though they would buckle each time a button was undone. His fingers moved in slow, teasing circles. The torture he was subjecting her to was such sweet misery. Hurry, please, she wanted to cry out, but the words simply would not come.

The next moment, as though he could read her thoughts, her skirt was swished down around her ankles and her petticoat was lifted over her head in a motion so swift it took her breath away.

"You're even more exquisite than I imagined," he mumbled, burying his head between her satiny breasts.

His hot, fiery hands cupped and massaged her passion-swollen crests and their peaks hardened instantly at the first flick of his tongue. His touch was maddening. Her senses reeled, completely out of control. One moment she felt as though her legs were about to give way beneath her. The next, she was certain she could easily spread wings and soar out to sea.

His hands had the power to enflame her flesh. His tongue teased and tantalized, filling her with sensations so exquisitely pleasurable she felt light-headed. Moans of pure ecstasy slipped from her. She bit her lip to stifle them, but it was pointless to try to conceal the tremendous impact of his love-making.

He knelt in front of her, his hands shaping her buttocks to steady her. Nipping gently en route, his lips seared a path down the center of her body, in and out of the tiny recess just below her waist, down to the patch of curly tendrils between her thighs. Not one curve or crevice was left unexplored. Passion flowed within her like sweet, liquid fire. Each touch of his tongue sent tremors through her.

One moment, she was afraid he'd never stop this sweet torture. The next, she feared he would. She knew she was losing touch with reality.

The beach began to spin round and round. A sweet, shuddering ecstasy exploded within her. Drained of strength, she dropped to her knees and fell back onto the blanket.

"That's only the beginning of the wonderful pleasure you are about to experience, my love," he assured her as he cradled her in his arms.

Unable to focus on anything but him, she watched as he undressed and tossed his shirt and trousers into the pile of clothes beside them. He was magnificent, even more beautiful than she had realized. When she had cleansed and bandaged his wounds, she had taken such pains to keep her eyes from roaming over his muscular body, but now, she wanted to look at it. Her eyes refused to be directed elsewhere.

He was tall and handsome and beautifully proportioned, stunningly virile. His legs were long and muscular, perfect for wrapping around her. Everything about him exuded power, raw, animal power. Such sensuality, she was sure, attracted women Undoubtedly, like herself, they would be only too willing to succumb to him.

She opened her arms wider. She wanted to experience the secrets of his body as he had familiarized himself with hers.

He came to her in one sudden burst of passion. Moaning her name over and over, he crushed her beneath him, wedging her deeper into the sand.

His kiss burned with urgency. The same need that had been building within her pulsated in him. His arousal was as demanding as her own. The rod of hot flesh piercing the inside of her thigh was firm and hard.

"Please, now. Now!" she cried, guiding him into her.

The instant he entered her, she gasped. The pain sobered her for an instant, but as he gradually aroused her again she told herself that now nothing—no one—could ever come between them.

Flesh against flesh, their bodies meshed as he guided her to the heights of passion, their hearts pounding in unison. She strove to prolong their passionate exchange, digging her fingers deeper and deeper into his inviting flesh. What is happening to me? she screamed silently. Then the flood of joy was uncontrollable, unbearable, totally devastating. She couldn't control it a moment longer. She felt herself surrendering to the tremendous pressure building inside her. Her entire body was racked by merciless spasms until, suddenly, something inside her exploded, and she soared into the heavens.

Chapter Seven

Dare basked in the warm aftermath of passion, every ounce of energy drained from her. Smiling contentedly, she snuggled closer to her love. He had given her more pleasure than she had imagined possible. Severing the last tie to girlhood had been more spectacular than Caroline had led her to believe. Thanks to Matt's tender guidance, her memory of the brief moments of pain had been softened by the ecstasy which followed them. He was certainly well experienced in the art of love-making, for he knew how to coax a response from every part of her. Not that she had needed coaxing, she recalled, sighing. It had never been a question of whether she would surrender but when she would do so. The joyous satisfaction he had given her might have to last for the rest of her life if . . .

Dare shook her head. Now was not the time to dwell on the future or on parting. That decision rested entirely with him. She had given herself freely because she loved him. That act of loving was in no way intended to be a trap. She loved him! *Love!* So much emotion was contained in that little four-letter word. *I love you*, she wanted to exclaim as loudly as she could, but when she formed the words the sound stayed locked inside her heart.

Her smile turned to a frown as she gazed at his face. How sad he looked! Lines of worry and tension creased his forehead.

"What's wrong?" she whispered into the darkness. "Did I . . . did I disappoint you?"

"You disappoint me?" The lines were instantly erased. "Never!" He gathered her close, his cheek resting against hers. "Silly girl! You're by far the most wonderful happening in my life in a long time." His jaw tensed; his voice became softer. "It is I who's been a disappointment to you. So much so that I stand a very good chance of losing you because of it."

Dare chuckled. "You couldn't lose me if you tried," she said, curling the blond tendrils springing up on his chest around her fingers. How wonderful he made her feel! How wanted!

His arms released her. "I haven't been entirely honest with you, Dare. As a matter of fact, there's been very little truth in anything I've told you."

The breeze suddenly stilled. Even the tide's gentle lapping seemed muted.

Her face paled. Suddenly she felt very ill. She pulled away and hugged her knees close to her chest to cover her shame.

"You see, my dearest, I am not the man you think

I am."

Her head lifted in weak protest. Her eyes pleaded, No, please don't.

She took a deep breath. He was about to confess everything. Her suspicions were about to be confirmed. Still she could not find the strength to listen. "I don't care who you are," she said trembling. "I know you're tender and kind and caring. That's all that matters."

"I wish it were that simple, but it isn't." His sigh was as doleful as her own. "I've done something that shames me, something completely unforgivable."

Overcome with her own guilt over having encouraged their intimacy despite her suspicions, Dare reached for her skirt and modestly covered herself. Her gaze drifted out to sea. There was no denying the role she had played, yet since they had experienced so much happiness together, it was only appropriate they share the guilt.

She gave a short nod and prepared herself for the worst.

"My name is not Matthew Colby. It's Chase . . . Chase Hamilton."

Dare said nothing. She just continued to stare out to sea, her face expressionless. She waited patiently, waited for the man to whom she had just vowed eternal love to tell her that he belonged to another.

"I'm not a journalist, either. I'm a captain in the United States Navy," he admitted solemnly. "And I've come to Key West at the request of the Assistant Secretary of the Navy, Theodore Roosevelt."

"Go on," she said dully. The sooner the truth, the whole truth, was out in the open the better.

His surprise was genuine. "Go on? Isn't that enough?"

Her astonishment matched his. "You mean, that's all you had to tell me?"

"Should there be more?"

Her head lifted. She risked looking into his eyes. "You mean you aren't sorry tonight happened?"

"Sorry?" He seemed more and more confused. "Sorry, you say? Why, I've never been happier!" he announced, his arms winding around her.

Dare sank against him, her head burrowed beneath his shoulder. "I had prepared myself for the worst. I feared you were going to tell me you regretted being unfaithful to someone else . . . to someone you love."

"But I love you."

Her eyes met his. His quiet declaration astounded her. "You do?" She could scarcely believe what she had just heard. "You love me?"

"Why, yes. I do. Is there something wrong with that?" he asked, his eyes dancing with amusement.

"No, nothing at all. I love you, too," she said quickly, unable to contain her joy. "I love you!" she exclaimed again, squeezing him with all her might.

A moment later she eased herself out of his grasp. "Now I'm afraid it's my turn to make a confession to you," she told him hesitantly. "You see, I've known all along that you weren't who you professed to be."

"Oh?"

Dare took a deep breath. "I know I shouldn't have, but at the time, I didn't see anything wrong." She sat up straight, her hands folded in her lap. She wasn't quite sure how to proceed. She'd simply die if he thought her actions were not completely innocent

120

and honest. "I checked your pockets for some clue as to your identity in case you . . . well in case you didn't make it, and your family had to be notified."

"Yes."

Her face flushed. "I found your watch. There was an inscription on the back. To—"

"To Chase. All my love forever, Nessa," he said, finishing the sentence for her.

Once again he pulled her close, his naked body sheltering hers from the cool breeze filtering through the palm fronds. "And you thought Nessa was my sweetheart or my wife? Of course, what else were you to think?" he asked quietly, his chin atop her head.

"Then she isn't?" Dare held her breath.

"No, she's neither my sweetheart nor my wife." He planted a row of tiny kisses along her brow.

Dare didn't have to look in his eyes to know he was telling her the truth. She felt as though a tremendous weight had been lifted from her. He was free!

"Admiral Sterling, Vanessa's father, has been a close friend to my father for as long as I can remember," he explained, his hands gently massaging the curve of her neck. "Because of this relationship, our families have spent a great deal of time together. Nessa's brother, Pierce, and I were roommates at Annapolis. I can assure you, however, that my feelings for Nessa are those I would have for a younger sister if I had one." A frown crossed his face. "However, I learned last summer that her feelings for me went much deeper than that. She had the idea that the Hamiltons and Sterlings should be united by marriage. Ours!"

"Why, then, was the watch the first thing you

121

reached for that morning when you asked for your clothes?" she asked, regretting the question the moment the words tumbled out of her mouth.

Chase started to shake his head, then caught himself and smiled. "Oh, yes, I do remember." Stretching behind him, he reached for his trousers and pulled the gold case from his pocket. "Open it," he said, handing the watch to her.

She looked puzzled.

"Just do it."

She unfastened the clasp. Even in the darkness she could imagine Nessa's beautiful, smiling face springing up to greet her.

"Take out the picture."

Fingers fumbling uncertainly, she did as he requested.

"Now, turn it over." He struck a match and held the light down to the picture. "Read it."

"Five one five three Morley." Puzzled, she looked up. "I don't understand. Is that a street address?"

"Hopefully, had the watch fallen into the wrong hands, that is the assumption that would have been made." He blew out the light and tossed the match into the sand.

"Wrong hands? It all sounds very secretive," she remarked, tucking herself next to him.

"It is. You see, I've been sent here on a top-secret assignment for our government," he revealed slowly. "Five one five three was part of my instructions."

"I understand," she said, her lips grazing on the warm flesh covering his shoulders. "Say no more. I'm sorry for being so inquisitive."

"No apologies necessary, my darling. You have a

right to know all there is to know about me."

She started to object. "But if it's confidential naval business—"

"I know you'll never betray me," he said confidently.

Her head rose from its cushion. "Never, I swear. No matter what."

Strong arms encircled her like a protective wall. "Today is the fifth day of the first month. The second five designates the pier number, the last digit the time. Morley is the name of the seaman my friend Charles Sigsbee was to send ashore to meet me."

"Sigsbee? The Captain of the *Maine*?" she inquired with interest.

He nodded. "That's correct. Do you know him?"

She shook her head. "I only know of him. We've never been introduced. Go on." She was anxious to hear more.

"Charles is another Annapolis comrade. He was a few years older than I and had the reputation of being as hard as nails on the plebes. At any rate, he was to be my contact once I arrived in Key West," he told her, his fingers caressing her arms as though her skin were covered in the finest silks. "He didn't know until today that I had been a passenger on board the Mallory liner."

She broke into a knowing smile. "I was wondering what you were up to this afternoon when I saw you in town. Especially after you told me you needed to stay in and rest," she reminded him playfully.

"You saw me?" he asked, grinning boyishly.

"Mm. I was on my home from visiting Uriah," she answered, hugging him closer. "At first I thought

123

you were leaving the Sea Palms and me for good, and didn't have the heart to tell me."

Gentle fingers combed her thick tresses. "Silly girl."

"I'm hardly a girl anymore," she reminded him, her words as sultry as her look.

His face came down to meet hers. "No, you're not. Not anymore," he agreed, his words fading into a mumbled groan the instant their lips met.

Limbs intertwined, they tumbled back onto the sand. The sweet, jasmine-scented darkness enfolded them.

Suddenly she drew back and laughed. "One more minor detail," she said, playfully holding him at bay.

"Which is?" he asked, nipping at her shoulder.

"Richard Davis loathes being called by any name other than his given one."

His strength devoured her. "I'll make a note of that."

She allowed herself to be absorbed by him, a raw, carnal craving overwhelming her once more. Every part of her was afire with an aching need to be consumed by his desire. Passion billowed in her like smoke, clouding her brain and dulling her senses. She could think of nothing but Chase. He was all that mattered. He was her life, and only he had the power to satisfy the urgent craving coursing through her.

His masterful touch sent her catapulting to levels of ecstasy not foretold by Caroline. Unwilling to delay a moment longer, she reached for him and guided him deep inside her. There would be time enough later for mutual caresses, but in that instant, she wanted to be consumed by him.

The pleasure he gave her was pure and explosive. Places she had never known existed inside her were aroused by his mastery. Every crevice of her body shook with wonderfully agonizing tremors. Her fingers clamped down on his firm buttocks. The louder she cried out for release, the deeper and harder his thrusts became. Finally, after what seemed an eternity of heavenly torment, she felt herself shatter into a million little pieces. She soared high and then floated back to earth.

His life force flowed, and she sank deeper into the sand, temporarily satiated. Sweet exhaustion flooded her limbs and she closed her eyes. Never again would she question Caroline's decision to run off to Savannah with the man she loved!

Too soon the clanging of the fire bell ended her Chase-filled dream and jolted her back to reality. She awakened instantly, and shot into a sitting position. The clamors and shouts sounded dangerously close. Overhead, the sky was the color of charcoal. A thick, foglike haze hid the stars from view.

Not the Sea Palms was her first panicky thought.

"Chase, wake up!" she exclaimed, shaking his shoulder.

"What's the . . . ?" His nose wrinkled. "There's a fire close by."

"Too close." She coughed as she frantically slipped her petticoat over her head. "It can't be the Sea Palms. It just can't be."

Pulling up his trousers en route, Chase scrambled up the sand dune behind them. "It's not," he shouted. "The flames are much farther away. Closer to the harbor, I think."

Her relief was short-lived. "The harbor? Dear God, that's almost as bad. Surely the warehouse isn't what's burning."

"Warehouse? Which warehouse?"

Buttoning her blouse became an exercise in dexterity. The fingers of one hand kept getting in the way of those of the other. "There's only one warehouse at the harbor, and that's where salvaged goods are stored," she explained, impatiently throwing her skirt over her head and fighting her way into it. "It isn't the cargo that concerns me," she said in a much softer tone. "It's Uriah. He's spending the night there."

"Uriah?" Chase grabbed hold of her hand. "Come on. We've no time to lose."

By the time they reached the town center a few minutes later pandemonium had erupted in the streets of Key West, and all her citizens were out in full force. Smoke rolled across the town in one giant cloud. At first glance, it looked like the entire commercial district was smoldering.

"What's burning?" shouted Dare at the top of her lungs to Mr. Pendleton, who was pacing the sidewalk in front of his newsstand.

"It's the warehouse," he yelled over the voices of the people clustered between them. "There was a loud explosion. Next thing I knew, the whole place was aflame."

Panic clawed at her heart. Breaking away from Chase, she elbowed her way through the mob, frantically searching for her old friend. "Has anyone seen Uriah?" she shouted.

No one replied.

First Mac, now Uriah! Dear God, no!

Horrible thoughts rushed through her mind. "No, not him too," she said aloud. She tried to pray, but the words caught in her throat.

An arm reached out from the crowd and pulled her back.

"Sorry, miss. Can't go any closer," a red-hatted fire official told her. "Restricted area."

Dare froze in her tracks. Heat stung her cheeks, and smoke teared her eyes. She couldn't believe what she was seeing. Only last week, at the town council meeting someone had suggested tearing down the old clapboard warehouse and replacing it with one made of brick. Less of a fire hazard, they had all agreed.

Dare covered her eyes. She just couldn't bear to look at the orange flames that must be dancing over her dear old friend at that very instant. He didn't have a chance to make it out of that inferno alive.

Sobbing uncontrollably, she threw herself against Chase when he finally caught up with her. "No one's seen him," she wailed. "He must be in there. Dear God!"

"Go ahead and cry, honey. Let it all out," he encouraged, cradling her close.

"Damnation!" boomed a voice. "Hell can't be much hotter than that."

Dare couldn't believe her ears. Only one Key West conch still retained the thick brogue of his native highlands.

"Uriah!" she exclaimed, laughing and crying at

127

the same time. She flung her arms around him. "I was so afraid you were caught in there."

He squeezed her close. Weathered age lines creased his bleary eyes. "Aye, lass. If'n I hadn't decided to step out for a bite to eat, I'd be burned to a crisp for sure."

"Have you any idea what happened?" she asked, composing herself.

"I'll be damned if I know." Uriah took off his cap and raked his fingers through his gray shag of hair. "I was on my way back from the café when I heard a godawful commotion. Next thing I knew the whole place was up in smoke. Whatever it was, once it started, there was no stoppin' it. That's fer certain," he added gravely.

Dare nodded in silent agreement. The building was too far gone to save. Repeated efforts of the fire brigade had proven futile. Even with the harbor so close at hand, not enough water could be pumped to extinguish the blaze. Thank Heavens the town's main business district lay across the street of crushed coral. She shuddered to think what might have happened if the fire could not have been contained in the harbor area.

"Damn! If'n it was goin' to burn, why couldn't it have waited till tomorrow?" stormed Uriah angrily as the three of them took one last look before walking away.

Tears welled in her eyes. His sentiments echoed her own. Why couldn't fate have dealt them a kinder blow? By nine o'clock tomorrow night, all the cargo salvaged from the Mallory liner would have been sold, and the future of the Sea Palms and of an aging mariner would have been guaranteed. As it was, she grimaced, Señor Ferrer would be expecting his money by the middle of next week. He had told her his terms would be the same as those set forth by the bank. Technically, the note wasn't due until spring, but she knew Eduardo Ferrer was notorious for reneging on his promises, especially when he stood to profit from others' misfortunes. Her frown deepened. If worse came to worse . . . She tried to block such a thought from her mind. Worse wouldn't come to worse! She simply would not allow it.

Linking an arm through Chase's, Dare held onto Uriah's elbow with her other hand. "Cheer up," she told her old friend. "All is not lost. At least you escaped without injury, and believe me, that means far more to me than the cargo from a hundred salvaged ships."

"I know, lass, and I appreciate ye sayin' it." His gruff tone cracked. "I just feel like I let you and my old friend down. Mac would have wanted me to make things easier for you. Damn it! I should never have left that building. Maybe if I hadn't none o' this would have happened."

"Don't be ridiculous!" she said sternly. "That place would have burned with or without you in it. You know that as well as I."

"Aye, I suppose it would have."

"Have you heard the news?" asked Mr. Pendleton as the three of them passed his storefront.

"What's that?" Chase queried, pausing in the street.

"Chief Monroe suspects arson is the cause of the fire."

"Arson?" the three said in unison.

129

"What makes him think that?" Chase stepped closer.

Pendleton peered over the top of his gold wire-rimmed glasses. "Don't rightly know. I just heard him saying something to Chief Seals about it looking like it was deliberately set." He turned his back to them for a moment and locked the door to his shop. "See you folks later," he said, slipping the key in his pocket and walking down the steps.

"Arson? Well, what do ye make of that?" Uriah said aloud.

Dare shook her head in disbelief. Arson! The thought that anyone would deliberately set fire to the warehouse had her completely baffled. "I don't care what the fire chief and the chief of police say," Dare declared a moment later, "they're dead wrong. Everyone in town knew the Mallory cargo was stored there."

"Maybe you've just answered your own question," suggested Chase as they threaded their way through the dispersing crowd. "Perhaps someone started the fire for that very reason. Maybe they were jealous they didn't get in on the haul."

"No. I simply refuse to believe that!" she argued. "There hasn't been so lucrative a haul in years. The salvagers wouldn't have been the only ones who'd have profited from the auctioning of the cargo. The entire town would have prospered."

Uriah was quick to agree. "When money's plentiful, businesses flourish."

Chase shrugged his shoulders. "Maybe so, but the fact remains if the chief's arson theory holds true, somebody had to strike that match, and if so he must

130

have had a mighty strong motive for doing so."

Dare said nothing. There was a lot of truth to Chase's deduction. Perhaps one person in town didn't want the goods auctioned off. But who? Why?

That same set of questions resounded in her head as they walked from one block to the next. Who? Why? Who could possibly gain by destroying an entire town's livelihood?

The rowdy sounds of the late-night festivities at the San Carlos Club blasted across the street. Dare's thoughts were interrupted by the loud strumming of a guitar and the clicking heels of dancers. Annoyed, she glanced in the direction of the building where the Cubans gathered.

Her pace slowed. Her pulse almost stopped the moment her eyes met the impaling stare of the formally attired Cuban standing stiffly outside the black wrought-iron gate. Had she not recognized him immediately, she could not have mistaken the pungent aroma of his harsh cigar.

The man lifted his hand in acknowledgment.

Dare's hold on Chase's arm tightened.

Of course, why could she not have put two and two together earlier? she asked herself, returning his pseudo friendly look with one of irate indignation. Eduardo Ferrer was the only individual in town who stood to lose from the sale of the Mallory liner's salvaged cargo.

Holding her head high, she purposely directed her gaze straight ahead as she passed within a few yards of him. He had as much to gain as she had to lose: the Sea Palms!

Chapter Eight

Rosy streamers of light peeped through the cracks in the shutters, rousing Dare from her contented slumber. She opened her eyes, then, smiling to herself, closed them. A satisfied sigh slipped through her lips. Chase was stretched out beside her just as he'd been on the very first morning he'd shared her bed, two weeks ago after the night of the warehouse fire.

Her heart skittered wildly. Each time she woke up next to him, it was as though she were doing so for the first time. Even when he was fast asleep, he fascinated her.

Ever so careful not to disturb him, she angled herself closer. Seeing him lying beside her, his body bronzed from the afternoons they had whiled away swimming and sunbathing nude on a tiny key just offshore, thrilled her just as much as it had the first time she had seen him in his natural state. He was the only man with whom she had ever been intimate. Still, she needed no comparisons to know he was truly a magnificent representative of the male sex. Her golden god, she had called him after one glorious afternoon of love-making on Christmas Tree Key. Her own Adonis! Even the gashes slashed in his flesh by the razor-sharp coral added character to his muscular chest.

How lucky she was to have him lying beside her, she mused, even if only for a little while. In the past fourteen days she had experienced the joy of love. Chase had been a skilled teacher, and she an eager pupil.

Her smile faded slowly. Just how much longer would she have him? she wondered. After all, it was just a matter of time before he was recalled to the nation's capital. She must not delude herself. Such deception could only lead to heartbreak. He had come to Key West on Navy business. When it was completed to Roosevelt's satisfaction, Chase would be ordered home. For her own peace of mind, the sooner she reconciled herself to that fact, the better. Chase wasn't hers forever. He was on loan from the Navy Department.

But he said he loved her, she reminded herself as she took in the steady up and down movement of his chest. Had those words been uttered in the ardor of a heated embrace, then she could have attributed that declaration to a moment of passion. But they had been spoken at times when the thought of sex had been far from their minds.

She chuckled softly. Just yesterday when they were at the bodega waiting for Señor Mendez to tally up their purchases, Chase had leaned over the candy counter and whispered those three wonderful words in her ear for no reason at all. *I love you.* How heavenly they sounded coming from him. *I love you.* Every time he said it, her insides went haywire.

A moment later, Chase opened his eyes.

She made no attempt to avoid contact with his passionate blue gaze.

Lazily, he grinned up at her. "Didn't anybody ever tell you it's bad manners to stare?" he teased, tangling his fingers in her hair and pulling her face to his.

"Plenty of times." Her lips were almost touching his. "But lately I've found that being bad definitely has its advantages."

"You don't say."

A vixenish smile curled her lips as Dare shook her hair free of his hand. "Oh, but I do say," she mumbled in her most provocative tone as she traced her tongue around the outline of his mouth.

"Mmmm. You'd better watch it," Chase cautioned her playfully as her full sensuous lips peppered kisses down his throat and across the blond fuzz matting his chest. "You keep that up, and you might just find yourself bargaining for a whole lot more than you can handle."

Her tongue blazed a trail down his ribs and past his slim, narrow hips. "That's just what I was counting on."

His tormented groan invited her to go even farther, to strive to give him as much pleasure as he had her. His body rose and fell beneath her, his heartbeat throbbing at every pressure point in his body.

Giving the covers an impatient kick, Chase rolled her over and pinned her between himself and the bed with one quick motion. His hands roamed over her, instinctively knowing the right places to stroke and fondle. He was now familiar with the intricacies of her body. Her breasts rose beneath his hands, their rosy peaks hardening like pebbles.

Gradually his hands descended, his lips following closely behind until his tongue slowly tantalized the soft mound of her womanhood. The pressure building inside her was explosive. Surely the fire at the warehouse could have been no hotter than the one rippling through her, she thought, biting her lip to stifle her cries of ecstasy.

Not a moment too soon, Chase fitted himself to her, bare flesh against bare flesh. Her limbs winding tightly around his, she guided him home. The flames inside her were soon burning out of control and waves of sheer ecstasy throbbed through her. Love flowed between them, sealing their unspoken vow that they would always belong together. Without one, the other would never be complete. Nothing and no one would ever change that.

She lay beside him unable to move from their bower of love. If she had her way, they'd lock themselves in her room and forget all about the political differences between the United States and Spain. Perhaps when relations between the two countries had been normalized, he could . . . She quickly discarded such notions. She should only be concerned with the present. Let the future take care of itself.

Filled with a tenderness she experienced only in

his arms, Dare watched her lover succumb to sleep. If only she could freeze that moment in time, perhaps their inevitable parting would be made less painful.

Careful not to disturb him, she slipped into her robe and tiptoed out of the room and down the stairs. Humming to herself, she made her way into the kitchen. Perhaps breakfast in bed would be just the enticement he needed to convince him that a thorough investigation of the pleasures they could share would prove far more stimulating than compiling information for the assistant secretary of the Navy.

Dare stopped short of the kitchen. She could hardly believe her eyes. Rummaging through the pantry was the old Bahamian Negress who had helped her enter the world and who had held her poor, dear mama's hand when she had slipped away to heaven.

"Calpurnia! What are you doing here?" she asked, pleasantly surprised.

"What does it look like I'm doing? I'm fixing your breakfast, of course," she said matter-of-factly, just as though she had never left Dare's employment. Her words were crisp and carefully enunciated. She spoke with a slight trace of a British accent, a reminder of her days on Abaco.

"You know what I mean," Dare scolded gently. Try as she might, she simply could not bring herself to reprimand the woman. Calpurnia had always been much more than an employee. She had been a member of her family for nearly four decades. "What about poor Mrs. Jarvis? Who's taking care of her?"

"Now just don't go fretting none about her, missy.

Mr. Jarvis brought his sister down from Miami." Saucer-sized eyes peered at Dare. "Besides, from what I been hearing lately, you're the one that needs taking care of."

"And just what is that supposed to mean?" asked Dare, her arms folded stubbornly over her chest.

"You know me, honey, I don't like to go repeating gossip." Calpurnia busied herself with her cooking, keeping one eye peeled behind her. "However, seeing as how I helped birth and raise you, I figured for appearances' sake I'd just move myself back into the Sea Palms just so folks around town'll know there's no hanky-panky going on under my nose." Her tone mellowed. "Don't you go worrying none about how you're going to pay my wages now because I don't want any money. Not one dime. Don't need it." Tiny tears glistened on her smooth, caramel-colored cheeks. "You and me, we family. We belong together. We all each other got left."

Dare hadn't the heart to object. What Calpurnia had said was true. They were family. Seeing her standing there, her tall, willowy form regally erect, she didn't doubt for a moment her mammy's old tales that she was a direct descendant of African King John Canoe.

"Oh, Calpurnia, what would I ever do without you?" she asked, raising herself on tiptoes to kiss her mammy's hollowed cheeks.

"Sure took you long enough to figure that one out." Calpurnia swatted Dare's backside with a dish rag, just the way she had done when Dare was a naughty little girl. "Now scat, you. Get on upstairs and make yourself presentable. I swear, traipsing around here half naked. What happened to all those manners the good sisters learned you?'' She followed her to the foot of the staircase. ''And you tell that young man of yours if he wants my approval,'' she yelled up, ''he'd better get hisself down here and bring a voracious appetite with him!''

An hour later, Chase pushed back from the huge mahogany captain's table that had been salvaged from a Dutch freighter four decades before. ''That was by far the finest meal I have ever eaten!'' he announced, his hands touching his stomach.

''You jus' wait 'til you taste my turtle steaks,'' returned the old Negress, her face beaming.

''My mouth's watering already.''

Dare could hardly contain her laughter. Chase definitely had a way about him. He had won Calpurnia's heart as quickly as he had won her own.

''Well, what do you think of him?'' asked Dare as soon as Chase left the room.

''Humph! I never did think I'd live to see the day when a Yankee would set foot inside this house,'' she declared with a grunt.

Dare rolled her eyes. ''Really, Calpurnia. The Civil War was over a good ten years before I was even born.''

The housekeeper said nothing. She went on clearing the table as though no query had been made.

''Well?'' prodded Dare impatiently, close on her heels.

''He sure can put away a mess of food.'' Her tray full, Calpurnia finally looked up and gave Dare a broad, pearly-toothed grin. ''Aside from the fact that he's a Yankee and that if he stays on he'll probably end up eating us out of house and home, I reckon he's jus' about the handsomest thing I ever have seen."

Dare's grin matched her old mammy's. Calpurnia's approval meant as much as Uriah's had. Those two were the only family she had left.

Calpurnia's smile faded. Her tone grew serious. "Now don't you go getting yourself hurt. You hear me? He's a fine man, but you gotta remember, child, that that same old ocean that brought him here is going to take him away."

Dare nodded sadly. She had told herself as much many times before.

Calpurnia gave her shoulder a rough squeeze. "Sure is good to be back home at the Sea Palms," she said, trying to cheer up her charge of twenty years. "That Mrs. Jarvis, cripple or not, she's the meanest old cuss I ever did see. Just couldn't do anything right to suit her."

Dare was only half listening. Calpurnia's earlier advice had recalled the same foreboding thought she mulled over at least a dozen times a day. Chase had already been in Key West for two weeks, far longer than she had ever dreamed. He has done what he came here to do, she mused. He's interviewed the Cuban expatriate dedicated to furthering the cause of Cuba Libre in order to determine whether the junta's claims against the Spanish are valid. However, even though his assignment is completed, he doesn't appear in any hurry to leave. Perhaps he is just awaiting further instruction from Roosevelt.

She was delighted by the delay, and if Chase objected to it, he certainly had a strange way of showing it. When he made love to her, it was obvious

140

that leaving Key West and her were far from his mind. When he spoke of the future, he always used the plural *we*.

Leaving Calpurnia to her chores, Dare retired to her study where she decided to catch up on her correspondence. Chase would probably not be back until noon. Every morning for the past two weeks, he had visited his friend, Charles Sigsbee, the captain of the *Maine*. Sometimes he discussed their conversations with her in great detail; at others he volunteered very little information about the gist of their meetings.

Frowning to herself, she took out her pad and pen from the desk. Something told her Chase's momentary depressions and blank stares were caused by his concern over the growing threat of war. The possibility of war breaking out sent shivers up and down her spine.

Ranting and raving at the top of his lungs, Uriah stormed into her study a little before noon.

Newspaper in hand, Chase charged in after him. "I'm just as convinced as you that Ferrer was behind the warehouse," he exclaimed, waving the paper, "but we can't demand that the police chief arrest him for arson unless we have proof to substantiate our accusations."

Red-faced and out of breath, Uriah threw himself into the wicker rocker. "He wants proof, does he?" he growled. "Why, by God, I'll give it to him. I'll beat the truth out of that slimy bastard if it's the last thing I do!"

Dare calmly sealed the letter she had just written to Caroline. "If you keep carrying on like this, you may not be around to beat up anybody. You know what Doc Edmundson said about your heart."

"Yeah, yeah, I know," he said, waving aside her concern.

Dare pushed her chair away from the desk, then turned it around to face them. "Now, tell me just what all this ruckus is about," she commanded in a tone usually reserved for difficult children.

"Here you go. The *Key West Herald*. Hot off the press," said Chase. He handed her the newspaper and then dropped onto the settee.

She read the headlines aloud. "ARSON BLAMED IN WAREHOUSE BLAZE." She looked up. "So? That's just what we concluded."

"Go on. Read the rest of it," urged Uriah, rocking impatiently.

Dare scanned the article, her eyes growing larger and larger with each sentence. "What do they mean by 'all leads have been discounted'?" She glanced from Uriah to Chase. Inside, her blood was boiling. "We told them all about Ferrer's plot to gain ownership of the Sea Palms. What does Chief Seals want before he'll bring charges? A signed confession from Ferrer?"

"Aye, lass. It certainly appears that way," agreed Uriah wearily.

"It says here that an empty kerosene tin was found inside," she said, "but that no one was seen going in or coming out of the building at the time of the blaze." Giving her head an angry shake, she threw the paper onto her desk. "I take it you've already had a few words with the police chief," she remarked wryly to Uriah.

142

His gray, shaggy head nodded forlornly. "Aye. I was at the station not more than a quarter of an hour ago."

"And?" she pressed him, anxious to hear all.

"Ferrer swears he was at the San Carlos Club from seven until midnight," continued Uriah. "Accordin' to him there are at least fifty people who'll back up his story."

Dare rested her head against the roll-top cushion and expelled an angry, frustrated sigh. "That's great. I'm sure all fifty of them just happen to work at the cigar factory."

"And if they don't vouch for him, they'll be out of a job," added Chase, just as bitterly.

"Even if he were there all night that doesn't mean he didn't put one of his boys up to it," Dare stated. "Ferrer's never been one to soil his hands doing his own dirty work."

Uriah sank into his chair, his arms hanging limply over the side. "I talked the chief into questionin' a few of those Cuban cutthroats, but it didn't do any good. When he questioned Ferrer about them, Ferrer just shrugged his shoulders and pleaded ignorance. Said he couldn't be held responsible for the actions of his employees."

"He might not be held responsible, but I'd wager the Sea Palms that he gave whoever lit that match a big bonus and a paid holiday in South America." After taking a few moments to cool down, she walked over to Uriah and rested her hands on his shoulders. "Don't worry," she told him as she gently kneaded the stiffness from his tired, old back. "We'll get to the bottom of this."

The old seaman gave her hand a fatherly pat. "'Tis you I'm worried about, lass. What's to become of the Sea Palms if we can't repay that cursed note?"

"We'll find a way to clear up our money worries. I promise. Besides," she continued, trying to mask her despair with a cheery smile, "the tourists are going to start coming down here any day now."

"I wouldn't count on that happening in the immediate future if I were you," Chase put in, frowning.

The gravity of his tone caught her off guard. His words sounded so dismal . . . so final. "What's that supposed to mean?" she asked quietly.

Chase cleared his throat. "I'm afraid relations between Washington and Madrid are steadily worsening."

Dare's cheeks suddenly paled. That news was just as distressing as the chief's refusal to prosecute Ferrer. She sat down beside him, one hand nervously reaching for the row of starched ruffles encircling her throat. War was inevitable! She had suspected as much all along. Day by day, it seemed that war had become less of a threat and more of a reality. "Go on," she urged. Taking a deep breath, she folded her hands in her lap and prepared herself for the worst.

"I personally am of the opinion that war with Spain is closer at hand than any of us suspect," Chase continued somberly. "As you are aware, Washington offered to mediate the controversy in Cuba, but Spain declined. Politely, of course, but nonetheless, they did decline." He looked at Uriah, then at Dare, his expression even more troubled when he met her gaze. "As a result of that refusal, relations have been very touchy. We're at the point now where the least disagreement could bring the entire situation to a head."

Dare gulped. "But from what I've been reading, it appears the dispute between the rebels and the army is on the verge of being resolved."

"Aye," interjected Uriah thoughtfully. "I feel the same way. The way I see it if we were so close to war, we'd have been in it three years ago when General Weyler was sent to Cuba as governor general."

Dare shivered. General Weyler, who had been dubbed the butcher by his friends as well as his enemies, had had a simple philosophy: There is no place for mercy in a war. He implemented that philosophy in Cuba. Rebel leaders and their followers were executed. Not even women and children were spared. And those who survived were not much better off. Conditions were deplorable. Misery and starvation were the rule rather than the exception. People dwelled in fortified towns and were treated no better than animals. Huge trenches, *trincheras*, surrounded each village and were manned with guards to keep the insurgents out and the reconcentrados in.

Taut worry lines pulled at Chase's mouth. "I, too, was certain that when Spain's liberal ministry came to power, the needless bloodshed would come to an end. The general consensus seemed to be that as soon as Weyler was recalled and replaced by Blanco, it would be but a matter of time before differences between the two world powers were ironed out."

"Then what makes you think otherwise now?" queried Dare.

"Seems to me Segasta and Blanco, too, have tried their damnedest to lend more of a sympathetic ear to the rebels," interjected Uriah.

"Be that as it may," began Chase, his tone growing graver with each word, "there are powers in Washington who would welcome an all-out confrontation with Spain, and the sooner the better!"

Dare fidgeted nervously in her seat. "Are you speaking as a citizen or as an officer in the Navy?"

"Both," he answered without hesitation.

She winced. She had been afraid that would be his answer. "You mean to say powers other than the press are encouraging an out and out confrontation?"

Chase nodded. "Our country has an estimated fifty million dollars invested in Cuba in addition to the one hundred million in annual trade that is at stake."

Uriah whistled softly. "If the truth were known, some of those greedy politicians don't give a darn about helping the Cubans. Why I'd bet the *Busy Lizzy*, what's left of her," he said with a chuckle, "that more than a few of them is in favor of a total U.S. takeover. You know they tried that in the fifties," he remarked knowingly, his index finger cutting the air, "but their little plan backfired on them."

Dare nodded in agreement. She hadn't been around then, but she knew her history. The Ostend Manifesto had practically guaranteed seizure of Cuba if Spain refused America's demands to sell. Its contents had justified American aggression. Luckily, former Secretary of State Marry had had the good sense to realize that if such a move were made, the

United States would be denounced by the entire world as a power monger.

"What about the president?" she asked, desperately searching for one ray of hope. "Surely McKinley will not deliberately plunge the States into war. After all, Grover Cleveland announced on numerous occasions that if Congress were to declare war on Spain, he, as commander in chief, would not issue the necessary orders to mobilize the army."

"Ah, but lass, ye must remember, this administration's policies do not have to agree with those of the former one," Uriah pointed out. "When the Republicans took charge last March, they came into office with a whole new set of rules."

"He's right," Chase concurred. "When they took charge, they brought with them a proposal to make the United States the strongest power in the world."

Dare sank against Chase's arm. "Ah, yes. Manifest Destiny, the belief that some nations are destined to expand their limits and extend sovereignty over others."

"For their own good," added Uriah quickly, his comment laced with sarcasm.

"Surely President McKinley will rely on his conscience rather than his politics to guide him," she said wistfully.

Chase had no reply.

"We can but hope, lass. We can but hope," echoed Uriah, shaking his gray head sadly.

"Tell me, Chase, in all honesty," Dare began, late that night as they lay in bed seeking solace from the impending war in each other's arms, "do you believe our country is on the verge of another war?"

His lips grazed the top of her head. "I fear the worst." His arms protectively enfolded her. "The president is caught in a rather precarious situation. His advisors are divided right down the middle. The overall feeling in Washington, as well as abroad, is that he could easily be swayed by either faction. Unfortunately for our country, he lacks the inner fortitude of most of his predecessors."

Dare pressed herself as close to him as she could get. She desired the comfort his warm body gave her. "Just last week, I saw an editorial cartoon in which he was portrayed as a pendulum. At the time, I had no idea just how accurate a picture that drawing presented."

"You're trembling," whispered Chase, drawing her shivering body tighter. "There's nothing to worry about. I'm here. I'll take care of you. I promise."

She burrowed her head into the hollow of his shoulder. "I know you will, my dearest. I know it." Dare swallowed hard. But for how long? she wanted to ask.

She had always prided herself on her fiery independence. Now was not the time to weaken, she reminded herself for the hundredth time. Chase or no Chase, war or no war, she and the Sea Palms would make it. They were survivors.

Suddenly, her problems with Ferrer seemed minute in comparison to an event which would affect much of the world. So many lives would be wasted by a pointless war. It would be a repeat of the

Civil War. Even though the Confederates and Yanks would be fighting side by side, the end result would be the same. Why couldn't those in power realize the futility of war, of killing?

Her arms tightened around him. Stay, just a little while longer, she pleaded silently. The thought of losing her island, her home, and the man she loved was just too much to endure. She knew she was strong. Accepting Mac's death had proven that, but now she had a feeling her strength was about to be tested even more! For the first time in her life, she wondered just how strong she really was!

Chapter Nine

Humming a lively tune, Dare bounded down the stairs, her feet high stepping in rhythm to the melody. In three short weeks, Captain Chase Millbrook Hamilton had far exceeded any of her preconceived notions concerning the perfect man. Mac had always assured her that when the right man came along, she'd know it in her heart. After the first night she'd spent locked in Chase's arms, both she and her heart were in total agreement. He was definitely the man with whom she wanted to spend the rest of her life. There was no doubt about it! He was her lover, her confidant, her friend. What more could a woman want in a man? Phillip may have set off fireworks for dear Caroline, but when she and Chase made love the sensations she experienced were cataclysmic.

Dare chuckled softly midway down the stairs. How surprised Caroline would be to read her last letter.

Her dearest friend would never believe the wonderful metamorphosis she had undergone in such a short time. Thanks to Chase, she was now a woman. What was it she had once told Caroline? Ah yes. A woman did not necessarily need a man in her life in order to be fulfilled. How wonderful it would be to eat those words! She had made a bet with Caroline that she would not under any circumstances marry before she was thirty. The prospect of losing that bet was now a welcome possibility. She couldn't think of a better reason to part with five dollars. Chase was the man she was destined to marry. He had to be. If she lived to be a hundred, what she felt for him could never be duplicated. After one night spent in his embrace she knew that. Other women, Nessa included, had in all probability loved him as fiercely as she did, but they had been unable to hold on to him. She'd not make the same mistakes as her predecessors.

Dare stopped suddenly at the bottom step and sniffed the air. Her smile quickly vanished. Fresh cigar smoke assailed her nostrils, and her nose twitched angrily. The aroma seemed to be coming from the study. Surely, not even Ferrer would have the gall to enter someone's home uninvited.

"Calpurnia," she called out. "Calpurnia!"

When no answer came, she lifted her skirt and stomped into her office, temper flaring and eyes glowering. Seeing Ferrer sitting on the settee with his cane propped in front of him and his hands folded stubbornly across the silver knob almost sent her into a tirade. She fought to keep control of her tongue. Losing her temper would only give him some satisfaction, she reminded herself, trying to conceal her rage.

He rose as she entered the room and gave a stiff bow. "I knocked, but no one answered," he said, leering despite his attempt to appear polite.

"Then did it not occur to you that perhaps no one was home?" Dare asked frostily.

He gave his shoulders an indifferent shrug. "The door was open so I decided to come in and wait." Bright white teeth glistened. "For all I knew, you were away, and your home was being vandalized."

Dare said nothing. She didn't believe him for a minute. Had Calpurnia stepped out for a quick visit to the market, she would have checked and double-checked the door to make sure it was secure. Her face flushed with anger, Dare sat down across from him. Hands primly crossed on her lap, she waited for him to state his business, her back as erect as that of her cane-seated chair. There was no need to ask him why he had come. She had expected him every day since the fire. How foolish she had been to tell him she would have the money to repay her debt so much sooner than was legally required. It hadn't taken him long to figure out the source of her sudden wealth. Nor had it taken him long to do something to deprive her of it.

Still smiling, Ferrer returned to his seat. He reached for his cigar, drew on it once, returned it to the ashtray, and leaned back against the pale blue cushions. "The day's loveliness is rivaled only by yours, my dear Dare."

The way he said her name made her cringe. How she loathed him! "I assume you did not come to the

Sea Palms to compare me with the weather," she said tersely. "If it's all the same to you, I'd prefer you get straight to the point."

"You are not going to offer me some refreshment? A cool drink, perhaps?" His thin-lipped smile resembled the sneer of a hungry animal.

Her reserve unbroken, Dare replied. "I do apologize, but as you've noticed, I'm sure, my housekeeper is out on an errand," she said, her voice calm and even.

Ferrer gave a curt nod. "As you wish." His smile disappeared. "I believe you and I have some unfinished business to settle," he informed her, his tone sharpening.

"You're referring of course to the note you purchased from the bank."

"But of course." Black beady eyes scrutinized every inch of her. Not one part of her body went unappraised.

Dare felt herself shivering beneath his impaling stare. He seemed to be undressing her with each scorching glance. He made her skin crawl. One look from him and she felt dirty all over. If hate could kill, he would die that very instant!

"It was my understanding that you would honor the same terms originally set forth by the bank," she said, silently refusing to allow him to bully her a moment longer.

"And it was my understanding that you were to repay the loan much sooner." Smiling confidently, he stroked his mustache. "If I am not mistaken, you were the one who first proposed an earlier date."

Dare met his pointed glare head-on. He knew

154

damned well the suggestion had been hers! "And you and I both know the reason why you were not paid on the day I specified. Correct?"

"I'm sure I don't know what you're talking about," he returned smoothly.

"Oh, but I'm sure you do!"

He feigned a look of surprise. "If you are referring to the fire—"

"I am. But then, I understand you know nothing about such matters," she added bitterly.

"Obviously, you are of the opinion that I do." His snakelike tongue slithered along his lower lip. "However, such matters are of no concern to me. What does concern me is that my investment is repaid, or that a suitable compromise is agreed upon, one satisfactory to both parties involved."

Her face flamed. "Just what exactly do you mean by a suitable compromise?"

Ferrer was in no hurry to answer her question.

Dare held her breath. There was no mistaking the gleam in his eye. He knew he had the upper hand. No doubt he was enjoying every minute of his advantage. She made up her mind not to avoid the intensity of his gaze. That would have increased the pleasure he was deriving from her predicament.

"I do not want your money," he said, sighing heavily. "My cigar factory and my numerous investments provide me with an income that is more than ample. And as far as my wanting to take possession of the Sea Palms, what use could I possibly have for a boardinghouse?" He laid his cane across his knees, his fingers skimming the onyx with tiny caresses. "You on the other hand, are in need of someone to look after your affairs as well as your needs. A protector, shall we say?"

Dare struggled to retain her composure. What he was slyly proposing disgusted her, yet his suggestion came as no surprise. After all, the man was totally without scruples. He had had the warehouse torched to make certain she would not get her hands on any of the proceeds from the auction. More than once, he had made it perfectly clear that he would stop at nothing to get what he wanted. If only she could stall him a little longer, she felt sure she could find some way out of her dilemma.

"Am I to assume then that you already have someone in mind who would act as my protector?" she asked, her face revealing no emotion.

"I would be more than willing to assume such a responsibility." His smile grew hungrier with each word.

"How kind of you," she mumbled bitterly. "Tell me, just what does being under your protection entail?"

Ferrer slicked a strand of hair back from his forehead. Beads of perspiration popped out on his cheeks. "You will want for nothing. Buy anything you desire and send the bill to me. If you do not wish to open up your home to outsiders, then don't. All your needs will be taken care of by me. All of them," he stressed, breathing heavily. His eyes swept down across her chest, boring holes through the yellow cotton blouse before they returned to her face.

It was all she could do to keep herself from pouncing on him and clawing his eyes out. "And in return?" she asked, keeping a tight grip on her anger.

How pleased with himself he was. "In return, you will be expected only to provide companionship to a man who would derive great pleasure from pampering and spoiling so beautiful a woman."

Companionship, indeed, she fumed. He wanted her to be his whore no matter how eloquently he propositioned her. And she would have none of that, no matter how desperate her situation might become.

"When must I give you my answer?" she asked, trying to sound sincere as she stalled for more time.

He waved his hand. "That is entirely up to you. However, I do ask that you remember on April fifteenth the Sea Palms and everything you possess will, by law, become mine. So it is to your advantage not to delay your decision." He rose slowly. "Needless to say, if you should wait until the day before to give me your answer, I shall still abide by my promise."

Everything about him repulsed her! Damn him. He knew he had her over a barrel. Everything had worked out just as he had planned.

His heels clicked together. "You will find, my dear, I am a very patient man." He reached for her hand.

Ignoring it, she lifted herself out of her seat. "Yes, I've been told that patience is a virtue, but whether or not it is one of yours remains to be seen." She knew she was treading on dangerous ground. Still, she couldn't bear him thinking she would jump at the chance to lie down and spread her legs for the sake of saving the Sea Palms. She would sooner torch her family home than have Ferrer possess it . . . or her.

"We shall see," he remarked in his usual snide

157

manner. "We shall see, indeed."

At the door, Ferrer did a quick about-face. "Ah, yes, one more thing," he began, a wolfish sneer contorting his face once again. "You would be wise to remember that your journalist friend will soon have about as much use for you as he would for yesterday's news. Don't despair, though," he said, his hand closing around her wrist in a viperish hold. "One man's cast-off is another man's gain."

Dare angrily jerked her arm away. If it would not give him satisfaction, she would slap his face. "Hell will freeze over before I enter into any sort of agreement with you, suitable or otherwise!"

His laugh was cold and calculating. "I shall remind you of those words the night of the fifteenth."

"You disgust me!" she spat, her eyes venting her hate. "I can think of no words foul enough to accurately describe you!"

His eyes flickered with amusement. "Be that as it may, dearest Dare, you have very little choice in the matter."

"I'm afraid I must disagree with you on that point!" exclaimed a voice from behind them.

Dare turned around. Chase was standing on the bottom landing. He looked like a man who never backed down to anyone or anything.

Ferrer's smile was quickly erased. He looked from one to the other, his mouth becoming even more set. "I fail to see how any of this concerns you, señor."

Chase proceeded down the remaining steps with deliberate slowness. "That is where you are wrong! This is my concern. However, I have better things to do with my time than to stand here and argue with you." He took out an envelope from his trouser pocket and offered it to the Cuban. "Here."

Ferrer gripped his cane with both hands. "You have nothing I want."

Chase shoved it into the pocket of Ferrer's coat. "One thousand dollars. Payment in full for the Sea Palms loan."

Dare's look of astonishment matched Ferrer's. "I'm sorry, but I, I can't allow you to do that," she told Chase softly. She reached for the envelope.

He diverted her arm. "Yes, you can, and you will. We shall discuss it later," he said, his words final.

"I'm afraid I cannot allow it, either," remarked Ferrer, reaching for the money.

"Why, of course, you'll take it," Chase told him with undisputed certainty. "It's all very simple. You bought the note from the bank, and I, in turn, am purchasing it from you." His grin was caustic. "Basic business practice, you see."

Cursing under his breath, Ferrer stepped toward the door.

"One more moment of your time, if you please." Cornering him, Chase took out a piece of paper from his pocket. "Before you leave, I'd like you to sign this."

"What is it?" Ferrer asked sharply.

Chase unfolded the paper and held it up for Ferrer to read. "A receipt for the money I just paid you," he answered. "As well as insurance for Miss MacDade that you won't forget ever receiving this several months from now."

Hate glared from Ferrer's dark, beady eyes. "I have no intention of signing this, or taking your money for that matter," he said, throwing the envelope down onto the floor.

Chase picked up the envelope, then stuffed it back into Ferrer's coat pocket. "There is where you are wrong," he calmly told him. "If you do not accept this money and sign this document, then I'll be left with no alternative but to tell every man involved in salvaging the Mallory liner all I know about the warehouse fire."

Ringlets of perspiration danced around Ferrer's eyes. "That's ridiculous. You know nothing about that fire. Neither do I for that matter," he added hastily.

Chase's smile was as cold as Ferrer's. "You're going to have to be more convincing than that when a drunken mob comes after you."

Expelling an angry grunt, Ferrer jerked a pen from his pocket and scribbled out his signature. "You may think you've gotten the best of me this time, señor, but don't count on it. People have died for less." His fingers gripped the cane so tightly their knuckles paled white. "You will be hearing from me. That's a promise. Both of you!" he hissed in Dare's direction. Then, turning quickly, Ferrer stomped outside.

"No-good bastard," mumbled Chase. "I should have broken every last bone in his body while I had the chance."

Dare released an exasperated sigh. "Oh, Chase. You shouldn't have paid off my debt. I'm perfectly capable of finding solutions to my problems." She didn't know whether to be annoyed or relieved. Once Chase left Key West, she'd be on her own again anyway.

His voice softened. "Oh, Dare. My sweet, sweet Dare," he said, his lips brushing over her forehead. "Come." He gently took her by the arm and guided her out onto the porch and into the swing. "I know you're capable of solving your own problems, and if I've offended you, I do apologize." One arm enclosed her shoulders, the hand of the other reached for her hands and covered them. "Please, don't be angry with me because I interfered in your affairs. I know how important the Sea Palms is to you, and I wouldn't have you lose it for anything in the world."

"I'm not angry," she said, her head nodding against his shoulder. "You have no idea how much I appreciate what you did for me. The Sea Palms is very important to me. As long as I have it, then Mac will live on. It's just that . . ." She hesitated. How could she put into words what she was feeling? "It's just that I don't want you to feel as though you're indebted to me for saving your life or . . . for anything." She swallowed hard.

Chase placed his cheek against hers, his breath fanning her lips. "You know as well as I that you could have taken that money from my pocket the day you rescued me and blamed its absence on the sea. I'd have been none the wiser. And as far as my being indebted to you for anything else," he continued, his cheek nuzzling hers, "all I can say to that is that if we were to spend the rest of our lives paying each other back, I'd be the last to complain."

Her heart, wildly out of control, pummeled her ribs. "Spend the rest of our years," he had said. Surely, that in itself was a proposal. Dare she hope? She waited anxiously for further mention of marriage, but nothing else was said. A little disappointed, she sank deeper into his hold. Marriage was an important step, she reminded herself. It was not to be taken lightly, nor was it something to go rushing into. Nessa, and who knew how many others before her, had vied for his name and in doing so had pushed him away. It was up to her to learn from the mistakes of those who'd preceded her in his arms.

"Ferrer was wrong," remarked Chase, interrupting her reverie a few minutes later. "I have no intention of casting you aside like yesterday's news."

Dare swallowed hard. He always seemed to have the uncanny ability to read her thoughts.

"You do believe me, don't you?" he queried.

She nodded.

"These three weeks I've spent with you have been the happiest weeks of my life." He tilted her head to his; his eyes searched deep into hers. "I have no way of knowing what the future has in store for either of us, but for the time being, you must trust me, and believe in me when I say that I would never, under any circumstances, cause you one moment of sorrow. I love you far too much to subject you to any grief at all."

"I believe you," she whispered, her eyes misting. "I love you, too."

He squeezed her close. "Then that's all that matters, my sweet Dare. That's all that matters."

Her arms instinctively wound themselves around him. I love him . . . he loves me . . . That's all that matters, she answered herself. Let the future take care of itself.

Dare pulled his head down to hers. As her honeyed

lips hungrily drank from his, raw desire spiraled through her. She grasped him tightly, her love. "I can't think of a better time than the present to start repaying my debts," she whispered as her tongue darted in and out of his ear.

His short, quick breaths came in unison with her own as his strong sensuous fingers shaped the narrowness of her waist, then rose until his thumbs traced tiny circles on the crests of her full breasts. "And I can't think of a time more appropriate than the present to collect."

Dare gave his cheek a quick peck, then rose quickly. "I thought you'd agree."

"Naturally," he said, grinning lazily at her.

"I'll just go in and pack us a lunch basket. It won't take a minute," she said cheerfully.

He stretched both arms across the back of the glider, and his smile widened. "Looks like a lovely day for a swim. Don't forget your suit."

"That's exactly what I intend to do." With that, she blew him a kiss and bolted into the house.

Chapter Ten

Dare lounged against the bow of the skiff while Chase rowed toward the tiny key which had been their retreat every afternoon for the past week. For seven gloriously wonderful days, Christmas Tree Key had been their own love nest. It was completely hidden from view by the tall, pointed casurinas for which it was named. Dare dangled one long, shapely leg over the side; the other rested atop Chase's knee. Her straw boater aslant over her eyes, she treated herself to a thorough perusal of the beautifully proportioned physique opposite her. Her own chest quivered with unconcealed delight each time the oars were dipped into the turquoise shimmers. Every strain and ripple of Chase's muscle-corded flesh was a sight on which to feast her eyes. Its raw, sensuous power never failed to elicit all sorts of strange stirrings inside her. A mere glance in his direction and gusts of desire vibrated through her. She knew his body as well as any woman could. Every minute detail of him fascinated her because contained within him was the power to give her pleasure she had not known existed . . . and he could devastate her if he so chose. Luckily, he was not the sort of man who prided himself on such behavior. The moment she had set eyes on him in the swirling waters, she'd known he was an exceptional man. How right she had been! Nothing—no one—would ever separate them, she vowed every day. And each time those words were spoken, she had more faith in them and in herself. She would never let him go. No matter what! Their lives had crossed by chance, and from that moment forward their destinies had been interwoven. She would do everything she could to make certain that would never change!

"I received word from Roosevelt that I'm to return to Washington on the twenty-sixth," remarked Chase without losing a single beat of his rowing.

Her heart sank to the bottom of the ocean. The twenty-sixth? But that was only two days away, she wanted to exclaim. Instead, she held her tongue. Tears stung her eyes, but she remained steadfast in her determination not to let them fall. How could he be so casual about the entire matter? she wailed silently.

"Really?" she finally managed to mumble.

Chase stopped rowing. He looked at her, confused yet amused. "Really?" he echoed. "Is that all I get? One lousy, little really?"

Dare gave her shoulders an annoyed shrug. Refusing to meet his gaze, she focused her sights on a gull winging its way home. He might think this was funny, but she was not the slightest bit amused.

"I asked to be assigned to Key West indefinitely," he said, picking up the oars and continuing to row. "And old Teddy's agreed that this is the place for me for the time being." His serious expression was replaced with a cheerful one.

Dare splashed him unmercifully. "You cad!" she exclaimed, laughing so hard she had to hold onto her sides. "Why didn't you say so? Why did you have to torture me? You let me think you were leaving. You knew I'd be upset!" Not quick to forgive, she sent another spray of water onto his face.

Chase grabbed her feet and bit her toe. "Easy. Don't go rocking the boat, or we'll both find ourselves swimming to shore."

She delivered a final kick and then jerked back her leg. "Why didn't you tell me sooner?"

"I was going to tell you a few days ago, but I decided to wait until I knew for sure." He leaned down and kissed her knee. "Had I known you would react so violently, I'd have written you a letter."

She threw both arms around him. "That's the most wonderful news I've had in ages!"

He offered his cheek for her to kiss. "Mmm. Keep that up and you'll never get rid of me."

"That's just what I keep hoping," she said lightly.

She sprinkled tiny kisses across his bronze, muscled chest, only to cease a moment later, her smile frozen on her face. A horrible thought had just crossed her mind. She was almost afraid to verbalize her fear. "Chase . . . Roosevelt's agreeing to let you stay here . . . well, does that mean the situation in Cuba has taken another bad turn?"

All traces of merriment disappeared from his face. "No one knows for sure one way or another. Unfortunately, that island's a powder keg just waiting to blow. The smallest occurrence could light its fuse." His eyes melted into hers. "At least one ray of happiness has come out of it."

Dare held her hand to his cheek. "You're right, my darling. So very right."

The tide carried them the rest of the way to shore. Dare said very little. Had Roosevelt granted Chase's request to stay in the Keys so that he'd be closer to Cuba in the event of war? She shuddered at such a thought. The prospect of life without Chase made her so miserable she wouldn't even try to imagine how she'd fare when he was no longer around. He was her life . . . her everything!

Chase had a way of knowing exactly what was on her mind. "We're not going to let Teddy or Ferrer or the Cubans spoil anything for us, now are we?" he asked cheerfully as he swung her out of the skiff and deposited her feetfirst onto the sand.

"Agreed!" She sidled closer to him. "Say, do you know something?"

"What's that?" he grinned.

"For a sailor, you're not half bad."

"Thanks . . . I think." He gave her backside a playful slap. "Last one in the water rows home."

"Hey, that's not fair." She tugged at her skirt. "All you're wearing is your trousers."

"Not for long." Laughing, he scrambled out of his trousers, then leapt out in front of her. "Hurry up, slowpoke!"

Her own laughter rang through the pines as Dare

dropped her petticoat onto the sand and took off down the beach after him. How wonderful it felt to have the sun's hot rays showering every inch of her body. Being a castaway on a deserted island definitely had its advantages, especially if she were stranded in the middle of nowhere with Chase, she decided as she loped along the surf in pursuit.

"Got you!" she screamed as she tackled him from behind.

They fell to the sand together, their bodies rolling into the water. Dare felt herself sinking deeper and deeper into the wet sand. The weight on top of her was a welcome burden.

"So what are you going to do with me now that you've caught me?" He lay over her, imprisoning her and driving her into the sand.

"Anything . . . everything," she moaned as she opened herself up to him. How wonderful it would be to be held by those strong arms and legs the rest of her life!

His kiss was hurried, almost as frantic as hers. The message it communicated to her was clear. He was just as anxious as she to take possession of what rightfully belonged to him.

Blood pumped hotter and faster through her veins. The wait was unbearable! She could think of little else but feasting on the limitless joys he had to offer. She wanted to gorge herself, to be completely satiated by his love.

As her yearning mounted, she moaned, "Love me, my darling. Love me, please." How desperately she wanted him.

Her hands roamed his back; her fingers dug into

the warm, inviting flesh of his buttocks. She felt like a woman deprived, her hunger that of a shark in a feeding frenzy. She had to have him.

"Love me," she pleaded, her words thick and her body flushed. "Love me as you've never loved any other woman."

His mouth smothered hers. "I do. I will."

"Now." Her legs climbed up his back. "Don't make me wait a moment longer."

His voice was teasing and playful. "You must, my darling. You must."

"I can't," she gasped.

"Show me what you want," he gently commanded, his tone lusty.

Dare was only too happy to oblige. The source of her pleasure pulsating hungrily in her hand, she guided him inside her. Her back arched to meet him, urging him to go deeper still, as his hips grinding into hers, he drove himself farther into her love chasm.

She met his thrusts with an urgency that demanded he claim her very body and soul. One part of her wanted to feel the core of her womanliness explode into thousands of delicious tremors, while the other wanted their moment to be suspended forever in time. She wanted to lie back, to let him make love to her slowly and sweetly, but she could not. Her own desire was overwhelming. Once her passions were unleashed, she could do nothing to harness them. She accepted him eagerly, wantonly.

The sweet surge of joy refused to be held back. The same delicious spasms which wracked her shivered through him at almost the same instant. His love flowed inside her like warm, molten liquid. She could feel it coursing through her, saturating every part of her.

Dare collapsed into the sand. Sweet exhaustion all but numbed her. A satisfied smile lingered on her lips. Not once in her adult years had she enjoyed such pleasure.

She closed her eyes, and a few moments later, she was only vaguely aware of being carried back to the cozy bower where they had spread their blanket, and of being laid ever so gently onto the bed of soft pine needles.

When she awakened later, Chase was lazing beside her, one arm draped over her, the other holding her hand. She looked into his face and smiled. His gaze focused intently on hers. The way he looked at her sent shivers cascading through her once again.

His blue eyes twinkled devilishly. "I had no idea I was tiring you out so," he said, his grin broadening. "You've been fast asleep for nearly an hour."

"I'm new at this. Remember." The tip of her tongue slowly trailed down his nose. "I'm sure, though, that the more time you devote to educating me in the finer points of love-making, the stronger my stamina will become." She threw one leg up over his hips and pulled him close. "As a matter of fact, I'd say that I'm just about to get my second wind."

"Oh, no," he protested, playfully pushing her aside. "I absolutely refuse to be used like a common sex slave."

Her teeth nipped at his shoulder. "Frankly, sir, I don't see that you have much of a choice in the matter."

"In that case I'll be delighted to comply with your wishes, my beautiful, wicked siren." Fingers, both gentle and rough, shaped the roundness of her breasts. "However, please, I beg of you, permit your lowly servant a morsel of food. I am famished. Without nourishment, I cannot possibly—"

She interrupted him with an elbow in his ribs. "All right, slave, I get the message." She lifted the lid of the picnic hamper and brought out a platter of fried chicken. After lunch you have no more excuses. Agreed?"

He rolled back his eyes. "Talk about battle fatigue."

Laughing, Dare stuffed a piece of chicken into his mouth. "Battle fatigue, my foot. You're loving every minute of it, and you know it!" He certainly wasn't alone in that. Still smiling, she helped herself to a drumstick.

"The *Maine*'s been ordered to Havana," announced Chase, midway through their meal.

Dare was stunned. She could not conceal her surprise or her disappointment. The news was completely unexpected. Just yesterday while dining aboard the *Maine* both Chase and Captain Sigsbee had assured her that talks between Spain and the United States were sure to resume at any moment.

"When did you learn that?" she asked finally.

"Charles told me this morning," he answered quietly, "when the *Maine* was taking on coal. I would have told you sooner, but I didn't want to ruin our outing."

Dare's appetite quickly vanished. "I don't understand. Why is it going? Everyone seemed so certain an end to the troubles was in sight."

His hand closed over hers. "According to the instructions Charles received late last night, the *Maine* is to be dispatched on a courtesy visit in the hope of resuming friendly naval relations with Spain. It seems Spanish authorities in Havana have been informed of the move and endorse it whole-heartedly."

"A courtesy visit?" asked Dare thoughtfully. "But she's a battleship, not a passenger ship."

Chase did nothing to mask his frown. "I know. That one detail concerns me as well. Why send an armored cruiser unless? . . ." He stopped suddenly.

"Unless what?" Dare was certain he had cut his statement short deliberately. "Go on. Unless what?"

It was obvious he was debating whether or not to tell her all he knew. "Unless Washington wants to pressure Spain into resolving the Cuban crisis once and for all."

"But what if that can't be done?" she asked, her heart as heavy as lead. "After all, public opinion has left the McKinley administration little choice but to recognize Cuban affairs and attempt to open dip-lomatic talks with Madrid."

"American lives and investments there must be protected at any cost," he added gravely. "My guess is that Consul General Lee requested an emergency call because the situation in Havana has become threat-ening."

Dare said nothing. His phrase kept echoing in her mind. "At any cost." A poor season for the Sea Palms would not be the only price she'd have to pay if the threat of war became a reality. Chase would have to return to active naval duty. If that happened, there was no guarantee that he would not join the countless ranks of casualties. A bullet or a marine mine could take him away from her forever.

She picked at the food remaining on her plate. For Chase's sake, she was determined to keep such dismal thoughts to herself. He had enough on his mind without having to share her own worries.

Finally, she could not remain silent a moment longer. "If there is a war, you'll have to fight even if the battles are on foreign soil, won't you?"

"Foreign sea," he corrected. "Not soil." His smile was strained. "I am a naval officer, my love. A career man. The obligation I have to my president and to my country cannot be shirked."

Dare nodded. She knew better than to argue with him. As far as he was concerned, obligations were not to be taken lightly. He had made a commitment, not to another woman, but to his country. She could never ask him to choose between her and his duty. Having Nessa as a rival for his devotion would have been far simpler.

Chase took her in his arms and gathered her close. Their hearts pounded in rhythm. "You do understand, don't you, my love?"

"Of course I do." She braved a smile for his benefit. "I suppose I should even be grateful for such international controversies."

"Grateful?" He seemed puzzled.

She pressed herself tightly against him. "That's right. Grateful. Had it not been for the problems between Spain and Cuba and the States, you'd never have been sent here, and I'd never have known the meaning of the word *love*."

"No, dearest, it is you who taught me the meaning of that word." He wound her long, dark tresses around his fingers. "And as far as my not having been sent here, I think you're wrong. That wouldn't have kept us apart. We'd still have found each other."

"You're right. We would have found each other. I just know it!" Dare snuggled close, her head burrowing into his chest. His words gave her solace. They would have found each other. By the same token, she reasoned, his heart throbbing in her ear, not even a war was going to come between them!

An hour later, as they silently watched the USS *Maine* steam out of the harbor, Dare sensed that one day soon Chase would be leaving too, and for the same reason. But he would not be leaving Key West alone, she vowed. Centuries ago, women had been able to accompany their lovers to sea. That was a tradition which needed reviving.

Chase waited until the *Maine* blended into the horizon before uttering a sound. "Now, what was it you were telling me before lunch about catching your second wind?" he asked, his words hot and eager in her ears.

Her palms ironed the warm flesh inside his thighs. "I wouldn't want you to think my interest in you is limited solely to the pleasures of your flesh," she said, her hand becoming more and more daring with each caress.

He slid back down onto the blanket, drawing her with him. "Are you trying to convince me it's my skill as a naval commander that appeals to you?"

Casting her eyes appraisingly over his body, she

175

said seductively, "That . . . and other things."

Chase moaned his approval. "My beautiful, shameless hussy. What am I ever going to do with you?"

Wriggling free of his hold, she threw a leg over him and rolled him onto his back. "Why don't you let me worry about that?" she asked as she straddled him.

"It appears I have very little choice in the matter."

Her firm breasts hovered temptingly above him. She offered him one, then the other. The peaks hardened instantly between his teeth.

Hair cascading onto his chest, Dare slid lengthwise over him, in a slow, teasing movement. "Shall we discuss the terms of surrender now?" she asked, blanketing him with her warmth.

"Ummm, keep that up and you can take whatever you want."

She peppered his stomach with kisses. "Thanks. Don't mind if I do."

With one swift movement, he rolled her off, and the next thing she knew, he was the one who had the upper hand.

She tried to free herself. "Hey, no fair!"

"There is no fairness in battle, my love," he told her as he pinned her shoulders flat into the sand. "First rule of war, never let down your defenses."

"And rule number two?" she asked, quite enjoying her position.

"Never underestimate the power of your enemy." With that, his body absorbed every bit of hers.

Encouraged by her cries of delight, he plunged deep into the bed of flame burning within her. With a furor akin to her own, he lay claim to what was his.

The sun and the pines and the ocean all spun round and round above her. Gripping him tightly, she held on for dear life. It took every ounce of energy she possessed to keep herself from being whirled out into the sky along with the rest of her surroundings. The sensations their passionate coupling evoked were powerful enough to catapult her into the blue.

I love you . . . I love you . . . I love you, she wanted to shout to the world, but a few minutes later a quiet sigh of contented satisfaction was all she could manage to get out.

Chapter Eleven

Darc awakened with a start. She tried to remember the dream that had so abruptly jolted her from sleep. It must have been terrifying because every inch of her was drenched in a cold sweat. She peered through the cracks in the shutter to her left. It was still dark. Daylight would not break for another hour at least.

Settling back under the covers, she reached out for Chase just as she had done every morning since she'd first wakened beside him. A moment later, she sat straight up. He was not there! All that remained beside her was the warm indentation in the spot where he had lain not too long ago.

Instantly rising, she ran down the stairs, her robe billowing around her like a sail caught in the wind. Calming herself with the assurance that he had probably awakened hungry and decided to feast on supper's leftovers, she raced to the back of the house. Hope turned to despair. The kitchen was deserted.

She began charging around the house opening and closing doors like a madwoman. It was no use! He was nowhere to be found. Dear God, where is he? she asked over and over.

Panic gripped her heart. The possibility that he had left to carry out some mission for the government crossed her mind. Surely, though, he would not have left her side without so much as a quiet good-bye kiss. Last evening, she remembered, he had spoken as though he felt the two of them would share the coming months. His plans—the trip they would take and the people he would introduce to her—had thoroughly captivated her. Surely such talk had not been the result of too much *vino* at the Café Cubano. Worse still, perhaps once the lights were out, he had had second thoughts and had decided to bow out gallantly before it was too late.

She came to a standstill before the door, listening. There was a noise, a sort of creaking sound, on the porch. She opened the door and glanced out. Relief overwhelmed her. Chase was slumped in one of the cane rockers. His chin cupped in his hands, he rocked slowly back and forth.

How foolish she had been to have thought him like the *Maine*'s sailors who were notorious for wooing women, bedding them, then disappearing when they had had their fill. She was ashamed of herself for even thinking something so absurd. Chase, she knew, took his commitments seriously. His promises were not idle conversation. She would do well to remember that in the future, she reminded herself as she slipped outside into the jasmine-scented air.

The sky was the color of blue smoke. A hint of

daylight filtered through the breaks in the low-hanging clouds.

She walked up behind him and laid her hands tenderly on his shoulders. "Good morning," she whispered.

He kissed her right hand. "What are you doing up so early, darling?"

His hand on hers, he guided her around the rocker and pulled her down onto his lap. Strong, masculine arms closed around her. "It's not even five o'clock yet."

"Mmm. Actually, it's a few minutes after," she told him as she covered a yawn. Feeling protected and secure in his embrace, she placed her head on his chest. The steady beating of his heart was like a lullaby in her ear. She sighed contentedly. "I was worried about you," she said finally. "You know I can't sleep anymore without you lying beside me."

For one split second, she regretted having told him how much she needed him. Not too long ago, she had intended to remain a totally independent woman. Of course, she hadn't counted on a man like Chase entering her life—a man who encouraged her to pursue her goals and not to settle for less than she wanted simply because of her sex. When she spoke of making the Sea Palms the most fashionable seaside resort in the United States, he did not laugh or tell her that without a man to manage it she would fail. He had confidence in her!

"Forgive me, dearest." His words drifted softly through the heavy cascade of hair which fell down her back. "My own sleep was troubled, and I didn't want to disturb you. The way I was tossing and turning, you'd have thought I was a fish out of water."

Dare nodded knowingly. It hadn't taken keen perception to sense he'd been restless for the past few days in spite of her efforts to get him to relax. The time they had spent together had provided her with some precious moments. She'd cherish them forever. Still, she couldn't deceive herself. He had become preoccupied. Good manners had prevented her from prying, but she suspected that Chase was longing to get off dry ground. The sea was calling to him, trying to lure him back. The temptation to set sail was becoming more difficult to resist with each passing day. Only a moment ago, he had likened himself to a fish out of water. The time when he would leave was soon approaching. And when it arrived, seeing him go would tear her heart out.

"You're anxious to resume your command, aren't you?" she asked. She was careful to keep her tone neutral and to avoid revealing her own feelings regarding his departure. If he really wanted to return to sea, she'd lose him for sure if she pleaded with him to stay.

"You know me well, don't you, my love?"

His hold tightened around her until she could hardly breathe.

"If you were not here," he told her, "I'd already have telegraphed Roosevelt to recruit someone else for his intelligence work and to reassign me to my ship."

"I certainly wouldn't want to stand in the way of our nation's defense," she somehow found the courage to say.

Deep, dark blue eyes reached into her soul. "Exactly what do you want?"

"You," she replied without blinking. "I want you."

"Then it's me you shall have!" His breath was hot against her neck. His masculine scent was so heady, so dizzying. She felt the warm, damp rush of arousal. There was no use denying how she felt. Even during a time of serious crisis, a time when the threat of his being taken from her was great, she could think of little else but her desire for him. She lived for those blissful moments of intimacy shared only by a man and woman in love. Each time they made love, there was a greater chance that he would leave within her a part of himself. She knew she wanted a child, his child, not as a means of ensnaring him but as a guarantee that a little bit of him would remain with her.

Her fingers flitted over her stomach. Nothing yet, but when there was, she'd know and she'd be able to pinpoint the exact moment of conception.

"What are you thinking, my sweet?" he asked, softly interrupting her thoughts.

"Of you, darling," she said, nuzzling closer. "Of you."

"And were your thoughts of me good thoughts or bad thoughts?"

A mischievous glow played in her dark, mellow eyes. "Why don't you be the judge of that?" Nimble fingers trailed down the front of his shirt popping open buttons along the way. His low, guttural sounds urged her on. Her eyes not straying from his face for an instant, Dare untied her robe. With a deliberately exaggerated slowness, she lay open the silken V, first one side then the other.

Hunger ablaze in his eyes, he pulled her to him, and his chest flattening hers with crushing force, he savagely took her lips.

Burning heat consumed her. She could feel his primal power hardening beneath her. She shifted her position ever so slightly and began rocking the chair with a slow, easy rhythm.

The next thing she knew, he was standing upright on the porch cradling her in his arms.

"I think we should continue part two in the privacy of our room, my sweet." His smile was devilish! "I wouldn't dream of tainting your reputation in public view."

Tremendous surges of desire flashed over her. The currents inside her thighs were urgent. He couldn't possibly bound up the stairs fast enough to suit her!

Almost two hours later, they emerged hand in hand from her room. Her face was aglow; her body still warm and moist from their love-making. She couldn't bear to wash away even the slightest trace of him.

At the base of the stairs, Chase gave her a chaste peck on the cheek. "Be back with the paper before the johnnycakes get cold."

"Just don't you go running off now," she said as she straightened his collar. "I've got big plans for you later this afternoon."

"Mmm. You've really got my curiosity aroused."

In an almost feline movement, she slinked against him. "That's not all I intend to arouse."

"Sounds interesting. Tell me more."

184

Dare gave his backside a flip. "Scat. Before I carry you up the stairs."

Standing at the door, the smile which had almost become a permanent part of her expression on her face, she followed his lengthy, decisive strides until he disappeared from view. How lucky she was to have so kind and gentle a man to initiate her into a world she had previously considered repulsive yet necessary. He had a knack of bringing out the most sensual side of her nature, a side of herself she had never before dreamed existed. Men like Chase were few and far between. If she spent the rest of her life searching, she'd never happen upon another. Not too long ago, she had viewed fate as her enemy. Now, it was her friend. Fate had brought her Chase, and when the time came, she was confident it would intercede to keep them together.

Happiness ballooning inside her, she skipped into the kitchen and greeted her housekeeper with a hug and an exuberant good morning.

Calpurnia, in turn, shoved a glass of green water into her hand. "Here, drink this."

Dare held the glass up to the window and studied the liquid inside. Its smell alone reminded her of a mangrove swamp. "What's in this stuff anyway?"

Calpurnia piled a stack of paper-thin johnnycakes onto a platter. "Just do as I told you, and don't ask questions."

"If I didn't know better, I'd say you were trying to poison me." Dare took one sip. The taste gagged her. It was all she could do to keep from spitting it out. "You've come up with some foul-tasting home remedies, but this one is by far the worst." She tossed the remaining liquid out the window. "I'll bet nothing grows on that spot from now on." She turned to Calpurnia, a broad grin on her mouth. "Sorry, but you'll just have to find somebody who's sick to try that potion on. I've never felt better in my life."

"Ummm, that's just what's been troubling me." Hands on her bony hips, the old Bahamian scowled accusingly at her mistress. "The way you and that sailor of yours been carrying on, I wouldn't be at all surprised if this place wasn't overrun with littl'uns this time next year."

Dare laughed. Obviously, she and Chase hadn't been as sly as she had thought. Rumpling the covers on his bed before helping him sneak up the stairs to her room hadn't quite done the trick. She should have known better than to try to pull a fast one on Calpurnia. That woman had the nose of a bloodhound and the eyes of an eagle.

"I thought you liked children," she said jokingly to Calpurnia.

"I do," grunted the Negress. "I like their mamas and papas, too. Even more if they're married."

"Now, Calpurnia, you told me you thought he was as fine a man as you had ever seen," she reminded her old mammy.

Calpurnia's hard exterior softened. "I just don't want to see you get yourself hurt. You're too young to go through life with regrets."

Dare took hold of a light brown arm. "He's not that kind of man. Really, he's not." A moment later, she lifted the glass and held it out to her old friend. "I know you've got some more of that vile-tasting stuff somewhere so how about giving me a refill?"

Calpurnia was only too happy to oblige. "You won't be sorry, I promise," she told Dare as she took a jarful of the green liquid from the pantry. "It's for the best."

"If it'd make you happy, I'd drink a gallon of it every morning." Holding her breath, she turned the glass up to her mouth. The taste of the bush medicine all but gagged her. When she was finished, she held up the glass. "See. All gone. Are you happy now?"

Calpurnia nodded. "Now all you got to do is get that sailor to put a ring on your finger, and I'll just be beside myself!"

Dare chuckled. She wouldn't mind that herself.

A few minutes later she watched as Calpurnia tightened the top on the jar and returned it to the pantry. How long had her housekeeper been up to such tricks? she wondered. Preventive doctoring the old woman had called it when she'd slipped a jar to Caroline before she ran off with Phillip. Knowing Calpurnia, she grinned to herself, she'd probably been spicing all the chowders with it since she'd returned.

"You're not mad at me, are you?" queried Calpurnia, noting her mistress's silence.

"Mad?" Dare flashed her a big smile. "Of course not. I know you have my best interests at heart."

Dare carried the platter of johnnycakes into the dining room a few minutes later. Of course, she wasn't mad at Calpurnia. How could she be? The ageless Bahamian had done far too much for her and her family to ever warrant a harsh word from anyone. Besides, she reasoned cheerfully, when the time was

187

right, Chase's seed would be firmly implanted inside her and nothing, not even Calpurnia's secret concoctions of herbs and roots, would prevent that.

From the very moment Chase stepped through the front door, Dare sensed something was wrong. His smile was strained, his eyes troubled.

They began their breakfast in silence. Even Calpurnia remarked that he must be coming down with something because he hardly touched a morsel of food on his plate. Finally, Dare could stand it no longer.

"All right. Out with it. What happened?" she asked, pushing back her plate. "I know something's bothering you so don't try to tell me it isn't."

Chase put down his fork and leaned back against the embroidered covering that topped the chair. Hands crossed over his stomach, he seemed to be debating whether or not to answer her question truthfully.

From the long, heavy sigh he expelled, Dare was certain his answer would be truthful.

"There is word from Washington that a personal letter written by the Spanish minister, de Lome, has been intercepted by a secret agent of the junta and sold to the *New York Journal*." His jaw tightened. "That accursed Hearst will have a field day with that piece of correspondence."

"Why? What's in it?" she asked, sitting on the edge of her chair.

"Nothing good, I'm afraid." His deepening frown added several years to his age. "It seems de Lome was foolish enough to write to his diplomat friend that Segasta was deliberately stalling for time, and that all those assurances he was giving McKinley about finding a solution and negotiating with the Cubans were completely meaningless."

"Good Lord! Those kinds of actions could have disastrous results for all three countries involved. Why on earth would he deceive the president?" She knew the answer to her question as she was asking it, and the reason behind such a move turned her stomach. She slumped down in her seat fearful that her breakfast was about to reverse its route. "Surely, Spain's leaders are not stalling so they can better prepare themselves for war?" She hesitated. "Are they?"

Chase's expression was as glum as her own. "It does appear that way. From all indications, they have neither respect nor faith in our president or in America. And there's more," added Chase after giving Dare several minutes to let it all sink in.

"I can't see how any other news could possibly be worse," she remarked drearily.

Chase nodded gravely. "It seems that de Lome committed an even more serious mistake when he referred to President McKinley as a 'weak bidder for the administration of the crowd.'"

Dare rolled back her eyes. "No, he didn't!"

"Yes, he did. Not only that," continued Chase, "but to make matters even worse, if that's possible, he accused McKinley of being an incompetent leader who was trying to stay in the good graces of the jingoes of his party."

Dare's eyebrows drew together. "Jingoes?"

"Politicians who have a belligerent foreign policy," he explained. "Warmongers." Chase slowly

189

shook his head. "I thought our diplomats were finally making some headway. That single note could easily set them back for months."

"Could the letter have been forged?" she questioned, adding that both the press and the rebels had much to gain if Americans thought Spain was being deliberately dishonest in her dealings.

Chase gave his shoulders a tired shrug. "It doesn't really matter whether the note was a forgery or not. The damage has already been done. Hearst has already seen to that!"

"Has Spain responded in any way to the letter being published?" she asked. At that moment, she didn't even want to dwell on the tremendous implications of such an act. Conflict between two world powers could easily set countries throughout the hemisphere to feuding.

"No one will even venture a guess as to how they will react. Not only are the Spanish people as a whole rather hot-blooded, they're unpredictable as well." He pushed his chair back from the table and stretched his legs all the way out in front of him. "Now, my guess is that they'll play it down as much as possible. They did recall de Lome the afternoon the letter hit the papers, but aside from that, no other acknowledgment has been made to date." He spoke with both confidence and authority. "I think they're probably just waiting for the entire incident to cool down before issuing a statement one way or another."

Dare thoughtfully reviewed all that she had been told. "Wait a minute. Doesn't it strike you a little odd that personal mail totally unrelated to government business was even intercepted in the first place?"

Chase nodded. "And that this particular piece of mail just happened to fall into the hands of one of Hearst's representatives," he said, completing her thought for her.

"Exactly," exclaimed Dare. "I'll bet the person who found the letter in his possession didn't do so merely by chance. Not only could the letter have been forged, it could have been stolen as well."

"That's all possible," he agreed. "But at this point in time, all those details are insignificant. The damage has already been done, and nothing can resolve the hard feelings."

Dare hesitated. She almost hated having to query him on this matter. "So where does that leave you?" she finally found the courage to ask.

"Leave me?" His confusion faded a moment later. "Ah, I see. You mean what will the consequences of the letter be as far as my mission is concerned?"

She nodded.

He lifted her hand to his mouth and kissed it. "I don't anticipate any change of plans to be quite honest with you."

"In that case, what do you anticipate?"

He rested her hand against his cheek and held it there. "My honest suspicion is that neither Spain nor America is very eager for an all-out confrontation." His voice became more confident as he continued. "I believe talks between the two countries will be strained, but they will nonetheless resume."

For the first time since Chase had returned from his morning stroll Dare breathed a sigh of relief. She desperately hoped his prediction would prove true. A resumption of peace talks would suit her just fine! Accepting the likelihood of war between such great powers was difficult enough, but having to resign herself to the possibility that Chase's days as a plainclothes naval officer were numbered would have been much harder.

Chapter Twelve

"Roosevelt has instructed me to travel to Havana as soon as possible and to apprise him of the situation there."

Dare was speechless. Her face waned to the same shade as the moon. Her feet suddenly stuck in the sand, and she could not summon strength to continue their stroll. The thick, inky darkness enveloping them was suddenly very oppressive.

"Don't I even get a 'really'?" he asked, trying to sound teasing.

Her eyes sought his through the blackness. "Dear God, you can't go. You just can't."

"It's no longer a question of whether I can or can't." His statement was gentle but firm. "I must. It's as simple as that."

Dare reluctantly nodded. Her quivering fingers laced through his steadier ones. She understood exactly what he meant by that remark. She herself had expressed her desire to keep the Sea Palms in words not at all unlike those he had just used. "What happened?" she asked as they resumed their walk. "I thought representatives from the three parties concerned were trying harder than ever to counteract the de Lome fiasco."

"They are. So they say." He draped his arm over her shoulder. "But the February ninth issue of the *Journal* won't be forgotten so easily."

His tone was bitter. Dare knew why. Leave it to Hearst and his damned editorials to stir up the most trouble at the worst possible time. When peaceful discussions at the conference table got a little dull, a little published propaganda would liven things up. Hearst's philosophy seemed to print anything regardless of the cost.

"If a circulation boost is what Hearst is after," Dare began as she reached up for his hand, "it seems to me matters would be a lot less complicated if he and Pulitzer would roll up their sleeves and slug it out amongst themselves."

"And leave international affairs to the experts." A forlorn sigh escaped him. "Unfortunately, the damage has already been done, and it's irreversible."

She was almost afraid to ask him to explain himself.

He pulled her closer into the shelter of his arms. "Public sentiment is more than ever in favor of sending our boys to Cuba. Americans can ridicule their president all they want, but let a foreigner do it, and that's cause enough to take up arms."

Dare laid her head on his shoulder. What a difference his presence had made in her life. Having him at her side gave her the courage to conquer the world if need be.

"I don't suppose you could tell Roosevelt you never received the telegram," she suggested, not quite sure if she were serious or joking.

Smiling, he shook his head. "You wouldn't want me to do that even if I could." His lips grazed her cheek. "Don't despair, darling. I'll only be gone a few days."

His promise did nothing to lift her mood. Seventy-two hours without him would be as long as an entire month. "I wish you didn't have to go," she mumbled into the night air.

He knelt in the sand and pulled her down with him. "But just think how much more you'll cherish my being in your arms after a short separation."

Her dark lashes fluttered. "I already cherish every moment I spend with you."

"And I you." Ever so tenderly, he cupped her face between his hands. "Look at it like this, my love, had it not been for Roosevelt and the whole lot of them, I'd never have come to Key West in the first place."

Her mood slowly began to lift. "Oh, I think you would have." A twinkle bright enough to rival any star's played in her eye. "Eventually."

"Think so, do you?"

Her words were full of confidence. "I know so." She drew her knees close to her chest, and hugging her legs stared out over the calm sea. The serenity was almost hypnotic. "Can you tell me what you'll be doing in Cuba, or are you sworn to secrecy?" she asked sadly.

"Actually I'm under a strict order of silence. But

seeing as how you, too, have a vested interest in this mission, I suppose I can risk Teddy's wrath just this once." The flippancy in his tone disappeared. His attitude sobered quickly. "I've been instructed to investigate and report on Spanish military strength in Cuba, without their knowledge, of course."

"You mean you're going there as a spy?" She shivered at the sound of that three-letter word. "That sounds terribly dangerous."

"Only if I'm caught in the act." He bundled her up in his arms. "Wouldn't want you catching a chill on my account."

At that moment, her health was the least of her concerns. "What would happen if you were caught in the act?" She was almost afraid to hear the answer. She visualized all sorts of cruel tortures and punishments.

"Undoubtedly, my Spanish would improve immensely!" he said lightly.

"Please, Chase, don't make jokes."

He gathered her even closer. "I'm sorry, sweetheart."

She found little consolation in his arms. "He would negotiate your release, wouldn't he?"

"He who?"

"Why, the president, of course."

She could feel the tension in his muscles.

"To be honest with you, Dare, you are privy to more information about my mission than the president himself."

Dare suddenly sat up straight. "You mean to say McKinley knows nothing of your assignment?"

Chase shook his head. "Neither does the secretary

196

of the Navy for that matter."

Dare could hardly believe her ears. "The secretary of the Navy knows nothing of this, either?"

"That's correct," he answered, deep concern evident in his tone. "The assignment was given to me during one of Long's absences."

Her entire body went rigid. She said nothing for a time. All she could think of was the tremendous risk involved in undertaking a mission of which neither the president nor the Navy was apprised. Suddenly a thought even more horrible shadowed her mind. "If the Spanish were to uncover your intelligence activity, then Roosevelt would be in no position to come to your defense, would he?"

"I accepted this mission knowing full well that if the Spanish found me out, Roosevelt would have no alternative but to disavow all knowledge of my activities."

His quiet acceptance of his fate did nothing to comfort her. If anything at all went wrong in Havana, Chase would be at the mercy of those who had made it perfectly clear U.S. intervention was not welcome.

"You mustn't worry on my account," he said softly.

"I can't help it." Her eyes began to mist despite her efforts to blink back the tears. "I couldn't face life without you."

"Hey, who says you're going to have to?" he whispered into her ear. "The prospect of us not being together is just as dismal for me as it is for you. I give you my solemn word as an officer and as a gentleman that nothing will happen to me. I swear it."

"How can you say that?" she sniffed. "You have no idea what the future holds."

His fingers became lost in her hair. "Oh, I think I have a pretty good idea of what the future has in store for me . . . for both of us."

At his words her heart leapt. *Us!* What a wonderful word that was. *Us!* The two of them! A pair! Surely there was only one way to interpret such a statement.

He kissed the top of her head. "I have a lot of confidence in myself. So must you."

She sank deeper into his arms. Feminine intuition told her he was referring to more than his mission. "I have all the confidence in the world in you," she said sincerely. "But that's not going to make my nights any the less sleepless while you're away."

"You won't be the only one counting minutes," he assured her with a kiss on the cheek.

"When do you leave?" she asked, dreading the answer.

"As soon as I can book passage on the next steamer over."

She felt a little guilty that the news she was about to deliver would not make him nearly as happy as it did her. "If that's the case, then I'm afraid you'll be waiting for quite a while. Occidental pulled their last ship off the Havana run last Monday."

His concern vanished quickly. "No matter. I'll just have to find another means of crossing. There are always Navy freighters, but by enlisting that sort of aid, I risk giving myself away." He considered a moment. "What about the tobacco boat? It's still making its runs, isn't it?"

198

Dare nodded. "But since Ferrer owns it, you could get your throat slashed before you've left port." Tapping a finger against her chin, she pretended to be deep in thought. "Of course there's always the press boat Hearst had brought down."

"Which is that?"

"The *Vamoose*," she answered. "It's tied up down at Lowe's Wharf."

"Somehow I don't think they'd take too kindly to the *World* press card I managed to scrape up. Any other ideas?"

She hesitated a moment before answering. It had been difficult not to tell Chase this idea first but he mustn't think her too anxious, nor must he read into her plan. "You know, the *Blue Runner*'s made that trip so many times I can't even count them," she remarked casually.

"Oh?"

She sensed that his interest was awakening. "Mac and I used to make monthly trade crossings and bring back everything from sugar cane to tiles. You know, you could borrow it if you like," she proceeded nonchalantly. "I'm sure Mac would be pleased to know it was being useful to the government." Repressing her chuckle nearly choked her. The day McKinley had been elected, Mac tied on a big one. "America will surely fall with that lily-livered sucker guiding her," he had said.

"Uriah knows the Gulf like he knows the back of his hand," she continued casually. "You'd have no trouble, I'm sure, getting him to crew for you."

"In that case, how can I refuse so generous an

199

offer?" commented Chase. "I promise you the *Blue Runner* will be returned in as fine shape as it is now."

Her finger to his lip, she drew back from his embrace. "Before you accept my kind offer too quickly, I think you should be made aware of the rest of the terms."

"Whatever terms you set forth will be exceedingly fair, I'm certain."

Dare wound her arms around his neck and presented him with a kiss that nearly toppled them both over backward. "Wonderful! When shall we set sail?"

His look was one of amusement mixed with surprise. "We? What's this we business?"

"You certainly don't expect me to let you go alone, do you?" she asked, feigning shock. "I mean, what guarantee do I have that I'll ever see either you or my boat again."

He did not share her amusement. "Surely you can't be serious, Dare. The sea's no place for a woman."

"That's just what Uriah preached to me the night I dragged you out of the water!" she exclaimed, a little miffed at such uncharacteristically masculine reasoning coming from him. "I can read the water and navigate by the stars as well as any sailor."

She paused and waited for a moment of reconsideration, but none came. Deciding to try a different approach, she scooted a little closer and let her fingers inch up the inside of his leg. Her tone mellowed. "Besides, what'll you do if you're way out at sea and get lonely?" she asked, aware that he was becoming aroused. "You know, one night on the

200

water can be longer than a half dozen on land.''

"Dare MacDade! Have you no shame at all!''

His words were hoarse and lusty. She was certain it wouldn't take him much longer to view the situation in a different light.

"Where you're concerned, my love, I am absolutely shameless.'' To prove her point she slipped her hand behind his belt and let her fingers massage his firm, hard belly. "Well, what do you say?''

"I really don't see that I have any choice in the matter,'' he replied in short, quick gasps.

"I thought you'd see things my way.'' Dare jumped to her feet and held out her arms to him. "Now that that's settled, what say we go back to the Sea Palms and formalize our agreement?''

"Oh? And what suggestions might you have for doing that?'' he asked as he pulled himself up.

Her fingertips tugged at the buttons on his shirt. "Something a lot more binding than a handshake, I promise.''

He offered her his arm. "Shall we, Miss Mac-Dade?''

She looped her arm through his. "By all means, Captain Hamilton. By all means!''

Laughing and playing like a pair of mischievous children, they ran up the beach kicking sand behind them. As they neared the Sea Palms, they bolted hand in hand into the street barely avoiding a carriage drawn by a runaway mule.

Dare paused on the front porch to catch her breath; then motioning for Chase to be quiet, she tiptoed inside.

Chase nodded in the direction of his room. Dare shook her head and pointed the way upstairs. Calpurnia already knew they were lovers, she reasoned silently, so why try to deceive her old mammy any longer. Despite the protests from her housekeeper, she knew the old Negress preferred Chase to any of the other Key West fellows who had come courting. "Even if he is a Yankee, he's a refined gentleman," she had overheard Calpurnia say to one of her friends. Calpurnia had also said Chase had class, and few men in the Keys possessed that!

Giggling uncontrollably with each creak of the old timbers, Dare scrambled up the stairs with Chase on her heels. No sooner had the door closed than she pounced on him.

Twenty eager fingers began tearing at garments. The quicker they worked, the more entangled their hands became. It seemed to Dare that it took her forever to get his shirt unbuttoned and off his arms although Chase whisked her wrap from her and disposed of her dress, her cottons, and petticoat in no time at all. She watched, her blood racing wildly, as he impatiently finished the task she had begun.

Passion seizing them, they came together in a quick rush of desire. Dare's nails dug into his back. She remembered Mrs. Lowe's well-meaning, motherly lectures to her and Caroline concerning a wife's duties to her husband. Grin and bear it, she had told the two of them. It is soon over.

Dare couldn't help but chuckle to herself. The longer the moments of bliss lasted the better. Poor Caroline! She hadn't learned her lessons too well either. No woman in her right mind would deny a man total access to her, she decided as they fell down onto the bed, their limbs entangled. At that instant, she could never imagine withholding such ecstasy from him or herself. What she and Chase shared night after night might be forbidden fruit, but she had already made up her mind to indulge her appetite to her heart's content.

His hands prowled over her familiarly. Her every curve and angle had been imprinted on his mind. Not one of her secret pleasure nooks and crannies had gone unnoticed. Those his fingers had skimmed past, his tongue's tip quickly found.

She writhed beneath him, her need growing. She urged him, pleaded with him, to cease the sweet torture and to lay claim to her once more, but he was in no great hurry.

Finally, after what seemed an eternity, he lifted her buttocks off the bed and guided himself home in a fiery act of passion that was both savage and gentle at the same time.

Her body rose and fell in unison with his, responding to his every move. Her thighs spread farther and farther apart until she was in as much control as he. Refusing him access to even the tiniest of spaces would be refusing herself infinite joy as well.

Moaning softly into her breasts, he gave a final thrust. Hurried, forceful quakes spasmed from one to the other, their intensity jolting them both.

He lay panting for a few minutes, his weight welcomed by her. Those few shared moments after love-making never failed to make her realize that just as she belonged to him, he belonged to her. She smoothed back blond tendrils from his damp forehead. Her eyes were too weary to remain open. Still, she saw him accurately in her mind's eye. His taste, his feel, and his smell were permanently ingrained in her senses.

Chapter Thirteen

The next dusk found the *Blue Runner* gracefully gliding through the Gulf Stream, her sails billowing and her lines flapping in the gusts of wind that followed close on her stern. Her stores held a full week of provisions, and enough tortoise shells and sponges had been loaded into her hold to convince the harbor officials that those aboard the Key West vessel had ventured to Havana to trade for sugar cane.

While Uriah and Chase planned their strategy for the following day, Dare stood on the bow and gazed ahead. The sky was a pearlescent haze like the ocean. There was not a cloud in sight. They had set sail on the tide, and barring any unforeseen problems or changes in the weather, they would sight Cuba by daybreak.

Exhaling a satisfied sigh, Dare stuffed her fists deeper into the pockets of her baggy trousers. Mac had told her countless times that, like himself, she had as much salt water racing through her veins as blood. At times like these with the briny foam stinging her cheeks, she was inclined to agree with him. She loved the sea and everything about it. Each breath of salty air she drew was more invigorating than the last. She understood what Uriah had told her after Mac's body had washed to shore. It wouldn't have been fitting for a man of the sea to leave this world any other way. According to her father's oldest chum, any other death would be humiliating for a seaman.

She stole a glance at her two companions. Judging by the loud exclamations coming from the cockpit, Chase and Uriah were engaged in a not-so-friendly battle of words. She couldn't help but chuckle. Chase's rank in the U.S. Navy meant nothing to Uriah, who was determined to run the *Blue Runner* the way he wanted and to have Chase crew for him. He still belted out his orders as though Chase were a lowly sailor.

A few minutes later, their heated exchange dwindled into the monotonous hum of conversation, and she turned her thoughts back to the sea, relieved that two of the most important people in her life were still on friendly terms. Time and time again, Mac had compared the sea to a fickle woman. How ironic, she mused, that the ocean would take one man from her life only to bring her another.

A warm, husky breath touched her neck. A pair of bronze arms circled her waist. "What's on your mind, honey?" he whispered as his lips grazed her cheek.

Snuggling back into his embrace, she drew his arms more tightly around her and laid her head against his chest. "The last time I was aboard the *Blue Runner* was the night the Mallory liner sank."

Chase rested his chin atop her head. "Six weeks ago." He expelled a heavy sigh. "It's hard to believe so much has happened in such a short period of time."

"You mean in regard to the crisis in Cuba?" Dare held her breath, hoping he would not say yes.

He didn't disappoint her. "No, I mean with you . . . with us." He turned her around to face him, his eyes taking in every detail of her face as though he might never see her again. "I feel as though you've been an integral part of my life for years, not just a few weeks." After a short, reflective pause, he grinned broadly. "Am I making any sense at all?"

Her arms drew him close. "Yes, you are," she whispered. "I know exactly what you mean. Since we've been together, these weeks have passed so quickly, but if we were apart . . ." She hesitated. Would he think her too presumptuous if she spoke her mind?

"Yes, my sweet," he encouraged softly.

She knew immediately there was no reason to keep her thoughts to herself. The gleam reflected in the blue pools of his eyes was inspired by the same feeling that lit her own gaze. "But if we were apart, that same amount of time would seem like six years at least."

She rested her head against his chest. There was still one question she wanted to ask. It had been gnawing at her for days, but she hadn't had the nerve to ask it. Never again will there be a moment quite so opportune, she told herself.

"What will happen when your mission is completed and you're called home?" The words were out before she knew it.

"You mean to us?"

She nodded, relieved that the question had been asked. Had she made a mistake by being so direct? she wondered, almost regretting her decision to do so when he offered no answer.

Tilting her head to his, he forced her to look at him. "I don't know when, but someday I may have to leave Key West. However, I swear, my love, I'll never leave you." His lips lowered to hers to seal his vow.

"I'll never leave you," he had said! The deeper their kiss, the faster those four words swirled inside her head. They needed no explanation. What she felt for him, he felt for her. The two of them had been destined to love.

"You believe that, don't you?" he asked the very instant his lips parted.

Her mouth ached for his. "I'd believe anything you told me." Even as she spoke, she was certain she would never have the occasion to regret having expressed such confidence.

She turned around and tucked her back against him, certain that she'd never know a happier moment. Not even the conflict brewing on Cuba could put a damper on her mood. "I'll never leave you," he had assured her. His words echoed in her mind and sent warm tingles down her spine. He loved her! She loved him! Their relationship had been bonded by the act of love. He possessed her, just as she possessed him. Perhaps the subject of marriage would come up . . . one day . . . but for the time being, having him beside her was enough. Instinct told her that his future would be hers, as hers would be his . . . with or without a formal ceremony. And her instinct was seldom wrong.

Strong, knowing fingers inching between the buttons of her shirt made her blood race. She sank deeper into him, needing his support, as his hands slowly and deliberately kneaded her breasts. Would the feel of his flesh on hers always excite her so? she wondered.

"I had no idea a fisherman's attire could be so enticing," he whispered, his breath warm on her ear, as one of his hands slipped behind the waistband of her trousers.

Dare chuckled to herself. Enticing, indeed. At sea she always dressed in simple, loose-fitting garb, and not once had she considered her outfit to be anything but practical.

Laughing provocatively, Dare pivoted out of his embrace. "If I were you, I wouldn't start something that can't be finished."

"Who says this can't be finished?" he asked, lounging against the railing.

Dare straightened her trousers and rebuttoned her shirt. "Me for one. Him for another," she said in a lower tone, pointing back to Uriah.

"You might be right." He glanced at the cockpit. "He didn't like me when I was Matthew Colby, and I get the feeling that since I revealed my true identity, he likes me even less."

Dare stole a quick kiss. "Neither your name nor your business has anything to do with him not liking you. He's figured out we're just a tad closer than friends, and that's what has him riled. Calpurnia, too, for that matter."

"Think she'll put one of her Obeah curses on me?" He chuckled.

"If she did, it would be no laughing matter, I assure you." Dare took hold of both his arms. "Uriah's the one you ought to be worrying about. He's been known to have made shark bait out of more than one Yankee in his day."

"Even if this Yankee's intentions are strictly honorable?"

"As far as he's concerned, a Yankee with honor hasn't been born yet," she replied in all seriousness.

"How do you feel about that?" asked Chase, his words filtering through her hair on the night breeze.

She melted against him one more time. "Oh, I don't think you're really from Washington." Playful fingers wound around the pale tendrils curling above his neck. "I think you were really born in the South and stolen by a band of carpetbaggers who whisked you up North and sold you to the highest bidder."

Chase threw back his head and let out a hearty laugh. "I must remember to tell that to the admiral. He'll be sure to get a kick out of it."

"The admiral?"

"My father," clarified Chase. "He's Washington born and bred, but he looks enough like your Robert E. Lee to be his twin."

"I'll reserve judgment and comment on that when I meet him." Dare bit her tongue the moment the words were out. How presumptuous of her to even think Chase would want her to meet his family! She held her breath and waited.

"Fair enough," he said without a moment's delay. "He'll love you."

She could hardly control the skittering inside her chest. "Oh, why do you say that?"

"Southern belles were always a weakness of the Hamilton men." His grin broadened. "Both my father and grandfather married Carolina darlings."

Dare poked him in the ribs. "See, I knew there was some Confederate blood somewhere in those veins."

"Unfortunately, the finer points of being a Southern gentleman have been overlooked during my school days." He pulled her inside the haven of his arms once again. "Think you could help broaden my education?"

Thick, sweeping lashes fluttered coyly. "Why, suh, I'd jus' be thrilled to help you any way I can."

Slim, powerful hips imprisoned her more supple ones. "I'll be at the top of the class, I promise."

"Practice makes perfect."

As his arms tightened around her she felt herself drawn to him once more. Snugly fit one to the other, their bodies began to make slow, undulating movements in rhythm with the waves. Dare pressed herself against him even tighter. Suddenly annoyed because the thin material of their clothing separated them, Dare stepped back and took hold of his hand.

"Would you be at all interested in a tour below?" Her eyes gleamed with playful passion. "Afterward, we could begin your lessons, and you could show me what an apt pupil you really are."

"I can think of nothing I'd rather do." His look was as passion-drugged as her own. "However," he said, breaking eye contact to glance over her shoulder, "I don't particularly relish the notion of personally satisfying some great white's hunger pains."

Dare sidled up against him, her body an offering and a promise. "I certainly have no intention of breathing a word of it to him. It can be our own little secret," she told Chase as she pinned him against the railing.

Chase looked once more in Uriah's direction. The old mariner appeared too lost in thought to be concerned with them. "Lead the way, my love, but remember, my loss is your loss as well."

Hand in hand, they crept across the deck, each creak of a timber freezing their movements in midair. Neither dared risk drawing a good, deep breath until they were down the hatch and safe from Uriah's disapproving eye.

When no footsteps scurried across the deck after them, Dare opened the door to her cabin.

"Welcome to my web said the spider to the fly," she whispered as she motioned him inside.

Ducking low, Chase squeezed between her and the door.

Anxious fingers began popping one button after another the moment he was inside. "I would imagine your quarters aboard your battleship are much larger than this," she remarked, running her nails down his chest.

"Much," he replied huskily. "But not nearly so cozy, I assure you."

Locked in a kiss as close as the cramped space, they fell back onto the bunk. In the confined space it took their combined efforts to remove their clothing.

Finally when no garments separated them, bare flesh melted together.

Sultry as an August evening, Dare lay beneath him, certain she could spend the rest of her life with their bodies interwoven and involved in the slow, erotic movements that promised the greater pleasure soon to be theirs.

Yearning for him to make her his own once more, Dare offered him her breasts, first one and then the other, and he accepted them with the greedy hunger of a suckling babe.

A moment later, completely at the mercy of her own needs, she was gratified when he made their union complete. As he thrust slowly and deliberately, her urgent moans drowned out all other sounds. Powerful sensations racked her body. Never had she felt so alive. Something definitely out of the ordinary had just happened to her, and she had a sneaking suspicion she knew exactly what it was. Poor Calpurnia! How upset she would be to learn that her swamp water had lost its potency!

Moments later, securely cocooned in Chase's arms, she lay with one hand on her stomach and the other on the curve of his shoulder. Glorious fatigue flowed through her. Even the least movement seemed unthinkable. Her eyes closed. If she were never again to know the joy of a man's love, she had experienced such bliss these past six weeks that it could suffice for a lifetime . . . maybe even two.

A few hours later Dare awakened from a sleep filled with dreams of her lover only to find herself alone. Without Chase scrunched up beside her, the tiny bunk seemed large and empty. She wondered if she would ever again be able to sleep alone, then she hoped she'd never have to go to bed without him beside her.

Rising to her feet, she scrambled into her clothes and dashed topside. Uriah was snoozing in the hammock Mac had strung out across the foredeck. According to Mac, there was nothing quite like being lulled to sleep by the water. He used to tell her that one night aboard the *Blue Runner* would do away with a week of restless ones in bed.

Dare smiled the moment she caught sight of Chase at the helm. His mere presence made her feel radiant. One glimpse of him, and a thousand little suns glowed inside her. She paused in the shadows and watched as he skillfully maneuvered the schooner along its course. He captained the *Blue Runner* with the same masterful finesse he demonstrated in love-making. How many before her had known the pleasure of his expertise? A month ago, such thoughts would have shattered her, but now they did not. He belonged to her. There would never be another man for her, or another woman for him. She'd be certain to be all he could possibly want.

Several moments passed, and still she could not avert her eyes from him. How handsome and how intent he looked! It was not at all hard to imagine Chase standing on the bridge of his ship shouting commands to his crew. How handsome he would look in full uniform. She smiled softly to herself. Even in the baggy, sun-bleached attire of a fisher-man, he was the finest-looking man she had ever seen.

Her gaze followed his out to sea, into the

tourmaline veil hovering around them. What thoughts are occupying him at this instant? she wondered. Could it be that like herself, he was reliving each and every second they'd spent in each other's arms?

He looked up suddenly and caught her eye.

She waved and proceeded toward him. "You were supposed to wake me up for my watch," she scolded gently as she kissed his chin. "I was to take the shift after Uriah. Remember?"

"But you were sleeping so soundly I just couldn't bring myself to disturb you."

She crossed her arms. "I don't believe that for one minute!"

The vibrant blue sparks in his eyes lit up his entire face. "All right. To be honest with you, I just couldn't wait to try my hand at sailing her. She's a real lady . . . just like her mistress," he added, his lips brushing her cheek.

Dare lovingly caressed the teakwood railing. "She's as fine a sailing vessel as they come. That's for sure. She'd weather any kind of gale or sea. You know, Mister Randolph Hearst himself tried to buy the *Blue Runner* a couple of years ago, but Mac wouldn't sell her."

"You don't say."

She nodded proudly. "That's right."

"What happened?"

Dare smiled. Mac had so loved to tell this story. What a pity he couldn't be with them now to recount it to the man she would one day wed.

"Shortly after Cuban rebels began making a stand against Spanish domination, two reporters from the

Journal came to Key West on assignment. Hearst's power boat, the *Vamoose*, was sent down later to take the pair to Havana. His boat was a long, narrow shell, built for speed in calm waters, nothing else. It just couldn't take the high winds and rough Gulf waters. Well, when Hearst heard of this, he was furious. His reporters were going to Havana one way or another even if he had to buy another boat."

"Which he did, of course."

She shook her head. "No, he didn't. He instructed his men to buy the finest ocean-going sailboat in all the Keys to get the job done, but that particular boat just wasn't for sale."

Chase was as amused as she. "So Mac wouldn't sell her, would he? I don't blame him. This one's a real beauty."

"My father could have been starving, but he wouldn't have sold her for any amount of money, and believe me," she laughed, "Hearst offered to pay him enough to buy ten *Blue Runner*s."

"Mac sounds like a man after my own heart." Chase's voice dropped. "I wish I could have known him."

A twinge of sadness overcame her, and her eyes began to tear. "I wish you could have. You two would have been great pals."

"Think so?"

She nodded. "I know so."

Hand on his elbow, Dare watched as he caressed the wheel with the same respect and gentle tenderness he always showed her. Like herself, the *Blue Runner* was eager to please and quick to respond to his loving touch.

An odd feeling of sadness tugged at her. Even though Chase had not said so, not in so many words, she could sense that he longed for the day when he would be instructed to resume his command of a ship like the *Maine*. Had he not been on special assignment for Roosevelt, he, not Sigsbee, would have brought the pride of the Navy into Havana harbor. Would fate have drawn them together under circumstances such as those? she wondered. Probably so. Fate would have seen to that.

She looked up suddenly at the sound of her name. "I'm sorry. What did you say?"

His smile was teasing. "I asked if one of those *Journal* reporters just happened to have been my good buddy Dick Davis?"

"Richard Davis," she corrected laughing. "And the answer is yes."

"Ah, so it was that little slip up that gave me away, huh?"

"That, plus a few other inconsistencies," she said as she wrapped both arms around his waist. Standing on her tiptoes, she could just barely rest her chin on his shoulder. "I certainly hope you learned your lesson."

"Which is?"

"Try as hard as you might, you can't put anything over on us island girls."

His words were as calm as the ocean. "Believe me, I never intend to deceive you again, not about anything."

Dare hugged him as tightly as she could. He was only verifying what she had known in her heart all along!

Chapter Fourteen

Dare stood beside Chase, her hand resting atop his. The time for her watch had long since come and gone, but Chase was none too anxious to relinquish his command. She didn't mind! Not in the least. He wooed and courted and caressed the *Blue Runner* with the devotion of a lover out to win his lady's hand. If Mac were looking down on them at that moment, he'd be sure to approve, she mused happily. Even Uriah seemed to have mellowed a bit after observing Chase at the helm.

It was twilight, the hazy lull before night finally gave in to an energetic dawning. The *Blue Runner*, her main sail lowered, drifted along her course. The sails would not be unfurled again until day had fully broken. There was no reason to hurry, Dare thought, tucking herself closer to her love. Spanish naval vessels had the reputation of greeting foreign vessels, especially those which tried to enter the harbor under the cloak of night, with a less than cordial welcome.

Focusing in the fuzzy light a quarter of an hour later, she finally distinguished what she had been waiting to see. Long and narrow and shaped like an irregular crescent, the largest island of the West Indies lay off the starboard bow. The well-rounded summits of Cuba's steep, sloped mountains reached for the sky. Off the north shore lay a long chain of islets, reefs, and coral keys; and dotting the coastline were rugged cliffs whose terraces looked like balconies cut into their rocky sides.

"You're certain we won't have any trouble getting past the harbor officials," queried Chase a short while later when the sails were again billowing tall and proud in the lazy gusts.

"There's no reason for them to suspect this particular trip is any different from the others the *Blue Runner* has made in the past fifteen years," she replied confidently.

Uriah pointed to the flag he had just hoisted. Emblazoned on the canvas was a painting of a huge queen conch that had been colored a bright pink. "Ye can rest assured they'll recognize that. Why, not too long ago, me and Mac was on a first-name basis with the whole lot of 'em."

Chase's vibrant blue gaze melted Dare's. "I just don't want my mission to endanger anyone," he said softly.

"I'm glad to hear you say that!" A mischievous gleam danced in her eyes. "I believe I've come up with a plan that will insure us safe passage out of the harbor as well."

The two men exchanged puzzled looks.

"A'right, lass, let's hear it."

Chase winked at the old salt. "I have a feeling she's going to tell us whether we want to hear it or not."

Dare took her time revealing her idea. She had carefully thought out her plan during the night while she had kept Chase company, and it seemed far less dangerous than his original intention to obtain information on the Spanish occupation single-handed.

Looking from one to the other, she began. "I am of the opinion that it would be in everyone's best interest if I were the one who gathered the information." She paused and held her breath, waiting for the response which was sure to come.

Chase let out a troubled groan. "Absolutely not! I have no—"

"Just hear me out," she interrupted calmly. "I have friends in Havana, a powerful Spanish family, who I feel certain are just as anxious as we are for this whole embittered mess to be concluded as soon as possible. I always visit the Cadallas when I am here so I am sure that any questions I might ask concerning the strengths and weaknesses of the Spanish army would be attributed to curiosity."

"She's got a good point there, lad," agreed Uriah, giving his grizzled whiskers a tug. "She could find out things that ye could be thrown into jail fer just mentionin'."

Chase held firm. "I should not have agreed to your coming along in the first place."

"Then just how would you have gotten here?" she teased. "Besides, need I remind you that I own the *Blue Runner*?"

"And need I remind you that as a captain in the United States Navy, I have the authority to commandeer any vessel for the service of our country."

Her mouth dropped open. "You wouldn't!"

"Probably not!" His chuckle turned to a belly-shaking laugh. "I may be a captain, but something tells me that you, Dare MacDade, would outrank me even if I were an admiral."

"I would be more than willing for the *Blue Runner* to aid in my country's defense," she said, unknotting her brow. "By the same token, I'd be equally willing to offer my services."

Their eyes held. No further words were exchanged. The quiet was uncomfortable.

Finally, it was Uriah who broke the awkward stillness. "Yer first lover's spat!" he teased good-naturedly. "What do ye make of that? Enough's enough. If the two of ye don't kiss and make up, I'll be damned if I don't throw ye both to the sharks."

"Well, what do you say to that?" asked Chase, leaning closer.

She could not suppress a grin. Sixty seconds was about as long as she'd been able to stay mad at him. "Given that ultimatum, I don't think either of us has much of a choice in the matter."

His lips brushed hers.

Currents of excitement flashed through her. His kiss, no matter how light, never failed to thrill her.

"See how much fun it is to make amends," piped up Uriah, slapping them both on the shoulders.

"Speaking of having no choice," she couldn't resist remarking a moment later, "you know as well as I that the risks involved if I do a bit of subtle spying will be minimal compared to those you, a complete stranger, would be taking.''

Frustrated, Chase looked to Uriah. "What am I going to do with this woman?"

"Ye may as well give in, lad. She's just like the rest of the MacDade clan—stubborn to the core. Ye'll not get any peace 'til she gets her way," he added, giving Dare a wink over his shoulder.

Chase expelled a contemplative sigh. "It certainly does appear that way, doesn't it?" He lifted Dare's right hand to his lips. His words were grave and quiet. "I'm sure I don't have to remind you that the mission you insist on volunteering to undertake is a very dangerous one. Since I cannot persuade you not to go, I want you to promise me that you'll be extremely careful. I don't want you to take any unnecessary risks. Understand?" His eyes caressed her. His voice lowered. "And keep in mind, will you, that as far as I'm concerned not even the most privileged piece of information is as valuable as you are."

"Oh, Chase," she murmured.

She hugged him and then disentangled herself from his embrace, saying, "Now, if you gentlemen will excuse me, I believe I shall go below and try to make myself a bit more presentable while you enter the harbor." She smiled to herself. Chase's blue eyes assured her that to him she was more than presentable already. Blowing a kiss over her shoulder, she disappeared down the hatch.

Gone were her tumbling tresses and fisherman's attire when she emerged from her cabin at a little past seven. The loose-fitting linens had been replaced with a white chiffon Panama skirt and a Cluny silk blouse the color of a conch pearl.

She struck a pose in front of Chase. "Well, how do I look?" she asked, patting her upswept hair and imitating the Gibson-girl stance she had seen advertised in fashion journals.

Appraising her appreciatively, he let out a low whistle. "I'd tell you my secrets any day of the week."

Laughing, she pirouetted several times in front of him, then sank into a low curtsy. "I take it then that I meet with your approval."

"Definitely! Do you always make your debut in Havana looking so stunning?" he asked, his tone playful.

"Only when I'm on government business."

Keeping one hand on the wheel, he gathered her in with the other. "I've never seen a more beautiful spy, or a more beautiful woman for that matter."

"Why, Captain Hamilton. I do declare," she said in her thickest Southern accent. "You have the makings of a fine Confederate gentleman after all."

Uriah stepped into the cockpit. "I believe it's time for me to take over now." He gave Chase a friendly shove that sent him even closer to Dare. "Ye've been having enough fun, lad. Now it's my turn."

"Aye, aye sir," returned Chase, saluting before he led Dare forward. "I almost forgot. I have a surprise for you," he told her after several minutes of starry-eyed exchanges on the bow. "Happy Valentine's Day."

She looked from him to the pink-ribboned box he had given her. "What is it?"

"You'll have to open it to find out."

She was so excited she could hardly untie the bow, and her breath caught the moment she lifted the top of the box. Lying on a bed of black velvet was a delicately woven gold chain, and dangling from it was an arrangement of tiny diamonds and rubies set in the shape of a heart.

"Well, say something. Do you like it or not?"

She didn't know whether to laugh or cry. "Oh, Chase, it's the most beautiful necklace in the whole world." She flung her arms around his neck. "And you are without a doubt the most wonderful man in the world."

"You deserve everything that's beautiful and wonderful, my love." He fastened the chain around her neck. "Beautiful and wonderful—I can think of no better adjectives to describe you, for you truly are all that's beautiful and wonderful."

"Oh, darling. I shall always love it." She lifted the heart to her lips and kissed it lightly before letting it drop back onto her blouse. "Just as I shall always love you."

His lips brushed the spot between her breasts where the pendant had settled. "Till death us do part," he whispered solemnly.

Her heart skittered wildly inside her chest. There was no doubt about it. He loved her as much as she loved him. "Till death us do part." Those five words said it all!

She guided his lips to hers, remembering his vow. "Even longer, my love. Always is forever."

He pulled her tight against him. "And a day."

"And a day," she echoed.

His arms hungrily devoured her.

She felt that she might burst from the happiness welling inside her.

Refusing to let go, she held him against her breasts long after his arms had released her. If only she could convince him to reverse their course and sail back to Key West! . . . Their task was indeed dangerous . . . but she reminded herself, completing the assignment was imperative for the security of their nation. Please, oh, please, don't let anything happen to him, she prayed silently.

"Hey, why the long face?" he asked. He held her at arms' length and gazed upon her with an adoration he made no effort to conceal. "I gave you the necklace to make you happy, not sad."

Her smile came naturally any time he was near. "I am happy. And do you know something? I have every intention of making you the happiest man who ever lived!"

"You've already done that, my love."

Standing arm in arm, they watched as the red-tiled roofs of the villas came into focus.

"The view of Havana from the sea is so picturesque. It looks like a huge mural," remarked Dare as she pointed out various points of interest.

On the peninsula to the west of the harbor was the white coral limestone city. Opposite it to the east stood Morro Castle.

"That's called the Bastille of Havana," she told him, pointing to the powerful fortress built during Spain's greatness in the sixteenth century.

"The harbor here is a natural one," she continued as the *Blue Runner* glided into the cut. "It's well protected from storms and winds, and is accessible to ships of any draft.''

Chase pointed to the iron gray monster that dwarfed the two cargo freighters anchored off her bow. "And there she is!" he exclaimed proudly. "She's a real beaut!"

Dare watched, her stomach tied in knots, as he saluted the *Maine*. Competing with a woman for his attentions would be far easier, she suspected.

A few minutes later, she noticed a native boat that looked like a wagon with a cover over it coming toward them. She breathed deeply. "Here comes the customs officer now. Let's keep our fingers crossed and hope he's friendly.''

"Oh, he will be once he gets a good look at you." A wicked glimmer lighting his eyes, Chase stripped off his shirt and slung it over his back. "Now if you will excuse me, I have some tortoise shells and sponges that need to be unloaded.''

The sight of his bare chest never failed to send her heart into a flutter. "Do a good job, lad, and I'll see there's a raise in it for you," she said, her lips puckered in a kiss.

"You're the boss!"

Parasol open, Dare strode across the deck to greet the customs boat. One of the men on it threw up a line, which Chase secured, and then the other officer, a crisply uniformed official with coal black hair and a drooping mustache, boarded the *Blue Runner*.

Relief flooded over Dare. At that moment, she wouldn't have been surprised to learn that her sigh had been heard on shore. Thank God, she knew him. He had cleared them many times before.

"State your business, please," instructed the

official as he crossed the deck heading toward Uriah.

Dare put on her friendliest smile and followed him. "Buenos días, Señor Valdez."

The officer turned quickly around. His stern expression was instantly replaced by one as affable as hers. "Señorita MacDade! So long since last I saw you." His smile disappeared. "Señor Cadalla told me of the death of your father. Please accept my condolences. He was a fine man. A tribute to all men of the sea."

"Thank you, Señor Valdez. You are very kind."

His hand reached out for her arm. "It must be very difficult for you to carry on."

She nodded. "I don't know what I would have done without Uriah these last few months."

Señor Valdez waved to Uriah, who returned his greeting.

"Tell me, how are Elena and those big, strapping sons of yours?" queried Dare the moment she noticed him looking in Chase's direction.

"Everyone is fine. My Elena is expecting another come May. This one will be a girl, we hope."

Her hand reached for her stomach. She couldn't help but wonder if perhaps she, too . . . "With eight boys already, I should certainly hope so," she said, returning her attention to the task at hand.

"Now all we need is eight girls!"

"Poor Elena!" laughed Dare.

His chuckle boomed across the deck. "What about their poor *padre*? I have to put food on the table to feed them all!" Still laughing, he opened his satchel.

Dare took that as the cue to get down to business. "We've come to Havana in the hope of selling some

228

of our sponge and shells," she casually began as she led him over to the bench. "There's not much of a market for anything in Key West these days."

"I fear conditions here are not much better." He scribbled a few sentences on the entrance papers. "If we did not have another on the way, I would move my family to Florida with the rest of our relatives."

"Then you have no hopes that the situation will improve?"

He nodded across the harbor to the Spanish battleship moored opposite the *Maine*. "With the *Alfonso* permanently stationed here, I fear conditions will become much worse before they get any better."

"I'm sorry to hear that." Her regret was genuine. "I have many fond memories of this island and her people. I hate seeing it all change."

"Cuba is strong! She will survive." His face dropped. "We can but hope her people will fare as well."

"They will, Señor Valdez. Like their home, her people are strong!"

He handed her one set of papers and kept the other for himself. "Enough talk of our problems. Today is the start of the Carnival. It is a time to celebrate and to rejoice in life. There will be time enough for sadness later." He gave Uriah the signal to take the boat the rest of the way into the harbor.

"Will you be staying with Señor Cadalla and his daughter?" he queried as he swung one leg over the side of the rail.

Dare untied the line and tossed it over the edge. "Yes, I will. I am hoping he will be able to advise me on some of my father's business affairs."

"I am certain he will be only too happy to assist you." Señor Valdez tossed one more curious look at Chase, who was bringing up huge tortoise shells half as large as himself.

Undoubtedly it would be in her best interest, Dare thought, to volunteer the information Valdez sought rather than have him query her about Chase's presence. She took another step toward the railing and leaned close to Valdez. "Uriah's been having a few problems with the bottle these days," she said, deliberately lowering her voice as she glanced over her shoulder at her old friend. "I had to hire this fellow to crew for us just in case he gets on one of his binges while we're here." Frowning, she shook her head. "Sure hope he works out. It's becoming harder and harder to get a sailor out of the saloons and back to the sea."

He nodded knowingly. "We are having the same problem here with our young men. Those that are sober enough to work run to the hills to join up with the rebels so they can become heroes." His head shook in disbelief. "Heroes. In a war that can never be lost or won."

Dare said nothing. She had heard from Señor Cadalla that Valdez's eldest son, Rodrigo, had run away from home to join the Maceo brothers, the leaders of a band of insurgents intent on liberating Cuba, in spite of the fact that his father was dead set against all the rebels believed.

Valdez shrugged his shoulders. "Ah, well, what is a father to do? He can raise his sons, but he cannot live their lives." His smile was weak. "Perhaps there are advantages to having daughters after all.''

"There are!'' she cheerfully assured him. "I have a feeling you'll be finding that out yourself before too long!''

"Perhaps.'' He dropped down into his boat. "Good day, Señorita Dare. If I can be of any further assistance, please do not hesitate to contact me.'' He waved a final time to Uriah. "I am certain I will see you at the rooster fights tonight. Until then!''

Dare felt her body relax as the boat made its way back to the customs house. So far, so good. If only the next two days went as smoothly, she mused, hoping that her good luck would not run out.

"Any problems?'' asked Chase, coming up behind her.

She shook her head. "It couldn't have gone smoother. He didn't suspect a thing.'' Staring off the port side, she motioned first to the *Maine*, then to the *Alfonso*. The two battleships were positioned so that the bow of one faced the bow of the other. At anchor, even with an expanse of water separating them, they looked as though they would fire on each other at any minute.

"They look ominous like that, don't they?'' she remarked.

"They're just keeping the peace,'' he returned, a hint of wryness in his tone.

"I wish you'd at least let me escort you to your friend's home,'' Chase told her a short while later after they had docked and her bags had been deposited on the wharf.

She squeezed his arm affectionately. "You worry too much. I'll be fine. Really. Chances are Señor

Valdez has already gotten word to the Cadalla household and their *volante* is on its way to meet me now. Besides," she added, unable to resist a wink, "with all the cargo that has to be unloaded, you and Uriah have your work cut out for you right here on the *Blue Runner*."

"Considering me and him's both a couple of sots," interjected Uriah, chuckling as he came across the deck. "Don't you worry none about her, lad. She'll be fine." He rammed his shoulder into Chase's in a playful gesture. "I'm goin' to keep ye so busy ye won't even know she's gone."

Chase let out a loud moan. "My poor back!"

"Who's talking about work, me man? Once our cargo's unloaded, the day's ours. As well as the night," he added, elbowing Chase in the stomach. "Just let me be your tour guide. We'll take in the cock fights first, then go on to the arena to see a matador or two get horned. Later, there's a great little café on the Prado with a couple of guitarristas and a half dozen or so pretty little señoritas who dance on your table."

"Umm. Sounds interesting. Tell me more."

Dare jabbed him in the ribs. "I don't care how many pretty little señoritas you dance with on tabletops, Captain Hamilton. You just make sure that you leave all the information gathering to me. Understood?"

"Aye, aye ma'am. Orders understood! For all intents and purposes, I'm just a lonely sailor out for a good time."

"Not too good." A wide grin on her face, she gave Uriah's scruffy cheek a kiss. "Keep him out of trouble, will you?"

"I'll do me best."

She turned to Chase and was about to kiss him when she heard someone calling her name. Her lips aching for Chase's, she forced herself around.

"Hello, Rosalía," she called down to Señor Cadalla's plump daughter. "I'll be right down."

"I suppose I'd better go now," she told Chase, her voice soft and longing. She dared not give him a farewell kiss, yet tonight would be the first night in six weeks that she had not spent in his arms. "I'll miss you." Her eyes penetrating his, she lifted the diamond and ruby heart to her mouth and grazed her lips across it. His stare locked onto hers in a look as impassioned as a kiss would have been. "Watch out for those señoritas!"

With that, she turned quickly and made her way to the dock before she had a chance to reconsider her offer to spy for the United States government.

Chapter Fifteen

"Who is that!" asked Rosalía, interested, wide-eyed, and all smiles. "He is *magnífico*!"

"Just a sailor we had to sign on for the trip," replied Dare, trying to keep her tone indifferent.

The young Spanish girl giggled. "If I were you, I'd hire him on permanently."

"Rosalía Cadalla!" she exclaimed, rumpling the short curls under the girl's black lace mantilla. "If your *padre* heard you talking like that he'd spank your backside for sure."

"You forget. I am sixteen now." She motioned to the boy tagging behind them to collect Dare's bags. "I am too old to turn over his knee. Now, he threatens to send me to the convent until he can arrange a suitable marriage."

Dare opened her mouth to sympathize with her young friend's dilemma, but she caught herself just in time. It was not her place to question Señor

Cadalla's intentions no matter how much she opposed marrying for any reason other than love. Family-arranged marriages were still a common practice among the Spanish aristocracy. The twentieth century might be rapidly dawning, but some age-old traditions remained, she reminded herself as they came to the end of the pier.

The streets of Havana were slowly coming to life. Negro newsboys were heralding the *Lucha*'s headlines. Peddlers leading donkeys carrying loads as large as they were hawked their wares in loud, singsong voices. Fruit and vegetable vendors had set up shop outside awning-shaded store fronts, and ice cream dealers pushed their carts. El Carternero, the breakfast man, was going from door to door selling a morning meal of fish, lettuce, and bean soup. Milk sellers were busy milking their cows in the middle of the street to assure their customers the product was fresh. Professional beggars had already begun to seek food that they would sell on the next corner. Sitting in front of a statue of Columbus was an old Negro man with a white scruffy beard. Dare recognized him immediately. He was Sam Racco, and his twelve fingers and eleven toes made him the most famous beggar in all of Cuba.

She followed as Rosalía led the way to a shiny black *volante* parked beside a scarlet spread of poincianas. Harnessed to the two-passenger carriage was a husky-legged Palomino. Atop it sat a driver who was wearing a black jacket with red shoulder ribbons that matched those braided into the horse's mane and tail.

The boy opened the door to the *volante* and shoved

236

the bags inside.

Rosalía handed him a few coins. *"Gracias,"* she said and then she motioned Dare inside.

"How is your father?" asked Dare, having settled herself comfortably into the thick, red velvet seat.

Rosalía tapped on the window, and the *volante* continued down Sea Wall Drive. "Healthy as a mule and just as stubborn!" she said with obvious affection. She took hold of Dare's hand. "He'll be so pleased to see you. You should have come for a visit much, much sooner."

Dare squeezed her friend's hand in response. No words were necessary. The Cadalla family knew of Mac's misfortune, and Señor Cadalla had taken the news of his death very hard. He had visited her twice in Key West since October and both times had tried to persuade her to come to Havana for a stay. Each time she had refused, using the Sea Palms as her excuse. Now, she could not help but feel a little guilty at scheming to take advantage of the Cadallas' friendship and hospitality in order to gather information for Chase. On the other hand, she reasoned silently, better her than him, for if he aroused the least bit of suspicion with his questions, he would be arrested and imprisoned in the Cavanos Fortress from which neither she nor Roosevelt himself would have a chance of extricating him.

As the *volante* turned down the palm-shaded Prado, Rosalía began chatting about her latest love. Nodding encouragingly from time to time, Dare settled back on the cushioned seat and took in the sights she had viewed many times before.

Its thick walls, narrow streets, and marble and

limestone buildings made Havana a distinctive city. Exotic tropical gardens and meticulously manicured grounds blended harmoniously, while above them regal-looking Royal Palms rose to heights of one hundred feet, their spreading, red-flowered tops dominating most of the scenery.

Havana had an exciting history. Mac had told Dare stories about the burning, plundering, and sacking of the city by the French and English, and by the pirates who prowled the nearby waters.

Surely her own people wouldn't risk its complete destruction for the sake of ridding the island of her motherland, she mused.

As they drove past the watchtower, Dare glanced up at the top, at the weather vane which was shaped like a woman. Inscribed on La Habana, according to Mac, was the sentence, MANY HAVE VISITED HAVANA WHO HAVE NOT SEEN HAVANA. Perhaps if this were rectified, she thought to herself, the city would not have to suffer the consequences of the dissension of her inhabitants.

Many of the buildings she passed brought back a flood of bittersweet memories of places she and her father had visited together. She remembered attending a party, as the Cadallas' guests, at the magnificent palace occupied by the governor general of Cuba. There, the floors were white marble, and the walls were curtained in red brocade outlined with gold threads. Outside in the courtyard the city guard paraded routinely each morning at nine o'clock. Beside the main palace stood the vice consul general's residence, and farther down, flanked on either side by massive stone towers, was Columbus

Cathedral, named in honor of the explorer whose remains rested there inside in a gold urn.

Dominating the center of the city was the Hotel Inglaterra. A dozen Americans were having breakfast in the café that fronted it because this hotel was the home of the American Consul General Fitzhugh Lee, as well as a temporary residence for most of the correspondents representing the leading newspapers of the States.

The *volante* came to a sudden stop moments later when a riderless horse charged from an alleyway. Its driver waited for the horse to be caught before proceeding. Dare straightened in her seat to gaze out at the commotion.

"It looks like the horse might have been spooked by those . . ." The words froze in her mouth. Not more than ten yards away, standing in front of the fountain at the town's center, were a Spanish officer in full uniform and a black-suited man carrying a silver-handled cane. Both men casually glanced up at the *volante* while continuing their conversation. Dare stared out the window in disbelief, then shrank back into her seat, and hid her face behind the curtain.

A half mile later as they turned into the Avenue of Palms which led up the mountain to the Cadalla villa, her face was still afire from the intensity of Ferrer's piercing glower.

Of all the rotten luck, she moaned to herself, her arms clasped protectively around her. Ferrer was the last person she expected to see in Havana, or wanted to see, for that matter. Granted, he had caused her no trouble at all since his money had been repaid, and he had even gone out of his way to avoid her, but she was not to be so easily fooled. Ferrer was not a man who accepted defeat gracefully. He was known to patiently bide his time until the opportunity to get even presented itself.

Her ears perked up upon hearing the name Rodrigo. She turned to Rosalía, suddenly very interested in the young girl's ramblings about her true love.

"Rodrigo Valdez?" she asked. "The son of the customs agent?"

"You know my Rodrigo?" she squealed excitedly.

Dare listened patiently while Rosalía sang the praises of her young patriot. She could not bring herself to share the girl's enthusiasm. No wonder Señor Cadalla, who was staunch in his position to remain neutral in the battle between the rebels and the Spaniards, was threatening to lock his only child in the convent until she was ready for marriage.

"Give me your solemn word that you will say nothing to Papa of what I have told you."

Dare promised without hesitation. She had no desire to break the news to Señor Cadalla that his daughter was in love with a rebel who probably belonged to the same band that had torched his tobacco fields last fall.

"How long has it been since you last saw your Rodrigo?" she asked, remembering the pain etched on Señor Valdez's brow when he had spoken to her of his son.

"Not since Christmas." Her sad brown eyes were quick to brighten. "I have been so depressed of late that I agreed to dance with Ramon at the ball tonight just to cheer myself up.''

"Ramon?"

Rose-hued cheeks rounded with delight. "Ramon Mendez, the vice consul's nephew. You should see him in his uniform!" she exclaimed, her big doe eyes rolling dramatically.

Dare laughed so hard she thought her sides would split. She didn't know whether she should be amused or relieved. Another couple of days and Rosalía would have forgotten all about her young rebel. Señor Cadalla's problems with his pampered, head-strong child would not be over until she was safely married and had children of her own, but hopefully, the next time she tried his patience, she would do so with another member of the Spanish aristocracy. Perhaps her infatuation with Ramon would get Rosalía back into her father's good graces . . . and keep the girl out of the convent for another few weeks, she added to herself as her laughter slowly dwindled into a chuckle by the time the *volante* began its last ascent.

Sitting alone atop a lush summit, the Casa Cadalla was the highest residence in all of Cuba. From its vantage point, the sprawling villa gave the ap-pearance of keeping a constant vigilance over the city, and to those standing on the Prado looking up, it resembled a giant, impregnable fortress. The carefully landscaped lawn surrounding it sustained more tropical and exotic plants than the Botanical Gardens. Enormously girthed silk cotton trees rivaled royal palms for supremacy in a forest of banyans, tamarinds, and royal piñons. Having been a frequent guest there over the past ten years, she was

241

as familiar with the house as she was her own. The interior of the spacious villa, with its burgundy brocades, sturdy mahoganies, exquisite tilework, and crystal chandeliers, was as elegant, if not more so, than that of the palace.

A pair of uniformed guards carrying rifles swung open the wrought-iron gate and motioned the *volante* inside. Two more were standing watch midway up the drive, and another pair was positioned outside the main entrance.

"Papa has become very security conscious ever since the rebels set fire to his fields," explained Rosalía in answer to Dare's curious survey of the men. "He refuses to let me leave the grounds unless a battalion of his men accompanies me and reports to him on everything I do and the names of each person I encounter."

"He just loves you and doesn't want anything to happen to you," Dare assured her. "Besides, the time will come when he won't be around to be so protective," she added softly.

"You're right," agreed Rosalía. "But that doesn't help me accept the fact that he's convinced a rebel band will kidnap me and hold me for ransom."

"Oh, I wouldn't dismiss that notion too lightly if I were you," advised Dare as she stepped down out of the *volante*. "Your father is one of the wealthiest men in Cuba, probably the wealthiest, and that reputation makes him the perfect target for kidnappers. As far as he's concerned, his richest holding is neither his home, his land, nor his businesses. It's you."

"Perhaps you can talk some sense into my daughter." The calm voice came from behind them.

"She refuses to listen to me. What do I know? I am only her father."

"Oh, Papa. Don't be silly!" exclaimed Rosalía, hugging her father. "You know I love you."

"*Sí*, and if I used the leather strap now and again, you might respect me as well." His anger faded quickly when he turned to Dare. "You have no idea how it pleases me to have you here." Hands on her shoulders, he gave each cheek a kiss. "I have been very worried about you."

Dare kissed his cheek with genuine affection. Keeping her smile was difficult. How he had aged the past few months. His tanned face seemed to have lost most of its rosy hue, and wrinkles creased his forehead and shadowed his eyes. The crow black mustache and full, thick hair that made him look so dashing now were flaked with gray. Even his smile looked a little haggard.

"I've been concerned about you two as well!" exclaimed Dare, trying to mask her surprise at his appearance. "The last time you were in Florida, you promised me you and Rosalía would come to the Sea Palms if the situation here failed to get better, and from all indications, matters here have worsened considerably."

With an arm tucked around each girl, Señor Cadalla escorted them into the courtyard. There, a pond filled with tropical fish was set in a garden thick with overhanging greenery, and a bamboo aviary containing an assortment of squawking parrots gave a junglelike atmosphere to the central area of the Cadalla Villa.

"I keep praying that the conflict between my

countrymen will cease, but so far my prayers have gone unanswered," remarked Cadalla wearily as he seated Dare and Rosalía in a wicker swing that hung down from the ceiling. "The rebels will not be satisfied until they have rid the island of the Spanish, and the military will not rest until the last insurgent is in the ground."

The *mayordomo* appeared with a pitcher of sangría and a tray of finger-sized cakes.

"*Gracias, Julio*," he told the butler before dismissing him. "But let us not talk of the island's political unrest. Tell me, in all honesty, *cara mía*, how you have been getting along these past few months."

Slowly sipping her drink, Dare gave him an account of what had been happening in her life and at the Sea Palms since his last visit in December. When describing the sinking of the Mallory liner, she did not mention Chase. She said that Ferrer's trickery had been foiled when Uriah had managed to scrape together money that had been owed to him throughout the years.

Cadalla's face puckered with disgust. "Eduardo Ferrer disgusts me!" he rasped between clenched teeth. "He has destroyed so many good men. His day will come, and not a moment too soon!"

"Papa says he is so low he would have to stand on a mountain to look a reptile in the eye," interjected Rosalía as she reached for another cake.

Dare's solemn expression became even graver. "I saw him here not more than an hour ago," she told Cadalla. "He was standing at the fountain with a Spanish officer when we drove past."

Señor Cadalla poured himself another glass of

sangría. "No doubt he was busy finalizing another business transaction with the military."

"What sort of transaction?" she asked.

"He smuggles in weapons for the rebels."

Dare was confused. "The rebels? Then why would he associate with the military?"

"In exchange for certain favors and privileges, sometimes even cash, Ferrer supplies the army with the details of his arms sale, and the army, in turn, surprises the rebels, confiscates the weapons, and Ferrer is free to carry on his business with the enemy with the army's consent." Cadalla took several, long swallows of his sangría. "Cuba's problems have made him a very wealthy man."

"Sounds to me as though he's party to a very dangerous game," frowned Dare. "Playing both sides can only guarantee his demise. Though I can't say I'd be any too sorry to see that happen," she added as an afterthought.

"As long as you are in Havana, I will see to it that his path does not cross yours," promised Cadalla. "I, myself, would like nothing better than to hasten his downfall."

At noon, Julio summoned them out onto the patio for a *merienda*. The meal brought back fond memories of the picnic supper Chase had spread out on the beach the first night they'd made love.

After flan and *café*, Cadalla pushed his chair back from the table and lit a cigar. "If it is agreeable with you," he proposed to Dare, drawing slowly on his smoke, "I will send some of my men down to your boat, collect the sponges and shells, and then distribute them myself. No one cheats me," he added with a wink.

"Not if they know what's good for them; right, papa?" joked Rosalía.

"Thank you, Señor Cadalla. I would appreciate that very much." Her gratitude was sincere, however she had learned from Mac years ago that the quickest way to insult this Spanish *amigo* was to refuse his assistance.

"Wonderful!" exclaimed Rosalía, taking Dare by the hand. "Now that business is settled, let's make plans for the masquerade ball. I am going dressed as a matador. I think Dare would make a beautiful flamenco dancer, don't you?" she asked her *padre*. Happiness and enthusiasm bubbled in her eyes. "Wait until you see the costume I have planned for you!"

Señor Cadalla waved his hand to silence her. "All this talk of a *mascarada*! What makes you so certain you are even going to be permitted to attend?"

Apple-plump cheeks fell. "Oh, but Papa, surely you cannot be serious. The consul general's masquerade ball is the biggest social event of the year. Please, do not deprive me of going," she pleaded, her wide eyes getting rounder with each word. "If you do, I shall just die!"

Dare chuckled softly. She couldn't imagine Señor Cadalla depriving his daughter of anything. He doted on her, and the fact that her mother had died when she was still an infant made him spoil her all the more.

His expression remained solemn throughout several long sighs. "I am sorry, Rosalía. Truly sorry, but you did go down to the city this morning without my permission and without your *duenna*."

"Papa, when the messenger came, you were already at the factory, and Maria was still sleeping. What kind of a hostess would I be if I were to permit a guest to travel unescorted to my home?"

His hard veneer began to crack. "I commend your sense of hospitality, but what excuses do you have for yesterday and the day before?"

Rosalía slumped back in her seat. Her head dropped. "You are right, Papa. As always!"

A spark of life shone in Cadalla's tired eyes. "Let's suppose for a moment I were to consent to your attending the *mascarada*, how would you costume me?"

Her round, cherubic face was all smiles once again. "If I am going as a matador, then it would only be fitting that you went as a bull."

"I will take your suggestion into consideration," he said, trying not to seem the least bit amused. "However, before we make all these elaborate plans, I think we should first consult our guest as to whether or not she would like to attend the festivities."

"Dare isn't a guest, Papa. She's family. And of course she wants to go, don't you?" asked Rosalía, hanging onto her *amiga*'s neck.

Cadalla motioned for silence. "I am quite certain she can speak for herself. Dare?"

"I would be most honored to go as your guest."

"There, then, it's settled!" exclaimed Rosalía. "See! Simple as that!"

Dare forced an enthusiastic smile. She wished it

247

could all be so simple. She really did want to attend the masquerade, but sharing the festivities with two very special people was not the most important reason she had for accepting their kind invitation. The opportunity to mingle with high-ranking Spanish officials privy to the very information Chase sought was one she could hardly afford to miss.

Chapter Sixteen

The Cadallas' fancy, custom-made carriage, reserved for special occasions, now joined the parade of shiny, black coaches winding their way to the Plaza Theater where the governor general was staging a masquerade ball for one hundred of Havana's leading citizens. Their manes and tails braided with red and black ribbons, four blond steeds towed the carriage, high-stepping their way down the Avenue of Palms. Inside the velvet-walled cab, Rosalía hadn't stopped chattering since the carriage rolled down the mountain, and Señor Cadalla, his everpresent look of stoicism on his face, just smiled and nodded in answer to his daughter's ramblings.

Attired in the red and black lace finery of a flamenco dancer, Dare sat with her nose pressed to the window. The sights and sounds enveloping them fascinated her. Carnival celebrants mobbed the streets. Some were robed in ornate costumes representative of centuries past, but most of the merry-makers had simply donned masks with grotesque faces in honor of the festivities. As was their evening custom, Cuban women stood at the windows of their houses and conversed with passersby. Men returning from the bullfights at the Regla were starting to gather at the café where they would sip coffee and cognac until midnight. On rooftop gardens through-out the city private carnival parties were taking place.

"All I hear is Ramon this, Ramon that," exclaimed Señor Cadalla good-naturedly as the procession rounded a corner. "What about your *padre?* Does not he deserve at least one dance with his little girl?"

Rosalía's voice rose several octaves. "Oh, Papa! Please, do not tease me in front of Ramon, and I beg of you do not call me your little girl."

Cadalla feigned a look of regret. "I knew this day would finally come, the day when another man would take my little girl's heart from me."

Rosalía sighed exasperatedly and looked to Dare for support.

Chuckling, Dare shook her head. "Oh no you don't! I am only an innocent bystander. My policy is to stay out of family discussions."

"Spoken like a true politician," remarked Cadalla, giving Dare a wink. "If only your president would take such a stand in matters not related to the United States."

Surprise written all over her face, she swallowed hard. Aside from expressing concern for the safety of her friends, she had not discussed the current situation or her political views. She suspected that

250

for the sake of friendship, Señor Cadalla had done likewise.

The Spanish gentleman reached for her hand. "I am sorry. That comment was completely uncalled for. Please accept my apologies." Smiling sheepishly, he gestured to his costume. "I should be wearing the suit of a jackass. No?"

"Don't be ridiculous!" she exclaimed cheerfully. "Do not give that remark a second thought. I myself have expressed such an opinion many times before. About the president, not your costume," she assured him laughing.

"You are very kind," he said, giving her arm a fatherly pat. "Very kind, indeed. Do not take an old man's talk to heart. The position I'm in . . ." He shook his head sadly, leaving his sentence uncompleted.

Her smile was neither forced nor strained. His elbow seemed the most natural rest for her hand at that moment. "There is no need for apologies or explanations. I can well understand your position."

His position, Dare recalled, had been the topic of more than one late-night conversation between him and her father. Mac had always respected the stand taken by his Spanish-speaking friend, and there had never been any doubt that the respect was mutual. The son of a Madrid banker, Caesar Cadalla had had no desire to pursue the profession of his father. As a young man he had come to Cuba, where he had soon married the daughter of a tobacco grower and had turned his wife's family's failing business into a prosperous one. Under his supervision, the Royal Tobacco Factory had eventually developed into the largest employer in all of Cuba.

After a long, thoughtful silence, Cadalla spoke. "It would be far less complicated if man could learn to live in harmony with his brothers."

Dare knew only too well what must be going through his mind at that moment. He had expressed much the same sentiments to Mac many times before. His allegiance was divided. The blood of the conquistadores flowed through his veins, but his heart belonged to Cuba.

At that moment, she, too, felt divided, a Judas on the one hand, a good Samaritan on the other.

She braved a big, enthusiastic smile for Rosalía and her father, then pressed her nose to the window once again. Her government desperately needed the information she might obtain at the masquerade. She knew Señor Cadalla was sincere in his fervent wish for peace. Still, she would have liked nothing better than to complain of a headache and excuse herself from attending the festivities.

Several minutes later, the carriage came to a halt in front of the Plaza. An enormous fountain made of pale blue marble marked the entrance to the theater. In its center atop a pedestal and showered by an effluence of bright, rainbow-colored lights, stood an alabaster sculpture of Queen Isabella.

A guard rushed out to the carriage and swung open the door. After checking the invitation Señor Cadalla presented to him, he offered Dare his hand.

Taking a deep breath, she slipped her black satin eye mask into place, held onto his hand, and stepped from the carriage.

"*Gracias, señor*," she mumbled, gathering her

fringed shawl close around her shoulders.

Rosalía followed, her cape draped over one shoulder. "Well, how do I look?" she asked as she charged ahead.

Dare caught up with her and straightened the front of her friend's tricornered hat. "Like you're ready to go to the Regla."

"Not without this you won't," Señor Cadalla called out. He tossed a red scarf to his daughter, then placed his bull mask over his head and began pawing at the ground.

Laughing, Rosalía grabbed hold of one arm and Dare the other.

"I hope my presence here doesn't offend your friends," whispered Dare, tightening her hold on Señor Cadalla as they strolled through the double arches. "I feel as though I am about to enter no man's land."

"You need not worry, cara mía. All those in attendance will be so preoccupied with your beauty and with fighting among themselves for the opportunity to dance with you, that no one will notice you are not Spanish."

"I hope you're right." For more reasons than one, she added silently.

Once inside the great hall, Rosalía impatiently scanned the crowd of masked partyers. Catching the eye of a conquistador, she motioned for him to join them. After proper introductions had been made, Ramon asked Señor Cadalla's permission to dance with his daughter. He grunted his reply, scarcely able to keep a straight face; then he burst into laughter the moment the couple hurried away.

"That daughter of mine!" he exclaimed, whirling Dare out onto the dance floor. "What am I going to do with her? Suitable husbands are not so easy to come by these days."

"Especially when the father has such great expectations of his future son-in-law," she managed to say before being spun around and around.

"Come. Let us get some refreshment," he suggested after the band had finished its third selection.

"Whatever you say," she laughed, completely worn out.

With Señor Cadalla holding her hand tightly, they threaded their way through the guests to an ornately sculptured fountain which showered champagne from each of its three tiers.

He handed her a glass of the sparkling wine, then took one for himself. "I see some friends I'd like you to meet." He nodded to their left to a pair dressed as gauchos.

"How can you tell friend from foe with everyone wearing masks?" she shouted into his ear.

"Some have already unmasked themselves. Just as I intend to do. This heat is stifling!" Handing her his goblet, he lifted the bull mask from off his head. "There. Much better. A man would have to be loco to go around in this all night," he said, wiping his face with a silk ruffled cuff. Carrying the bull head by the gold ring pierced through its nose, he led her over to a couple whom she first mistook for father and daughter.

"I would like you both to meet the daughter of a very old, very dear friend of mine," he said, introducing her after a few polite pleasantries had

254

been exchanged. "General Arola and his wife."

Dare smiled politely. She knew from the name that General Arola was the mayor of Havana. "I am very pleased to make your acquaintance," she said in Spanish.

The general bowed low. "The pleasure is ours, señorita."

His wife managed a cordial smile but said nothing.

Sensing that the young woman, who appeared to be about her own age, had no intention of striking up a conversation, Dare stood patiently by while the two men discussed possible reasons why several of the town's leading citizens had been eliminated from the attendance list.

She chanced a side-glance at the pale-featured woman a moment later. Her dark eyes flickered with recognition. Of course! General Arola had married a young American. What was her name? . . . Elsa Tobin. That was it!

She remembered the scandal the marriage had caused. Hearst and Pulitzer had both played that story for all it was worth. American beauty weds Spanish thorn, the headlines had read.

As Dare gazed at her, the other American woman's look became more open. There was something sad, almost wistful, about her feline-colored eyes. Deciding to give it another try, Dare turned back to her. "I am afraid Rosalia's idea for my costume is not very original after all," she said, motioning to a half dozen other flamenco dancers standing nearby.

Señora Arola nodded. Her smile was bland.

It took only a few seconds for the problem to finally dawn on Dare. She repeated in English what she had just said. "Your idea to come as a cowgirl was much more clever."

The other woman's eyes came alive. Suddenly they were a sparkling emerald green. "This outfit might be clever, but I am afraid my Spanish leaves much to be desired." Taking Dare by the arm, she led her a few feet away from the two men. "I was beginning to think I was the last American left in Cuba," she remarked, fanning herself with her hat. "My name's Elsa." She chuckled. "I suppose you've figured that out already. Anyway," she continued, all smiles, "you've no idea how wonderful it is to meet you. You couldn't have come along at a better time. I had already decided that in exactly fifteen more minutes I was going to develop a horrible headache. Now, I shall wait an hour at least."

Dare immediately felt at ease with the young woman. Liking her came quite naturally. "How long have you lived here?"

"Years," she replied, sighing heavily. "Actually only one, but it's gone by so slowly. Don't get me wrong. My husband is the world's last great romantic. I dearly love him." She threw a bitter scowl into the crowd. "It's his countrymen I have trouble with."

"What kind of trouble?"

"Because I am an American, everyone thinks I'm a spy." Her smile was troubled. "Poor Bernardo spends as much time defending me as he devotes to running the city."

After mumbling something in her husband's ear, she took Dare's hand and led her out onto the terrace.

"What brings you to Cuba? . . ." Elsa hesitated,

then smiled. "For a moment I thought the champagne had gone to my head because I couldn't remember your name. Now I realize Caesar introduced you only as the daughter of a great friend."

Dare chuckled. She, too, had noticed that her name had delicately been eliminated. "Dare MacDade," she said, grinning. "Not a very Spanish name, is it?"

Elsa clapped her hands together in amusement. "No it isn't. It's about as Spanish as Elsa."

A waiter brought them two more goblets of champagne and seated them at one of the tiny iron tables.

"So what brings you to this tropical paradise?" she asked after her first ladylike sip.

"Business," replied Dare before proceeding to tell Elsa in great detail what a tremendous help Señor Cadalla had been in finding a market for her sponges and tortoise shells. She was surprised at how easy telling her well-rehearsed lie had become. Practice makes perfect, she thought wryly.

Elsa proved to be a sincerely interested listener, and with a little encouragement, Dare found herself telling the mayor's wife all about Key West and the Sea Palms.

"I've never been to Key West," remarked Elsa, motioning for the waiter to bring more champagne. "I've heard so much about it, though. Perhaps Bernardo will take me there for a visit once hostilities between our countries have cooled."

Dare frowned into her goblet. "I fear that time will be long in coming."

Elsa was quick to disagree. "Until just recently, I shared your pessimism, but my husband is convinced that the two countries' political differences will soon be resolved, and friendly relations will resume." She leaned back in her chair, her arms hugging her waist. "Believe me, if he thought otherwise, he'd put me on the *Maine* himself."

"I am surprised the *Maine*'s appearance hasn't created more of a commotion," remarked Dare, having waited patiently for just such an opportunity to present itself.

"Oh, but it did when it first steamed into the harbor." Elsa leaned over the table. Her voice became hardly more than a whisper. "Authorities here were convinced an ulterior motive was behind the *Maine*'s visit, but they decided to deal with its arrival diplomatically."

"Oh?"

Elsa nodded. "That's right. Bernardo said that several Spanish naval commanders called on the commander of the *Maine*, and salutes were exchanged. The following day, General Lee and Captain Sigsbee and several of his officers visited the governor general at his home, and when General Parrado and his staff returned the visit, they were entertained like royalty on the *Maine*." She paused for several short sips of champagne. "Mm. And that's not all. Bernardo said that General Parrado was extremely pleased with the reception they had been given and that he expressed much admiration for the splendid battleship and her commander."

Dare breathed a sigh of relief. Thank God for that, she thought, keeping her words to herself. Such news would be certain to please Chase. Perhaps the resumption of friendly relations was well on its way after all!

Elsa positioned her hat back in place atop her blond ringlets. "I suppose we really should be returning to the party." She giggled softly. "Heavens, if word got out that you're an American, too, all sorts of rumors would start to circulate about us being spies and plotting to overthrow the Spanish."

Nodding in agreement, Dare stood up beside her newly acquired friend. "I'm afraid I don't know the first thing about plotting an overthrow." Her chuckle was half-hearted. Pulling her shawl together with one hand, she offered Elsa the other. "You really must come to Key West, and I insist that you and your husband stay at the Sea Palms as my guest."

Elsa gave her hand a firm squeeze. "You are most kind. I fully intend to take you up on that offer." She waved to her husband, who had just motioned for her to join him. "Oh, my. He's let General Blanco corner him again. General or not, that man is such a boor. I feel one of my most horrible headaches coming on. See you in Key West." With a sly wink and a kiss on the cheek, Elsa hurried across the room to join her husband.

Dare scanned the crowd for the Cadallas, but neither Rosalía nor her father were to be found. Seizing this opportunity to mingle with the Spanish aristocracy, she moved from one group to another pretending to be in search of her friends, her eyes wide open and her ears alert for any bit of interesting news she might pick up.

A small gathering of military officers who had congregated in the far corner of the room underneath a portrait of King Alfonso piqued her interest. She proceeded toward them, slowly weaving her way through the crowd.

A billiards game going on in the room behind these men afforded her the opportunity to listen to their conversation while feigning an interest in the game.

A tap on her shoulder a short while later interrupted her translation of what was being said. Thinking that this was just another young gentleman asking for a dance, she turned around, smiling and ready to make her apologies.

Her heart sank.

She knew immediately who was wearing the loose brown robes of a monk. The hood hid most of his face, but those piercing, cold eyes could belong to only one man.

She stepped back, stopping only when her shoulder made contact with the column behind her. Her voice sounded steadier than she felt. "Señor Ferrer, what are you doing here?"

"That same question could very well be asked of you." Like his eyes, his smile was hard and calculating. "Your friend, Señor Cadalla, just informed me that from now on I could purchase my tobacco elsewhere. But I suppose you know nothing of that."

"You're correct. I do not." She drew her shawl more tightly around her shoulders. "If you will excuse me . . ."

He blocked her exit. "Not so fast."

Even with the shawl concealing her from his prying eyes, she could still feel his gaze puncturing her flesh. "Really, Señor, business matters concerning the Royal Tobacco Factory are of no consequence to me."

"Exactly what is of consequence to you?" A loose-fitting sleeve cornered her between the column and the wall. "Perhaps a naval captain who comes to Key West under the guise of a journalist?"

Her eyes remained wide open. She restrained herself from blinking, certain that even the slightest twitch would give her away. "If you have a point to make, please do so." Her resolve held firm. Chase had feared a leak at the telegraph office, and Ferrer's remark only proved his suspicions.

He closed the short distance separating them. His chest hovered threateningly close to her own.

She felt the column at her back. A sudden move was out of the question. A cry for help would be sure to draw unwanted attention to herself. Ferrer, she was certain, would like nothing more than to see her weak and vulnerable. Frantic, she searched the crowd for her friends. They were nowhere to be found, and the few officers who did look her way and take note of her predicament snickered.

Ferrer's pearly-toothed grin was laced with poison. "General Parrado would be extremely offended if he knew an American naval captain had been smuggled into Havana under false pretenses." He stroked his mustache. "Of course, there's really no reason for him to know, now is there? After all, your Captain Hamilton could have accompanied you for no other reason than to be of assistance." His other arm imprisoned her. "However, the possibility still remains that your voyage here had nothing to do with sponges and shells." He inched closer, a knowing leer affixed to his lips. His depraved eyes gleamed, evil and lustful.

One last step and his body had all but devoured hers.

"No one knows that but I." His breath smelled of rum and stale cigar smoke. "I am certain a woman as beautiful as you can find some way to persuade me to keep what I know to myself."

He pinned her against the column. "I am willing to forget all our past problems as well. There's no need for hostility between friends."

His proximity filled her with revulsion. Her head swam and she felt nauseous.

His eyes began to glaze. Short, rapid gasps punctuated his barely audible words. "Why force me to take that which you would be only too happy to give freely?" One hand tore at her shawl; the other dove between her breasts. "You want me between your legs as much as I want to be there."

Eyes venting her hatred, she knocked his hand away. "I'd see you in hell first!" she rasped between clenched teeth.

"Not in hell," he laughed. "In room two ten. Casa Cortez. Midnight tomorrow night."

Her nostrils flared. "I wouldn't wager on that if I were you," she spat.

"You will be there," he said confidently. "And your legs will spread like those of any other *puta*. They do it for money; you will do it to insure that I will not go to the authorities Wednesday morning with what I know." His eyes raked over her one final time. "I apologize for the delay, but I have business elsewhere tonight." Rough hands cupped her face,

262

their pressure nearly cracking her cheekbones. "Don't look so disgusted. You will enjoy every minute of it I promise. You will be pleading for more long after I have had my fill of you!" Hot lips blistered her mouth before his hands dropped back to his sides. Clicking his heels, he bowed low. "Until then, my lovely, I shall remain your most humble servant."

Chapter Seventeen

Dare hung on to the door of the *volante* certain that the next time it swung around a corner or dipped into a rut she would be badly jostled. The driver had been instructed to return her to the harbor *pronto*, and from the speed they were traveling, it was apparent he did not take Señor Cadalla's orders lightly.

Grasping her bag, she sat back on the plush velvet upholstery and tried to relax. Surely another five minutes and this mad ride would end. She would be so glad to get back to the ship, but she wanted to arrive there in one piece, she decided, struggling to keep her seat. She had collected so much information she could hardly remember it all, and Chase and Uriah were sure to be worried about her. She had promised she'd be back by noon. Already she was nearly seven hours overdue. Of course, she'd just have to make them understand her tardiness was unavoidable.

Dawn had been breaking by the time they'd returned from the party and settled down in their rooms. Rosalía had awakened at noon with a horrible headache—nothing less than what she deserved for consuming so much champagne, her *duenna* had chided. As much as Dare had wanted to return to the *Blue Runner*, she had felt that she could not desert her young friend. She had promised to stay until Señor Cadalla arrived home at six o'clock, and when he did, he had brought a friend with him, a Captain Eulate. Upon learning that Captain Eulate commanded the Spanish cruiser, the *Vizcaya*, she had not objected too strongly when they had all insisted she stay for coffee. Once Chase had been briefed on the contents of their conversation, she felt certain he'd view the delay as a blessing in disguise.

At last, the horse was slowing to a walk. Chancing to look out the window, she soon realized why. Total chaos reigned throughout the city. The streets of Havana were even more congested on this second night of Carnival than they had been the first. All two hundred and fifty thousand of its inhabitants were out in full force, running wild in the streets. More than once the driver had to crack his whip to clear a path for the carriage.

The harbor was the one part of the city the revelers did not seek out. On the waterfront the commotion in the city sounded like nothing more than a faraway rumble.

The *volante* came to a halt at the end of Sea Wall Drive, where the driver dismounted and hurried around to open her door.

"There's no reason for you to walk me all the way

266

to the boat," she told him as he brought out her bag. "I can manage from here, thank you."

"Señor Cadalla, he told me to see you safely to your boat," said the man in broken English. Grinning, he motioned her ahead. "Pedro be in much trouble if he doan listen to the boss."

Dare acquiesced with a chuckle. She understood exactly what Pedro meant. A finer, more respectable man could not be found in all Cuba, but once his wrath had been provoked, Señor Cadalla was slow to forgive and even slower to forget. "In that case, lead the way."

She stopped midway down the dock. There was no mistaking the identity of the two lone figures pacing back and forth along the pier where the *Blue Runner* was tied. She waved to them, but remembering she was not alone, she restrained her enthusiasm.

"Where've ye been, lass? We've been worried sick over ye!" exclaimed Uriah, hurrying to meet them.

Chase lingered behind, his hands stuffed in his pockets, relief untensing his brow.

Pedro handed him her bags, then bidding a final farewell in Spanish, he ran back up the dock to where the *volante* was parked.

Chase waited until they were aboard the ship and hidden from view by the shadows before gathering her to his chest. "God, I've been so worried about you!" he exclaimed, as she burrowed into his arms. "It was bad enough when you didn't make it back by noon, but when you still hadn't returned by dusk, I began to imagine all sorts of horrible things had happened to you."

His concern was touching. "If I can expect a

homecoming like this every time I'm out of your sight for a day or two," she began, all too happy to collapse in his embrace, "then I shall have to arrange to be absent more often."

"Don't you dare!" he exclaimed, his words soft and husky in her ear. "I've been going crazy. I was getting ready to come after you myself."

Uriah observed their reunion with a sly smile. "He's been like a caged animal stalking up and down the deck just waiting for the opportunity to pounce," he told her. "Ye're lucky ye came back when ye did. I couldn't have kept him confined to quarters much longer."

"When you hear all the information I have for you, you'll be glad I stayed away those extra hours," she said. "There might even be a promotion in it for you when Roosevelt hears how brilliantly you executed your mission."

His smile was quick to fade. His look became one of complete seriousness. "Believe me, no news, no matter how important to our national defense, is worth endangering your life. I could have kicked myself for letting you assume my responsibility in the first place."

Dare tossed him a smile which was teasing and mischievous. "The way I remember it you had very little choice in the matter, Captain Hamilton."

"That's right," concurred Uriah, his hands resting atop his thick middle. "She had ye by the privates. That for sure!"

"Uriah!" exclaimed Dare.

"Can't help it," grinned the kind, weathered face. "'Tis true."

"I can't argue with you there!" Chase scratched his unshaven chin. "All I can say is that the news had better be worth a day and a night of worrying about you."

Dare pinched his cheek. "What about all those pretty señoritas? Surely they managed to alleviate some of your troubles."

One blond brow lifted high. "Oh, they did . . . but only temporarily."

Uriah slapped Chase on the back. "Ye got yourself into this one, lad. I reckon I'll go on down to the *cantina* and get us some supper while ye get yerself out of this mess."

Her smile froze. "Don't be too long," she told Uriah, undecided as to whether or not she should tell him about her encounter with Ferrer. "I, uh, I'd like to set sail as soon as we can."

"Somethin' wrong, lass?"

Dare looked from one to the other contemplating her decision. "I suppose I might as well tell you."

"Tell us what?" urged Chase.

"Come on, lass. Speak up."

"I went to a masquerade ball with the Cadallas' last night, and I saw Ferrer." Her gaze dropped to the deck. She hadn't the heart to give them a complete account of that confrontation. Her flesh still felt all dirty and slimy from his touch, as if no amount of soap and water or perfume could ever wash away that horrible feeling.

Chase lifted her chin, forcing her eyes to meet his. "And?"

She repeated what she had learned about Ferrer's military and rebel connections and his business

269

dealings with each. "Anyway," she continued, sighing a troubled sigh, "when I saw him last night, he made it a point to let me know that he had learned your real identity." Her hold on his hand tightened. "He knows that you're a captain in the Navy, as well."

"There's no reason to let that upset you," he told her as he peppered kisses across her fingers. "A lot of people suspected all along I wasn't a journalist. I was always having to borrow a pad and pencil from the person I was interviewing," he chuckled.

"Somethin' tells me it isn't that simple," piped up Uriah, his narrow lids squinting together. "Come on, lass. Tell all."

"Having to reveal your identity may have no dire consequences in Key West, but here . . ." She couldn't bring herself to go on.

"Aye, I see what ye mean," said Uriah, his shaggy head bobbing up and down. "Ye'd be shot as a spy fer sure."

"Ferrer threatened to expose me to some of his friends in the military, didn't he?" Chase's jaw tensed. His fist balled into a knot, and he slammed it into the boom. "That son of a bitch! Needless to say he had a little exchange of favors already planned!"

Dare nodded. "To insure his silence, I'm to meet him at the Casa Cortez at midnight."

"I've a good mind to meet him under the covers meself!" Uriah patted the pearl-handled knife tucked under his belt. "With a slit throat, he wouldn't be able to do much talking a'tall."

"His throat's not all I'll slit!" exclaimed Chase. "By the time I finish with him that whiny voice of his will be a few octaves higher."

Dare kept a firm hold on both their arms. "I don't care what you slit. As a matter of fact, I'll help you myself, but for God's sake, let's wait until we get back home. There, at least, we can deal with him on our own territory and on our own terms. Here, we'd have to contend with his military friends as well."

"Yer right, lass." Uriah chuckled. "But what I wouldn't give to be able to hide in his bed and see the look on his ugly face when he turns down the covers and finds me and me knife ready and waiting. And willing," he added, bursting into a laugh.

"If you'd like we could arrange a homecoming like that for him when he gets back to Key West, but for now," she said, her eyes and voice pleading, "let's shove off. Please."

Chase shook his head. "We can't. Not right yet anyway."

"Why?" she asked impatiently. "What do you mean?"

"Charles informed me last night that I'm to report to him all the information you were able to obtain so he can telegraph it to Washington tonight." The look in his eyes was one of sincere regret. "I'm sorry."

Her face paled. For the moment, Ferrer was forgotten. "Charles? Where did you see him?" she asked, suspecting she already knew the answer. "Oh, Chase, you didn't! Not after giving me your word! You promised you wouldn't take any unnecessary risks."

"It wasn't my choice," he said, softly but firmly. "I know it's hard for you to accept, but I have a duty to the Navy. The decision wasn't mine to make, but I was, nonetheless, responsible for carrying

Her tone was a blend of anger and co
what if someone spotted you?" H
cautioned her against pursuing the issue. They had
had that very same discussion many times before.
Experience had proven that it was pointless to
oppose what he adamantly believed. Still, she
couldn't help but resent the Navy and its assistant
secretary for placing the man she loved in so
dangerous a position.

Violet eyes glared at blue, both pairs simmering.

It was she who lowered her gaze, nodding sadly
and telling herself it was better to lose the battle than
the war. At least in the long run, she'd still have him
if she gave in. She hoped!

"It's one thing to be a naval officer on board a
vessel that cruises into an unfriendly port," she
began shakily, her lids blinking to control the tears
forming behind them, "but to go sneaking into a
hostile port pretending to be someone you're not is a
different set of circumstances entirely. Had you been
caught . . ." She couldn't go on. Just thinking about
the price he would have paid—execution Spanish
style, blindfolded and shot at sunrise—made her
shiver.

A few minutes later, she found the courage to look
him in the eye. On the outside, her eyes were dry, but
she felt tears would burst forth at any moment.

"You're right, of course," she said, breaking the
awkward stillness.

It was his turn to falter. "Am I? I sure as hell hope
so." His frown as troubled as her own, he took hold of
both her hands. Rough fingers closed tightly around

smooth, delicate ones. "I've put too much on the line to be otherwise." His lips grazed hers. "Trust me, please."

"Back before ye can miss me," piped up Uriah as he went ambling across the deck, his plump cheeks apple red.

"Take your time," grinned Chase, his eyes not leaving hers for a moment. "Take your time."

Dare smiled. Her fears were quickly forgotten. Neither Ferrer nor the hostile Spanish could spoil this moment. There was no mistaking Chase's intention; she felt the same need. This was not the first time a sudden craving for him had overcome her, nor would it be the last!

"If you would be so kind as to step below to my quarters, sir, I am certain I can provide you with information which will win you a commendation."

He gave a low bow. "Madame, I am at your disposal."

"That, Captain Hamilton, is just what I wanted to hear. Shall we?"

Looping her arm through his, she led him below into the darkness enveloping the lower deck. It wasn't even necessary to see where she was going. She could sense every twist and turn. She knew that old ship as well as she knew the back of her hand.

Chase kicked the door closed once they were inside her cabin. "You did say something about a commendation, didn't you?"

"First, you have to earn it." She was already taking off her dress. "Make love to me, darling."

"That will undoubtedly be the most delicious assignment I've ever been given!"

273

His trousers joined a heap of ruffles and lace finery a moment later. "You see," he said, closing the distance between them once again, "as far as I'm concerned, you are my life. Past, present or future!"

That was all she wanted to hear!

Hungrily reaching out to him, her arms winding tightly around his neck, Dare fell back onto the bed, pulling him down with her. She'd do her damnedest to see to it that he never regretted those words!

Her long, shapely legs scissored around him as her fingers dug into his back. Sometimes she loved the playful romping that preceded their love-making, but not now, not tonight. Now she wanted to be joined with him as quickly as possible. Only then could the storm building inside her be allayed. And Chase was as eager to couple as she.

A satisfied moan rumbled deep inside her throat as he entered her. Then their bodies rose and fell in perfect unison, her back arching high to meet each deliciously penetrating thrust. One moment, she found herself soaring. The next, she was plummeting. Over and over, she cried out for release until, finally, a downpour of fiery sensations consumed her.

"Now that you've had your way with me," said Dare, snuggling contentedly into the crook of Chase's arm, "I imagine you're anxious to get down to business."

He held her close.

She could tell by the feel of his mouth on her cheek that his lips were spread in a wide smile.

"Now that you mention it, I do have better things to do with my time than dally in bed all night with some insatiable tigress who leaves claw marks all over my poor back. My time would be better spent elsewhere," he added, his chin tousling her hair.

"On the *Maine*, perhaps?" Dare expelled a heavy-hearted sigh. Why ruin so beautiful a moment? "Oh, well, some women lose their men to gambling or to booze," she said, trying to sound cheerful. "Some to other women. But me? Me, I have to compete with an old metal tub. Poor me!"

"Poor you," he agreed, placing a kiss on each eye. "Now, are you going to give me any valuable information or am I going to have to resort to cruel and unusual punishment to get it out of you?"

"I surrender!" Frowning and smiling at the same time, she settled into his embrace. The quicker he left, the sooner he'd get back, she reasoned. "All right, Captain Hamilton, sir, where shall I begin?"

"Why don't you start by telling me about your friend Cadalla? How does he fit into the political picture here?"

"He doesn't fit at all." Laying her head on his shoulder, she stared out the porthole into the thick darkness hovering off the bow. The constellation of Orion was overhead, the Pleiades arranged nearby.

"Like the majority of people in Cuba," she explained, "he just wants to see an end to the violence and bloodshed as soon as possible. According to him, families and allegiances have been divided long enough. All Cubans must unite and band together for the common good of their land." She used the exact words Señor Cadalla had so many times in the past.

"So what does he think about Segasta?" queried

Chase thoughtfully.

Dare drew his arms tighter around her. "He feels the prime minister has made as many concessions to the rebels as he can without completely bowing to their demands. Contrary to what is publicized, Segasta is in favor of autonomy just as long as the change to self-government is a gradual one rather than a radical takeover. According to Señor Cadalla, Spain is reluctant to announce her position on this matter for fear of losing her last stronghold in the Atlantic to America."

"Losing Cuba to America!" exclaimed Chase, obviously surprised. "Why, the very notion is ridiculous. I've never heard anything like it. Losing Cuba to us, indeed! Why, we're not imperialists."

Dare did not respond. She had wondered many times whether, if America did intervene, her leaders would not be tempted to step into the motherland role they had just forced Spain to vacate?

His questions continued. "How about military occupancy? Is it as extensive as we have been led to believe?"

Dare nodded. "That's just about the only subject the journalists haven't exaggerated. Spanish forces number close to . . . I believe Captain Eulate said they were close to two hundred thousand."

Chase whistled softly.

"Even with such strength," she continued, "the military is scarcely able to hold more than the major seaports. Most villages are already in the hands of the insurgents."

"Hmmm. I suspect Roosevelt will be pleased to hear that," he remarked before making his next inquiry. "Any speculation on the reasons for their lack of success?"

Once again, she nodded. She felt rather pleased with herself. It seemed she had learned more valuable information from discreetly circulating at the party than she had thought. "Morale among the troops is extremely low," she told him. "Not only have they been stationed far away from home in a land that, for the most part, resents their presence, but their equipment is old and barely serviceable, and day-to-day supplies are growing increasingly more difficult to obtain."

"Interesting," commented Chase slowly. His chin rested gently on the top of her head. "From what you've found out, it would be safe to surmise that their resources are rather limited."

"Apparently the situation has already drained the country's treasury much more heavily than they care to admit, and they simply cannot finance a war. For that reason, Vitorio seems to think that Spain will elect to withdraw from Cuba entirely rather than provoke a confrontation with the United States," she informed him, remembering how impressed she had been with the Spanish captain's sincerity.

"Vitorio? Who's that?" queried Chase.

She sensed his concern was more than professional. "Captain Eulate insisted we address him by his given name." She snickered softly at the prospect of Chase being jealous. "You know, he was a very, very nice man," she couldn't resist adding.

"Ah, fraternizing with the enemy, were you?"

She could tell his joking was not all that genuine. "He's not the enemy, leastwise, not yet. Besides," she pointed out playfully, "my instructions were to obtain information. How I did so was up to me. No one offered any suggestions as to how I was to go about it."

"How old's this Vitorio character anyway?"

"Would Roosevelt be interested in his age, do you suppose?" she teased. "In the interest of national security, I'd say he's probably forty or so."

"That's good." He seemed relieved. "Definitely too old for you."

"You're nearly ten years older than I," she pointed out laughing. "So what difference does another decade make?"

His teeth nipped her ear. "Ten years older makes a better lover, but twenty years, well, that's a different matter entirely."

"Why, Chase Hamilton, I do believe you're jealous."

His hug nearly took her breath away. "You bet I am. Now before I ravage that lusty young body of yours why don't you see if you can remember anything else your dear Vitorio might have mentioned?"

"He isn't my Vitorio!" she exclaimed, chuckling. "But for your information, along with complimenting a certain captain's choice of feminine companionship, he voiced a great deal of respect for the United States fleet, especially for the *Maine*."

"Oh?"

"He said that he and the other officers who were entertained by Captain Sigsbee were most impressed by the ship. As a matter of fact, I got the feeling they were all quite envious."

"Envious," he repeated thoughtfully. "That's the same conclusion Charles made."

"So tell me about Captain Sigsbee," she said, sitting up and folding her legs beneath her. "Does he seem to be in good spirits?".

"Yes and no." His tone suddenly grew very serious. "He's been concerned over being misinformed about the Spanish reaction to a courtesy call. Can't say as I blame him."

"Misinformed? How so?"

"Contrary to what he had been led to believe," began Chase, "the Spanish government had in fact requested the *Maine*'s visit be postponed for a while because they didn't want the rebels thinking the U.S. had sent the ship to intervene on their behalf." Frowning, he continued. "When General Lee telegraphed Washington asking for a delay, he was politely informed by Secretary Day that the *Maine* had already received orders to sail, and he wasn't about to recall her."

"I was under the impression her arrival was treated quite cordially," she said, then proceeded to tell him of Elsa Tobin Arola and the conversation she'd had with her the night before.

"Everything she said is true," confirmed Chase. "The Spanish authorities have been most civil toward the *Maine* under the circumstances. One might even go so far as to say they've bent over backward to be accommodating," he said as he massaged her breasts with a tenderness which was both gentle and possessive. "When a better anchorage spot came open several days ago, the commander of the *Alfonso* declined it so that Sigsbee

279

could change his anchorage to buoy four. Not only that, but Charles and his men were entertained royally at the palace and aboard the *Alfonso*, and when the *Maine* reciprocated, the Spanish commanders and officials couldn't have been more friendly."

He kissed the nape of her neck, then pulled her back down. "Charles has remarked several times that hostilities between the two countries were temporarily forgotten in light of the fact that these men shared common bonds, being men of the sea and performing duties for their respective homelands."

Dare curled up beside him, her head resting on his chest. No sound was more pleasant than the beating of his heart against her ear, she decided happily. God, how she loved him! "A relationship such as the one you've just described does sound encouraging," she agreed as she sprinkled kisses across his chest. "Let's just hope that the same men who sat opposite each other at the captain's table won't soon be facing each other as adversaries."

"I guess time will tell." Soft kisses filtered through her hair. "As much as I hate to leave, my darling, I must. Charles is waiting for the report."

"Are you sure there's absolutely nothing I can do to detain you?" she asked teasingly shortly after donning her baggy fisherman's attire.

Even in the dark, she could sense his smile was troubled.

"Another course of that delicious meal I just feasted on might very well do the trick," he replied, trying to sound cheerful, "but I do have—"

Dare silenced him with a kiss. "Shhh. Only joking.

I'm well aware of the fact that you have a job to do."

"I'll be back shortly. An hour at the most."

Hand in hand, they returned topside.

"I suspect that when I get back, I'll be famished." He gave her shoulder a squeeze. "And enchiladas and sangría aren't exactly what I have in mind to satisfy my hunger."

"Don't you worry," she told him, her hand on his chest. "I'll hold supper for you."

A feral gleam played in his eyes. "You do that."

She watched in silence as he lowered the dinghy over the edge. Her heart grew heavier with each passing moment. How could she explain the dread gnawing away at her? She didn't understand it herself. Don't go, she wanted to plead, but her better judgment restrained her from doing or saying something she might later regret.

A moment later, she gave his arm one last squeeze and forced herself to step back. "I love you."

"My precious Dare . . ." He blew her a kiss. "I love you too." Swinging himself over the edge, he dropped down into the dinghy. "In an hour. Promise!"

She threw him the line, then with a final wave and the words *I love you* still affixed to her lips, she watched gloomily as he rowed into the night.

Tears she could no longer contain streamed freely down her cheeks. Try as she might, she just could not shake the foreboding feeling overpowering her.

"He will come back," she whispered into the silent night. "He has to. He just has to!"

She lifted her head to the heavens. The stars had become shadowed by thick clouds which a light land breeze had wafted out to sea. "Please, dear God, please, don't let anything happen to him."

Holding tightly to the diamond and ruby heart, she paced across the deck, bow to stern, stern to bow. She had a feeling her feet were about to cover a lot of miles in the next hour. Undoubtedly, the next sixty minutes would be the longest she would ever spend.

Chapter Eighteen

"Sit down, lass," Uriah ordered gently. "The way ye keep pacin' back and forth, ye're goin' to wear the deck plumb out."

Pacing mechanically in front of him, Dare released a worried sigh. "What time is it now?"

"Five minutes later than the last time ye asked me. Sit down, will ye? Ye're givin' me the jitters."

After another long look in the direction of the *Maine*, she lowered herself down onto the bench, then sprang back up in the same movement. Her hands dug deep into the pockets of her cut-off breeches. "Oh, Uriah, I wish he were back."

"Starvin' yerself isn't goin' to get him back any faster," he told her, offering her an enchilada. "Here. Eat this. Ye're goin' to need that strength when it comes yer turn to keep watch."

Her chin dropped to her chest. "I can't. I'm too worried to eat."

He uncorked the bottle of sangría. "Then at least take a swig of this. It'll calm yer nerves."

She shook her head. "The only thing that's going to calm my nerves is rounding the point at Fort Taylor, and knowing the Sea Palms is just around the next bend. We're ready to shove off, aren't we?"

"Aye, for the tenth time. I swear lass, what's eatin' at ye? Ye're actin' like there ain't going to be no tomorrow."

Her gaze drifted in the direction of the *Maine* and settled onto the hazy shadow of the battleship. If only it weren't so dark . . . then she could watch for him as he came rowing back.

"Ah," nodded Uriah knowingly. "He hasn't been gone an hour, and ye're behavin' like he's been away fer days. Settle down. We'll be well on our way out of this hellhole before Ferrer figures out he's been had," he assured her before turning the bottle up to his mouth.

She kicked the air in front of her. Ferrer was the least of her worries. Both hands raked through the thick mass of dark tresses that cascaded around her shoulders in a breeze-caressed disarray. "Damn it! What's taking him so long? He promised me he'd be back by ten."

"And I'm sure he will be. But ye gotta give the poor lad another half hour before ye start cussin' at him."

She paused a moment to listen to a distant bugle sounding taps and then sat down on the bench beside her old friend, her back slumped against the boom. "You're right. I'm being silly. Silly. Silly." She cracked a tiny smile. "He's barely had time to row out there, much less report to Charles and get back here."

An arm covered with gray hair enveloped her. "He may not be here to protect ye, but I am. Ye jes don't worry none, ye hear me. If that snake Ferrer does come after ye, he'll have a little surprise waitin' fer him," promised Uriah as he gave his knife a pat.

"Oh, Uriah, it isn't Ferrer, or the Spanish for that matter, that bothers me," she remarked softly as she laid her head on his shoulder.

"'Tis not?"

She fought to keep her eyes dry. "Uriah," she began a few moments later. "Do you remember the day Mac drowned?"

"Aye. I'll never forget it if I live to be a hundred."

"Do you remember what I told you when you dropped by the house that afternoon?"

"Aye." Gray eyes began to blear. "Ye told me ye had this terrible feelin' that a storm was brewin' out at sea, and Mac shoulda stayed at home. Had he listened to ye, he'd—"

She completed the sentence for him, her words choked with sobs. "He'd be here with us right this minute." Her head lifted. Eyes too blurred to focus stared into the inky black off the starboard side. The *Maine* was little more than a silhouette atop the water. The shape of the Ward line steamer, the *City of Washington*, which lay astern the *Maine* could hardly be distinguished, and the *Alfonso* was not visible in the darkness.

"You know, Uriah, I had that same feeling right before Chase left," she announced after a pause.

"Heh. Ye're imaginin' things, lass." He reached underneath the bench and brought out a silver flask. "Here. Best thing in the world fer the jitters.

285

And fer whatever else ails ye as well."

She looked at the flask for a moment, then reached for it. "Oh, all right. Just as long as it isn't some of Calpurnia's swamp water." She took a long, hard gulp, then splattered it over the deck. "Good God A'mighty, Uriah. Are you trying to poison me?" she coughed. "This isn't sangría. It's whiskey," she exclaimed, wiping her mouth with her sleeve.

"'Tis and there's none finer!" he remarked chuckling. "And ye must admit, it does wonders fer taking yer mind off yer problems."

Fist balled, she belted him in the shoulder. "You old devil, you. Why didn't you tell me it wasn't sangría?" she laughingly demanded.

"Ye didn't ask me."

Suddenly, with no warning, a deafening blast thundered across the skies.

Her laugh froze in her throat; her heart plummeted.

"Dear Mother o' God," exclaimed Uriah, looking around the harbor in wide-eyed wonderment. "What do ye suppose is goin' on?"

Before she had a chance to reply, gale force waves battered head-on into the sides of the *Blue Runner* and sent a mountain of water crashing over the rails. The boat began to rock as though it were pitching and lunging on the high seas.

Dare struggled to keep her hold on the boom. It felt as if the very bowels of the ocean were being regurgitated. "Uriah?" she called out.

"Don't worry 'bout me, lass," he shouted back. "Just hang on."

A second discharge erupted, then a third, all

sounding like a mighty herd of horses had come stampeding across the heavens.

Holding on to the boom lest she be sent clear over the edge by one of the waves sweeping across the deck, Dare frantically surveyed her surroundings for some explanation of the sudden explosions.

The bay was now lit by a sharp, bright light that hurt her eyes. Countless multi-colored flares soared into the air like Fourth of July rockets bombarding the skies. Ships, barely distinguishable earlier, were as visible now as if it were daylight.

A low-hanging mass of smoke had settled near the Ward freighter. At first glance, Dare was certain that the freighter had blown an engine, but a moment later, when the cloud began to lift, she realized that the *City of Washington* was intact. Her relief was short-lived. It was not the freighter that had vanished into the thick, hazy fumes that were darker than the night. It was the USS *Maine!*

For one split second, her legs were as heavy as lead. They refused to move. Try as she might she could not budge them.

Then, suddenly, her feet were flying out from under her, and she was sliding over the wet boards in slow motion.

Another dull, sullen roar split the air. Closing her eyes against the intense glare, Dare made one last lunge for the railing and grabbed hold.

When she forced open her eyes a moment later, her heart stopped in midbeat. Her trembling legs refused to support her weight a moment longer, and she sank down to the deck, not believing what she had just seen.

The bow of the *Maine* had disa████ ████ ██m-
pletely. Her foremast and smaller st█████ ████ en,
and flames were raging across her ██████

She wanted to yell to Uriah, to scream out for
Chase at the top of her lungs, but no sound came.

Seconds later a dead calm hung over the water like
a shroud. Cries of *"Abandon ship!"* echoed across the
bay.

Before she had a chance to catch her breath and
turn around to look for Uriah, loud reports echoed at
rapid intervals. The next moment, fragments were
flying through the air, penetrating the eerie quiet
with whistling sounds.

Another giant wave hit the boat broadside and sent
Uriah sprawling across the deck in her direction.

"What in bloody tarnation is goin' on out there?"

"It's the *Maine*," said Dare, her words hardly a
whisper. "Good Lord, I believe she's sinking."

Even as she verbalized the disaster, she could not
believe what she had just seen. Surely it was all a
dream, a horrible, horrible nightmare from which
she would soon awaken. But she knew she would not
awaken. She was already awake, and nothing could
change what she had just witnessed. The USS *Maine*
had been blown clear out of the water. Right before
her eyes, the pride of the United States Navy had been
reduced to nothing more than a great mass of twisted
iron.

Her legs gave way beneath her, and she crumpled
to the deck in a quivering heap. Chase was out there
somewhere, but where? If the mighty battleship
could not withstand what had ripped it in two, then
surely a man could not survive such an impact. Dear

God, if Chase had been on that ship . . .

She couldn't let herself think such terrible thoughts, for if she did, they would surely come true.

Her head dropped between her knees. Somewhere out there Chase was struggling for survival if he were not already . . .

Her fists pounded the deck. "He can't be dead. I won't let him die."

Uriah gathered her in his arms and caressed her with fatherly tenderness. "Shhh, lassie. Take it easy. Everythin' will be all right."

"Don't let him die!" she screamed, pounding her old friend's chest with all her might. "Dear God. He can't die! I won't let him."

She collapsed against Uriah, her words scarcely more than sobs. Had it been only six weeks ago that she had wailed these same words, she wondered as she tried to calm herself. Six weeks. A short time to have developed such lasting ties with someone. She couldn't know him any better had she known him all her life.

Uriah gently rocked her back and forth in his arms. "Go ahead, lassie. Cry 'til yer heart's content. Get it all out. It'll do ye good."

I love you. Till death us do part. Always. Forever and a day.

His words of love reverberated inside her head louder and longer than any of the sounds blasting across the harbor. If only she had been able to convince him to set sail the moment she'd returned from the Cadallas', he'd still be alive. Perhaps if she had not tarried so long over coffee that evening . . .

She cursed herself over and over. How stupid she

had been to keep her foreboding dread to herself. Rather than risk losing him by insisting they leave Havana immediately. Losing him would have been painful, but at least he would be alive, not blown to pieces. Had he been confronted with a choice between her or the Navy, and had he chosen the Navy, then life without him would be only tolerable at best, but living with the knowledge that their separation had been provoked by death, a death for which she indirectly bore the responsibility, would make her existence unbearable.

Suddenly, she had an idea. Perhaps he was not dead after all. Maybe he was fighting to stay afloat just long enough for her to get out there to him. Maybe he still had a chance.

She came alive instantly. "Quick, Uriah. We've got to go get him. I'll get the lines."

Uriah held on to her and wouldn't let her go despite her kicking and screaming. "Don't be a fool, Dare!" he yelled over her own shouts. "We get any closer we risk bein' blown out of the water ourselves."

"I can't let him die! Let me go! I won't! I won't!"

A stinging slap across her cheeks jolted her back to reality.

"Sorry I had to hit you, lass, but somethin' had to bring ye back to yer senses."

She nodded.

Her whole body felt numb. She cried until the tears would no longer fall and Chase's name was but a sob caught in her throat. Chase was lost to her forever.

Her head burrowed deeper into Uriah's chest. She'd gladly give her own life to change what she knew fate had decreed. What a cruel trick to let Chase survive one life-threatening ordeal only to let him fall victim to the next.

"Dare . . . Dare . . . Dare."

Good Lord, now she was hearing him call out to her.

"Dare . . . Dare . . . Dare . . ."

She covered her ears with her hands. How plainly she could hear him pleading for her to be his salvation once more.

A moment later, she lifted her head from Uriah's shoulder.

"Dare!"

There, she had heard it again. This time, the sound was less muffled and much, much closer.

"Uriah, do you hear what I hear? It's Chase. He's calling me."

He tried to guide her head back down. "Just rest, lass. Another couple of minutes, and we'll make up our mind what to do."

She jerked free of his arms. "I'm not imagining it, Uriah. I hear Chase. He's calling me." Breaking away from his hold, she ran as far forward as she could without falling overboard.

She stared down into the water. "Chase, I'm here."

Suddenly, her face erupted into smiles. Her tears became tears of joy. Swimming toward her with long, powerful strokes was Chase.

"It's him!" she shouted to Uriah. "Quick, get a rope."

Uriah threw a line over the rail, and the next moment, the two of them were reeling Chase in.

"Oh, Chase, my darling," she exclaimed, flinging

her arms around him and covering his cold, wet face with kisses. "Thank God, you're alive. I just knew you went down with the *Maine*. I thought you were dead for sure."

"So did I," he managed, gasping for breath.

Uriah spread a blanket over his shoulders. "What happened out there, lad?"

"I wish I knew." His words were directed to the spot of ocean where the *Maine* had lain at anchor, quiet and peaceful, less than an hour before. "I was rowing back to the *Blue Runner*. I was nearly here. Then I heard an explosion." He dropped down onto the bench at middeck. "I didn't have time to respond before a wave washed the boat right out from under me."

Dare bundled the blanket tightly around his shoulders. "Poor darling. You're freezing. You'll come down with pneumonia for sure if we don't get you into some dry clothes."

Lips blue and shivering, he stared back at the spot where the *Maine* had been, looking as though he had seen a ghost. "Pneumonia, you say? I only pray they'll be so lucky."

Dare held him close, silently vowing never to let him out of her sight again. His body was so cold, so unresponsive. His hands remained by his sides. When he looked at her, it was as though she weren't even there. The louder the noises from the city streets became, the tighter her arms wrapped around him, but still he did not react.

From their vantage point on the bridge, it looked as if the events offshore had plunged the entire city into pandemonium. Everywhere she looked, crowds were pushing and shoving their way to the harbor. Despite police efforts to restrict them, the mobs broke through the hastily erected barricades and elbowed their way onto the pier stopping only when they could proceed no farther.

"What's happening out there?" a man wearing a devil's mask called out from the next dock.

"The *Alfonso* just sank the *Maine*." The reply, in Spanish, came from someone in the crowd.

"Good, we didn't ask her to come here in the first place," shouted another reveler amid cheers and applause.

Dare squeezed herself against Chase. "War? Could that be true?"

"No. The *Alfonso* was nowhere near the *Maine* when she went down. As a matter of fact, the captain had changed his point of anchorage just—" Chase's words were less confident as he concluded his sentence—"just before supper."

Dare knew what was going through his mind; the same thought that had entered hers at the same instant. Was it possible the captain of the *Alfonso* had changed buoys because he knew what would happen at exactly nine forty?

"Look, there goes the *Alfonso* now," shouted Dare, pointing to the ominous Spanish battleship plowing its way to the place where buoy number four had once been. "What do you suppose it's doing out there?"

"It looks like it's . . . yes, it is." A sigh of relief accompanied his words. "The *Alfonso*'s leading the rescue efforts."

"Thank the good Lord for that!" softly exclaimed

Uriah. "If there'd been any question as to its whereabouts when all this was going on, there'd be hell to pay for sure."

Dare, too, breathed a sigh of relief. A ship wouldn't rescue survivors from a vessel it had been instrumental in sinking.

"Isn't there something we can do to help?" she asked, watching as a fleet of small boats sped across the bay to assist the *Alfonso*, the *City of Washington*, and the customs and police patrols in the search for survivors.

Chase shook his head. "I think we'd be better off to just wait and see what happens. For the time being, the most we can do is watch," he repeated dismally. "Just watch."

"And pray," Uriah added, his tone grave.

"Yes, that too," concurred Chase.

Dare paced back and forth across the deck just as she had done when she had thought Chase had been lost to her forever. Watch and pray. Little else could be done as she maintained her vigilance for most of the night. Watch and pray.

"Why don't you try to get some sleep?" Chase suggested.

Dare shook her head. She wanted to remain with him. His body was beside hers, but he had withdrawn. She couldn't blame him. He had far more on his mind than the two of them. Still, she'd decided long ago that her place was with him, and there she would stay until he told her otherwise.

"You sure?" he asked. "I don't know how much longer this is going to go on."

"It doesn't matter. I'll stay. I'm not tired. Be-

294

sides . . ." She hesitated.

"Besides what?" he asked, his attention on the next load of bodies being brought to shore.

"I'd rather be here with you." She couldn't take her eyes from the scene at the main dock. How many of those bodies were still breathing, she wondered, and how many had just not been able to stay afloat long enough.

Chase turned and walked away. Dare followed. She supposed that, like herself, he could not go through another half hour of seeing the dead being separated from the living, of looking at those whose limbs had been blown away.

Avoiding her eyes, Chase said. "Go below. I'll be down as soon as all this calms down."

No longer worried about rejection, she pulled him close. "I'm staying right here with you." Even in the dark she could tell the entire ordeal had scarred him in a way that was not physically evident. "We'll go through this together."

He said nothing. Then his arms opened wide, and she stepped inside. No words were necessary. As far as she was concerned, that one gesture said it all.

"We're going to be waiting a long time," he told her after holding her for a while.

"I know."

The last word they'd received had reported only a dozen men found alive. There were still three hundred and forty odd men to be located. And most of those had probably been blown up with their ship.

Chase led her over to the cockpit bench. She sat down, relieved that he was with her. Thank God, he was not one of those men who were not yet accounted for. Head on his shoulder, she closed her eyes, telling herself it was just for a moment.

When her eyes opened, she had no idea how long she had been asleep, but the scene in the bay had changed little. The crews of the *Alfonso* and the *City of Washington* were still combing the water, and power boats were rushing to shore only to head back out again once their loads had been delivered.

Rubbing her eyes, she sat up straight and threw back the blanket that had been spread over her.

"Where's Chase?" she asked Uriah, who was leaning over the bow, his body slumped and his eyes gazing far out to sea.

"Uriah?" she called out his name again.

Her old friend turned around. "I wonder if anyone has even imagined what's goin' to be made of all this up in Washington?"

"What do you think will happen?" she asked, joining him on the bow.

"All hell's goin' to break loose. I can tell ye that much right now," he said confidently. "Ye jus' mark my words. What Congress and McKinley don't start, Hearst and Pulitzer will."

"I hope you're wrong," she said quietly. God, how she hoped he was wrong. "Chase didn't leave the *Blue Runner*, did he?" she asked, panic suddenly seizing her.

"No, I'm here," he called out from the pier.

Thank God! she thought to herself as she went running across the deck.

Through the darkness, she could see that he was not alone. There was someone with him. A man. It looked . . . It was!

"Charles!" she exclaimed, leaping off the boat and onto the pier. "We've been so worried about you. Thank God, you're safe!"

"Yes, thank God," he echoed, his voice heavy and grim.

Chase took his friend by the arm. "Let's get on the boat. We can see what's going on from there."

Nodding, Charles allowed himself to be escorted aboard the *Blue Runner*.

He seemed to be in a daze, as if he knew what had transpired during the course of the evening, but couldn't bring himself to accept it.

Dare went below to fetch them all some hot coffee. When she came topside, Uriah was waiting for her.

"Here, put a little o' this in the mugs," he said, adding some whiskey to the hot brew. "It'll do everybody a world o' good."

"She's gone," she heard Sigsbee say as she joined them. "They called her the staunchest vessel in the whole fleet. Said nothing could bring her down. But something did," he said, his face buried in his hands. "I can't believe it. I still can't believe it."

"Here, drink this," she told him, handing him a mug, "It'll make you feel better."

He looked at her like she was crazy. "I have just lost my ship. Believe me, nothing, not this or anything else, will make me feel any better."

"I know that, Charles," she said gently, "but it'll do you a world of good to get something hot in you."

Poor man, she mused, watching as he used both shaking hands to guide the mug to his mouth. Poor, poor man. He had aged twenty years at least since she'd seen him in Key West harbor. Only eight years

297

Chase's senior, he looked old enough to be his father. His features were pale, so much paler than she remembered. The half dozen or so times she had been in his company, he had looked so crisp and starched, so Navy, so much in control. Now, he looked helpless, almost pathetic. His blond hair was matted against his scalp, and bits of seaweed clung to the thin strands. His glasses' left lens was cracked, and the wire rims were bent out of shape. His dress whites were covered with mud, sand, silt, and blood.

"Shouldn't we get a doctor down here to look after that?" she inquired, concerned about the fresh blood on his shoulder.

He shook his head. "Flesh wound. Nothing. Nothing in comparison to what most of my men are suffering."

She nodded and became quiet. She had a feeling most of the blood splattered over him came from the men he'd been trying to save. How many of those had still been breathing when he'd tried to pull them off the vessel or get them out of the water? she wondered.

"What happened, lad?" queried Uriah. "Have ye been able to figure out yet just what went wrong?"

Charles shook his head. "I have my own conjectures, but I'd prefer not to voice them until I'm certain they are correct. No doubt though the wires from here to Key West and from there to Washington will be running all night with so-called firsthand accounts," he said wryly. "Those press boats that went out were more interested in getting stories than they were in helping to pull in survivors."

"Ye think it was the Spanish?" pressed Uriah, trading his mug of coffee for a silver flask.

Charles took his time answering. "If so," he said finally, "I don't see why they sent one of their own into the water after me." He inhaled several gulps of air then exhaled them slowly. "You're lucky you got out when you did," he told Chase. "Good thing you didn't stick around for the ten o'clock poker game."

Chase tried to smile, but could not. "Yeah, tell me about it." He waited until his fellow officer had lifted his head from his knees before asking the next question. "Just what did happen after I left?"

The tired face went blank. "I don't know. That's the God's truth." He leaned back against the railing. "After I saw you off, I went down to my quarters and started writing my wife a letter. Suddenly, without the least bit of warning, a series of sharp vibrations and violent rendings shook the ship."

His gray face contorted as though he were suffering horribly. Remembering the evening's terrible events was causing him excruciating pain.

"I made my way in the dark through long passageways, groping from side to side. Somehow, I managed to get to the poop deck. I ordered all high explosives flooded, and then directed boats to be lowered to rescue the drowning and the wounded. By that point there was no more confusion than a general call to arms would produce."

He looked from Dare to Chase to Uriah, then back to Chase. He seemed confused, as though he had not yet fully comprehended what had happened. "Three detonations. Three. And my ship was gone!"

He struggled to keep his eyes free of tears. "It happened so fast. Perhaps if there had been more time . . . if I had acted more quickly . . . No, nothing can change the outcome. The *Maine* and my crewmen who perished with her are no more."

He hung his head. When he looked up a short while later, he asked, "Did I tell you that the explosions occurred far forward? Right under the crew's quarters. That's why I lost nearly all my sailors. Can you imagine how horrible it must have been for those poor devils? At one minute they're sitting on their bunks playing cards, bragging about their girls back home, and in the next, the face or arm or leg of a buddy has been blown away. Just like that."

His words were mixed with sobs that he tried to contain. "Before coming here, I went down to the hospital to visit the few survivors. Some were badly burned. Others were permanently scarred or had lost a limb. The same plea resounded throughout each ward. "Please, God, let me die. Let me die."

He looked as though he would break down.

Dare turned to Chase, her eyes begging him to somehow lessen his friend's anguish, but he made no effort to silence Charles. Instead, he nodded, urging his friend to go on, to get it all out of his system while he was still among friends and would not be reprimanded for being emotional.

"You know when we first steamed into Havana Harbor the morning of the twenty-fifth, I selected my anchorage site myself." His words were punctuated with heavy sighs. "The dockmaster suggested I change to a better location a few days back. Then, this very evening, the *Alfonso* decided to put a little distance between the two warships. I can't help but wonder if any of this would have happened if I had

300

stayed put."

Chase leaned closer. "You see a significance there?"

He hung his head once more. "At this point, old friend, I don't know what's significant and what isn't."

"Ye know accordin' to the locals, gossip has it that the Spanish put a submarine mine under buoy four."

"How do you figure that?" questioned Dare.

"While ye were sleepin' and Chase was mullin' the situation over, I decided to stretch me legs a bit," he answered, "so I walked up the pier and over to the next dock. Our friend Valdez was there. That's what he had heard."

"Spanish sympathizers or the Spanish military?" she asked.

Chase nodded. "That's right. There's a lot of difference between the two."

"Especially as far as declaring war is concerned," added Charles.

Uriah shook his head. "He didn't say one way or the other. Probably jus' a lot of talk. For all anybody knows, it could even have been the rebels. Lord knows they stand to gain just as much as Spain's got to lose if the United States does storm Havana on account of this."

"That's right," remarked Dare thoughtfully. "It's Carnival season, and with everybody going around in masks, no one could tell the rebels from the loyalists."

"All the particulars will be sorted out later," remarked Charles grimly. "The fact remains, my ship has been sunk, and a good many of my men have been lost. They trusted me, looked to me for protection, and I let them down. Perhaps if I—"

"You could have done nothing—I repeat, nothing—that would have altered the events of tonight." Chase's words of assurance were strong and emphatic. Placing an arm around his friend's shoulders, his fingers roughly kneaded his friend's back. "Shape up, man," he ordered, forcing Charles to look him squarely in the eye. "If you start blaming yourself now for what happened, you'll go through life feeling responsible for something that was out of your hands completely. You are still the captain of the USS *Maine*. Understand?"

Taking a moment to compose herself, Charles stood up. He held himself tall and proud. "Yes, you're right. One hundred percent correct." He took a deep breath. "Ship or no ship, I am still the commander of the *Maine*. I owe it to my men, those who made it, those who did not, to carry on in a manner they would expect and respect."

Chapter Nineteen

Dare glanced up from the March issue of *Ladies' Home Journal* as Chase stomped up onto the porch. "Oh dear," she sighed, putting away her magazine. "From the looks of it, you've had quite a morning at the naval building."

He took off his jacket, tossed it into the glider, then rolled up his sleeves. "The admiral always did tell me not to play poker because my face would be sure to give me away." He gave her cheek a quick peck, then sat down on the porch. His back fit snugly into the crook of her legs, and one arm rested on each of her knees.

"Poor darling." She began massaging the tension from his shoulders. She wanted to ask about the ruling of the committee appointed to investigate the *Maine*'s sinking, but decided to wait. "How's that?"

"Ah, that feels wonderful. You have ten years to put in," he said as he stretched out his legs.

"And when the ten years is up?" She leaned down to kiss the top of his head. "Any ideas?"

He turned up his cheek for a kiss. "What say I renew your contract for fifty years? Maybe, sixty? How's that?"

"Oh, I think I'd better think that over," she told him.

"The pay might not be much, but consider if you will all the hidden rewards." He chuckled softly. "Although I'm afraid I've gotten a bit negligent in that department lately, have I not?"

She laughed. "I'd be the last person to argue with you there." Her voice softened. "But you've had a lot on your mind. I understand. Now, you just sit back and relax, and I'll take care of the rest." She resumed the massage, her fingers penetrating deep into his skin. "Goodness. You're all tied up in knots."

"I hope I never have to go through another five weeks like these."

She vigorously kneaded the flesh underneath his collar, thinking that she couldn't agree with him more. So much had happened the past five weeks; much more than she had ever thought possible!

Of the three hundred and fifty-three men aboard the *Maine* when it sank to the bottom of Havana harbor, only eighty-seven survived. The Ward line steamer and a lighthouse tender, the *Mangrove*, transported them to Key West where the mother superior of the convent of Mary Immaculate placed the school and convent at government disposal for use as a military hospital.

Word of the disaster had spread like wildfire. The

immediate and lasting response was a desire for revenge. "Remember the *Maine*! To hell with Spain" had become a national cry to arms. Emotionalism outweighed objectivity. The president's disposition toward peace was more popular aboard than at home. His own political party was overwhelmingly in favor of war and had assured him both privately and through the press that if he continued his stand for peace he didn't have a chance of serving a second term.

Within a week, a fleet of United States Navy ships was mobilized in Key West where all military and naval operations would be coordinated. A flotilla of newspaper boats had arrived two days before with correspondents from all the major papers. Many of the hometown tabloids were represented as well. Big city journalists and small-town reporters alike clamored for war. "Cu Be or not cu be!! That is the key westion" wrote one reporter anxiously awaiting orders to carry on to Cuba.

Dare's fingers sank deeper into Chase's flesh as she thought of the future. Not since the animosity between Spain and America first began to build had the outlook for peace appeared so bleak. All indications pointed to war. Ten days after the sinking of the *Maine*, Roosevelt, in Chase's words, had taken it upon himself while Secretary of the Navy Long was on vacation to cable Admiral Dewey with orders to proceed to Hong Kong and fill up his coal bunkers, and in the event of war, to make certain that the Spanish squadron did not get beyond the Asiatic coast. A week and a half later, Congress had allocated fifty million dollars for the national defense. That in itself was a sign they anticipated war.

Her sighs as heavy and as troubled as Chase's, she continued working out the tautness between his shoulders. He was not the only one who had been tied up in knots lately. She had suffered right along with him. Much to her chagrin, the Navy Department had notified Chase that when the Norfolk shipyard completed the *Titan*, the brand-new battleship would steam down to Key West to meet its new commander. Chase! It was bad enough knowing that he'd be spending more nights aboard his ship than in her bed, but the news that the *Titan* would be the first battleship to cruise out of Key West harbor if war were declared really worried her. Lately, she had joked that Chase was just on loan from the Navy, but she feared that what had been said in jest would soon prove true.

Had the news from the two courts of inquiry been encouraging, he would already have told her the results. Knowing that the opposite was true made her feel apprehensive. The inclination to peace or war might very well have been determined that morning.

Curious, she decided to take her chances and, after a deep breath, casually asked her question. "So tell me, what rulings did the court make?" She held her breath and kept her fingers crossed. "Can you tell me, or is it top secret?"

"Hardly." He gave the hand on his shoulder an affectionate pat, then pulled himself up. "By the time the press gets wind of it, it'll be broadcast around the world anyway." He dragged a rocking chair across the porch and positioned it next to Dare's. "Which would you rather hear first: the findings of the Spanish panel or the American one?"

"Let's hear what Spain has to say," she replied, preparing herself for the worst. "I'll save the crucial one for last."

"That's about the size of it." One hand on hers, he began. "The board of Spanish naval officers has attributed the *Maine*'s disaster to accidental internal combustion."

She let out a few breaths. The news wasn't nearly as bad as she had thought. "Since she had just taken on a full load of coal, I'd say that was a rather feasible deduction."

"I'm not quite sure just what to make of it," said Chase after a few moments of deliberation. "Perhaps they feel such a ruling will lessen suspicions regarding their guilt."

"Their original intention, if you remember, was to bring in an independent group of officers from a number of countries to investigate the matter," she quickly reminded him, "but the United States Navy Department objected to their proposal."

"Granted," he allowed. "On the other hand, Spanish representatives refused to let American divers examine the wreckage. Could be they were afraid something might be found down there," he added softly as if thinking out loud.

Dare sank back in her seat. Or of evidence that might be planted, she thought. At the risk of sounding unpatriotic, she kept this thought to herself. She loved her country as much as the next person, but she was aware that the majority of Americans wanted war, and she knew how far many so-called patriots would go to insure that the

Bourbon flag was hurled out of this hemisphere.

"You know, Chase, that theory of spontaneous combustion isn't inconceivable. As a matter of fact, it sounds a lot like what happened three years ago with the *Cincinnati* right here in Key West. Remember?"

He nodded. "That's right. Luckily, smoke was spotted coming from the magazine. Otherwise, she'd have been blown out of the water just—"

"Just like the *Maine*," she said, taking the words from his mouth.

"I'm sure the U.S. board of inquiry came up with a completely different theory. Right?" she asked.

He nodded. "They think she sank because a submarine mine was planted near her bow." Elbows propped on the arms of the rocker, he burrowed his chin between his hands. "They accused the harbor officials in Havana of gross negligence, but did not go so far as to hold Spain directly responsible for what happened."

She let out a deep breath. "Well, that's certainly encouraging. I was expecting far worse, weren't you?"

Chase stared into space, a dazed expression fixed on his face.

Dare reached for his arm. "Chase, darling, are you all right?"

He nodded. "Just thinking. During the five days the court was in session Charles was not called on once to give his account of that night."

"Odd," she remarked slowly. "You would have thought he'd have been their primary source of information."

"Yes, one would have thought so." After a short

pause he looked up. "At any rate, he still has cause to celebrate. Neither he nor his crew was held responsible for any event which transpired that night."

"Thank God. Perhaps that will ease his mind some."

"Yes, let's hope so," he commented, his voice becoming a bit distant.

"What do you suppose will happen once the findings of the courts have been released to the public?" asked Dare later in the day as they took their afternoon stroll down the beach.

"I wish I knew." He picked up a stone and sent it skipping over the water. "But if you want my opinion, I'd be willing to bet on the likelihood of war."

Lifting the hem of her skirt high above her ankles, Dare shuffled through the surf without missing a beat. His prediction came as no surprise. She had expected as much. Had the findings of the U.S. court of inquiry proved beyond a shadow of a doubt that Spain had in no way been responsible for what happened, the result would have been the same. War! The American public would have it no other way. Hostility had been building far longer than five weeks. Mac had told her of an incident that had occurred a few years before she'd been born. An American merchant ship had been overtaken at sea by a Spanish gunboat. The crew and passengers of the *Virginius* had been taken prisoner and shot in Cuba. Just last week one of the *Journal's* reporters had played a joke that revived the hostilities regarding this affair. To add a little excitement to the uneventful news he cabled to his paper, he reported that a ship called the *Virginia*, loaded with silver bullion and coconuts, had been sunk by the Spanish army. The public was outraged. Even the retraction printed by the *Journal* the next day did nothing to quiet their screaming demands for revenge.

Dare wound her hand around Chase's waist as they paused a few minutes later to watch a pair of dolphins play follow the leader in the shallows a short distance away.

"Wouldn't it be wonderful if life were that simple," she remarked, laying her head on his shoulder.

His lips lingered on her forehead for a long while. "Unfortunately, man is too complex a creature, my love. The price, I suppose, one pays for progress."

"Ay, yes. Progress," she repeated with a sigh. "It seems the word has become almost synonymous with war."

"Chase," exclaimed Dare as they resumed their walk, "I have a marvelous idea. Let's get the boat and row over to Christmas Tree Key. That'll keep our minds off the dilemma we face here."

"Maybe for a while, but once we return our problems will be waiting to be solved," he said, his words heavy.

"Oh, please," she urged, grabbing his hands. "We used to have such fun over there. Our own little kingdom, you used to call it. How about it?"

He shook his head. "Not today, dearest. I just don't have the time. Sorry."

Her enthusiasm quickly faded. *No* seemed to be his favorite word lately, and the fact that he had a lot on his mind his favorite excuse.

She let out a heavy sigh. There'd be other days, she told herself wistfully. Perhaps there'd even be other nights, nights when his desire would again flame out of control.

"You understand, don't you, Dare?"

She tried to put up a cheerful front. After all, she reminded herself, she was a twenty-year-old woman, not a petulant child prone to temper tantrums when she didn't get her way. "Of course, I understand, Chase," she assured him, attempting to sound very adult. "Honestly, I do."

"You'd make a horrible poker player, too," he said, half grinning. Hands deep in the pocket of his trousers, he walked on slowly. "I've a meeting with Commander Forsyth scheduled for four o'clock. It's imperative I attend. We'll, uh, we'll be planning strategy for our first line of naval defense, just in case the Spanish decide to venture past the neutral zone and into the waters of south Florida."

She started to latch on to his arm, then decided against doing so and let her hand drop to her side. "Of course. The first line of defense is very important," she said, none too convincingly.

He turned her to him. "I can almost hear what's going on inside that pretty little head of yours, Dare MacDade," he said, taking her face between his hands and forcing her eyes to make contact with his. "And you can just cease such thoughts this very minute."

"I don't know what you—"

Before she could finish her sentence, his arms had seized her and imprisoned her against his chest. His mouth pressed to hers, he devoured her lips in a kiss

311

that sucked the very breath from her.

When he finally released her, he grinned sheepishly. "I'll bet you thought I'd forgotten just how that was supposed to be done."

She was at a loss for words. All she could do was look at him, a half-dazed expression on her face. A kiss like that could easily be the ruination of many a young, virtuous woman. "I, uh, I suppose you only needed to refresh your memory a bit," she finally managed.

Sky blue eyes gleamed hungrily at her, turning her knees to jelly.

"That's only the start of it," he said, his gaze hot and passionate. "I'm a quick learner, and I relearn even faster."

Before she could object, he lifted her into his arms and, amid laughing protests, swung her round and round until they both collapsed in a dizzy heap on the sand.

"What was all that about?" When she finally caught her breath, she laughed so hard she thought her sides would split. "Oh, Chase, I do believe you've gone mad."

"Oh, I have, my darling, and it's all your fault," he told her as he covered her face with sandy kisses. "I've gone mad over you." He pulled her into a sitting position and brushed the sand from her blouse. "I just want to make sure you know that: one, I love you very, very much; two, regardless of what you think, I have by no stretch of the imagination lost interest in you. I'd be a fool if I ever did. Three, you are very, very sensuous, and a man would have to be insane to turn down an outing on Christmas Tree Key with you, or anywhere else for that matter. Number four—"

Lips pressed to hers again, he gave her a kiss, long and deep, that reached right into her heart.

"And number four," he continued, "I want you to know there's a lot more where that came from."

After checking the time, he pulled her to her feet. "It's a quarter to four, my sweet. Commander Forsyth isn't a man who enjoys being kept waiting."

"Sounds as though he and I have something in common," she returned quickly.

He pinched her backside. "Hey, watch it! Do I detect a bit of sarcasm in that remark?"

She chuckled. "A bit, perhaps." With her skirt hiked high above her knees, she struck a provocative pose. "Tell me, what does Commander Forsyth offer you that I don't?"

"Not one thing, I assure you." He dropped onto his knees and ran kisses up and down her legs. "Except for the fact that he could break me if he knew I was dallying on the beach with you instead of plotting our course of action." Rising, he kissed the tip of her nose. "Let's hurry, love, minutes are ticking away."

"But you forget. We've yet to plot our course of action." Arms around his neck, she nibbled at his ear lobe. "You know, your office is less than five minutes away. The Sea Palms is even closer." She tucked herself against him to emphasize her point. The pressure she felt against her leg told her that he would need very little persuading. "What about it, sailor? Can I possibly interest you in five minutes of pure heaven?"

His hands circled her hips. "You make temptation

awfully hard to resist."

"Then why bother?" Her tongue darted in and out of his ear. "Well?"

"Mmmmm. You are shameless, aren't you, my love?"

Her lips peppered kisses down his neck. "Need I remind you that you made me that way?"

"I know, I know." His tone became serious. "And I curse myself every day when I think that my ignoring you so much of the time could very easily fling you into another man's arms."

"Never. Not in a million years." She looped an arm through his. "Like it or not, you're stuck with me."

He lifted her hand to his lips and kissed each finger. "I don't like it. I love it. And I love you."

"But you have to go, right?"

He nodded.

Her cheerful mood did not desert her. "I'll not stand in the way of my country's defense."

"What a good sport you are, my sweet!"

She wiggled a finger in front of his nose. "You just remember that you owe me a conference too."

He kissed her lips with a resounding smack. "I owe you so many it may take me the rest of my life to pay up."

"I'll hold you to that." She smiled to herself. This was the Chase with whom she had fallen in love. Poor baby, he does have so much pressure on him these days, she thought, reminding herself to be much more understanding in the future. Otherwise . . . Perish the thought! Nothing would ever come between them.

Arriving back at the Sea Palms, Dare helped Chase into his jacket and then straightened his collar. God, he was handsome, she mused, lovingly smoothing back his hair. She doubted that, in the entire history of the U.S. Navy, any officer had done so much justice to his uniform.

He took her in his arms again and kissed her lightly. "I'll hurry home to you. Promise!"

His words thrilled her. Home! If only he would make the Sea Palms his home for the rest of his life! Nothing would make her happier.

"And when I get here," he continued, squeezing her fingers as he released her, "I want to find you all dressed up in your prettiest party dress because you and I are going out on the town. We'll have ourselves a night to remember."

"Every night I spend with you is a night to remember." After a light kiss, she pushed him toward the steps. "Now scat before Commander Forsyth comes looking for you."

Humming to herself, she leaned over the balustrade and followed his every movement up the street. Just before he rounded the corner, he turned and blew her a kiss. Feeling on top of the world, she blew it back to him along with a whispered, "I love you."

Then she settled into the rocker. Legs crossed and one hand shading her eyes from the sun, she resumed reading the article. Each time she turned a page, her free hand brought the ruby and diamond heart to her mouth for a soft kiss.

A short while later, overwhelmed by the eeriest feeling that someone's eyes were studying her, she looked up. Cane in one hand, cigar in the other,

Ferrer stood at the end of the walk. Dressed in his usual morbid black, he looked as though he had just come from a funeral. But the way he is smiling, the funeral is likely to be someone else's, she thought bitterly.

Their eyes locked in venomous stares, her glare every bit as poisonous as Ferrer's. How she loathed him! She did not doubt that he had informed the Spanish authorities of Chase's presence. Probably the sinking of the *Maine* had prevented them from acting on his information.

Her chin lifted defiantly. She was determined not to cower before him. Would she never be rid of him? she wondered angrily. Would he always be there to taunt her?

As though he read her mind, he smiled, an icy smile that sent cold chills racing up her back. I will always be here to torment you, the smile seemed to say.

After a curt nod and a tip of his hat, he tapped his way down the street.

She could no longer concentrate on the article. She felt that she hadn't seen the last of him. Perhaps he was too leery of Chase's wrath to venture off the street today, but there would be other days. What thoughts passed behind those cruel, calculating eyes of his? she asked herself. No pleasant ones she would wager.

She stood up. Ferrer could even cast clouds on a brilliantly resplendent day. No sense worrying about him. He'd make his move soon enough, and when he did, he would choose the time. Like most predators, he received as much pleasure from stalking his prey as he did from closing in.

She went into the house and closed the door behind her. Then, remembering Ferrer's nasty habit of walking into homes uninvited, she latched both locks.

Calpurnia met her at the stairs with a glass in her hand. "You forgot to drink this."

Chuckling to herself, Dare debated whether or not to tell her old mammy that her Bahamas bush medicine wasn't as potent as it used to be.

Calpurnia shoved the potion at her. "Drink it."

Dare took her housekeeper by the arm and sat her down on the bottom landing. "I'm not quite sure how to tell you this, Calpurnia, but that little concoction of yours didn't do the trick. I'm expecting."

Calpurnia's caramel-colored expression remained unchanged. "'Course it didn't work. It can't unless you swallow it."

"Then what's that?"

The old woman's face broke into a smile. "This is to make sure that li'l chile comes into this world kicking and hollering at the top of his lungs."

Dare did as she was told. Calpurnia had nursed many expectant mothers through their pregnancies, and she'd delivered more babies than Doc Edmundson. Both mother and child always came through.

"How'd you know?" she asked when she had downed all of the mixture.

"Oh, I could tell right away," boasted the Negress. "'Specially when you started making up at supper for what you couldn't keep down at breakfast."

"Oh, dear, I hope Chase didn't notice that."

"He didn't," her housekeeper assured her. "Men never can figure it out until the last."

Dare nodded. She hoped Calpurnia was right! Chase had enough on his mind.

She reached for the old woman's hand. "Dear, sweet Calpurnia. You have a potion for everything, don't you?"

"They's just one thing I don't know, and that's how I'm ever going to go about getting you and Captain Hamilton wed in time."

Dare set the glass down on a step. "You mustn't say anything to him about the baby. Promise me you won't. When the time's right, I'll tell him myself."

"Humph. That chile could be half grown by then."

Dare looked deep into Calpurnia's big, doe eyes. "Promise!"

Calpurnia gave a begrudging nod. "Whatever you say, but you just make sure you tell him before he goes off to Washington next week."

The color drained from Dare's face. "Washington? Where'd you hear that?"

"Him and that commander friend of his was talking about it last night after supper." Calpurnia eyed her suspiciously. "He hasn't said a word about it to you, now has he?"

Dare shook her head. Experience had taught her Calpurnia was not easily deceived. "No, he hasn't, but I'm sure he will. He'll tell me tonight, I'm certain."

"Humph! I should hope so. No decent man would go running off like that leaving behind people who depend on him."

"Now don't you go badmouthing him, Calpurnia. You love him as much as I do, now don't you?"

She shrugged her tired shoulders. "Maybe I do, and maybe I don't. But I'll tell you one thing. He goes off without telling you, he'd better not come back tomcatting around here, or I'll have a thing or two to say to him."

Dare responded confidently. "He won't go running off. He's not like that. He loves me just as much as I love him."

Calpurnia rolled back her eyes. "They say love's blind, you know."

"Maybe it is, maybe it isn't," returned Dare smiling, "but one thing's sure. Both of us went into it with our eyes wide open."

Several grunts serving as a response, Calpurnia returned to the kitchen, leaving Dare to sit on the steps with only her thoughts for company.

What Calpurnia had said about Chase running off didn't bother her. Chase was definitely a notch or two above most men in that respect. What did concern her was that he had had all last night and a good part of the afternoon to tell her of his plans to go to Washington, but he had not mentioned them. Why? Something that important couldn't have slipped his mind. Granted, he had been under a tremendous amount of strain lately, but he had remarked many times that he thrived on pressure.

Well—she sighed—he'd tell her when he got good and ready, and in the meantime . . .

One hand reached for her stomach. And in the meantime what? she wondered.

She positioned herself on the step so that her back

319

rested against one bannister, her feet touching the other, just the way she used to curl up on the stairs when she was a little girl. And in the meantime, she decided, she wouldn't add to the pressure on Chase by telling him about the babe. "Our baby," she said aloud, smiling as she caressed her stomach.

Nothing had changed yet. Any increase in her size was strictly her imagination. According to Calpurnia, her mother hadn't started showing until her sixth month. Poor Mac hadn't even guessed she was expecting. Perhaps she'd be like her mother, she concluded hopefully. That way she could take her time breaking the news of his future fatherhood to Chase.

Her arms folded protectively around her middle. She really didn't care if she started showing in six months or three. The changes her body would undergo would be exciting and fascinating. To think there was a little baby growing in there!

How would Chase react? she wondered. Surely, he'd be just as happy as she was.

Dare frowned suddenly. But what if he wasn't? She hadn't even considered that possibility. Suppose he interpreted this as a ploy to trap him.

Still frowning, Dare rose slowly and started up the stairs. She still had a little time left before worrying about that, she decided.

A grin tugged at her lips. First things first, she told herself as she turned and went back down. Finding out why he had made plans to go home without mentioning them to her demanded all her attention for the time being. She decided how she was going to go about obtaining the information she wanted! The way to a man's heart might be through his stomach just as Calpurnia said, but that was by no means the only route available. Something ran a close second.

"Hey, Calpurnia. What's for supper?" she called out on her way to the kitchen.

The housekeeper's pearly-toothed grin gleamed excitedly. "Seeing as how we need to work on Captain Hamilton a lot these next couple a days, I thought we'd start off by having all his favorites." Her eyes big and round, she proceeded to recite the menu. "Thought we'd begin with a little conch chowder. You know how he loves that! Then maybe a little conch salad to get him in a real good mood, but I figure my lobster in cream sauce will be what does the trick. Why, I'll bet he gets right down on his knees tonight and proposes." Her finger tapped the corner of her mouth. "Now what on earth am I going to fix for dessert? He has such a sweet tooth."

"Anything. You be the judge of that. Whatever you decide on will be delicious, I'm sure." Dare turned around quickly before the smile twitching at her lips gave her away. If everything went as she planned, they wouldn't get past the main course.

"Oh, one more thing Calpurnia," she said before leaving the Negress to her work. "Why don't you take the night off? I can serve dinner myself."

Calpurnia laughed. "I know 'xactly what you up to, girl," she said, shaking her finger. "And don't you think for one minute I don't know what's going on in that devious little head of yours." She gave Dare a rough hug. "Don't you worry none. As soon as I'm finished in here, I'm going to take myself to the church social."

Dare kissed Calpurnia's wrinkled cheek. "I don't know what I'd do without you."

"Jus' don't you ever try. Now get out of here, and leave the rest to me. You go get yourself all doodied up for Cap'n Chase Hamilton of the United States Navy." Calpurnia flipped the dish towel at Dare's backside.

Feeling as though she could conquer the world, Dare stepped out of the cedar tub after a luxurious, hour-long soak in jasmine-scented water.

Poor Chase, she giggled aloud as she peered inside her wardrobe in search of an appropriate outfit for the evening. He had no earthly idea of what was going on. How surprised he'd be when he walked through the bedroom door—no, not surprised, flabbergasted—to find a table set up with all his favorite foods and her in a seductive pose atop the bed. Just thinking about the treat she had in store for him sent her into a fit of laughter. She couldn't wait!

Still chuckling, she pulled out an aqua-colored gown with ecru lace cuffs and a wide fancy collar. She held it up to her and stood before the mirror; then shaking her head, she slipped the hanger back onto the rack. The gown would be perfect for an evening out on the town, but it was not really suitable for what she had in mind.

Hurriedly, she flipped through the rest of her dresses. Nothing really struck her fancy. She needed something simple, but exotic . . . innocent . . . but a bit wicked.

A moment later, she closed the door to the

wardrobe. She knew exactly what would fit that bill perfectly. She rummaged through the teak trunk at the foot of her bed. It was filled with keepsakes from Mac's many sailing adventures. In it she found exactly what she had in mind.

Her face aglow with anticipation of the wonderful pleasures the evening would bring, she slipped out of her everyday robe and into a white silk kimono decorated with handpainted, red firebreathing dragons. Its softness caressed her bare skin as she tied the wide red sash around her waist.

She brushed her hair until it shone and its long, coffee-colored tresses were full and thick, then she dabbed some perfume behind each ear. She looked in the mirror and smiled. The kimono was just right. It was simple, but exotic . . . innocent, but with a hint of wickedness!

An hour later she tood at the window impatiently, waiting for Chase. Her insides were warm and tingly, and every time she thought of the joys to come, she burst into giggles. She felt as eager and as excited as a bride on her wedding night.

She glanced behind her. A table for two was elegantly set with fine china and English goblets. A bottle of wine was chilling in a bucket, and two candles were just waiting to be lit.

Finally, after what seemed a very long time, she spotted him coming down the street. His walk had a bounce to it, and his strides were long and hurried. Good, she remarked to herself as she closed the shutter. He was just as anxious to get home as she was to have him there. She couldn't wait to see the look on his face when he walked through the door.

After checking to make sure that no last-minute preparation was overlooked, she turned down the bed and positioned herself in the center, her legs curled beneath her and her back against the mahogany headboard. Chase should be coming up the walk now, she mused, trying to envision his progress.

The front door opened and closed.

"Dare, I'm home."

Her heart skittered wildly. She fanned her hair out around her shoulders and waited, almost bursting with excitement. "I'm up here," she called out, her voice trembling.

A moment later, she heard familiar footsteps bounding up the stairs. She loosened the folds of silk around her neck and shoulders and leaned back, eyes opened wide, her rose-petal lips pursed sensuously.

The brass knob turned, and the door swung open.

"Hello, sailor," she said, her greeting hoarse and lusty.

Chase stopped just inside the door. For a moment he didn't move. Finally, his wide-open mouth lengthened into an approving smile. "Well, hello, dragon lady."

She patted the space beside her. "Care to join me?"

Before the last two words of her invitation had been uttered, he was halfway across the room, leaving a trail—shoes, cap, and jacket—behind him. "I'm not the sort of fellow who has to be asked twice." Grinning from ear to ear, he settled down in front of her, his legs crossed Indian style. "I take it we're not going out tonight?"

Her lashes fluttered coyly. "Would you be too disappointed if we stayed home?"

"Disappointed?" He lifted her hand to his mouth and kissed it. "I can think of nothing that would please me more. After all, the food at the Sea Palms is the finest in town, and the service, well, the service here is second to none," he announced, eying her with obvious delight.

"I was hoping you'd see things my way."

Two brilliant blue pools sparkled like the ocean at midday. "Was there ever any doubt in your mind?"

"No, never." She motioned to the ice bucket. "May I pour you a . . . ?"

He didn't give her a chance to complete her offer. Hot lips sought hers. "The wine right here is much more to my liking," he said between sips.

Soft moans rose in her throat as she drew him to her. God, how she loved him!

His lips set the room spinning and she spun with it.

Head tilted back, she silently pleaded with him not to stop at her mouth but to work his way down her entire length showering hundreds of kisses along the way.

A layer of silk between his teeth, he slid the soft material off one shoulder, then the other while he gently laid her back on the bed. Untying the sash, he tenderly parted the silk.

"You become more beautiful with each passing day." His eyes devoured her, sparing not one part of her body.

His mouth sought her breasts, the tip of his tongue circling the summit of each and peaking their rosy tips.

"Don't forget this one," she said, her words barely

a whisper as she offered him her left breast.

"I won't," he returned, cupping the warm flesh between his hands. "I certainly wouldn't want this one to get jealous, now would I?"

She closed her eyes, luxuriating in the wonderful sensations he was arousing in her.

When she finally opened her eyes, he was unbuttoning his shirt. "Don't. Let me," she insisted as she took over the task his fingers had begun.

Wriggling free of his shirt, he looked deep in her eyes and then kissed her probingly before his lips and tongue traced a fiery path down to the spot he had been caressing moments earlier.

Once again, she found herself lying flat on her back while his devastating tongue explored her. Finally, she could endure the pleasurable torment no longer. "Chase . . . my darling," she whispered. "Please, make love to me. It's been so long."

"Too long," he agreed as he rid himself of his trousers. "What a fool I've been for taking my problems to bed instead of you."

"Then why don't we make up for all those wasted hours tonight?" she suggested, leading him into the curve of her thighs.

"You luscious vixen! How could I refuse you anything?"

Chuckling ever so softly, she wrapped her legs tightly around his. She did not doubt that next week she'd be in Washington with him.

Her body melted into his, his skin lapping up hers. Nothing else mattered. He was her world; he was her life. Each yielding to the other, they were one, two separate entities joined together by the unbridled desire they shared. Her body was his, his hers. The hot blood coursing through her veins had only seconds before been routed through his. The sweat forming on his sun-bleached brow had first beaded on hers, and the beat of his heart and the rhythm of her pulse were one and the same. One moment his powerful body robbed her of energy. The next he replenished it with his strength. Even if she were never to be loved again, memories of moments like these would last a lifetime.

Surrendering gladly to his skillful love-making, she writhed beneath him, longing for utter satisfaction. With an urgency rivaling his own, she drew him deeper into her. She wanted him to have all of her. Only he could give her the pleasure she sought. Only he could take her to the clouds and let her float back to earth. Only he . . .

Her eyes heavy with desire, hooded closed as the lovers succumbed totally to the passion overwhelming them. A moment later, a colorburst of stars exploded before her eyes. Her body knew only the sensations flooding through it and then she was being hurled into oblivion.

Slowly she returned to lie silently in his arms. Had she known how to phrase what she was feeling at that instant, she doubted she would have had the strength to say it. They drifted into sleep and woke in about an hour, neither knowing which one had stirred first.

"Now that we've had our appetizer, shall we adjourn to the table for the rest of our meal?" she suggested.

"Appetizer?" repeated Chase. The hand nearest her began stroking the territory he had just claimed with an unmistakable possessiveness. "Honey, I just had a seven-course gourmet meal." He bridged her legs with his. "I have a better idea. Why don't we just stay right here and I'll serve us supper in bed?" Head lowered, he kissed the pink crests topping her breasts. "That way when it comes time for dessert, we'll already be here. Agreed?"

Her nod was an enthusiastic as her smile. She couldn't have planned the evening better. Something told her that he wouldn't be the least bit annoyed when he learned that Calpurnia had forgotten to whip up a dessert.

Chapter Twenty

Dressed in a stylish, three-piece tailored suit Chase had insisted on buying for her during a shopping spree in Atlanta, Dare sat in a high-backed, velvet chair in the dining car, sipping hot tea. Washington, Washington, Washington chugged the locomotive as it labored along the tracks toward their destination. Even though she was nearly there, she still couldn't believe her good fortune. She was en route to the nation's capital with Chase. A few minutes ago the conductor had passed through the car announcing the estimated time of arrival: one o'clock, right after lunch. They had just come through the mining town of Wheeling, West Virginia, as they sat down to breakfast. It wouldn't be long now!

She was so excited, she could hardly eat her fried potatoes and eggs, but Chase was having no trouble at all putting away his waffles and sausages. Occasionally he glanced over the top of his newspaper and winked. How lucky she was to have him! More than one person had remarked that they looked so happy, they had to be newlyweds. Chase had not corrected them, and neither had she. She really did feel as if they were on their honeymoon.

The past five days had been like a wonderful dream. Snug and cozy in a sleeping compartment that encouraged togetherness, they had made love each night as the wheels rolling over the tracks drowned out her cries of ecstasy.

She smiled to herself as she remembered that it hadn't taken much persuasion to wangle an invitation from Chase. Her feminine wiles had seen to that! Two days before he was scheduled to sail from Key West to Tampa where he was to board the train, he had finally gotten around to breaking the news to her that he had been called to Washington to deliver his final report to Roosevelt regarding the Cuban situation and the tragedy that had befallen the *Maine*. The prospect of his leaving seemed just as dismal to him as it did to her, and when she'd casually suggested she would love to see the cherry blossoms in bloom, he had replied that there was no time like the present. Uriah had moved into the Sea Palms the day before she left, and with him and Calpurnia looking after it, she had no qualms about taking a short vacation. With those two in charge, the resort couldn't be in better hands. No sooner had Uriah dropped his bags on the front porch than he was out drumming up business—reporters and Navy wives who had traveled south to be near their husbands. Her life was finally getting back to normal, and she had Chase to thank for that. If it took the rest of her life to pay him back, she wouldn't mind.

She had seen so much of the South the past few days, and Chase had proved an excellent guide. She would have been content to curl up on one of the big, soft lounges while the scenery unfolded before her eyes. But Chase had taken it upon himself to give her geography lessons and to throw in a history lesson or two.

Gainesville's rolling hills and its white-fenced pastures in which horses raced the train gave way to the red clay flatlands of Macon on the first day of their journey north. Vast expanses of lush greenery marked the sites where old cotton plantations had once stood. Reaching Atlanta had proved delightful. It was a city in full bloom. Gardens alive with flowering peach trees, dogwoods, and azaleas provided settings more spectacular than the solid gold dome topping the capitol building. A four-hour stopover had given them a chance to explore the city firsthand, and they had visited the finest women's shop where Chase had insisted on purchasing nearly every outfit she tried on. That night the climb from North Georgia to Chattanooga was so steep the train almost stopped as it huffed and puffed its way into Tennessee. She had awakened more than once, frightened that the train, unable to make the hills, was speeding back down the slopes. But the train had made it into the long tunnels cut through the sides of the West Virginia mountains and had headed on into the coal fields. Indeed, the smoke from the coal mines had been left billowing behind them only a few hours before.

As Dare realized how close they were to Washington, her excitement mounted. They were almost there. Next stop, Washington.

Chase folded the newspaper and reached across the table for her hands. "Know something? I'm glad you coerced me into bringing you along."

"Just who coerced who? You're the one who did the inviting, and don't you forget that!"

"True," he agreed, "but let's not forget that you were the one who did all the arm twisting."

Her mouth flew open. "Why, Chase Hamilton! You ought to be ashamed of yourself for saying such things. I didn't pressure you and you know it."

"You're right. Poor choice of words." He leaned across his plate. Glancing at the table across from them, he lowered his voice. "But you can't deny the fact that you did take advantage of me when I was most vulnerable."

Her chuckle faded to a concerned sigh. "What if your family doesn't like me?"

"What if they do?"

"I'm serious, Chase. That really does have me a bit worried."

He warmed her hands between his. "Why shouldn't they like you? You're beautiful, sweet, witty, brave . . . not to mention the fact that you saved their darling son from Neptune's evil clutches." He blew her a kiss. "You worry too much, my angel. Trust me. They will love you. Just as much as I do. I promise."

"And what about Vanessa?" Mischievous sparkles danced in her violet eyes. "Think she'll love me, too?"

"Let's not push our luck."

"Chase, tell me something. Did you ever? . . ." She hesitated. There was no tactful way to ask what she wanted to know. "What I mean is, you and Nessa, did the two of you ever? . . ."

"No. Never," he answered before she had a chance to complete her question. "I could no more go to bed with her than I could with my sister, if I had one."

"Speaking of beds, what sort of sleeping arrangements do you think we'll have at your home?"

He chuckled. "Obviously not what we're used to. However I feel certain between the two of us we can find a solution to the dilemma of separate beds."

She suppressed her giggles when the waiter came to collect the plates. Imagining Chase tiptoeing from one end of the corridor to the other, like a thief in his own house, set her off again.

"For that reason," he began, kissing the palm of each of her hands, "I think we should make good use of the present sleeping arrangements."

She was quick to agree. "By all means. So do I."

Once again she had to struggle to keep from bursting into laughter because most of their sleeping had been done in the observation car.

Taking a deep breath, she pushed herself back from the table, her silly grin replaced by a serious mature look. She stole a glance at the matronly woman beside her, then cleared her throat. "Do be a dear and escort me back to our quarters," she told Chase, fanning herself with her napkin. "I feel another of my deadful headaches coming on."

He was quick to catch on. "Why, of course, dearest. A little nap is just what you need then," he said, pulling out her chair.

"A little nap is not exactly what I had in mind!" she exclaimed, throwing her arms around him the moment their door closed.

"It isn't?"

She slipped his jacket off his shoulders. "Heavens no! Who'd want to sleep when there are far more stimulating activities to engage in."

Leaning against the door, he unbuttoned his left cuff. "For instance?"

"Oh, I thought I might do a little reading." She stepped out of her skirt. "Maybe even a little embroidering."

He took a step toward her. "But that will only make your head ache even more."

Closing the distance between them, she reached for his belt and unclasped the buckle. "Have you any suggestions?"

"No, not right this minute." He took the pins out of her hair and let it fall in a long silken mass, then he fluffed it out around her shoulders. "But I feel certain if we put our heads together, we'll come up with something."

Her lips lightly brushed his. "Yes, you're clever."

"I've been told that," he said as he stepped out of his trousers and into her arms. "And on more than one occasion, I might add."

"Mmmm. I wouldn't doubt that for a moment." Her arms slowly wound around him.

A devilish sparkle in his eyes, he motioned to the tiny bed. "Shall we?"

Still hanging on to him, she took a few steps back. "Who am I to deny you anything?"

"Ah, the perfect woman." With tenderness, he set

her on the bed. "And to think, all these years I've assumed there was no such thing."

"I'm the exception, not the rule," she said, welcoming his weight gladly.

"You're telling me."

Her heart hammered against her chest with such force that she thought it would burst through her ribs. When he smothered her with his virility she lost all self-control. One kiss and she was suddenly transformed into a woman who would stop at nothing to bring pleasure to her man. Her inhibitions had been wiped away that first night when he had made her a woman in every sense of the word. But even a woman specially trained in the art of love-making could not have given or received more pleasure.

A light tap sounded at the door.

Chase made no attempt to alter his position. "Yes?"

Dare had to stuff the corner of the quilt into her mouth to keep from laughing hysterically.

"It's Louis, suh, yore porter."

Eager, adventuresome fingers explored the velvet soft tuft between her thighs. "Would it be too much of an imposition to have you come back in, say, an hour or so? Mrs. Hamilton is quite ill at the moment."

Mrs. Hamilton! The name had a wonderful ring to it. Mrs. Chase Hamilton. Dare Hamilton. How lovely they both sounded. Perhaps one day . . . She sighed happily to herself.

"No imposition, suh. None a'tall. Can I bring yer missus any medicine?"

Chase's eyes melted into Dare's. "No, thank you.

She has all the medicine she needs right here."

"Very well, suh. Hope yuh feel better, m'am."

"Thank you. I'm sure I will," she said, trying to make her voice frail. As soon as the footsteps faded, she maneuvered herself over him and began to move up and down very, very slowly, her movements setting the pace for his.

"I do believe I've discovered the sure-fire remedy for headaches," she said, her words interspersed with gasps.

"We might even go so far as to say that you have come upon a universal cure for whatever ails you." Smiling, he rolled her back over without missing a beat. Then his strokes became harder and faster.

An hour later, still warm and moist from their love-making, Dare glided back into the coach, her arm looped through his.

A pink glove reached out for her midway down the aisle. "Feeling better, dear?" asked a heavy-set woman.

Recognizing her as the lady who had sat opposite her in the dining car, Dare smiled politely and touched her temple. "Oh, yes. Much, much better, thank you. A little rest makes me as good as new."

"Oh, I'm so glad," she heard the woman say.

"So am I," whispered Chase as they made their way to their seats.

The remainder of the morning seemed to drag by. Midmorning tea and coffee was followed by a lunch of salt beef and cabbage. Dare could hardly do more than pick at her food. How she hoped Chase's family liked her! What if they didn't approve of her? What then? She chuckled. One would have thought she were meeting her perspective in-laws. Maybe she was! She could hope. All the more reason to make a good impression, she told herself, vowing to be the perfect lady.

She fidgeted in her seat. Unfortunately being the perfect lady required that she wear a corset. According to everything she had read about ladies' fashions, no lady of decency would be caught in public without one on. Women in Key West were so much more practical than their northern counterparts, she decided. Fashion was more often than not sacrificed for comfort's sake. There, the tropical temperature prevented them from wearing anything more than a drawstring petticoat and a camisole under their garments.

Would she ever be able to take one good, deep breath during her stay in the nation's capital, she wondered. A hand reached protectively for her stomach. More than once during the course of her trip, she had felt a bit faint. Still, making a good impression on Chase's parents was incentive enough to endure this discomfort for as long as necessary, providing little Chase was in no danger of being suffocated!

She chuckled softly. Little Chase! What would she do if he turned out to be a girl?

Head turned away from Chase, she pretended to be engrossed in a scene outside the window. How could she possibly explain to him why she was giggling, she mused, a big grin on her face.

From a distance, it seemed that the entire city of Washington had dressed up in its Sunday best just to greet her. Blooming cherry trees canopied the last quarter-mile of track with an awning of pale pink petals.

At last, the moment she'd been awaiting had arrived. The train reduced its speed until it was barely moving. After a few jolts and several sharp screeches, the brakes locked and the whistle of steam announced their arrival.

Dare stood. One hand pulled at her skirt while the other tugged at the smoke gray strip of velvet cuffing her jacket's sleeves.

Chase observed her with a smile. "Just be yourself, my love." With that bit of advice, he hooked his arm through hers.

Frowning, she examined her reflection in the window one more time. "Are you sure I look all right?" she asked, smoothing the powder blue frill on her blouse.

"You do not." He kissed the tip of her ear. "You look stunning. Absolutely, beyond a shadow of a doubt, positively stunning. Ready?"

She took as deep a breath as her supporting undergarment would allow. "Ready as I'll ever be."

"That's my girl."

Head held high, she stepped off the train into the beehive of activity outside. On the tracks opposite theirs, trains were getting up steam. One smartly dressed conductor was threading his way through the crowds swinging the chain of his pocket watch and barking loudly, "All aboard. Baltimore, New York express. All aboard."

Gentlemen wearing high stiff collars that held their necks rigid and ladies who looked as if they had just stepped from the pages of a fashion book hurried about, rushing to catch their trains.

"I wired the admiral and told him to expect us," shouted Chase, patting her hand. "He's in this mob

338

somewhere, I expect."

Dare nodded her acknowledgment. She could scarcely hear herself think, much less carry on a conversation. The admiral. How strange to address one's father by his naval rank. She grinned. No stranger than her calling her father Mac.

Eyes wide and alert, not wanting to miss a single thing, she held tight to Chase as they made their way up a long flight of stairs. She found herself in a large, open area which seemed to be built in old, Southern colonial style with ornate, white granite columns supporting a high ceiling.

The commotion inside the station was even more chaotic than on the red-bricked walkways outside. Shoeshine boys were spit-polishing shoes right on the spot. Newspaper boys, food vendors, and tobacco dealers sold and collected for their products without causing their customers to miss a single step. Quite a change from the easy, laid back atmosphere in which she had spent her whole life.

The almost frantic hustle and bustle around her made her cling even tighter to Chase's arm. Everyone seemed to be moving purposefully. No one was just ambling along enjoying the scenery. No one stopped; no one chatted. Eyes focused in front of them, these people went about their business with methodical precision, all but running over each other as they went on their way.

Never before had she been exposed to such a hodgepodge of people. How cosmopolitan it all seemed! Washington was surely a melting pot for all cultures, for nearly all nations were represented right here in the station. She supposed that stemmed from the fact that after the Civil War, the United States had risen from the fifth to the first nation in the world and as a result, immigrants flocked to big cities to look for work.

Dare paused for a moment to take everything in. How incredible her surroundings seemed; how naive she had been to think that life in Key West was representative of life anywhere else in the United States.

She shook her head in disbelief a few moments later. "Well, would you look at that!"

"What?" asked Chase, glancing around to see what had aroused her attention.

She pointed to three doors standing alongside each other and read the signs on each aloud. "Ladies . . . Gentlemen . . . Coloreds."

"What do you find so amusing about signs on washroom doors?" he asked, taking her arm.

She chuckled. "All that talk about equality! To think, you Yanks freed the slaves from us Simon Legrees and then when they came North you decided they weren't equal after all."

"I believe the proper terminology is equal but separate."

"Oh, I see." Her grin broadened. "I'm surprised you all just didn't up and decide that some of us are just a little bit more equal than others."

"Point well made." His right arm encircling her waist, he squeezed her close. "If I were you, I'd go a little easy on the you alls. You are in enemy territory, my Southern belle."

Her lashes fluttered. "Ah, but suh, I have you to protect me."

"Wait right here."

Before she could question his motives, he had

abandoned her, leaving her beside one of the white granite columns. When he returned a moment later, one hand was held behind his back.

"For you," he said, presenting her with a little bouquet of violets. "Flowers for a flower."

"Oh, Chase. They're beautiful." She kissed the tip of his chin. "So are you."

He pinned the bouquet to her jacket's velvet lapel. "There. Nothing's too good for my violet-eyed beauty."

"You're so wonderful." Sighing, she snuggled close to him. To heck with what Calpurnia said about public displays of affection. "I love you so much."

"Not as much as I love you."

Her smile spread. Care to make a bet on that? she was about to ask when he suddenly lifted his arm and waved.

Dare looked up. Standing at the far exit was an older man sporting a huge goatee and a snow-white moustache. She knew instantly that he had to be the famous admiral she had heard so much about, a man adored by his friends and respected by his enemies, Chase had said.

Her pulsebeat doubled. She'd settle for just a bit of kindness from him and his wife. Wondering where Mrs. Hamilton was and deciding that the admiral looked harmless enough, she lengthened her strides to keep up with Chase.

The admiral made his way toward them, his hand pressed against his left side as though he were in some sort of discomfort. According to Chase, a rowdy boys' game had left an arrowhead lodged in his side, and there it had remained for half a century.

"Chase, my boy. Glad to see you!" he exclaimed in between the handshake and the hug. "Your mother couldn't come. She's a little under the weather. Sends her love, though, and said to tell you she'd see you at supper."

Dare stood patiently by, not wanting to interrupt the father-son reunion and waiting until Chase held out his arm to her before making the move to join them.

The admiral's eyes, an even deeper shade of blue than this son's, caught a sparkle of light when Chase made the introductions. "I was wondering when you were going to get around to doing the honors." He gave a decorous bow. "From Chase's letters, I feel as though I know you already. I must say if I were twenty years younger I'd send the boy home alone."

Dare was thrilled. She hadn't expected so pleasant a surprise. "I can't tell you how happy I am to meet you, Mister Hamilton, sir," she said, succumbing to an urge to kiss his plump cheek. "I can see now why Chase is such a charmer."

Her remark obviously pleased him. "Mr. Hamilton, sir—pshaw! Call me Admiral." He gave her a little nudge. "You can even call me Horace if you'd like, though God knows why my mama saddled a tyke with a name like that." He threw his arms around her. "Welcome to Washington, Dare." He winked over his shoulder at his son. "Southern women! Can't beat them. You don't mind if we forgo the formalities, do you Dare?" he asked, giving her another kiss. "I always told my son, go to sea to find adventure, and go South to find a woman. I can see now that he took my advice in both instances."

Dare returned his hug with genuine affection. She

342

couldn't stop grinning. Just as Chase had promised, she had fallen in love with the admiral instantly. How silly she had been to worry about him being a rough and tough ogre who ruled his family with an iron hand. "You're every bit as wonderful as your son said you were," she couldn't resist telling him.

"And so are you!" he returned jovially. "Not many heroines in the world, and I'm glad my son managed to latch on to one of them."

She beamed from ear to ear. "There aren't many knights in shining armor left in the nineteenth century," she said, taking hold of Chase's arm. "Thank heavens I found one who even has a little rebel blood in him."

"Oh, Chase! Chase!" called a feminine voice from behind them.

"Looks like the rest of the welcoming committee has arrived." The admiral grazed a knuckle over Dare's chin. "Though I can't say I expect her to be all that pleased to see you," he said chuckling.

Dare's smile wilted and her heart almost stopped beating. There was no mistaking the identity of the young woman who had just floated into the station as if she were making a grand entrance at a high society ball. Nessa's picture definitely did not do her justice. She was ten times more beautiful in person. Wasp-waisted and puff-shouldered, she had the figure of a Gibson girl. Heads turned as she walked by. Men were obviously in awe of such a creature. How could they help but be? Dare wondered unhappily.

How dowdy I must look by comparison, mused Dare. Her own gray traveling suit that she had thought so fashionable struck her as something a matron would wear once she'd seen Chase's old love glide into the room in a mint green gown, and with an ostrich plume of the same color curled in the top of her slant-brimmed hat.

She looked at Chase, studying his reaction. Was it her imagination or had his face really lit up at the sight of Nessa? Were the words resounding in her head echoing in his as well? *Yours forever. Yours forever. Yours forever.*

"Oh, Chase, darling, darling, welcome home," exclaimed Nessa, her arms winding tightly around his neck. "I've missed you terribly. What a cad you are to keep popping in and out of my life at a moment's notice." She kissed him hard on the center of his mouth. "Mmmmmm," she exclaimed, smacking her lips. "I can see right now I'm going to have to have a nice, long talk with Uncle Teddy and convince him to let me keep you here for a while. Washington is just not the same without you." To emphasize her point, she gave him another kiss, this one even harder and longer.

Chase looked at Dare as if to say, What am I supposed to do? "Hello, Nessa. Beautiful as ever, I see," he said, his enthusiasm held to a minimum.

Dare cringed, and her temperature suddenly shot up. A kiss like that was definitely not the kind a sister would give her brother, nor was the look of total devotion in Nessa's partially hooded eyes. She couldn't really tell whether Chase was embarrassed or amused by Nessa's brazen display of affection. One thing was obvious, Miss Nessa Sterling had no intention of acknowledging Dare's presence. To her Dare MacDade was nothing more than an intruder.

Finally Chase nodded in Dare's direction, and

when his arm possessively encircled her waist, Dare breathed a sigh of relief. She snuggled close to him. After all, what had she expected? That he would ignore her, or worse still pretend she was just someone he had assisted in getting off the train?

At last Nessa turned to her, her manner cooling considerably. "When the admiral told me Chase was bringing home a friend, I had no idea that friend would be someone other than a Navy buddy." Her amber eyes blazed. "My name is Vanessa Sterling," she said, her sugar-coated voice spiced with vinegar. "But then I suppose he's told you all about me."

Dare offered her hand. She was determined not to be made a fool of. "Why, no, he hasn't," she said, smiling sweetly. "As a matter of fact, I don't recall him mentioning anything about you." She could have sworn she heard the admiral stifle a chuckle. "But no matter. My name's Dare MacDade, and I am very pleased to meet you." She lifted her head triumphantly. There! She could hold her own, even with a Washington socialite!

For a moment, Nessa looked as though she didn't know quite how to react. She took Dare's hand, gave it a weak shake, and released it quickly, almost as though she were afraid of contracting some horrible Southern disease. She repeated her name. "Dare, hummm. What an unusual name for a girl."

Chase's eyes glowed with love when his gaze left Nessa and focused on Dare. "An unusual name for a most unusual woman."

Trunks and bags collected, the four of them headed toward the huge, glass doors.

Nessa offered Chase her arm.

The admiral took hold of it instead. "Come along,

everyone. There are sights in Washington far more exciting than the depot. Isn't that right, Vanessa, dear?"

While the admiral hailed a cab and Nessa complained about the delay, Chase drew Dare close. His warm breath fanned her cheeks, and his whispers made her shiver. "I know what you're thinking, and you're wrong!"

Dare bit her lip to keep from smiling. She had to admit the thought had crossed her mind. "Oh, am I?" she asked, keeping her eyes focused straight ahead on a WELCOME TO THE NATION'S CAPITAL banner strung across the front of the building opposite the station.

His hold around her middle tightened. "Friends. That's all she and I ever were. I give you my word."

His thumb was inching up. Keeping a straight face became increasingly difficult for Dare as the thumb rose even more. "Your word? You mean your word as an officer and a gentleman."

He nodded. "Absolutely."

She turned to him. Her face expressionless save for the slight arch of one brow. "How about the word of Matthew Colby, reporter *extraordinaire*." Her stoic look gave way to a smile. "What do you suppose that's worth these days?"

His words drifted lightly through her hair. "You just wait until I get you home."

"I can hardly wait." Her answer was less than enthusiastic. "You'll go to your room, and I to mine. What fun!"

"You're wrong there," he said, straightening his stance as their cab pulled to the curb. "The fun starts afterward. Guarantee it!''

It was nearly five o'clock by the time their whirlwind tour of the city was completed and the cab pulled up in front of a colonial-style residence that looked more like an ancestral home than the stately mansion she had envisioned. Although Chase had never come right out and said so, she had suspected all along that the Hamiltons were no average, run-of-the-mill Navy family, but she certainly had not expected their home to be so grand.

A pair of servants dressed in identical white outfits and wearing black bow ties unloaded their bags and carried them on ahead.

''I suspect you'll be wanting to freshen up a bit, my dear,'' remarked the admiral, one arm around her, the other around his son. ''Why don't you show her to the guest suite, my boy, and I'll go see if Mother's up and about. We can make the proper introductions later. Say, in about an hour or so?'' Hands stuffed into his pockets, he strolled away, but not before giving his son a sharp glance.

''What was all that about?'' queried Dare, laughing as they climbed the marble staircase.

Chase tucked his arm around her waist. ''Ah, ha. So that sly glance of his didn't go unnoticed after all.''

''You bet it didn't. Now, 'fess up.''

''Oh, I wouldn't be too concerned if I were you,'' advised Chase as caressing fingers inched their way up her side. ''After all, he was a Navy man himself!''

A moment later, he nodded to the door on her right.

"That's the guest suite," he said as he kept on walking.

Butterflies flitted wildly in her stomach. "Might I be so bold as to inquire where you're taking me?"

"To my room, of course. After all, I did guarantee you lots of fun and excitement." He nibbled on her ear. "Any objections?"

She snuggled close. "Nary a one!"

"Good." He pushed a door open and, swooping her up in his arms, swung her over the threshold and deposited her inside.

She burrowed her head deep into the lapel of his coat to keep from rousing the entire household with her laughter.

Their clothes were quickly discarded and they reached hungrily for the other, falling onto the bed in a tangled mass of bare, hot flesh. Words of longing rushed from their mouths while their hands explored and excited each other's bodies.

Her fingers made brazen by the wanton stirrings inside her, she let her hand stray down over his chest to the curly mat of tendrils that led to the source of her pleasure. His maleness was hard and ready. Passion pulsated through it.

In a moment his lips sought her female center, leaving nothing untasted. She could think of no words to describe the sensations shooting through her. She wanted to lie back and be inundated by his manliness.

Smiling, Chase slid back up, his sensuous frame gliding over her and promising still more pleasure. Her love spilled out to him, and slowly, ever so slowly, he once again began to arouse her most secret of places.

Chapter Twenty-One

Dare fell across her bed, exhausted by another afternoon of shopping and sightseeing. Where on earth had she ever gotten the notion that Chase's mother was a frail, sickly sort of woman who had more bad days than good? When the admiral had met them at the station nearly a week ago and apologized for his wife's absence, saying that she was under the weather, Dare had immediately envisioned someone who lounged in bed all morning with a cold compress on her head and a bottle of Doctor Hostetter's Celebrated Stomach Bitters within arm's reach. How wrong she had been!

Pale and willowy, with dark shadows under her eyes, Mrs. Hamilton appeared to be anything but the picture of health. However, after seeing her in action, Dare had decided that athletic would be a fit adjective for her. The woman was a powerhouse of energy. When everyone else was ready for a rest, she was still going strong. A real talker, she stopped only long enough to catch her breath. The poor admiral couldn't get a word in edgewise.

Nevertheless, Dare had fallen in love with Chase's mother, who had informed her only a few minutes after formal introductions had been made that she would prefer to be called Mattie, not Mrs. Hamilton. From that moment on the two of them were fast friends.

Chase spent every day on Capitol Hill conferring with Secretary Long and Assistant Secretary Roosevelt, who she later learned just happened to be Nessa's uncle. Even with Chase's busy schedule, she hadn't found time to be bored. Five minutes after the noon meals were over, Mattie was going out the door, a purse in one hand and Dare in the other.

The prescription for good health and a long life, according to Mattie, was never to ride when you could walk. With that in mind, Monday, Tuesday, and Wednesday had been devoted to touring the city on foot. One had to be a marathon runner to keep up with Mattie. Stomach in, chest out, head up, and legs extended in a brisk stride, she trotted up and down the avenues which had been designed to converge on Pennsylvania Avenue.

Mattie, it turned out, was a walking encyclopedia on Washington, and after three days of her lecturing, Dare felt she knew as much, or more, about the city's history as many Washingtonians. The United States, she had learned, was the first nation in the world to plan a capital city exclusively for the government seat, and the city which resulted had been named in honor of the nation's first president.

The first point of interest they had visited had been

the Capitol, which was set on the brow of a hill above the Potomac. Its central building, constructed of Virginia sandstone, had a statue of freedom poised atop the iron dome surmounting it. The extension wings, marble edifices, were the home of the Senate and the House.

From there, they had walked to the executive mansion. According to Mattie, the two-story home of the president had been painted white to hide the fire marks that resulted when the British had attacked it some eighty years before.

Quite a few points of interest could be seen from Dare's bedroom window, especially the obelisk-shaped Washington Monument that dominated the entire skyline of the city. Mattie had pointed out the places on the surrounding hills where defense forts had been built during the Civil War to protect the city from a Confederate invasion. The war itself always had been and always would be a sore subject in the Hamilton family, Mattie had informed Dare in a voice that still retained its Deep South drawl.

After the historical tour, Mattie had taken Dare on a tour of the ladies' garment district where the items manufactured and sold included the latest gowns from Paris, pongee silk parasols, and bloomers that looked like Turkish harem pants. Convinced that Mattie was making purchases for a niece whose family had fallen on hard times, Dare had agreed to model any outfits that appealed to her only to find these clothes boxed and sitting atop her bed when she arrived home.

Sighing wearily, but contentedly, Dare swung her legs from the bed to the Oriental rug carpeting the room. There was really no time for fatigue. In another three hours she was to be a guest at the Sterlings' dinner party. The President himself had been invited, or so Mattie had said. Although Dare would like nothing better than to "develop" a splitting headache and stay home, she knew Chase would be expected to attend anyway, so she would be left at home wondering just what Nessa was up to. The ashen-haired vamp had made no bones about it; Chase was hers! The poisonous glares she targeted at Dare from time to time were murderous. Dare trusted Chase implicitly. It was Nessa she worried about. The way Roosevelt's niece saw it, she'd had Chase first, and her hold on him was permanent, the till-death-do-us-part kind.

Chase was a big boy, and he could take care of himself, but there was no sense in putting temptation in the way of a handsome, healthy, and virile man, Dare reasoned.

Rising to her feet, a smile on her face, she surveyed her surroundings, her home away from home. She missed the Sea Palms terribly, but she really had become quite fond of the room Mattie had given her. Plump pillows, cushions, and spreads—all a corn-flower blue which reminded her of Chase's vibrant eyes—covered her bed, the settee, and the chairs. Getting used to the tassels and curlicues adorning the dark oak pieces had taken some doing, but once she'd become accustomed to the more contemporary styles of decorating, she found she felt at home.

Her room was so conveniently close to Chase's, she could not help but wonder if the sleeping arrangements had been deliberate or coincidental. Surely the admiral and his wife suspected the relationship was more than platonic, but they hadn't made an issue of that. She was glad, for she had come to love and respect Chase's parents. It didn't take someone with a keen perception to see that they thought just as much of her, and she wouldn't want anything to lessen their opinion of her.

How silly she had been to worry they'd have no time alone during their stay in Washington. As it turned out, they were spending even more hours together than they'd shared in Key West the week before they'd left. He came to her room every evening following an after dinner cigar with his father and he left in time to be found in his own bed when the admiral appeared for the early morning father-son chat which had become a ritual over the years. When he arrived in the late afternoon after his meetings on the hill, he'd slip into her room and stay until it was time to dress for dinner, then they'd meet in the parlor over a chaste, innocent kiss in front of the old folks.

A subtle tap at the door told her that this evening was no exception. Her fatigue vanished at once. With renewed strength, she flung open the door and fell into his arms. The kiss they shared was long and hard and deep, the kind one would expect after a much longer separation.

Later as they lay in each other's arms, Chase asked, "What exciting adventures did my mother direct you on today?"

Dare rolled over onto the pillow. "Mattie took me to a meeting at her ladies' club."

"That's my Mattie for you. Always has her son's best interests at heart. I suppose you learned how to make a man's home his castle. Correct?"

"Not exactly." She burrowed even closer. How safe

and secure she felt ensconced in his arms. "Actually, I learned how to become a totally liberated woman."

His response was one of mild amusement. "You what?"

She nodded. "You heard me right. Making the home a castle and a man its king was not on the agenda. As a matter of fact, neither was anything else having to do with the traditional role of woman." She sat back up. "In case you're interested, the topic of today's lecture was abandoning childrearing for a career."

"Sounds like Stanton and Anthony are at it again. Well, what did you think?"

"Personally, I think it's a lot of fuss over nothing. There's no reason why a woman can't have a family and a career. I know that when I . . ." She stopped suddenly, her face turning several shades of red.

"When you what?"

She gave a few indifferent shrugs of the shoulder. "When I marry and have children, I still want to have an active interest in the Sea Palms." She held her breath and waited for a response, hopefully one that included a proposal. When none came, she settled down beside him. The person who described patience as a virtue was definitely not waiting for the father of her child to propose.

"Did you do anything else interesting?" he asked, bundling her close.

She gave way to a smile in spite of herself. Poor Chase, he had no idea of what was going on. She could not blame him for her well-kept secrets.

"Nothing as interesting as you are," she replied as he drew little heart-shaped designs over the satiny breast nearest him.

"You've no idea, my love, just how glad I am you said that." Starting at her mouth and proceeding ever so slowly, he nipped a trail of kisses between her rose-crested hills, his lips descending caressingly to further excite her. Then, worshipping her body with lips that nibbled and teased, and his hands which pampered every curve and rise, he retraced the path just taken.

Her flesh came alive under the hot wetness of his lips and the mastery of his touch. No longer was she in control of her own body. It hollowed and arched in response to his, twisting and turning at the pleasure he so expertly bestowed. What power he had over her! Smiling ever so softly, she reached for him. He wasn't the only one who wielded power. Her position could hardly be described as vulnerable.

Pinioned beneath him, crushed by the wonderful force of his weight, she permitted herself one moment of luxuriating in his arms. How she loved getting drunk on the manly essence he exuded! Her emotions drugged and senses intoxicated, she felt that she could float all the way down to the Keys on her euphoric cloud.

Another moment she delayed, indulging herself deliciously, then she clamped both legs around him tightly and, desire pulsing through her, she arched high to meet his entry. He was a most welcome guest, and the reception she intended to give him would be unlike any other he had ever received, just as his love-making, though familiar, had new and exciting elements so that each time was more explosive than the last.

She gave of herself freely and proudly, refraining from nothing, and desiring only his total satisfaction in return. Her name a continuous moan on his lips, he drove himself home, to the place where he belonged at that moment and forever. Her fervency grew as he plunged deeper, pleasuring and tormenting her until they scaled peaks of pleasure seldom attained by mere mortals.

When she awakened from the sleep that had claimed her, Chase was leaning over her, fully dressed, planting a row of kisses across her breasts.

"Time to get ready for the party, sweetheart," he whispered, his breath warm and sweet against her skin.

"Anything you say, my darling."

"Oh, if Susan B. Anthony could hear you now!" He blew her a kiss on his way out, then closed the door softly behind him.

A knock sounded a short while later as she was making last-minute touches to her appearance.

"It's just me, dear," called out Mattie.

"It's open," Dare replied, struggling to fasten the row of snaps closing the back of her evening gown.

"Here, let me help you," offered Mattie, peach silk rustling as she rushed to help. "There. How's that?"

"Thanks," Dare smiled gratefully. "I'm afraid left to my own devices, I'd have been in here all night."

"Oh, Chase would have lent you a hand, I'm sure. You look stunning, my dear," Mattie exclaimed without giving Dare a chance to determine whether her previous remark had been as casual as it seemed. "Absolutely stunning!" Taking Dare in hand, she walked her over to the mirror. "What do you think?"

Dare was speechless. She could hardly believe the reflection staring back at her was her own. Very few girlish traits remained. She really had bloomed into a striking-looking woman ever since the first of the year. Of course she herself couldn't take all the credit for the change. Chase deserved a great deal of it. Being in love had brought a rosy hue to her cheeks and a sparkle to her eyes.

Not even Nessa with all her Parisian finery would be able to hold a candle to her tonight, she vowed. Never again would that tigress make her feel dowdy and unsophisticated. She could hold her own with any woman, Roosevelt's niece included!

Her hairdo was sleek, her locks brushed smoothly up in back and secured in a huge loop atop her head. Every hair was in its place. A pinch of rouge, a bit of color to define the heart shape of her mouth, and a pat or two of the powder puff had worked wonders.

Lifting her gown a bit, she whirled in front of the mirror, surveying her image from every possible angle. Try as hard as she could, she simply could not find a single flaw.

Exquisite was the only word she could find to describe her gown. Chase's big blue eyes would become even larger at the sight of it. Hopefully, he'd be so busy ogling her, he wouldn't be able to spare the energy to give Nessa the time of day. The saleslady had called it a princess gown, and it certainly was elegant enough to be worn by royalty. Cut in many gores and seams that extended from shoulder to the hem, the lavender silk clung to her hourglass curves as though it had been made just for her. Its sleeves were short, fitted puffs, and the dainty little frill sculpting the square-cut neck seemed to play peeka-boo with the ripe fullness beneath.

Something told her Mattie had directed her to the gown with this particular evening in mind. Though she had not said so, not in so many words, Chase's mother gave Dare the distinct impression that she wasn't overly fond of Nessa and would like nothing better than to see Admiral Sterling's daughter upstaged by someone else, namely her!

"My son will undoubtedly be the luckiest man at the party tonight," announced Mattie, squeezing Dare's shoulders.

"Second luckiest." She kissed the powdered cheek. "The admiral takes first honors for that."

"Oh, how you go on!" she exclaimed cheerfully, smoothing the bodice of her high-necked gown. "Shall we?"

Dare kissed her necklace for good luck. "By all means. We certainly can't keep our charming escorts waiting, now can we?"

Both the admiral and his son stood at attention when they walked down the stairs.

"I can see you and I are going to have ourselves quite an evening keeping these luscious creatures from being snatched right out from under our noses, my boy." The admiral lifted his wife's hand to his mouth. "My dear, you seem to get lovelier with each day that passes."

"And you, Horace, darling, are every bit as handsome now as you were that Christmas morning when you came courting me." She straightened his tie, then gave his goatee an affectionate tug. "Maybe even a tad more so."

"What's the matter, son. Cat got your tongue?" chuckled the admiral after downing the rest of his bourbon. "You were talking forty miles an hour not five minutes ago."

Chase walked slowly toward Dare, a boyish grin on his lips and a million stars aglow in his eyes. "That was before this lovely lady walked into the room. I fear she's left me all but speechless."

How patrician he looked coming toward her in his high shoes and creaseless trousers! She would have liked nothing better than to throw her arms around him and cover him with kisses, but she confined her response to a demure nod.

"Why thank you, Chase. You are most kind."

She turned up her cheek.

His lips brushed over it.

His masculine scent was so intoxicating that she almost reeled out of control.

"Please, allow me," he said, reaching for her boa.

His eyes certain to read the most intimate of her thoughts, he arranged the fluffy purple feathers around her shoulders. Lingering fingers made her bare flesh tingle with the promise of what the night had in store.

"Would that I were those diamonds and rubies," whispered Chase, his gaze centered on the expanse of smooth skin between her breasts.

An arm curved around her waist, he ushered her outside to the awaiting cab. A stolen kiss in the shadows left her feeling her legs were going to give way beneath her at any minute.

The Sterlings' butler, a rigid, unsmiling man, met them at the door of the rambling, white brick colonial. His European countenance expressionless, he took their wraps and pointed the way into the living room where most of the guests had already assembled on horsehair-covered sofas and lounges.

The Sterlings' living room could easily have been mistaken for an art museum, for paintings of all colors, shapes, and sizes—many of them idealizing women—decorated the walls. Oriental vases and pagoda-shaped ornaments rested on baroque tables, while bamboo jardinieres overflowed with wax flowers, and artists' easels displaying chromolithographs stood in every corner.

Mattie waved to one of her friends who was standing beside a monstrosity of a piano. "Lucy," she called. She tucked her arm around her husband's. "Come along, Horace. Let's leave these two lovebirds alone for a while."

Dare chuckled to herself. Alone, did she say? How on earth could that be the case in a room filled with a hundred people at least?

A waiter brought over a tray. "Champagne?"

Chase presented one of the tulip glasses to her, then reached for another. "Thank you." Smiling, he lifted his glass to hers. "May I propose a toast to the future Mrs. Hamilton?"

Deep violet eyes stared at him in disbelief. An appropriate answer would simply not come. How long she had waited to hear him say those two words, *Mrs. Hamilton!*

He was amused by her shocked expression. "Well, Miss MacDade, do you or don't you accept?"

"Why, Captain Hamilton, I would be a fool not to."

Excitement coursed through her veins. Now she could tell him of little Chase without having to worry that he would think she was trapping him.

He clicked his glass against hers. "I couldn't agree

with you more."

The tinkle of their glasses could be heard all over the room, she was sure, as could the pounding of her heart.

She sipped her champagne very, very slowly. She was already high, and she reminded herself, their child was a little young to start indulging in strong drink.

An arm around her shoulders, Chase led her to a tiny alcove the other guests had yet to find. "How do you like July the third?"

"Since it's my birthday, I like it just fine." Her grin froze. July the third was three months away. If they waited until then, she'd be five months along. Oh dear, she sighed to herself. She'd be showing for sure. "You know, darling, I'm not the least opposed to long engagements, but personally I'd like to get the formalities over as soon as possible."

"Why? We've already had our honeymoon night!" he reminded her, his teeth nipping at her ear lobe.

"Many times," she added, laughing. "But it's just that I, that I'm—"

"Afraid I'll run out the night before?" He nuzzled her neck, his warm breath raising her temperature another few degrees. "I know the Sea Palms is very, very special to you, so I'd like to be married there. We'll be living there afterward anyway."

"We'll what? Oh, Chase, you don't mean it!" she squealed delightedly as she flung her arms around him. "How—why—what happened?"

"Commander Forsyth is resigning, and I've been selected to replace him. I found out just this afternoon."

She felt as though she were going to float up right through the second floor. "That's wonderful!" she exclaimed, holding on to him to anchor herself. "I love the Sea Palms so much. Almost as much as I love you." She kissed his mouth full and hard. "But why do we have to wait three whole months? Why not get married as soon as we get home?"

"Three months isn't going to make a big difference. Married or not, we'll still be sleeping in the same bed." Another quick kiss, then he turned up his glass. "Mother and the admiral will be visiting her relatives in North Carolina along about then, so they could just come on down from there. You don't mind, do you?"

"Mind? Oh, darling, don't be ridiculous. I wouldn't dream of marrying you without Mattie and the admiral being there. Really!" She paused, seeking strength. There was simply no way around it. He had to be told!

"Chase, darling, there's something I should have told you already, but I wasn't really sure. I mean, I was sure, but I wasn't sure if I should tell you." One hand steadying the palpitations in her stomach, she took a deep breath. "You and I, I mean we . . . what I mean to say is that . . ." She sought his eyes, desperately needing his reassurance to continue. "Chase?"

He said nothing.

"Chase?" She followed the path his eyes had taken. He wasn't even listening!

A hush had fallen over the entire crowd a moment earlier, and now she knew the reason why every man, Chase included, was standing with his mouth agape.

Chapter Twenty-Two

Breezing down the stairs in a red, skin-tight gown with a plunging neckline that left very little to the imagination was Nessa. Dare sensed the reason why Nessa had chosen that exact moment to make her entrance. She thrived on being the center of attention, and at that instant, all eyes would be on her.

Her amber gaze sought Chase's immediately and her eyes stayed focused on him throughout her descent.

Chase finally managed to tear himself away from the spectacle on the stairs. "I'm sorry, darling. You were saying?"

Her heart sank. "Never mind," she said softly. "It can wait." Wait for a time when Nessa isn't around to steal the show, she mused, disheartened.

Her hips swaying suggestively, Nessa headed straight for them. "Chase, darling. Handsome as ever I see," she purred. Full, pouting lips brushed his mouth. "Hello, Dare," she said dully, her fingers toying with the brass buttons on Chase's jacket.

Gripping her glass, Dare resisted the urge to sling the champagne right onto Nessa's cleavage to cool her panting chest. She felt as though she might explode at any moment. There was no mistaking the message Nessa intended to convey. *Get away. He's all mine!* Seeing Nessa rubbing herself against Chase like a bitch in heat made Dare's blood boil. At that instant, she would have liked nothing better than to throw a temper tantrum and demand she be taken home. Good sense cautioned her to stifle her rage. Any negative reaction, and she would be playing right into Nessa's scheme. She would not be a pawn in anyone's game!

Composing herself, Dare smiled sweetly at her foe. "Nessa, darling, how chic you look!"

"Red is your favorite color, isn't it, Chase?" Turning around very slowly, her breasts thrust out, Nessa modeled her gown for him. "It's your favorite style, too. Tight and cut very, very low."

Dare cringed. The woman made her livid, acting as though she wasn't even there. Hardly an inch separated them. Nessa was so close to him. How she'd love to beat some manners into that hussy!

Chase looked red under the collar. "Honestly, Nessa, the way you're carrying on, you'll have everyone here thinking we were a hell of a lot more than friends."

"Well?" Smiling demurely, she fluttered her pale lashes.

Chase gave an uncomfortable chuckle. Returning her hands to her sides, he stepped back. "I swear,

364

Vanessa, what am I ever going to do with you?"

"Anything you like." Each syllable was clearly enunciated, leaving no doubt at all as to what she had in mind.

For the first time since she'd joined them, Nessa turned to Dare. A triumphant gleam flickered in her yellow-brown eyes.

Their hard, amber gaze reminded Dare of a cat ready to pounce and claw out the eyes of some unsuspecting creature. Catty eyes! How appropriate for a catty woman, thought Dare silently. She envisioned Nessa flexing her talons at someone who stood between her and Chase.

"Chase darling, would you mind terribly getting me a glass of champagne?"

He glanced at Dare.

She held out her glass. "Yes, I believe I'd like a glass as well."

The smile on Nessa's face lasted only until Chase's back was turned. "He and I go back a long way, and I'm not going to let you or any other little island girl take what's mine. Have I made myself clear?"

"Had I seen your brand on him, I'd have thought twice before accepting his marriage proposal."

"You're lying!" hissed Nessa. "He wouldn't marry you. Not when he can have me!"

It had taken some time, but at last Dare saw Nessa for what she really was. She wasn't a rival. She was just a spoiled, pampered child who was used to getting anything she wanted.

Dare gave her shoulders an indifferent shrug. "Might I suggest you take that matter up with him instead of me? After all, he told me something quite different."

"I don't believe you." Nessa crossed her arms. "When did he ask you?"

"Not more than five minutes ago." Dare didn't bat an eye. "As a matter of fact, he asked me as you were coming down the stairs." Give or take a few seconds, Dare mused, still smiling.

Eyes venting hate, Nessa tossed her blond head. "I wouldn't start making any wedding plans if I were you. Not just yet. I don't discard anything or anyone until I've had my fill!" Without waiting for a response, she stomped away.

"What happened to Nessa?" queried Chase when he returned with the champagne.

Dare smiled. He didn't sound the least bit concerned. "Oh, she saw someone she had to talk to." She took a sip of her drink. Until I've had my fill, Nessa had said. What could she possibly have meant by that? Still, two things were clear: she was a poor loser, and anyone who bested her would surely pay!

"Just as well." He nuzzled her cheek with the stem of his glass. "I like having you all to myself."

"Chase, old man, how the hell are you!" The ebullient voice came from across the room.

"As you were saying?" Dare watched as a droopy-mustached man headed toward them with rapid, energetic strides.

Chase shook his head. "I would have preferred a few more of these in me before going another round with him."

"Another round?" queried Dare. "Who is he?"

"Theodore Roosevelt at your service, madame." His stocky body bowed low. One eye winked behind bottle-thick glasses. "I'm positive we've never met before because if we had, I'd never have forgotten you."

"Mr. Roosevelt, I'd like you to meet my fiancée, Dare MacDade," said Chase stiffly.

"So this is the Key West beauty I've been hearing so much about? Miss MacDade, I am enchanted," he announced, reaching for her hand.

Dare sighed happily. Fiancée! What a wonderful sound that word had. "The pleasure is mine, sir," she said, realizing that the two men were waiting for her to make an appropriate remark. Fiancée! How wonderful it sounded!

"I do believe meeting you has given me just the incentive I need to put the Navy yards in the Keys first on my list of inspection." He motioned for a waiter and lifted a glass of champagne from the tray. "Ahhh." He took a long sip. "You sure know how to pick them, son. Who'd have believed it? The elusive bachelor is getting married." He took another gulp. "Hot damn! That news is sure to start a ruckus in this house." Once again he turned up his glass. "Here's to the happy couple."

"Thank you, sir," said Dare, wondering why Chase seemed none too friendly toward the man who had sent him to Key West in the first place.

"I'll tell you what, young lady," boomed Roosevelt, patting his mouth with his handkerchief. "If I were you, damned if I wouldn't stay up North awhile. Things are going to get mighty hot in Key West the next month or so."

His prediction took her by surprise. "What do you mean?"

"What do I mean? Why, Miss MacDade, we, the United States of America, are going to have us one bully little war on our hands in no time." His head thrust forward. "Yes sireee! It won't be long before we'll be a having us a war!"

"Aren't you being just a little overzealous?" Chase spoke up. "After all, the president has yet to—"

"President? You call that white-livered cur a President." Roosevelt's jaw muscles worked furiously. "Why he has about as much backbone as a chocolate éclair. A president with any gumption at all would already have given the command to invade that miserable hellhole and avenge our boys who sacrificed their lives so their fellow man can enjoy an existence free of oppression." He paused to catch a second wind. "Damn it, Chase. You're a Navy man. Why you oppose me makes no sense to me!"

"It isn't you I oppose," said Chase, calmly. "I do not believe we should rush blindly into something that could have catastrophic results for the entire world."

Dare stood quietly by. From what Chase had told her of his meetings with the Assistant Secretary of the Navy, she gathered the two of them had been feuding all week.

"Like it or not, sir, the United States is simply not prepared to go to battle," argued Chase.

"Not prepared?" echoed Roosevelt, his tone as indignant as the arch of his bushy brow. "I'm disappointed in you! How can you think such a thing, much less say it? We'd be fighting to liberate our fellow man. God would be on our side. How could we go wrong? How could we not end up the victor? Heh? I ask you that!"

"I'm relieved God will be on our side, sir. We'll definitely need all the help we can get." Chase exhaled an exasperated sigh. "You know as well as I that our Navy has yet to prove itself under fire. The only action the regular Army's seen is a few Indian skirmishes. We have no general staff, no war college, and the National Guard is more a social club than a military organization."

Roosevelt's neck was as red as the heavy portieres draping the exit behind them. "Thank God you're the exception rather than the rule as far as officers are concerned. That's all I can say."

"You know as well as I the only reason they're in favor of a war is because promotions have been so slow ever since the War between the States," wrangled Chase, becoming just as heated under the collar.

"What about those who aren't officers? Heh?" His hands moved as fast as his mouth. "How can you account for those hundreds of letters I receive every day from Harvard students, Indians, Wall Street brokers, polo players, convicts, cowpunchers—just to name a few—who are writing in to volunteer." His head thrust forward even more. "You heard me right. To volunteer! Why, if there is a war, and I fully expect the outbreak of one in the near future, I have every intention of resigning my position and recruiting every last one of them for my regiment of volunteers!"

Dare squeezed Chase's arm. People were staring at them. The loud discussion was making her quite uncomfortable.

Chase was quick to pick up the message. "You're not going to change how I feel, Teddy, and I've long since stopped trying to reason with you."

Roosevelt proceeded as though he hadn't heard a word. "And speaking of the War between the States, think of the morale booster it would be for the Rebs and Yanks to all be fighting on the same side for the same cause."

Chase shook his head. His voice remained at a normal pitch. "And when young boys are brought home in flag-draped caskets, what will you tell their mothers? They did their part to boost morale?" His smile was grave. "You have your convictions, I have mine. Let's just leave it at that, shall we?"

"We're both as stubborn as two old mules," laughed Roosevelt. "And seeing as how I'm not going to change your mind, and hell would have to freeze over before you'd change mine, we might as well call a truce and enjoy this little do." He smoothed the tips of his mustache. "There'll be plenty of time later for long faces. You know, young lady, I'd be mighty honored if I could have the first dance of the evening with you." He offered her his arm. "You don't mind, do you, old man?"

Without giving either a chance to reply, he whisked her away to the adjoining room where the band had just struck up a lively tune.

"I hope the talk of war didn't make you uncomfortable, Miss MacDade," remarked Roosevelt as he led her out onto the dance floor.

"Talk does not make me uncomfortable at all," she replied, placing one hand on his shoulder and the other in his hand. "It's the action resulting from such talk that upsets me."

"I understand you witnessed the *Maine*'s sinking." Holding her at a polite arm's length, he glided her around the room.

"I did."

"Then tell me this if you will. Do you not think Spain should suffer for so unforgivable an act?"

"If they were responsible, I feel that some sort of action should be taken. However," she added, feeling protective of her friends, the Cadallas, and the many other kind Spanish people living in Cuba, "if it is proven that Spain was not responsible, then I do not feel the action taken against the *Maine* should be used as an excuse for glory seekers to go to Cuba to make a name for themselves."

His walrus mustache lifted. "Is that what you think I am, Miss MacDade? A glory seeker?"

Dare grinned. In spite of his brash nature, he was a very likeable fellow. Even Chase had said as much after their worst row on Thursday. "Your niece told me that you would be president one day. After seeing, and hearing, you in action, I'm inclined to agree with her."

His mouth broadened to reveal large, white teeth. "That, young lady, is the best compliment I'm likely to be paid all evening."

When the dance had ended, he led her over to the spot where they had left Chase. "Looks like he's deserted you, my dear. Can't for the life of me see why he'd do something foolish like that." He motioned for the waiter. "But don't you fret. You couldn't be in better hands."

Half listening, she scanned the room for Chase and

breathed a sigh of relief when she saw him dancing with his mother. When she'd discovered the alcove empty, she had imagined Nessa had snared him. Smiling, she gave him and Mattie a cheery wave.

After fanning herself with her handkerchief, she turned her attention back to Nessa's uncle. "Mrs. Hamilton told me the president was supposed to be in attendance tonight. Would you be so kind as to point him out to me? I've never met a president before."

"Lately, I've been trying to stay as far away from him as I can." He chuckled. "To be honest with you, I think he's been trying just as hard to avoid me." He raked his fingers through thick, close-cropped waves. "Why settle for just meeting the twenty-fifth President of the United States when you've gone and danced with the twenty-sixth?"

Dare laughed. "I suppose there's some sense to such reasoning."

"Damn right there is!" His hearty laughter dwindled down into a chuckle. "You must think me an awfully brash fellow."

"Awfully," she agreed, still laughing. "But then, I still think you're an excellent dancer."

"Thank you, madame. Coming from so graceful a lady as you, I am honored indeed." He made a grand, sweeping bow. "The agility you saw exhibited on the dance floor came from my days in the ring." He pulled at his ears. "These cauliflowers came from boxing as well."

A moment later, his good humor vanished. He pointed to a pale, clean shaven man who had just entered the room. "Speaking of the president, there he is now." He gave her a gentle nudge. "You remember this occasion. Three years from now, you can boast of having made both our acquaintances on the same evening." He opened his watch, then snapped it closed. "Hmm. He's only an hour and a half late tonight. That's better than usual."

"I imagine running a country the size of the United States can be very time consuming," she quipped, unable to resist.

"Indeed. Especially if you spend most of your time on your knees," he returned quickly.

"I beg your pardon."

"On his knees. You know, praying." He took off his glasses and patted the sweat beading his lids. "He told the cabinet day before yesterday that he was waiting for God to give him a sign as to where his destiny lay, with war or with peace."

"God certainly is busy these days." She stared straight ahead without blinking. "Between soldiering and divine intervention, that is."

He slapped his hands on his knees and roared good-naturedly. "That Chase is some lucky cuss! Haven't seen a girl with so much spunk since—" his voice softened—"since my Alice."

A few minutes later, she pointed to the crowd gathering at the base of the stairs. "He's certainly drawing quite an audience," she remarked. "I think I'll get a little closer so I can hear what's going on."

"You wouldn't mind if I didn't join you, would you? After all, I do hear that nonsense day in and day out." He gave her hand a parting kiss. "I'll look you up when I come through Key West with the troops," he promised. "You haven't heard or seen the last of

Theodore Roosevelt. Not by a long shot," he winked.

"I know. I'd be disappointed if I had." She kissed his cheek, then made her way to the spot where the crowd had assembled and wove her way to the front.

Had there been any doubt about it before, there certainly was none now! Roosevelt and McKinley were as different as night from day. Where one was ebullient and aggressive, the other was reserved, rather subdued. The worry lines etched deep into his face gave McKinley's already pale features an even more troubled expression. Even the cleft in his chin, the one mark of distinction possessed by his otherwise ordinary face, looked weak in comparison to Roosevelt's less conspicuous one.

Roosevelt did, indeed, seem the more likely of the two to direct a nation's affairs, she had to admit. The only drawback she saw was his rally-round-the-flag attitude. As much as they had hit it off, there was no denying it. If there were no battles going on, he'd create one. He was just too aggressive to be in so sensitive a position. She could almost hear him pleading with Congress: *Just one bully little war. Just one! Just one for the sake of boosting the morale of our boys in blue!*

"Many of my colleagues disagree with me," she heard McKinley begin in a monotone that could have easily bored the stuffed owl on the mantle to tears, "but I feel that we, the people of the United States of America, have the power to intervene in Cuba, forcibly if we must, without going so far as to recognize the independence of the present insurgent government, and that is the message I shall strive to deliver to Congress tomorrow morning."

The burst of applause was like a stimulant inciting him to continue.

"We must put an end to the bloodshed, to the barbarism, to the starvation inflicted upon those who beg us on bended knees to aid their struggle for independence." His speech gained momentum. "The situation in Cuba is intolerable! It is deplorable! And you, good citizens, should be aware that at this very moment, our own peace and tranquillity is being threatened by such a menace."

From the fervency of his announcement, one would have thought he were addressing both houses of Congress. She wondered why he would choose a party to air his views regarding national affairs.

Dare couldn't help but smile to herself. Keeping her mind on the subject McKinley was addressing was impossible. After Roosevelt's earlier description of his adversary, she had difficulty picturing him as anything other than a chocolate éclair.

Thumbs tucked under his arms, the president hotly pursued the issue at hand. "We owe it to our neighbors across the way to give them protection. It is our God-given responsibility to end the misery there and the atrocities that are being committed."

The applause became louder and lasted longer as his speech progressed. With each additional clap of enthusiasm, his confidence increased. "We have a duty to intervene, and America is one nation who does not shirk her responsibilities!"

A loud burst of cheers erupted throughout the gathering.

Even had Dare been in agreement, she would not have shared the crowd's thunderous ardor. Did they really know just what they were encouraging? Surely not! No one in his right mind would be so elated at the prospect of dead soldiers strewn across a battlefield!

The louder the hurrahs grew, the more outspoken the usually taciturn man became.

"As President of the United States, I shall not shirk my responsibility. Tomorrow I intend to address Congress and present my request that we do everything in our power to bring an end to the Civil War in Cuba."

"Hip hip hurrah! Hip hip hurrah!" went up a noisy round of shouts.

Dare could do little more than shake her head. That sort of enthusiasm was exhibited at sports events, not in response to a declaration that would send young men to foreign soil to die—one that would probably cause many civilian casualties as well. My God, she wondered disgustedly, was mankind really so depraved?

She looked behind her. Teddy Roosevelt was shouting loudest of all. He'd have his bully little war.

"What about Spain?" asked an enterprising young voice from the rear of the audience. "Many of us were under the impression they had agreed to all the United States' demands."

McKinley puffed up like a frog. "I, young man, do not know the full details of anything Spain may have agreed to."

Dare sucked in her breath. What a remark for the nation's leader to make! It sounded like an out-and-out lie. Spain had agreed to America's demands! Why, she and Chase had discussed that earlier in the day. Could it be that the president was not presenting a completely accurate picture to his listeners?

"Will there be war, Mr. President?" boomed a hearty voice behind her.

"The likelihood of such an occurrence grieves me deeply," remarked the president solemnly. "However, if we find ourselves in a position where it cannot be avoided, yes, war will be our only alternative."

Once again a round of cheers and applause erupted throughout the gathering.

Dare felt as though she needed to sit down. There was no longer a question as to where McKinley's destiny might lie.

"To hell with Spain. Remember the *Maine*. To hell with Spain. Remember the *Maine*," fervently chanted most of those around her. "To hell with Spain. Remember the *Maine*."

"We'll show those bastards!" exuberantly declared one fellow. "We'll show them who's going to sink who to the bottom of the ocean from now on."

Finally, she could take no more. She had had enough!

Gathering her skirt, she pushed her way through the mob. She would be willing to bet that tonight was the first time Roosevelt had been upstaged by McKinley.

She returned to the ballroom, anxious to report to Chase what she had just heard.

Mattie was standing beside the piano with her friend, Lucy. From the looks of it the admiral was in the middle of recounting one of his hand-waving tales to his cronies for the umpteenth time. But where was Chase? What on earth had happened to him?

Had he come looking for her after his dance with his mother, it would have been easy to find her right up there where the president was the center of attention.

"Dare! What a pleasant surprise seeing you here!"

She looked up, puzzled that a stranger, and such a sinfully handsome one at that, addressed her with such familiarity. A moment later, a glimmer of recognition flickered in her eyes. Of course. He was Nessa's actor friend. "Mr. Gilette. Yes, this is indeed a pleasant surprise."

"Bill, I insist." Emerald green eyes lit up with rakish twinkles. "And where might the lucky Captain Hamilton be?" he inquired, his gaze following hers around the room.

She continued her visual survey. Chase had to be there somewhere! "I'm afraid I can no more answer that question than you," she replied, a little disappointed. "He'll be back directly, I'm sure."

"What a fool to leave so lovely a woman standing all alone." He offered her his arm. "I would be grateful, my dear, if you would consent to dance with me. I know I am not a suitable replacement for your captain, but I will be ever so much more attentive."

"Well, I don't know." She scoured the room once more. There was no sign of Chase anywhere! Perhaps he had gone to the buffet, or maybe he had stepped out for a smoke with one of his Navy friends. "I really should wait here," she finally told the actor. "Chase is sure to come looking for me shortly."

Gilette took her hand. "Seeing you in another man's arms would bring him running, I promise. I know it certainly would me." With a devil-may-care smile on his lips, he whisked her into his arms and onto the dance floor.

He held her close, too close! His thick, mutton-chop sideburns prickled her cheek. His hand explored the hollow of her back, his fingers running up and down her spine familiarly. She didn't know whether to be angry or amused. It really was quite funny! The touch of another man failed to arouse her.

"If we are to continue the dance, Mr. Gilette, would you please refrain from so viperish a hold?" she asked in a matter-of-fact tone. "I assure you, I am not going to vanish into thin air."

No sooner were her words out than her partner complied with her request. But at the same moment, she would have given anything if she could have uttered a few magical words and disappeared!

Not more than three couples away, in plain view of everyone, were Nessa and Chase. What they were doing could hardly be called dancing. It looked more like coupling! Nessa's arms were tightly locked around his neck, and her shapely body was pressed deeply into his. Her moves were far from subtle. They taunted and teased, conveying her expectations loudly and clearly. Her head tilted back, eyes glazed, and her creamy breasts almost exposed, she was totally oblivious to anyone's—everyone's—presence. *Yours forever*. There was no doubt about the truth of those two words any longer.

Damn Nessa, fumed Dare, seething despite her artificial smile. What she reserved for private moments that hussy was putting on public display.

Curses on you, too, Chase Hamilton, she wanted to shout at the top of her lungs. True, most of the men there would give their right arms to be maneuvered into such a position, and Chase really didn't look thrilled at having been selected for such a treat; still, he didn't have to tolerate her rubbing herself all over him like some bitch in heat!

Not a moment too soon, the dance ended and Gilette graced her cheek with a kiss. "Thank you very much, Dare. You made me a very happy man."

She did her best to put up a cheery front. It was bad enough to see Nessa attempting to seduce Chase, but to reveal her feeling to her rival's escort would only make her look ridiculous. Besides, Gilette seemed the sort of man who'd enjoy a good laugh over her predicament later.

"I wonder if I might prevail upon you to fetch me a glass of champagne."

Bowing low, he kissed each fingertip of her right hand. "I would pluck the moon from the sky this very instant if I knew it would make you happy."

She smiled sweetly. "Actually, for the time being, I would really much rather have the champagne."

"Your lowly servant will return before he's missed."

Undoubtedly, she mumbled under her breath. Now, to the matter at hand! Standing on tiptoe, she peered over the heads of the dancers who blocked her view. Wait, where had they gone? She searched the room again and again. They had been there just a moment ago, she decided, annoyed, but they certainly hadn't lost any time getting away from the crowd.

Gilette returned with her drink and made a grand display of presenting it to her. "Ah, to whet such lovely lips myself."

She was so preoccupied she took the glass from him and thanked him only when most of its contents had been drunk.

Over the rim of the glass she saw Gilette's eyes grow bigger and bigger. "Is something wrong?" she asked, trying to track his stare.

His hasty smile was none too convincing. "Something wrong? Oh, no, of course not. Nothing at all." His gaze still riveted to the spot that the piqued his interest, he took her elbow and steered her away from the direction they were facing.

Turning back around, she sought whatever it was that had held him captivated.

The little smile she had managed to feign withered immediately. Her world was about to collapse!

Hand in hand, Nessa and Chase had just retreated into a room opposite the ballroom and, after a quick glance behind them, had closed the door.

"I'm ever so sorry, Dare," mumbled Gilette. "I was hoping I could distract you from seeing that."

His arm around her shoulder did little to console her. Had she not seen it with her own eyes, she would never have believed it . . . Chase and Nessa stealing away for a quiet little rendezvous while she stood looking on like a fool.

"There must be some perfectly logical explanation for what we saw," she reasoned aloud, trying to rid her mind of conjured-up images which had no business there, images of Chase and Nessa entangled in a heated lover's embrace which could easily lead to . . . No, get a hold of yourself, she thought. There has to be a reasonable explanation.

Gilette's words were patronizing. "Yes, yes of course. You're right. There is some explanation for what we just saw. I'm certain when the two of them come out of there, they'll let us in on their little secret."

"Yes, their little secret," she repeated under her breath.

Something about him at that moment struck her as very, very odd. After all, he had just as much cause as she to feel humiliated and embarrassed. No man likes to have his companion throwing herself at another man, especially with a roomful of people looking on. Yet Bill Gilette seemed to be taking it all in stride. Come to think of it, the entire incident had been so well timed it could have been a brilliantly directed scene from a play. Except this time, the ending would not be the one the two stars expected!

"You poor dear," she said in a voice just as condescending as his. "How selfish I am to have only my own concern at heart. I can see you're suffering as much as I. Perhaps even more."

Her words took him by surprise. He stared at her as though she were crazy.

Dare smiled to herself. Was it possible the great Thespian had forgotten his next line. "I overheard Nessa discussing your problem with Chase, and I want you to know that . . ."

"Problem? What problem?" he interrupted. "What are you talking about? I have no problems."

She patted his hand. "Don't worry. I won't say a word to anyone. I wouldn't dream of breathing a peep." Finally, she felt as though she had the upper hand. At last, she had control of the situation. "I'd have never guessed. Not in a hundred years. And I feel certain not one woman in this room would have suspected."

"Know what? What are you talking about?" His hand reached up to cover the violent throbbing in his temple. "Surely you don't mean to say that—"

A forefinger across his lips silenced him. "There, there. Don't get yourself in such an uproar." She bit her tongue to keep from laughing. "I think you're fascinating just the way you are. It doesn't mean a thing to me that you won't . . . that you can't . . . I mean, just because you're not particularly interested in women is no reason to—"

"Not particularly interested in women?" he blared, then quickly lowered his voice when he saw he had sparked some curiosity in those around him. "Is that what she told him? That I was not particularly interested in women? Well, who the hell am I supposed to be interested in anyway?"

"Shhh. You don't have to curse me," she rasped, desperately trying to contain her chuckles.

"I apologize." He tugged fiercely at his high, stiff collar. "I can't believe she'd tell him such a thing. Good God, I am an actor. My reputation could be destroyed if my public were to believe such a lie." He paused for a moment, shaking his head in disbelief. "Why that little tramp! If anyone should know what kind of man I am, it would be her. Just what did she think we were doing in my dressing room all those afternoons? Playing tiddledywinks?" He took her glass from her hand and downed what remained. "I believe I shall take my leave of Miss Vanessa Sterling. Now and forever! If you will excuse me, good-bye and good night."

"I'll make your apologies," she called after him. She wondered if Gilette had ever made such a dramatic exit from the stage. Perhaps he could be prevailed upon to let her audition for his next production. After all, he should be the first to admit her performance was even more brilliant than his.

And Nessa! How surprised she would be the next time she went for a matinee in Gilette's dressing room. How she'd love to see the look on her face when he started hurling accusations at her. Serves her right, she told herself, trying to allay a tinge of guilt for having lied. That blond, cat-eyed seductress definitely had it coming. If she got only a fraction of what she deserved, then justice would be served.

Poor Chase! That poor darling!

She charged across to the room to where the next act was being staged. What sort of mess had he gotten himself into? One thing was certain. With Nessa as director, it would be a scene which could not easily be explained to an audience.

She could not help but wonder what might have transpired had she played out the scene with Gilette as Nessa had planned. The possibilities for endings would have been unlimited, but they all would have had one aspect in common, namely Nessa making good on her threats that Chase was not to be had by any woman except herself.

She could almost hear Gilette reciting the seduction monologue now. Chase would have been kept occupied until precisely the right instant, and when he went in search of her he would have found Gilette's arms consoling her. The other approach

Nessa and her cohort might have taken would have been to direct an unsuspecting Dare to the room in which Nessa and Chase were secreted. What a kick Nessa would have gotten out of that one! Too bad there would be no such fun! Still, Nessa was going to get the surprise of her life.

The door had been left ajar. Purposely no doubt, she decided as she ventured inside on tiptoe and took refuge behind a pair of earthenware urns which stood taller than she.

Slinking into the shadows, she realized that this room was a most unusual place for a romantic tryst. It looked like a zoo, but only the animals' heads were visible. Mounted on the wall opposite her were a rhino, a tiger, a hippo, and a deer.

Vance Sterling was apparently a big game hunter like his brother-in-law, Roosevelt. Undoubtedly this room was reserved for the mementos he had brought home from deepest, darkest Africa.

How appropriate it was that Nessa should have chosen such a setting in which to seduce Chase! The only problem was that Chase could not be brought down and bagged as easily as the trophies on the wall. Miss Sterling would find that out soon enough. On that she would stake her life.

Nessa stood on one side of the room, Chase on the other. Neither looked very happy.

"I don't care what you say, Chase darling. You can't marry her," whined Nessa, her hands pleading. "I simply won't allow it. I'm the one who loves you, who really loves you, and you know that you love me. Just look at us. We're perfect for each other. A match made in heaven. Remember? That's what everyone said about us at the Christmas ball. We're so much alike, you and I. Look at all we have in common. The Navy is just as much a part of my life as it is yours. Oh, Chase, think how I'll be able to help boost your career once we're married. Think of it!" She closed the distance between them with long strides. "I love you," she said, flinging herself against him. "I love you. If you reject me, I'll kill myself, I swear."

His hands remained in his pockets. He made no effort to comfort her. The look on his face revealed nothing but tolerance.

Dare sucked in her breath and waited. She could feel the hair on the back of her neck standing straight up. She'd just as soon have him tangle with a wildcat than have him caught in Nessa's deadly claws.

"Oh, Vanessa!" His sigh was troubled. "You will always be a very, very dear friend," began Chase, his body still straight and stiff, "but that is all. Period! We've been over this time and time again long before Dare even came into my life. What you've professed to feel for me for so many years is just an infatuation. You'll get over it. I promise!"

She stepped back. "Infatuation? You mean, like a schoolgirl crush?"

He nodded. "That's right. A schoolgirl crush."

Her voice grew even more sultry. "There's only one problem with that. I'm hardly a girl." Her feline eyes widened then narrowed. Gazing directly at him, she lowered her plunging neckline even more until the thin red straps had fallen off her shoulders.

She slinked closer to him, sleek as a jungle cat stalking its prey. "I'm over twenty-one. I'm hardly a girl, Chase, but you were always too proper and

386

polite to find that out." Her voice became little more than a purr. "As you can see, I am a woman. If you ever had any doubt about that before, perhaps this will convince you once and for all." A hand supported each breast. "See, I truly am a woman, a woman in every sense of the word . . . a woman who loves you desperately . . . one who will do anything, anything at all, to please you."

She walked into him, stopping only when she could go no farther. Breasts lifted high, she flicked her fingertips across the crests. "Take them. They're yours. You can do with them as you will. You can do with me anything you desire." Her right hand caressed his neck.

He shook her hand off, his expression stone faced. "This is ridiculous. You say you're a woman, but you're acting like a child, and a very spoiled one at that. Now come on. Make yourself decent, and let's get back to the party before someone comes in here."

"And gets the wrong idea?" she teased, her laugh taunting. "Where's your sense of adventure, Captain? I thought you loved the challenge of living dangerously. Make love to me here, my darling. Right on the bearskin rug. No one will disturb us. I've seen to that already."

"Cover yourself, Nessa, and let's get out of here. This little talk of yours has gotten way out of hand."

"Why don't you cover me with yourself? I'd like that, wouldn't you?" Her eyes were all but closed, her lips pursed for a kiss. "Take off your clothes. Let me see the great Chase Hamilton."

"No."

"Why?"

"Because I am not interested," he answered, enunciating each word slowly and clearly. "Do you understand?"

Both of her arms went around his waist.

From where she was standing, Dare could see Nessa's fingers kneading into Chase's dinner jacket.

"Give me one good reason," she persisted. "I've been told I'm beautiful and desirable and woman enough for any man. Damn it, Chase, I want you! And you want me. You may not want to admit it, but I know you do. You've always wanted me."

He shook his head. "You're wrong."

"Why don't you want me? Give me a reason, any reason."

"I've given you a dozen already." His tone grew more and more impatient. "Don't be so childish. You say you're a woman, so act like one."

Head burrowed in his dark velvet lapel, she began to sob.

"I am not the right man for you, dear Nessa," he told her, his voice sounding a bit more tolerant. "But you will find him one day, and when you do, you'll look back on this evening and have a good laugh when you realize once and for all that I never really was what you wanted."

"Oh, but you are." Her head rose and her eyes flamed. "And one way or another, I'll have you."

He walked away, leaving her standing for a second with her arms still outstretched. "Enough of this nonsense. I am going back to the party. If you don't want to come, fine. It's up to you."

"You're right. It is up to me, and don't you forget that."

The sound of something ripping made Chase whirl. "What the hell?"

Dare's mouth flew open. The top half of Nessa's gown, what there was of it, lay in two shreds around her waist. Surely, she wouldn't resort to something so obvious to get her way! mused Dare.

But Nessa stood there, her breasts rising and falling in anger, her smile wicked and deadly. "You say you want me to go out there with you? Fine. I shall, and you can explain to Bill and to my father and to the president and to my Uncle Teddy just how my gown got in such a horrible condition."

Chase opened the door wide. "After you, Vanessa," he said, his arm sweeping through the entrance.

Surprised, she quickly turned away.

The door closed.

Dare expelled a relieved sigh. She wanted to kiss Chase for calling Vanessa's bluff. There would be time for that later, she mused, smiling to herself.

What a man! How many others would have declined so sweet an invitation? Not many, she thought, in answer to her own question. As a matter of fact, she'd bet just about anything that Chase was more the exception than the rule.

She decided she wouldn't mention a word to him about witnessing the incident. If he wanted to tell her about it, fine. She'd listen. But if he didn't, that was all right, too. She already knew everything about the rendezvous. He was not an easy prey to womanly wiles. He had his own temptress, one who was a lady in public and a tigress in the bedroom.

Nessa picked up a goblet and slung it across the room. The glass struck one of the urns and shattered into tiny little pieces at Dare's feet. "Damn him! Damn him! Damn him!" Arms clutching her waist, Nessa kicked the sofa, then fell down onto it. "I'll fix that bastard!"

Dare stepped out from behind her hiding place. "If I were you, Nessa, I wouldn't do anything of the sort."

Ruby red lips parted wide. "How long have you been here?" she demanded, covering herself with a pillow.

"Long enough." Head held high, Dare stepped toward the door, then turned back calmly. "Looks like he's one trophy you're not going to be able to add to your collection." One dark brow arched in amusement. "He'll just have to be the one that got away!"

Chapter Twenty-Three

Fanning herself with a palm frond and searching the sky for respite from the scorching temperature, Dare sat on the front steps and waited, as she had done every evening for the past six weeks, for Chase to return home from the Navy building. Now that he was the commander, he had to spend twelve to fifteen hours a day working, sometimes even more if transports were slow in arriving or if a Spanish patrol boat had been sighted a little too close to American waters.

Of course, it could be worse, she told herself as she dabbed at a bead of perspiration with the sleeve of her blouse. Had the *Titan*'s arrival not been delayed for reasons known only by the War Department, he could have been sleeping on the battleship rather than with her at the Sea Palms. A more terrible thought struck her. He might already have left with the fleet that had set off for Cuba last week.

Six weeks, she repeated, half aloud. It was already June, and a sweltering one at that. Even the fish had to be panting. June! What on earth had happened to the month between June and April? Had it come and gone so quickly? It was hard to believe the trip to Washington had happened so long ago. Six weeks! So much had happened . . . and it had happened so quickly!

Several days before leaving the capital city, Chase had arrived home from Capitol Hill with the news that Congress had just passed three resolutions. These recognized Cuba as an independent country, demanded Spain's immediate withdrawal, and gave the president authorization to employ U.S. armed forces to achieve those ends. Because the United States had been criticized by other countries for attempting to do the same thing for which it condemned Spain—establish and maintain an empire—a fourth resolution was adopted as an amendment to the three. The Teller Resolution, Chase explained, assured such critics that the U.S. had no intention of exercising sovereignty, jurisdiction, or control over Cuba. In short, the amendment guaranteed Cuba would be left to her people and not annexed by her neighbor to the northwest. Several days after the president delivered his four points to Congress, Admiral Sampson sailed to Cuba with orders to blockade the ports. Chase had been in Washington at the time; otherwise, he would have joined Sampson's squadron which consisted of two battleships, an armored cruiser, three monitors and three cruisers, seven gunboats, six torpedo boats, a pair of armed tubs, an armed lighthouse tender, and a supply steamer. These ships covered an eight-mile spread when they sailed from Key West. And on the day they sailed, a cablegram was sent to Dewey in the Far East instructing him to commence operations. Capture or Destroy, read his orders.

Hair held high off her neck, Dare remembered the events which followed. During the following week the United States declared war on Spain. On the homefront, the headlines came as no great surprise. Only hours after the public had learned of the declaration, a Spanish steamer was captured off the Keys and the first prisoners were taken, and as far as most Americans were concerned—certainly the journalists—victory would soon come.

Never had the states been so united, wrote one patriotic reporter. Never had McKinley been so much in favor with the American people. He could have appointed himself dictator, and no one would have voiced the least objection.

The orders Chase received instructed him to take command of the Key West base on May first, or as soon thereafter as possible, leaving them little time to get home. The partings were sad, and the good-byes hurried. Mattie and the admiral promised to be down by July third for the big event. Though she did not voice her doubts, Dare did not share their optimistic belief that the war would soon be over. She had not thought so then, and she certainly did not think so now. The Spanish were not about to roll over and play dead. They had far too much at stake, namely a four-centuries-old empire.

At every depot where the Tampa-bound locomotive stopped boys intending to volunteer were added to the list of passengers. Certainly the trip between Washington and the west coast of Florida had been rich in experiences she could not forget. The troops already on board and the young men who intended to volunteer were treated like national heroes. Townsfolk turned out at the stations in their Sunday best to wave the lads in blue on to victory. Bibles and boxed chicken suppers were distributed by the pretty girls. Bands marched and paraded to "Hail, Hail, the Gang's All Here," and the "gang" went off to war as if they were going off to a church picnic.

At one stop, she remembered, the D.A.R. presented the colors to the captain of one departing group of volunteers. In the middle of the ceremony, a young boy who looked no older than fourteen rushed out of the crowd pleading with the captain to let him join up. The captain asked the boy how much he weighed, and when he was told one hundred and twenty-five pounds, he suggested the boy fill his pockets with enough rocks to reach the hundred-and-thirty-pound weight requirement. The lad did as the captain suggested, and when the train pulled out of the little West Virginia hamlet he was right there on board with the rest of the men going off to fight.

Many times since she had lain awake wondering what had ever become of that freckle-faced youngster once he had reached his destination. Too soon and too cruelly, she feared, he had learned the meaning of growing up.

While the send-offs were glamorous, the volunteer proving grounds were anything but. Just last week, Chase had brought home news that at Chickamauga a third of the volunteers had been wiped out by canned meat that was spoiled, and an equal number were still violently ill. Even from the train's window, she had seen that the health and sanitary conditions in Chickamauga were abominable. The training grounds in Tampa were no better. The city lacked an adequate supply of drinking water even for its own inhabitants, and filth flowed in the streets where the soldiers had pitched their tents.

It had taken twice the normal time to get from Tampa to Key West. All steamers and motor launches had been commandeered by the army to transport troops, and had General Shafter not recognized Chase and arranged for their passage, she would probably be sitting on the steps of the Tampa Bay Hotel at this very minute.

Poor General Shafter! Even now, she had to stifle a laugh when she thought of him. Nothing about him was very general-like. He was over sixty and very obese, and he coped so badly with the intense Florida heat, Dare wondered if he'd last until he reached Cuba. And if he did, how he would be able to plan an entire military offense in tropical weather which lent itself to sickness and exhaustion? His acting assistant general, millionaire John Jacob Astor, was a character too! He was nearly as much of a personality as Roosevelt. Tall and slim and a smoker of big cigars, he informed them at least a half-dozen times that he had volunteered to set an example to the younger generation and to look for adventure!

Adventure! If she heard that word once more in relation to the war, she would scream! Man does not go around killing other human beings in the name of adventure. Religious and political differences might very well have caused past wars, but when in history had one been fought purely for adventure?

Adventure! Undoubtedly that had motivated Roosevelt to quit his post as assistant secretary of the Navy and to recruit men as he had said he would for his Rough Riders. The quest for excitement had led stockbrokers, Indian fighters, bartenders, and Harvard grads to answer his call for a special kind of man.

Dare stood up, stretched, looked down the street, then sat back down again. Still, no sign of Chase, and he had promised to come home early for an outing on Christmas Tree Key. Poor darling! She really couldn't be too hard on him. No sooner had he taken command of his post than word had arrived that Admiral Cervera, the leader of the Spanish Atlantic fleet, had been ordered to proceed to Cuba. European intelligence agents had reported that the Spanish admiral had objected bitterly to the government demand. It was bad enough that his vessels were decaying hulks with wooden decks which would burst into flames at the first hit, but he had no charts of American waters. Despite his protests, his fleet of four armored cruisers and three destroyers headed to Cuba to protect Spain's stronghold. His powerful new cruiser, the *Cristobal Colon*, had to get underway without her main gun turrets which had never arrived from Italy. Spain's main concern was that Cervera restore a bit of their national pride after the humiliating defeat Dewey had inflicted upon them in Manila. According to the *Journal*, Dewey had hammered the pitiful Spanish hulks into scrap iron. Four hundred Spanish casualties had resulted, whereas one American sailor had died from a heart attack. To add insult to injury, the U.S. fleet had even taken three and a half hours off for breakfast! How do you like the *Journal*'s little war? chortled Hearst.

After such a decisive victory, the Navy's main objective had been to stop or to capture Cervera, and the Flying Squadron, under the leadership of Commodore Schley, had undertaken the challenge. Yet Cervera and his flotilla had been able to elude them and had managed to limp into Santiago Harbor. As it turned out, the Armada was not to have the last laugh, for the Flying Squadron bottled it up in the harbor without a single shot being fired. The U.S. forces could not gain entrance into the waterway, but neither could Cervera get out. Later, when a rumor circulated that Cervera was planning an escape, the U.S. carrier, *Merrimack*, had been deliberately sunk at the entrance to the harbor.

An American victory at sea was inevitable, so the papers forecast, and as far as Dare was concerned, nothing could please her more! Just so the war ended! Her wedding day was a month away, and the last mention Chase had made of it had been in Washington. Many times she had wanted to tell him about their child, but the right moment to do so never seemed to present itself. First Nessa's shocking descent down the stairs had prevented her confession, and then war news had become their main topic of conversation and Chase's primary interest. He was as loving and devoted as he had ever been, but it seemed that she no longer took precedence in his mind. Rightly so, she realized, for as commander of the largest and busiest naval port in the country, he had much responsibility. He didn't have time to notice that she was absent from the breakfast table, or to sense how moody and how prone to depression she had become. Thank heavens no physical changes had yet given her secret away. If Calpurnia were right, which she usually was, then she still had another month or so before he would find out . . . unless she told him. She did not doubt that he would marry her, pregnant or not, and not out of obligation, either, but for love. Adding one more load to the burdens already weighing him down hardly seemed fair, she reasoned, leaning back and resting her elbows on the step behind. The arrival of the *Titan* was long overdue, and in the meantime, Chase had to watch at least fifty of the Navy's best ships steam toward Cuba. While he wasn't particularly enthusiastic about fighting in a war that he had begun to regard as a glory seekers' war, he was still a Navy man at heart, and every bit as eager as his peers to prove his ship and crew were the best America had to offer. Even he admitted such a longing was rather childish, but that didn't keep him from feeling glum about having to sit out the first phase of the naval offensive. The past two weeks he had seemed to be living for the day when his ferocious battleship steamed into port. Then, he'd set off to Cuba, to tangle with Spain's "invincible" armada.

Dare's head drooped. She realized she mustn't allow herself to dwell on Chase's departure. The *Titan* would soon arrive, and Chase would put out to sea. Those were his orders, so she might as well resign herself to the inevitable. Other Navy wives had to; she could, too. After all it wouldn't be long before she was his wife.

Calpurnia brought out a glass of lemonade. "Why don't you come sit in the shade for a spell?" she asked, handing Dare the cool refreshment. "A woman in your condition oughtn't to expose herself to such heat."

Dare did as she was told for once without putting up a fuss. After all, she reasoned, she could argue until she was blue in the face, and Calpurnia would still not take no for an answer. Nobody knew more about women carrying babies than Calpurnia!

Uriah stepped onto the porch at sundown. "How ye doin' there, lass?" he asked, giving her a hug that was not as hearty as his embraces used to be.

"Never better." She eyed Calpurnia suspiciously, wondering if she had taken it upon herself to let Uriah in on their little secret.

"Doan you be cutting them eyes at me, missy. I know what you be thinking and you is wrong!"

"What's all that about?" queried Uriah after Calpurnia had retreated inside the house.

Dare shrugged her shoulders. "Don't ask me. She's been acting a little strange lately ever since the last of the reporters left for Cuba. I think she enjoyed having all those hungry men staying here those few weeks."

"She did. Doted over each and every last one of 'em like they were her sons." The amusement was quick to leave his voice. "Chase tells me once you two're married, the Sea Palms will no longer be a resort."

"That's right," she said, remembering how pleased she had been when Chase had proposed that very thing. "It'll be nice with just the four of us here."

"Four?"

"You, Calpurnia, Chase, and I." Dare chuckled. "What did you think we were going to do? Boot you out in the street?"

The ruddy flesh beneath his scraggly beard blushed. "How was I to know? I mean, Calpurnia's always been here to look after ye."

"So have you, Uriah Robertson." She squeezed his arm. "Like it or not, you're stuck with us, and there's no way out of it." She took another sip, then pulled down the brim of her boater to shield her eyes from the sun. "Chase tells me you've got quite a profitable little business going for yourself piloting the press boats beyond the reef."

He grinned. "I was tempted to let the *Alamanda* hit one when I found out the mighty Hearst, hisself, was on board."

"Wouldn't have done any good at all," she told him, latching onto his arm and keeping her hand there. "He'd have struck out swimming, and knowing how bullheaded he is, he would have probably made it."

"And beaten everybody else in the process." Uriah took off his cap, flattened his mop of gray, then put it back on again. "Speakin' of goin' for a swim, I heard some of the lads down at the dock talkin' 'bout our friend Ferrer. Seems he double-crossed the wrong person last night and ended up with his throat slit and a rock around his neck." He spat out into the yard. "I 'spect he'll turn up in a fisherman's net sooner or later."

Her face was expressionless. A man's death was hardly cause for joy. On the other hand, it was hard to grieve over one who preyed on those who were most vulnerable. As Mac would have said had he been sitting on the porch with them, the old vulture got just what was due him.

She searched the street for some sign of Chase. It was after seven. So much for their afternoon outing to Christmas Tree Key.

Uriah stroked his grizzled whiskers. "If ye're

400

lookin' for Chase, lass, 'tis me guess he won't be home until very late."

"Oh?" She sank down in the swing. Even without asking, she had a sneaking suspicion why. That great gray monster she had spotted on the horizon at midday had obviously not been the supply ship they were expecting. Damn! The *Titan* had arrived. That was the news she had spent the last six weeks dreading to hear.

Uriah gave her knee a fatherly pat. "Cheer up, lass. Word is that the *Titan* will stay put right here in the Keys in case the Spanish try an invasion of South Florida."

His words did little to cheer her. None of his news had given her much cause to celebrate. Damn the Spanish, the *Titan*, McKinley, Roosevelt! Damn the whole lot of them! There had to be a better way to settle international disputes. There just had to be, and whoever had come up with the notion of war in the first place should be shot at sunrise. The entire concept of killing other living beings to prove supremacy was absolutely ridiculous. There was simply no rhyme or reason to any of it.

Eight o'clock came and went, and at nine, there was still no sign of Chase. By ten, Uriah had retired to his room and Calpurnia to hers. Taking a supper tray filled with double portions of minced lobster and peas and rice, since according to Calpurnia she was eating for two now, Dare headed for the office. Leaving the door open in case she was asleep when Chase finally came home, she curled up on the couch with her supper and reread a letter the Cadallas had posted three months before but which had just arrived. Anticipating the Court of Inquiry's ruling,

Caesar and Rosaliá had left to visit family in Madrid. Thank God they were a safe distance away from the fighting!

The feel of warm lips brushing across her cheek roused her. "Ummm. What time is it?" she asked, rubbing her eyes.

"Late, very, very late," he whispered, mussing her hair with kisses. "I guess Uriah told you the *Titan* came into port."

Dare nodded. How excited he sounded. Just like a kid who had acquired a new toy. "That's wonderful," she said, minus the enthusiasm. "You must be very happy."

"I am." He kissed her again. "But you're not, are you? Hey, what's for supper? I'm starved."

I don't know what you're having, but I'm going to have a baby! How tempted she was to just blurt it out. To get it all out in the open, but she couldn't. Not now. Maybe later. Maybe tomorrow.

Instead, she pulled herself up with a yawn. "Calpurnia's got a plate all ready for you," she said, trying to sound happy and cheerful. After all, she told herself, no man liked coming home to a complaining woman, especially when she was still his fiancée, she mused chuckling.

He took her in his arms. This time his kiss was no light, airy wisp. It was hard and long and passionate and centered smack dab on her mouth. "I love it when you chuckle secretively."

"Makes you wonder what I'm scheming about, right?" She helped him out of his jacket and hung it over the back of a chair. "You must be exhausted, honey, so why don't you just stretch out, and I'll bring in your supper."

"Better watch it, or you'll fall out of grace with your friends Stanton and Anthony."

"Being in your good graces is all I care about." Arms around him, she squeezed him tight.

God, she'd die, just die, if anything ever happened to him, she thought. She'd much rather see him alive in Nessa's arms than killed by a Spanish bullet.

"Bring it upstairs, will you?" he asked, opening his eyes to find her gazing at him. "I haven't had supper in bed for the longest while."

"Anything you say, master."

He caught her arm as she turned away to leave. "Hey, one more thing. About Christmas Tree Key this afternoon, I'll make it up to you, I promise."

"I'll hold you to it."

A short while later when she delivered his supper to their room, it was she he reached for instead of the tray. Eager hands caressed and explored the shapely body beneath her cambric nightgown.

"Hey, I thought you said you were starved," she reminded him.

"Oh, I did, but I didn't say for what."

Ever so gently, he eased the lobster-pink linen over her head and onto the bedpost. His tongue retraced the route the fine cambric had taken while strong, powerful hands began a rousing expedition over hills and valleys that had known no pleasures until he had traveled them.

Moaning his name over and over, she fell back onto the pillows, her body ready for him, his touch eliciting lightninglike flashes of desire until she exploded from the magnificent pressure.

Cradling her in his arms, he burrowed his head between her breasts and feasted on all the delicacies he found there.

"Is it my imagination, or are those beautiful creatures becoming fuller and rounder?" he asked, finally surfacing after the longest while.

She hesitated. How easy it would be to tell him now. After all, passion was not the only reason her breasts would swell. If he learned of little Chase the romance of the moment would only be heightened. After a few moments of debate, she shook her head. She had to wait. For what, she wasn't quite certain, but now was not the time.

She rolled over on top of him straddling his chest. "Obviously, they want to please you."

"Mmmm. Who am I to argue?"

She breathed a sigh of relief. Thank heavens there'd be no reason for further explanation.

Her lips skimmed a trail of tiny kisses across his rock-hard thighs. Daring and devilish, she tantalized him until he could take no more, and the hot flesh between his legs had swollen to its fullest.

Grabbing hold of the warm, soft cushioning of her hips, he slid her up over his belly, rolled onto her and drove himself home.

In a matter of seconds the bed had been transformed into a magic carpet, and they were whisked into a whirl of fantasies and pleasures few mortals ever enjoy.

Floating back down to earth on a feathery cloud, Dare stretched out on his chest, completely satiated by the sweet, warm honey that had flowed from his loins to hers. On her lips was a smile of satisfaction. There were just some pleasures the mighty *Titan* would never be able to duplicate!

Chapter Twenty-Four

Tie and shirt collar loosened, Chase stomped across the porch one week later on the hottest morning ever recorded in town. He took turns stuffing his hands into his pants pockets or using them to rub the back of his neck.

"There is nothing, not one thing, you can say that will make me change my mind. The answer is no, no, no, no and *no*."

"Whatever you say, dear." Dare sat in the glider fanning herself with the hem of her skirt. "I've never known it to be so hot. There's not even so much as a breeze. Wouldn't you like another glass of lemonade?"

He plopped down in the swing beside her. "We are not talking about the weather, nor are we discussing lemonade. We are talking about that Scottish stubborn streak of yours, Dare MacDade, which will not permit you to take *no* for an answer."

"Don't be ridiculous. Of course I can take no for an answer. I just did." Hyacinth eyes blinked innocently. "You just told me I couldn't go to Santiago with you, and I accept your decision. Really I do," she assured him calmly. "There is a war going on, and if Admiral Cervera were to attempt an escape, then the *Titan* would be right in the middle of the fighting. A woman would only get in the way." She poured herself another glass of lemonade. "See. I do understand, so aren't you going to apologize for saying I'm stubborn? Cheers."

"Not in the least, because you are!" He cast a suspicious glance in her direction. "Something's going on behind those mesmerizing eyes of yours. What it is, I'm not quite certain, but I wish to hell I knew."

She fitted her arms around him. "Why, Captain Hamilton. Am I correct in assuming you don't trust me?"

"No farther than I can throw you."

"What a perfectly horrible thing to say to your intended!" Head resting on his shoulder, she snuggled close. "What if I told you the only thing I'm thinking about right now is what a wonderful reunion we'll have when you get home."

"Not only are you as obstinate as an old mule, you're a terrible liar!" He kissed the tip of her nose; then with a satisfied groan, he gathered her even closer. "Maybe I am being a little tough on you." His words filtered through her curls. "After all, what are you going to do? Stow away on a battleship?"

Dare chuckled. If he only knew!

"What time do you leave port?" she asked, her head

pressed into his shoulder.

"Five o'clock this evening, but I have to be on board by four for a staff meeting," he replied.

"I hope you'll at least agree to let me walk you down and see you off," she said, winding her arms tightly about him.

He helped himself to her glass. "Better than that. I'll give you a guided tour beforehand. How does that sound?"

"Perfectly grand." She brushed her cheek across his close-shaven one. Poor Chase. He had no way of knowing he had just solved the only problem standing in the way of her plan's success.

She unbuttoned the second, third, and fourth buttons of his shirt. Her fingers crept inside, their soft tips tingling from the field of rough hair prickling them. "Since we have only a few hours to spare until then . . ."

Bright blue eyes came alive. "Yes?"

"And since both of us could do with a little more than a good-bye kiss."

"Say no more, my sweet." He was on his feet in an instant.

She found herself in his arms the next. "No wonder they made you a captain at such a young age. You learn fast."

"Flattery will get you everything."

Her eyes twinkled naughtily. "Except to Santiago."

"I'll hurry home, darling. I promise," he vowed on the way up the stairs. "You know how I hate being separated from you even if it's only for a night."

She pushed the door shut behind them.

As he laid her on the bed, he said, "Let's make this an afternoon to remember?"

"Oh, it will be." She pulled him down with her. "That I promise."

Later in the day, after lunching at the Jefferson Hotel, the two of them strolled arm in arm to the red brick building that housed the Navy offices.

What a handsome couple they made! she mused happily, catching a glimpse of him and herself in a store window. She had not missed the envious looks thrown their way by a few of the town's most eligible young women. Chase was positively gorgeous in his dress whites, and she seemed to compliment him perfectly with her shell pink blouse and her skirt with white and pink vertical stripes.

How lucky she was, she thought, hardly able to contain herself. Captain Chase Hamilton, USN, was a man any woman would give herself to for one night of ecstasy, yet she had been the one chosen for that one night as well as all the others in their lives.

"What's in there?" he asked, nodding to the huge straw bag by her side.

"Oh, just a surprise for you, my love," she replied without missing a step. "But you can't open it until you're far out at sea."

"Mmm, if it were just a little bigger I'd think that you were going to stuff yourself in there."

"Chase, darling, don't be ridiculous!" she grinned.

He squeezed her hand. "Only teasing you, my love. Only teasing."

Before they stepped from the dock onto the gangplank, he guided her around to face him. "I'm very proud of you for not making a fuss."

She thought she would surely give herself away. For a second, all sorts of guilty feelings overwhelmed her. Excuses or not, she was scheming to deceive him. In that respect, she was no better than Nessa. On the other hand, she reminded herself, she had made a vow that they would never again be separated, and she had every intention of keeping that promise. Nothing or no one was going to come between them again, and that included a war!

"I understand, Chase," she said softly. "Really I do. You have an obligation to the Navy, to your country, to your president, and you mustn't let them down." In a stronger voice she added, "We must all do what we feel is right."

"I have an obligation to you too, my love." Her face cupped in his hands, he probed deep into her gaze. "Sometimes that which we love the most is that which we most slight."

"You haven't slighted me, my darling. Not in the least." The longer he expressed sorrow about having to leave her, the more wretched she felt. "Not another word about it," she urged sweetly. "You have to do what you feel is right." And so do I, she wanted to cry out. And so do I. But he would never understand.

"What a lucky devil I am!" He started to kiss her; then seeing that they were the object of some of his crew's attentions, he delivered a perfectly respectable kiss on her cheek.

She tilted her other cheek to him. "Silly boy, I've been trying to tell you that for months!"

"Aren't you going to show me where the great captain sleeps?" she asked, a while later after having toured the ship from stem to stern.

Chase checked the time. "Well, it's nearly four now," he frowned.

She tugged at his arm. "Oh, come on. We'll have plenty of time. You can get one of your men to escort me off the *Titan*. That should save you some time. After all, you did promise," she reminded him sweetly.

"All right. One quick peek, then off you go." He leaned closer, his breath fanning her face with a dizzying warmth. "And don't you go getting any ideas, either. I hardly think Admiral Sampson would understand my tardiness in Santiago if I used you as an excuse." His eyes melted into hers. "Then again, maybe he would."

His quarters were more spacious than she had imagined. The cabin was nearly the size of the room they had shared for the past five months and it contained a bed, a washstand, a bureau, a bookcase filled with leather-bound volumes, and a huge roll-top desk with a sprawling chair. However, the object she had hoped to find there was missing. There was no wardrobe. Damn! Oh, well, there had to be a closet somewhere. After all, he couldn't command a ship in a wrinkled uniform. Perhaps the trunk at the foot of his bed would do. Hmmm.

"Seen enough?"

"What? Oh, yes." Winding her arms around his neck, she imitated Nessa's distinctive little pout. "Everything except what I came here to see," she answered, her hands shaping his firm backside.

He pressed hard against her.

She could feel his source of pleasure hardening rapidly.

"Oh, and what is that?" he asked.

She replied with a long, soul-searching kiss. "You're a smart man. I'll bet you can figure that out," she said when they finally managed to pry their lips away.

He pulled her to him again, this time even more forcefully. "Perhaps you'd better give me another hint." He lifted her breasts, weighing one in each hand, as he covered her lips with his.

The ship's bells sounded four o'clock.

Dare smiled to herself. Everything was proceeding right on schedule.

Disentangling herself from his arms, she took several steps back. "Your meeting! I had forgotten all about it." After straightening her skirt, rebuttoning her blouse, and patting her hair back into place, she hooked her arm through his. "As much as I hate having to say good-bye, my darling, I suppose we must."

"I'll be back before you have a chance to miss me," he whispered, his hot words sending her blood pounding through her veins. "You'll not be out of my thoughts, not even for a minute."

She flung her arms around him once more. "And you will be with me every moment as well."

She smiled to herself. Truer words were never uttered. If he only knew!

She forced herself away from him once more. Dabbing at her eye, she swallowed hard, then turned away. "I'm ready."

Eyes focused straight ahead, she walked out of his cabin without glancing behind her to the spot where she had dropped her big straw bag.

Once topside, Chase motioned to a sailor nearby. "Ensign Drury?"

The young man hastened to them. "Yes, sir!" He saluted.

"Escort the lady back to her home, please."

"Aye, aye, sir. Ma'am."

Chase nodded for him to wait by the gangplank.

"I'll expect you to come home in time to make an honest woman out of me, Captain Hamilton," she told him, her arms longing to coil around him once more.

"The very hour I return, I promise I shall do just that." He pressed his forefinger to his lips, then to hers. "Good-bye, my love. Until then."

Dare watched until he disappeared below; then she counted to fifty for good measure before walking down the gangplank on the arm of the young ensign.

She stopped abruptly midway down. "Oh, dear, I left my bag on board." Her dark lashes fluttered innocently in the sailor's chubby face. "Do you think I could possibly, I mean, you wouldn't mind terribly if I went after it, would you, Lieutenant?"

He looked pleased. "I'm not a lieutenant, ma'am. Least not yet."

She looked surprised. "Oh, I'm amazed you're not one already. You do have a certain leadership quality about you."

He was suddenly six feet tall. "Well, thank you, ma'am." His eyes lit up even more. "If you'd like, I will fetch your bag for you if you can remember where you left it."

"Oh, could you? That would be so kind." She quickly scanned the deck for Chase. He was nowhere in sight. "I feel certain I left it beside that big gun on the quarterdeck."

He thrust his chest out proudly. "Don't worry about it. I'll find it for you."

"Thank you, Lieutenant . . . I mean, Ensign Drury."

She waited until he was a safe distance away before letting her giggle escape. She had just taken a page out of Nessa's book, and had executed her move with as much finesse as Miss Sterling would have displayed.

Hands locked behind her back, she strolled around the deck eying her surroundings with a curious fascination. Then, when no one was watching, she scrambled down the hatch and retraced the route Chase had taken to his quarters.

"All right, Dare, I know you're in here somewhere, so you might as well come out and save me the trouble of coming after you."

Dare pushed back the lid of the huge old trunk in which she had spent the night, curled up in an uncomfortable ball. She waited for him to help her out, but when he made no effort to assist her, she struggled out on her own. Gone was her summer dress, and in its place was the baggy sponger's attire she had worn to Havana. For a moment, she hesitated to meet his gaze; then realizing his bed had been slept in, she faced him defiantly.

"You knew I was in that, that coffin all along, didn't you?" she demanded, hands on her hips. "And you let me sleep there knowing how sore I'd be in the morning? That is lower than low!"

"When Drury came back and told me you had

disappeared after sending him running all over this ship on a wild-goose chase, I figured you were going to pull a stunt like this," he announced smugly as he sat down at his desk and began shuffling through some papers. "And as far as your being uncomfortable, I'd say that any discomfort you might have experienced served you right!"

Her eyes swept the floor. "You're really angry with me, aren't you?"

He turned his chair around and his eyes opened wide. "Angry? Now whatever would give you an idea like that?" he asked, his gestures as overstated as the tone of his voice. "Why should I be upset? Not only will I have a mutiny on my hands when word gets out that my fiancée is aboard, but I could, in all probability, lose command of the *Titan*. But why should that upset you?"

"I don't expect you or your crew or all the admirals in the Navy to understand this," she said as she began walking slowly toward him, "but I nearly lost you on two different occasions, and I don't intend to let that happen again." She stopped only when her knees touched his. "I'm sorry, but I can't help the way I feel."

He stared at her in disbelief.

She was certain she saw glimmers of love reflected in his deep blue gaze.

"If we're blown up, I suppose you'd want to die with me, wouldn't you?" he asked, straining to keep his frown.

Head lifted, her gaze absorbed his. "If it were that or spend the rest of my life without you, yes, yes, I would."

Her intuition told her that he was longing to reach out to her, to touch her, to comfort her, and that it took every last ounce of restraint he possessed to keep from doing so. She eased up on the desk and folded her hands in her lap. Suddenly, she lifted her gaze. "Why did you sail knowing I was on board?"

"Not because I wanted you here. And don't you look so hurt. I don't want you here because I love you." His bark dwindled into a purr. "I figured if you were determined to accompany me, then nothing I could say or do would keep you from it. I wouldn't have put it past you to sail the *Blue Runner* right through the blockade."

"The thought did cross my mind," she said reluctantly, "but Uriah told me we'd never make it through the submarine mines. One hit and we'd sink plumb to the bottom."

Chase rolled his eyes. "I should have known!"

Arms crossed at her waist, she scooted farther back on the desk. "So what are you going to do with me now? Feed me to the sharks?"

"Don't give me any ideas!" A mischievous twinkle sparkled in his eyes. "Actually, I've decided to reward your devious exploits with free passage to Santiago aboard the battleship, the *Titan*."

"Oh, Chase, that's wonderful!" she exclaimed, throwing her arms around him. "I knew you'd understand."

"Not so fast," he said, freeing himself from her grip. "You haven't heard the conditions yet."

"Whatever they are, I shall agree to them most happily!" Anything, anything at all just to be able to remain by his side, she mused happily. Anything.

"Good, then I shall send word to the *Olivette* that you are on your way."

Her brows wrinkled in confusion. "But that's the ship that transports the press and the wounded. Why send me there?"

"To keep you safe! That's the one ship that won't be a torpedo target."

Her eyes were pleading. "Why can't I stay here with you? I'm willing to take my chances."

"I know, but I don't want you to. Besides, a battleship is no place for a woman. Neither is a war!" he added sternly.

"What about Kate Watkins and Anne Benjamin?" she asked, remembering the two lady journalists they had met in Tampa. One had been assigned to cover the war for the *Toronto Mail and Express*, the other for *Leslies'*.

"The battleground is like an office to them."

She thought a moment longer. "All right, then what about Mrs. Babcock? She's just your average, run-of-the-mill woman. Just like me."

A smile tugged at his mouth. "Believe me, Dare MacDade, when I say that nothing about you is average. Now, who's this Mrs. Babcock?"

"We met her on the train coming down. Remember? Her husband is a corporal with the seventy-first New York. She follows him wherever he goes and tends to the wounded."

"Ah yes. Now I remember." He scratched his chin thoughtfully. "Next thing you'll be telling me that Mrs. Babcock is expecting a baby."

His gaze imprisoned hers. There was no way she could escape from it. She sat there stunned and open-mouthed.

416

Had he belted her one with his fist, she could be no more stunned.

It took her some moments to recover sufficiently to utter even the shortest question. "You know?"

"Of course I know. What do you take me for, an idiot?" he asked gently.

"Why didn't you say something?"

"That very same question might well be directed to you."

Her head shook slowly. "I don't know what to say."

"That'll be a first." His laugh dwindled into a sigh. "Why didn't you tell me?"

"Oh, I tried. I tried many times, but I just couldn't bring myself to break the news to you. Either the timing was all wrong, or something else came up, and I . . . I just lost my nerve." Finally finding the courage to meet his eyes, she tried to smile. "I really just lost my nerve."

Resting his arms on her legs, he leaned over her. "And what, might I inquire, were you afraid of? That I'd abandon you, the both of you, five minutes after finding out?"

She shook her head. "No, that thought never once crossed my mind, I swear."

"Then what?"

She held his hand close to her cheek. "You've been under such a tremendous strain, what with the war and all, I just couldn't bring myself to add another worry to your burden."

Head lowered, he kissed her rounded stomach, then massaged it ever so gently with his chin. "Neither you nor our child would ever qualify as a burden."

Her mood lifted. Perhaps . . . "Then, I, that is, we, can stay?"

"I'll give you my answer in Santiago." He checked his watch. "If my calculations are correct, that should be sometime within the next hour and a half."

Dare's grin broadened. Somewhere in his frustrated sigh, she had detected a trace of amusement. Her hand crept up his leg, her fingers tenderly digging into the flesh beneath his trousers. "And in the meantime?"

His hand halted the course of hers. "And in the meantime, I have a ship to command."

She moved from the desk to the bed on which she curled up. "If you should change your mind," she said, patting the empty space beside her, "you know where to find me."

His smile faded. "Oh, I forgot." After a thoughtful stroke of his close-shaven cheek, he added, "I'll have Lieutenant Roberts move a cot in here immediately."

"A cot? Whatever for?"

He eased down onto the bed, keeping as far away from her as he could. "A woman in your condition really shouldn't be disturbed," he said, blue eyes gleaming.

Arms coiled tightly around his neck, she pulled him down to her. "Come here, sailor, and I'll show you just what kind of condition I'm in."

"Ah, woman, you are going to be the undoing of me yet."

One brass button after another popped open.

"Oh, but what fun you're going to have being undone," she promised, smothering him with kisses.

418

Chapter Twenty-Five

Hands in her pockets, Dare left Chase on the bridge and strolled across the deck. The sun felt hot on her face. It was only a little past six and already the early morning cloud mist had been burned away by the glaring warmth. Heat rose like steam across the glasslike calm of the ocean. The air was still, uncomfortably still. Not even the tiniest cloud was visible. Smoke from the ships' stacks rose in columns and pillared the sky.

A few of the seamen called to her by name as she walked by. One hand shielding her eyes from the sun, she waved to each one and exchanged a cheerful hello. It hadn't taken her long to make friends with most of them. Her protective instinct had been instantly aroused by the younger ones, many of whom had never been on a ship before. Luckily, not one of the boys had put up a fuss about her being on board. As one sailor put it, most of their sweethearts back home would never dream of putting to sea with their men, and she should be commended for her devotion, not chastised. After learning that his men had adopted her as their ship's mascot, Chase relented on his threat to banish her to the *Olivette*. Whether or not he would be admonished by Admiral Sampson remained to be seen, but one thing was certain: Chase was as proud of her decision to accompany him as the rest of his crew. More than once she had caught him looking at her with a glow in his eyes that had not been present before. Although he would rather swim back to Key West before admitting it, her decision to stow away had been a big boost to his morale. As he had told her many times before, he liked a woman with spunk, and she was by no means deficient in that department. Mac had seen to that. "Just because you were born a girl is no reason you can't be every bit as courageous as a boy," was his favorite piece of advice. She often wondered if that had been the reason he had insisted on calling her Dare. Mac, God bless him, would certainly be proud of her now had he lived. She had a feeling that wherever he was, he knew, and he was probably strutting up and down saying, "That's my daughter."

"Good morning, Ensign Drury. Sure going to be a hot one."

The chubby-faced ensign dropped his eyes to the deck. Red-cheeked and head lowered, he quickly shuffled away, the way he always did whenever she was near. Poor lad! If only she could convince him that she wanted to be friends! Word of her presence had spread like wildfire among the crew of the *Titan* as it had to the crews of every other ship in the harbor. Poor Ensign Drury had been made the laughingstock of the entire fleet, and it was all her fault. Still if she had to do it over again, she would not have proceeded any differently. The means she had chosen might not be all that blameless, but it had achieved her end. At least she was with her man, not sitting on the porch of the Sea Palms wringing her hands and waiting for a bit of news.

She wasn't quite sure how, but she would make it up to the poor fellow. Once they returned home, perhaps she would invite him over for one of Calpurnia's delicious, home-cooked meals. Better yet, she would invite Josh Curry's daughter, Annabelle, to join them. They should be close in age, and one was every bit as shy as the other, so they should get along just like two peas in a pod! Just thinking about what a fine pair they would make eased her conscience considerably!

Stepping out onto the bow, she leaned over the railing and gazed at the scene that had greeted her every morning for the past five days. Every time she looked at the island, the sight confronting her became harder and harder to believe. Gone were the lush vegetation and fertile greenery of Cuban valleys. In its place lay the brown, burnt rubble of what had been a healthy crop. Once beautiful villas had fallen into charred ruins. Those that had managed to survive were nothing more than walls without roofs. Had Casa Cadalla suffered a similar fate, she wondered.

It seemed the only features of the landscape to escape devastation were the royal palms. With their tall, stately trunks and spreading, green-plumed branches, they still reigned over the setting.

Nothing else remained the same. Even the mountains had changed. Their summits, which rose high into the clouds, were topped with Spanish blockhouses, and as far as the eye could see, the same pagodalike structures ran up and down the coastline like railroad depots.

From where she was standing, she had an unobstructed view of Santiago. Built on a hill, the city sloped down to the harbor. Scalloped tiles roofed houses which were built low and protected from intruders by the black, wrought-iron grates that laced the windows.

One week had passed since the *Titan* had joined the semicircular arrangement of battleships and cruisers assigned to keep Cervera and the Spanish fleet bottled up inside the harbor. One entire week! Seven full days! During that time, June had dragged into July, and the temperature had become worse than unbearable. Those first few days could easily have qualified as hell on earth. Last week had been a blessing in comparison to the heat wave they were experiencing now. Not even a hint of a breeze stirred Old Glory, and the only shimmer in the ocean came when a fish struck the surface.

Even though she kept such thoughts to herself, she was beginning to wonder if those in charge knew what they were doing, and if they indeed knew, whether or not they had the right reasons for doing it. Each day brought with it events which were sure to make headlines in the newspapers back home and in most of those around the world. Rumor had it that

Spain had scraped together a third squadron to send to the Philippines. In retaliation, Hearst had ordered his European representative to sink a blockship in the Suez Canal, but Spain recalled the squadron just in time. After enduring choppy seas which had caused most of the mules and horses to be thrown overboard to the sharks and which had left the majority of his troops deathly ill, General Shafter's regulars, accompanied by a batallion of national guardsmen and the Rough Riders, landed on the Cuban shores and marched to Santiago. From all indications, the arrival of the army had been nothing short of a disaster and a pitifully funny one at that. Total chaos reigned. Supplies were insufficient and communications were so horribly inefficient that no one, not even the War Department, knew what was going on. The troops were not the least bit prepared for combat in the tropics. Basic essentials such as khaki uniforms, mosquito netting, and hammocks had been omitted from supply requisitions. Most of the soldiers had landed in their winter uniforms, which were woolen infernos under the tropic sun, and a few days after landing, men began fainting at roll call and growing more and more delirious as the day progressed due to malaria and other tropical diseases.

Each night, all those aboard the ships anxiously awaited news of what was happening elsewhere in the Spanish empire. A German squadron comman-der, five days before, had refused to obey Dewey's harbor regulations in Manila Bay and had conspired to seize the islands for his own country. Luckily, a British ship in the vicinity had intervened, and the ties between America and England had been strengthened considerably by this one move.

The Pacific island of Guam, taken early in the war because the Spanish officer in charge had mistakenly thought the shots fired on him were courtesy shots, had been annexed the last day of June. According to press releases, Guam had been taken because Mrs. McKinley had expressed a troubled concern to her husband about the poor heathen natives who ran around there half naked. Agreeing wholeheartedly with his wife, the president had announced that an inner voice had told him it was his duty to civilize and Christianize the entire Philippine islands.

Word had spread that Hawaii, too, was about to be annexed because it was needed as a coaling station. Chase, however, said that the U.S. could use it without taking such drastic measures.

Could there be some truth to the earlier criticisms that McKinley and his administration wanted an empire all their own, Dare was beginning to wonder. Had they condemned one week something they practiced the next? From all indications, Puerto Rico was about to be occupied as well. It didn't take a military genius to figure out that in the event Spain did surrender, all the possessions it had lost in the process would belong to the victor. Even Chase was beginning to question the motives of his superiors!

One or two more days, a week at the most, and the conflict in Cuba would be over. So Chase had said! Time was running out for Cervera, and he and his fleet were the last hope Spain had. Just yesterday, the American army had stormed the Spanish outposts of El Caney and San Juan Heights. Teddy's Terrors, as

424

the Rough Riders had been renamed, were in the thick of the action. Despite stubborn Spanish resistance and heavy casualties, the United States' forces had succeeded in capturing the summit and had begun closing in on the city itself. General Toral had been asked to agree to a surrender, but as of yet, no answer had been given. His action seemed contingent on Cervera, and at that moment the guns of every ship in the horseshoe formation were pointed right at the fleet inside the harbor.

Nearest to shore on the west was Commodore Schley and his armored cruiser, the *Brooklyn*. Next came the battleships, *Texas*, *Iowa*, and *Titan*, all three looking straight up the narrow line of the harbor and poised to attack at the first sign of life within. The *Oregon*, famous for her long run around the Cape, was positioned off their starboard side, and beside it lay the *New York*, Admiral Sampson's flagship. Completing the wide semicircle was the *Indiana*. A pair of converted yachts, the *Vixen* and the *Gloucester*, were stationed close in shore, one at each end of the formation.

With the Heights under U.S. occupation, Admiral Cervera's options were limited. He could surrender his entire fleet, or he could make one last gallant effort to charge the blockade. The speculation among the officers was that the Spanish admiral would choose to surrender. Chase, on the other hand, disagreed, and his prediction of what would happen had resulted in her not closing her eyes all last night. He was of the opinion that when four hundred years of greatness ended, it would not happen as the result of a surrender. It was no secret that Cervera wanted to haul down his colors rather than waste the lives of his men on a last show of gallantry. Like any good commander, explained Chase, Cervera knew when he was trapped and he recognized that any action short of surrender could result in a needless bloodbath. However, according to messages intercepted in Europe, the Spanish government was at odds with the commander of their Spanish fleet and had insisted he do otherwise.

Until this explosive situation was resolved, the *Titan* and the rest of the U.S. ships would man their battle stations and keep their crews on emergency alert.

A strong pair of arms encircling Dare's waist disrupted her thoughts. She leaned back against the familiar broad chest. Her arms held his, encouraging him to tighten his grasp. In the confines of the captain's quarters, Chase had no reservations about displaying his affection, but in front of his men, he was very reserved. She wondered what had prompted his change of mind.

"Do you know what today is?" he asked, his hands slipping between the buttons of her shirt as he pulled her back against him.

Dare smiled, pressing herself closer to him.

"Let me see," she said slowly, her finger tapping her chin. "Today is Sunday, the third of July. Hmmm. Is there something else special about today?"

"Isn't it your birthday?" he asked, his eyes innocent and wide.

"Ah, yes, so it is." One shoulder lifted matter-of-factly. "How silly of me to forget so important a day!

Good heavens! I'm twenty years old today. Fancy that!"

He nibbled at her ear, his fingers becoming more and more daring as they explored her breasts. "Happy birthday."

She chuckled. Admiral Cervera was certainly getting an eyeful. Perhaps at that very moment, he was telling his officers to break through the blockade because the captain of the *Titan* was distracted.

He repeated her age, very thoughtfully and very slowly. "Ummm. I love you. Even if you are getting old." Cupping both breasts, he vigorously massaged each ripe mound. "I don't suppose you'd remember what spectacular event was supposed to have occurred on this day, would you?"

"Hmmm. Spectacular event. Don't tell me. Let me guess." Pretending to be deep in thought, she squeezed his hands even tighter. "Do you think I could persuade you to give me just one teeny-weeny hint?"

In answer, he hummed a few bars of the wedding march. "Sound familiar?"

"Oh, that," she said with an indifferent snap of her fingers. "I knew all along you wouldn't marry me. As Calpurnia always said, why buy the cow when you can get the milk free?" Evicting his hands, she turned around to face him. "You know something, Captain Hamilton? I wouldn't be surprised if you had sent word to your friend, Pascual, to start a little commotion out there just so you'd have a good excuse for backing out."

"Why, Dare MacDade. You ought to be ashamed of yourself for even thinking such thoughts. Is that all the confidence you have in me?"

Grinning, she shrugged her shoulders. "I am truly at a loss for words."

"Maybe this will put a few back in your mouth." He fished into the pocket of his trousers. "What do you think of it?" he asked, unclasping his fingers to reveal a diamond and ruby band. "It just so happens I had this little trinket in my pocket, and since I can't step into town to pick out a birthday present, I guess this will just have to do."

"Oh, Chase, it's beautiful!"

He slipped it midway down her third finger, then quickly slid it back off. "Wait a minute! Why didn't I think of this before?"

"What are you talking about?" she demanded playfully, trying to get to his pocket. "You give me back that ring, or I'll scream at the top of my lungs that you're trying to take all kinds of unmentionable liberties with me."

He dangled the ring in front of her nose one last time, then dropped it into his pocket. "As I was about to say before I was so rudely interrupted, the smart thing for me to do would be to let this ring serve two purposes: number one, a birthday present; and number two, a wedding ring. How does that suit you?"

"Unless you're planning on celebrating both events on the same day, I'd say that was pretty chintzy of you."

His sigh was long and hard and deliberate. "I've been known to go to just about any extreme to save a few dollars."

The impact of what he was proposing was slow

sinking in, but when it did, she had to steady herself against the railing to keep her legs from crumbling beneath her. "Do you mean? . . . I mean, is it possible . . . but what about? . . ." There were a million questions she was dying to ask, but not one progressed beyond a few, incoherent mumblings. "Really?" was all she could manage. "You really mean it?"

"Of course I really mean it," he replied, joining in her laughter. "We decided on a July third wedding, and a July third wedding we shall have." His voice lowered, as did his hand. Gentle fingers affectionately shaped her rounded stomach. "How many other children can boast that they were in attendance when their parents tied the knot?"

"You have just made me the happiest person in the entire world!" she exclaimed, sniffling and giggling at the same time.

His lips brushed hers. "No, my darling. Second happiest."

A moment later, Chase straightened himself to his full height. "Incidentally, my crew has expressed the sentiment that if I don't hurry up and make an honest woman out of you, I'll be hanging from the yardarm by sunset."

Her eyes twinkled. "We certainly wouldn't want to leave the *Titan* captainless, now would we?"

He shook his head. "Not on your life, or mine, whichever the case may be."

"Care to tell me your plans, or do you intend to surprise me?" she inquired, holding tightly onto his hand as though she were afraid of letting go.

"There's a chaplain aboard the *Iowa*, and Fighting

Bob Evans is going to let me borrow him for a little while this afternoon."

"This afternoon?" Her hand went to her head and patted the loose braid hanging down her back. "Goodness, I've a million things to do before then."

Grabbing hold of her shoulders, he pulled her face to his and planted a kiss at the tip of her nose. "Just think of this ceremony as a practice session. When we get back to the Sea Palms, we'll go through the whole rigamarole all over again. Agreed?"

She nodded. "Agreed. One more question, though. Do I have to wait until we're back in Key West before I can wear that gorgeous ring?"

He thought for a moment, then shook his head. "No, but you will have to wait until the 'I do's' are said."

"How about the wedding night?" she teased. "When do you propose we have that? Before or after?"

"Before or after what?"

"The ceremony, silly," she answered, still giggling.

"But I thought we'd already celebrated that."

Dare nodded. "Many times over, but not on the day of our wedding." Arms wound tight around his hips, she slipped a hand into his crisp, white pocket.

"Hey, no fair!" he exclaimed, jerking it out and examining it. He felt in his pocket to make sure the ring was still there. "What a low, underhanded trick to play. And we're not even married yet. How do you like that!"

Her tongue outlined the shape of his lips. "As my old friend Nessa would say, you certainly can't blame

430

a girl for trying."

"Speaking of trying, what was that you were saying a moment ago about celebrating our wedding night a little early?"

She feigned a look of shock. "Why, Captain Hamilton, just what kind of a lady do you take me for?"

"Meet me below in ten minutes, and I'll show you."

She was about to tell him he had a date when a movement at the end of the line distracted her. Her smile was quick to fade. She motioned to the eastern end of the formation where the *New York* was pulling out of its place. "What do you suppose is going on out there?"

Chase shook his head. "I have no idea what Admiral Sampson is up to now."

A signal flag went up on Sampson's flagship.

Chase read it aloud. "Disregard motion of commander in chief." He turned back to Dare. "He must be going to Sibbony for another meeting with Shafter."

"Reckon what that means?"

He looked toward the harbor, then to the empty spot in the formation. "I wouldn't even venture a guess."

Dare watched as the flagship rounded the point and disappeared from sight. Her stomach felt a little queasy. If Cervera were going to try to make a run for it, a better opportunity might never present itself.

Taking her hands in his, he gave each a quick squeeze. "Ten minutes?" he asked softly.

Her grin was deliciously wicked. "I thought you

had a ship to run."

"Even the captain has to take an hour off now and then for a quick nap."

She blew him a kiss. "Napping is the one thing you won't be doing."

She watched, smiling, as he returned to his men. What a handsome commander he made! Even his presence demanded respect and attention!

Humming happily to herself, she completed her brisk, morning stroll. All she could think of was that in five hours—three hundred minutes—she would become Mrs. Chase Hamilton. Five hours! If only she could speed up time!

Ten minutes later, she started down the companion ladder when suddenly a round of signal guns from the *Iowa* brought her scrambling topside.

Sailors tumbled down ladders to their battle stations. Engines were pounding at full strength, and the signal that the enemy was emerging had been hoisted up the masthead. Only when she saw the same signal flag fluttering from the other ships as well did she realize that they were not in the middle of a drill. The chaotic commotion was real! Admiral Cervera was chancing the impossible. He was about to attempt an escape.

She scurried across to the bow for a better look. By the time she got there, Cervera's flagship, the *Maria Teresa*, was coming out of the long, narrow channel under a full head of steam. Smoke poured from her funnels, and Spain's red-and-gold battle flags waved high.

There was no mistaking her course. Passing between the hilly coastline, the *Maria Teresa* was

432

heading directly for the open sea.

Swinging into view a moment later were the *Vizcaya*, the *Cristobal Colon*, and the *Oquendo*. Rounding the turn in their wake were Spain's two dreaded torpedo-boat destroyers, the *Furor* and the *Pluton*.

She reached for her heart-shaped pendant, seeking comfort. If she maintained her present heading, the *Maria Teresa* would ram right into the *Titan*.

Since the U.S. fleet had trapped Cervera, it had been under a standing order. In the event of escape, *charge*.

Clouds of smoke poured from the funnels of the United States' battleships, but not one made a move to break formation.

"Get below," shouted Chase as he ran across the deck.

Ignoring his command, Dare rushed to his side. "What's going on? Why aren't we making some kind of a move?"

"We can't. Not until the order's given." Chase pointed to the *Brooklyn*. "With Sampson gone, Commodore Schley is the officer in charge, and until he sounds the command, we keep our position." He shouted for his men to stand ready to fire, then yelled at the *Brooklyn*. "Damn it Schley. Now's your chance to prove what you're made of."

His voice was drowned out by the roar of the engines, but he went right on yelling. "Show the department you should have been made an admiral instead of one of your underlings."

His eyes fixed on the *Brooklyn*, he paced back and forth across the bow. "Damn it, man, do something!"

Like his crew, he stood waiting, watching, praying for the command to open fire.

Dare, too, stood by, not knowing what to do. Schley had to make a move and make it fast. Now, he was the one who was running out of time. The *Maria Teresa* was almost head to head with him. She could not turn west until she had safely maneuvered around El Diamante, but once that hidden shoal had been cleared, the open sea was hers for the taking!

They were still waiting when the *Maria Teresa* swung westward and opened fire at long range.

Suddenly, a loud cheer erupted from the men aboard the *Titan* and from their comrades. Commodore Schley had just raised another signal flag. Its ensignia bore the command they all wanted to see.

"Follow the flag!" Chase's voice rang out loud and clear. He whirled around to her. "And you, get below."

"I'm staying, Chase. I'm staying with you."

He opened his mouth to protest, but instead made his way to the bridge, pulling her along with him. Not long afterward, they stood perched on their vantage point watching as the *Maria Teresa* cleared the sand bar and dropped off her two civilian pilots. Then, one by one, the three cruisers following on her stern swung westward as well.

Suddenly, a melee erupted as American ships rushed to converge on Spanish vessels. The chase was on! The *Brooklyn* was first in the file. The *Texas* was sandwiched between the *Iowa* and the *Oregon*. The *Titan* jolted into fifth position, only a long jump away from the *Oregon*'s stern.

Holding tightly to Chase's arm, Dare stole a quick

434

glance behind them. The *Indiana* and the two converted yachts were bringing up the rear. Farther away, a flotilla of press boats labored to catch up, and behind them, just offshore, the *New York* was straining to rejoin the fleet.

Dare's attention returned to the activity ahead where pursued and pursuers raced westward full steam ahead.

For the longest while, it seemed doubtful that the battleships could muster enough speed to overtake the Spanish hulks. Then, just when their chances looked bleakest, the American gunners let go with their artillery.

Dare covered her ears. The thunder of the cannonade, reverberating to the depths of the sea and returning to the surface, was enough to blow them all out of the water.

Pandemonium ensued. Cervera and his vessels pressed forward raggedly, determined not to go down without a fight, while the best of the U.S. Navy wove in and out of line to keep from being exposed to each other's cross fire.

Dare held tight to Chase's arm. More than once, she had been tempted to run below and wait out the battle and, just as many times, she had vowed to hold firm. Her place was by her man, and that was just where she intended to stay!

Just when it looked as though the *Maria Teresa* would escape, she began losing speed. Steam filled her decks, and several earth-shattering explosions followed. When the smoke around her finally cleared, her entire midsection was engulfed in flames. She drifted toward the beach, staggering and rolling, her flag burning as if it were paper. Her sister ship, the *Oquendo*, fared no better. She, too, quickly became a floating furnace doomed by the wall of rocks jutting out from the island.

Shrouded by smoke from the other two, the *Pluton* ran onto the rocks and blew up.

Dare held her breath as the *Gloucester* made ready to attack the remaining destroyer. The yacht was no match for a torpedo boat that could destroy ships ten times its size. Still, only six hundred yards away from its mark, what had once been a millionaire's pleasure boat somehow managed to elude every single shell aimed at it. Meanwhile the *Furor* took a hit in her bow and went steaming round and round out of control. The smoke began to lift, and through the haze, she could see a white rag waving from the stern. In response to their surrender, the *Gloucester* set out to rescue the survivors. Not long after the *Furor* exploded and sank, the *Colon* lost power and ran aground on the coast beside what remained of the flagship and the *Oquendo*. Her colors were hauled down amid the cheers and applause of the American crews.

Chase silenced his crew. "Full steam to the west," he blared.

The next thing Dare knew, the *Titan* had made a sharp, ninety-degree turn that nearly sent her and everyone aboard toppling over.

Dare grabbed hold of the railing to keep from being plunged into the fiery water. She didn't have to ask what was about to happen. The *Vizcaya* had almost slipped by them once, and she was not going to get a second try. With all guns pointed at the

Spanish cruiser, the *Iowa*, the *Texas*, and the *Titan* took off after the last remnant of the once-great fleet, their artillery pounding at her sides.

Each shot fired, Dare prayed, would be the last, yet only when the *Vizcaya*'s wooden decks were covered with flames did the merciless barrage cease.

The crew of the *Titan* cheered as she passed the burning wreck.

Dare closed her eyes. Death was hardly cause to celebrate.

"Hush, boys," shouted Chase at the top of his lungs. "Those poor devils are dying."

The stench of burning flesh and the sudden realization that the corpses brushing the bow of the *Titan* were faceless quieted those few men who had disregarded their captain's demand for silence.

Rescue efforts were begun, and the crew proceeded with these chores without so much as congratulatory slaps on their buddies' backs.

Feeling as though her insides were about to come spewing forth in one violent rush, Dare turned her back on all that she had seen. She could take no more. The gruesome scenes she had just witnessed would plague her nights for as long as she lived.

"I think I shall go below," she said, her voice weak.

Nodding somberly, Chase took her arm, but a call from the crowd gathering at the stern drew his attention.

"Go on. I can manage," she assured him.

Leaning against a main turret for support, she watched as a chair was hoisted over the side of the *Titan*. Strapped to the chair was a Spanish officer. A blood-soaked handkerchief was wrapped around his head.

Dare inched closer for a better look. Could it be? . . . No, surely it was not.

She nearly lost her footing.

Dear God, it was! Poor Captain Eulate! She had been so caught up by the action, she had not realized until that very moment she had drunk coffee with the captain of the *Vizcaya*. He, too, had preferred milk in his, and like her he had reached for the chocolate pastries instead of the ones filled with fruit. They were not so different after all.

She swallowed her tears. It was too late to feel pangs of guilt. At least he was alive.

Refusing Chase's offer of assistance, Captain Eulate eased himself to his feet with greatly labored movements. Without uttering a sound, he removed his sword from its belt, kissed the hilt, then presented it to Chase.

Dare watched, her heart swelling with pride, as Chase returned the sword to its rightful owner.

The Spanish commander bowed low in gratitude. Drawing himself to his full height, he lifted his right arm high above his head and saluted his vessel. "*Adiós*, Vizcaya," he said softly, his voice cracking.

As though his ship had been awaiting his farewell, her forward magazines exploded, and less than a minute later, the *Vizcaya* was no more.

A lone bugle from a nearby vessel trumpeted the end of four centuries of greatness.

Troubled, Dare shook her head. That which had taken four hundred years to achieve had been demolished in only four hours.

Captain Eulate gave one last solemn nod; then he

allowed Chase and a young lieutenant to help him across the deck.

Dare held her breath as they shuffled past. The Spaniard's dark, grief-stricken gaze settled on her briefly, before he focused his attention one last time on the spot where his ship had gone down.

Not the slightest glimmer of recognition had flickered in his eyes. For that she would be eternally grateful. The time for renewing friendships would come later.

Her steps as heavy as the burden weighing on her heart, Dare made her way below. There was something about Captain Eulate's expression—she couldn't quite put her mind on just what—that left her with the distinct feeling he had known from the moment the *Vizcaya* came tearing out of the harbor — that the invincible armada was coming out to die.

Chapter Twenty-Six

Breakfast tray in hand, Dare tiptoed into the bedroom, a rush of memories flooding her thoughts. Had anyone told her the half-drowned man she had pulled from the ocean would be her husband in six months' time, she wouldn't have blinked twice. Even then, she had known their paths had been destined to cross. What fate had ordered, no human being could undo. He was her life! She couldn't even begin to imagine an existence without her handsome Viking.

Leaving the tray on the trunk, she eased back into bed and tucked herself as close to him as she could. If they slept together every night for the next fifty years, she would never be able to get close enough. The blood rushing through his veins supplied her with a life-giving force too.

Smiling to herself, she held out her left hand for the first of the many inspections she would make that day. Catching the morning light, the diamonds and rubies awakened to sparkle atop their bed of gold.

Three days ago, they had formalized the vows they had exchanged the night their love had first been consummated. Held on the beach at sunset, the ceremony had been simple. Uriah had given her away while Calpurnia had stoically looked on. Mattie and the admiral had cabled that they would not attend the wedding but would be in attendance at the birth of their first grandchild in November. She had worn her mother's wedding dress, its pearl-white satin now ivory. Even after the seams had been let out as far as they could go, the gown still fit a little snug around the hips, but as Chase had jokingly told her, considering the circumstances, that was to be expected. Wondering what the minister's reaction would be in four months when he would be asked to baptize their child brought a grin to her lips.

After they had been pronounced man and wife, it had seemed only appropriate that they row out to Christmas Tree Key, drink champagne by moonlight, and toast each other's happiness.

The future was theirs. The days and months and years to come took precedence in her thoughts. Last week's happenings seemed far in her past, and she would do well to leave them there. Yesterday's War News segment of the *Key West Herald* had brought everything into focus one last time. Its photographs and reports had featured the surrender of Santiago. Even now, it was hard to believe she had been at the center of it all.

The surrender ceremony had been held in the main plaza. A *World* reporter had tried to get an official photograph of the signing, but an angry General

442

Shafter had ordered him away. The general's sentiment seemed to express that of most of the American military present. "Leave them with their dignity," he had blared. "That is all they have left." William Hearst, wearing a boater and bow tie, was present to cover the signing firsthand. She and Chase had happened to stroll by just in time to catch the tail end of his interview with Roosevelt. Battle had done nothing to humble the ebullient Teddy. Head thrust forward and jaw working vigorously, he told of how he had been the only officer present when the Heights were stormed and taken. Admiral Sampson, who had come straggling back too late to resume command of his fleet, announced to the correspondents that the great Naval victory in the harbor of Santiago would be his Fourth of July present to the good people of America. Commodore Schley, not to be outdone, delivered a heartrending eulogy lamenting the death of the only American, one of his own crew, who had been decapitated by a shell from the *Vizcaya*.

Careful not to disturb his sound sleep, Dare laid her head on Chase's chest. His heartbeat was just like him, forceful, yet gentle. How wonderful it was going to be to awaken every morning of her life to the feel of curly blond sprigs tickling some part of her body.

Yes, it was indeed time to put the war behind them. Conditions for an armistice were already being negotiated. If the history books made any mention of it at all, the Spanish-American War would probably be likened to a comedy of errors. Four hundred men had lost their lives to the enemy's bullets. Five thousand had died as a result of disease-causing bacteria.

Easing back onto the pillow, Dare brushed a pale tendril from Chase's forehead. Nothing would please her more than to spend all day right there watching him sleep.

Her lips brushed his cheek's early morning stubble. She hated to awaken him, but she must. Secretary of the Navy Long was scheduled to arrive at eight, and the commander of the base in Key West had to be there to greet him.

Chase sighed, but his lids remained hooded over his eyes.

"Darling, time to get up," Dare said softly, her mouth grazing his.

His eyes opened lazily. A blue more magnificent than that of the Gulf greeted her. "What do you mean, time to get up? I'm on my honeymoon."

"Tell that to Secretary Long." What she had intended as a slap on his buttock turned into a kneading caress, and she drew her hand away only to have it returned by him.

"I intend to do just that," he remarked, burrowing his head between soft, creamy mounds which were all too eager to pillow him. "Right after I submit my resignation."

Her fingers ceased their wicked massage. Surely she had misunderstood him. He couldn't have possibly said what she thought she had heard.

His tongue trailed kisses across her full, ripe breasts, calling her rosy tips to attention. "You see, my love, I have recently come to the conclusion that the Navy does not offer me the kind of life suitable for a married man. Now that I'm no longer a bachelor, having a different woman in every port has lost its appeal." A strong leg slid ever so gently up her thigh. His warm, bare flesh melted into hers. "I have decided that my place is right here in the Keys with my island girl, and that if you still want to, we'll make the Sea Palms the most fashionable place to winter on the east coast. A real vacationer's paradise."

"Oh, Chase, do you mean it?"

He nodded. His eyes melted into hers, setting their violet shades afire. "With all my heart, my love."

"But what about those five generations of Hamilton sailors?"

With tender, loving strokes, he caressed the swell beneath her waist. "The sixth generation of Hamiltons can start a tradition of its own."

A roving breeze strayed in from the ocean, bringing with its cooling wisps the promise of love and happiness.

Dare enclosed him in her arms. Never before had she dreamed such happiness existed. She had found her own paradise in his embrace!

GET A *FREE* BOOK!

Just answer the following questions and Zebra will send you one of the four books listed on the back—*absolutely free!*

1. Where do you buy paperback books? (*Circle one or more*)
   Supermarket   Convenience Store   Newsstand
   Drugstore   Bookstore   Other

2. How many paperback books do you buy a month? _____
   a year? _____

3. What magazines do you buy? _____
   _____

4. Where do you buy magazines? (*Circle one or more*)
   Supermarket   Convenience Store   Newsstand
   Drugstore   Bookstore   Subscription   Other

5. What newspapers do you buy? _____
   _____

6. Where do you buy newspapers? (*Circle one or more*)
   Supermarket   Convenience Store   Newsstand
   Drugstore   Bookstore   Home Delivery   Other

7. Do you buy paperback books in the same place you buy
   your magazines and newspapers? _____ yes _____ no

8. Where do you buy Zebra books? (*Circle one or more*)
   Supermarket   Convenience Store   Newsstand
   Drugstore   Bookstore   Other

9. If you circled Bookstore in #8, is this because you couldn't
   find Zebra books at your supermarket, drugstore, newsstand, etc.? _____ yes _____ no

10. Would you spend $6.95 for a large format historical ro-
    mance? _____ yes _____ no

11. What is the title of your favorite Zebra cover?
    _____

(*continues on the reverse side*)

GET A *FREE* BOOK!
(*see reverse side*)

12. What is the title of your favorite cover on any paperback?

_____

13. Who is your favorite Zebra author?

_____

14. Who is your favorite author?

_____

15. What radio or TV shows do you listen to or watch?

_____

16. Do you work outside your home? _____ yes _____ no

Send me the following book—*absolutely free!* (Check only one)

_____ PASSION'S DREAM by Casey Stuart

_____ STORM TIDE by Patricia Rae

_____ PASSION'S PLEASURE by Valerie Giscard

_____ SAVAGE EMBRACE by Alexis Boyard

Mail my book to—

name: _____

address: _____

_____

_____

Tear out and mail questionnaire to Zebra Books, 475 Park Avenue South, New York, New York 10016. Allow 4-6 weeks for delivery. Offer expires July 1, 1985. Offer limited to one per customer.